THE CHATELAINE

KATE HEARTFIELD is a *Sunday Times* bestselling author and a former journalist. Her debut novel won Canada's Aurora Award, and her novellas, stories, and games have been shortlisted for the Nebula, Locus, Crawford, Sunburst, and Aurora Awards. Kate lives near Ottawa, Canada.

ALSO BY KATE HEARTFIELD

The Embroidered Book
The Valkyrie

THE CHATELAINE

KATE HEARTFIELD

HARPER
Voyager

Harper*Voyager*
An imprint of
HarperCollins*Publishers* Ltd
1 London Bridge Street
London SE1 9GF

www.harpercollins.co.uk

HarperCollins*Publishers*
Macken House
39/40 Mayor Street Upper
Dublin 1
D01 C9W8
Ireland

First published as *Armed in Her Fashion* in Canada in 2018 by ChiZine
Publications
First published by HarperCollins*Publishers* 2023
1

A catalogue record for this book is available from the British Library

ISBN: 978-0-00-856785-9

Typeset in Meridien by Palimpsest Book Production Ltd, Falkirk, Stirlingshire

Printed and bound in the UK using 100% renewable electricity
by CPI Group (UK) Ltd

MIX
Paper | Supporting
responsible forestry
FSC
www.fsc.org   FSC™ C007454

This book is produced from independently certified FSC™ paper
to ensure responsible forest management.

For more information visit: www.harpercollins.co.uk/green

For Xavier, who loves history.

But tel me this: why hydestow, with sorwe,
The keyes of thy cheste awey from me?
It is my good as wel as thyn, pardee!

—Chaucer, *The Wife of Bath's Tale*

PROLOGUE

Bruges, 1302

Supper was salt herring again, skinny and bony. Margriet grabbed her herring by the tail and dangled it over Nicholas's plate, the fish-skin rippling silver in the light of one candle. Her brother frowned and pushed her little headless fish away. He probably thought himself too big to play floppy-swords, now that he was fourteen, now that there were French soldiers in the streets with real swords at their belts.

Margriet shrugged, lifting the fish to her mouth with a roar before devouring it.

Nobody laughed. They were all so grumpy these days. Mother frowned, Katharina rolled her eyes, and Father did not react at all, gazing wearily at the candle.

'Is there any bread tonight, Mother?' Katharina asked.

Mother shook her head. 'I'm sorry, darling. Perhaps this summer the harvest will be better.'

'It won't matter how good the harvest is,' muttered

Nicholas. 'Flanders could become as rich as Cockaigne, with fat pigs running everywhere, ready for roasting. It wouldn't matter to us because we'd have no coin to buy any of it. The damned French king will tax every morsel that passes through the gates of Bruges.'

Margriet's stomach growled at the mention of roast meat.

'Hush,' Mother said. 'Nicholas, you must not say such things, especially not outside the house. Your father must be seen as neutral in all this. A boatman needs customers; he needs trade. He cannot make enemies of the other guildsmen or the wealthy families. He must be neither Claw nor Lily, for the time being, until things are settled.'

'The Bible says a man cannot serve two masters,' said Nicholas.

'No, he cannot,' Mother said sharply. 'But he may serve none, if he's careful. In times like these, if a man chooses a side, he has already lost.'

'I wonder why lilies and why claws,' Katharina said.

'I know,' said Margriet, swallowing her fish. 'It's because the French king wears a lily on his shield and the count of Flanders has a lion on his.'

'I know, of course,' Katharina spat. 'What I mean is, I wonder why the king and the count chose those symbols in the first place.'

'Oh.' Margriet didn't know the answer to that.

'You're such a show-off,' Katharina said.

'It is a little unseemly, Margriet, this habit of yours,' Mother said. 'You need not be so hasty to show the world every time you think you know the answer to a question.'

Margriet's eyes stung.

'That's why you don't have any friends,' Katharina said.

'I'd rather have no friends than no brains,' Margriet shot back.

'Girls, girls,' Mother said, sighing.

Father gazed at Mother's face. It was a beautiful, disappointed face, like the image of the Madonna in the Church of Our Lady.

'Children, be peaceful, for heaven's sake,' he said. 'You're only restless because you have nothing to tire you out, now that the crane is shut down. I am sure it will start up again soon. You won't be cooped up much longer.'

Margriet ate the last of her herring, licking her salty, fishy fingers. She hoped the Bruges crane would be out of order for a while yet. She took her turn once a week like the other boatmen's children, but she hated walking in the wheel that powered the crane, walking and getting nowhere. Still, the crane helped Father and the other boatmen load their wares.

She preferred the days Father took her as a helper in his boat. She would float along, dipping her fingers in the soft green water of the canals. She collected bits of wood and feathers from the surface. Each day she chose one of her treasures to ride along in the pocket tied beneath her apron. She was good at finding, good at watching. That was how she had spotted the giant serpent that lived in the canals.

No one else knew it was there, for the creature was invisible. But Margriet was clever and could read its rippling traces on the surface of the water. She tossed a twig onto what she guessed was its back and found that the twig disappeared too.

Manoeuvring the boat through a clump of weeds, her father only scolded when she tried to show him. 'Don't pester me while I work. The Minnewater monster is nothing more than a story, no more real than Reynard the Fox, or Ysingrim the Wolf.'

Margriet didn't talk about the serpent with anyone after that, but she watched for it. Often, she spotted it near the Minnewater, the widest part of the canal near the southern wall where Father moored his boat.

Nicholas was complaining again.

'I would rather fight than walk in a crane like a beast.'

'Well, that's too bad,' Mother said. 'If there is any fighting you must stay out of it. When the killing is over, we'll make our peace with the victor. I will not lose another child to this war. I have asked God to spare my children and I believe he will if I keep them out of it.'

'You won't lose me, Mother, don't worry. I'm a good fighter. I'll be a good soldier.'

'Will you now?' Mother asked, her voice high and strange. 'And in whose army? Perhaps you have not noticed that the count is a prisoner in Paris? And the men of Bruges who fought for their city are exiled, wandering out there somewhere, or dead? Perhaps you'd rather be a Lily, and fight for the French king?'

Mother clapped her hand over her own mouth, but Margriet couldn't tell if she was trying to stop herself from crying or from talking.

'If I met the French king, I'd show him a thing or two,' said Margriet, because things were awful.

'Oh ho, is that so?' Nicholas asked, smiling. 'You, an eleven-year-old girl?'

Margriet nodded, continuing to talk to keep him smiling. 'I'd trick him. I'd sneak up on him in his sleep and cut his head off like a chicken's.'

'Show-off,' Katharina mouthed.

Her mother made another of her noises but dropped her hands.

'Really, Margriet. Such a thing for a girl to say.'

Nicholas was not smiling any more. He and Father looked at each other across the table, then looked away.

Margriet chewed her lip and vowed to say nothing more until morning. She wondered if anyone would notice.

Before bed, Mother took the distaffs and wool out of the basket. Katharina and Margriet used short distaffs but Mother's was as tall as a broom-handle. The speed of her spinning was the subject of stories and rumours as far away as Ghent, Father said.

Margriet did not have her mother's talent. The wool bunched at the top of the distaff and tugged, and her spindle banged between her knees.

'I can't see what I'm doing with only one candle,' she complained.

She remembered too late, her vow of silence.

'We don't need to see to spin,' Mother said.

'Maybe you don't, Mother, but I do.'

'Oh, I swear, I'll have to file the edges of your tongue one of these days. Pull that yarn off and start fresh. It's about to snap anyway.'

Margriet tugged the wool apart. She stuffed a long line of bunched, ugly yarn deep into her pocket, to join the feather.

Father and Nicholas came upstairs. Father's face was grave; he held a lantern.

'Bedtime?' Mother asked.

Father said, 'You get the girls into bed. Nicholas and I are going to check on the boat.'

'Now? It's past Compline.'

'Yes, and we'll have to have the boat ready by cockcrow for whatever use the French might require, else it will look as if we're staying home on purpose. With all these soldiers tramping through town I shouldn't wonder if someone's put a hole through it or done some other mischief.'

Mother pursed her lips. 'Must you take Nicholas?'

'I might need his help. I'm not taking him far. Just to the Minnewater.'

She said nothing and bowed her head.

After Father left, Mother made no sign to get the children into bed. She kept spinning so the girls did too.

'I'll tell you a story, shall I?' Mother said.

'Reynard,' Margriet said.

'You always want Reynard,' Katharina argued.

'You chose yesterday. I want Reynard.'

'All right. Katharina, don't argue with your sister. Where shall I start, Margriet?'

'From the beginning.'

Katharina sighed heavily.

'It was Whitsuntide,' Mother began, 'and the trees were all dressed in green, when King Nobel the Lion decided he would have a great feast. He summoned to his court one of every kind of animal to speak for their kin. They would spread word throughout the land, of the king's generosity . . .'

Father and Nicholas had still not returned when Mother stopped, saying as she always did that Reynard had got in quite enough trouble for one day and would get in more tomorrow. She kissed them goodnight and knelt to pray by the big bed near the staircase. Katharina and Margriet cuddled under the covers. Spring had come to the days but not yet to the nights.

The girls' bed was near the outer wall where the house jutted over the street. As if it were right beneath them, they heard men laughing and shouting in French. A woman screamed.

Katharina sniffed. 'I'm frightened, Margriet.'

Margriet put her arm around her.

Margriet woke to the sound of something clattering against the shutters. She eased herself out of bed and walked to the window, her skin all gooseflesh. She opened the shutter a crack.

A group of women stood below. She recognized one as the wife of the baker who sold the twisted bread. Margriet liked the bread but not the baker. He once told her that she was destined to be a shrew and a scold.

The baker's wife, in any case, did not seem timid. She called up in a hoarse whisper, 'Our exiles are back in the city. The Claws are rising! Tell your men that if they go toward the Belfry they're sure to meet up with the others. Tell them to bring knives and axes. We'll be rid of these French pigs by dawn.'

Margriet nodded and turned to see if anyone had heard. The open window let in a little moonlight. Her mother still knelt by her bed, but her head and arm rested on it. She had fallen asleep praying. Nicholas's bed was empty. He had shared that bed with his brother Jan, before Jan went off to fight against the French. Jan died on the field.

Father and Nicholas were still out there. They must be warned. They must get out of the streets, away from the fighting. They might not have heard about it yet, since the Minnewater was at the edge of the city, far from the Belfry in the city centre. But the fighting would come this way eventually, for the castle the French were building was also in the south.

Margriet slipped on her cloak and shoes. She tiptoed past her mother's bed and down the stairs.

The half-moon lit the cobbles on Casteelstrate and the ripples on the Minnewater at the end of it. Though Margriet heard shouts and noises, her own street was deserted. Please God, she prayed. Please let me reach them in time and bring them home before the fighting comes.

Where Casteelstrate met Assebrouckstrate, under the sign of a cobbler's shop, a swarm of men shoved and punched a wiry, redheaded man.

'Wait, stop!' cried one of the bullies. 'Let's give this young fellow a fair trial.'

Margriet pressed herself into a recess between two houses. How to get past them? It would take forever to go around by other streets.

The mob of angry men pushed their victim to the ground.

'Say the words in proper Flemish! Say, *"scilt ende vrient"*. Shield and friend!'

'Say it, traitor, say it now!'

The poor fellow only sobbed and stammered.

'He can't say it.'

'He can't say it because he's French. He's one of them.'

'I'm not, no,' the trembling Frenchman stammered in heavily accented Flemish.

'Come on, come on, speak up. You'll have to say it sooner or later.' The ringleader repeated these instructions in French. The bullies laughed. Their torches threw shadows on the buildings. The red-haired man murmured something Margriet could not hear.

A raised club cast a long shadow on the torchlit house. The Frenchman screamed as it fell with a thud. Margriet put her hand to her mouth. The man groaned in pain. She ought to go home, to comfort Mother and Katharina, who must surely have woken by now. But Father and Nicholas were out there somewhere, and although they could pronounce 'scilt ende vrient' properly, like anyone born and bred in Bruges, they had not chosen sides. They worked with the Lilies – had been seen carting their goods and bowing their heads to them. Mother always urged the two to stay neutral, to work with anyone.

'*Scilt ende vrient!*' the Frenchman burbled. But he had neither shield nor friend. The c and the v were wrong; it was all wrong.

Margriet could not see him any more, for the shouting bullies surrounded him. The attackers wheeled and staggered from the sheer force of their own kicks and blows. Finally, they stumbled down the street, shouting in some wordless tongue.

Margriet left her hiding spot and ran. It was a relief to match the pace of her legs to the pace of her heart. Her feet slipped in a patch of something wet – offal or night waste – but she righted herself and kept running. Panting, she raced to the water's edge.

The Minnewater, where the Bruges canals opened into a wide expanse, lapped quietly in the moonlight as if all were well with the world. Its sour smell was as familiar as her sister's breath, her mother's bosom.

There was no one at the water's edge.

And Father's boat was gone.

Margriet walked the length of the mooring wall, inspecting each boat. Things looked different at night; perhaps she was simply not recognizing it. No, the boat was gone. And her father and brother with it.

Margriet turned in a circle, peering down streets and alleys that led to the centre of the city. Father and Nicholas were out there. She was a clever girl. She would find a way to get them safely home. In the morning this nightmare would be over, and one side or the other would be in command of the city. She would accompany Father in the boat as usual, trailing her fingers through sunlit water.

She bit her thumbnail, staring into the water. The moonlight bounced off swirling ripples at a strange, impossible angle. The canal serpent! Nicholas and Father were bound to be near a canal. Perhaps the serpent could help her find them. It would be faster than paddling! Besides, if a twig became invisible upon its back, what else might become so?

Margriet knelt on the stone wall, gripping the slimy edge, watching the swirling waters. In the rippling movement of the swells, she could see the outline of the creature quite clearly. It was long, huge; as broad as a horse. It could carry three people on its back!

Margriet asked God to bless her enterprise and untied a good long rope from the closest boat. Her fingers grew cold, and she struggled with the wet knot. Next, she pulled the balled-up yarn from her pocket, doubled it and used it to retie the boat. It would not hold, this disgraceful yarn she had spun, but she had to make some effort. She was a boatman's daughter. It was one thing to borrow a rope and another to let a boat drift away.

Now, what sort of knot did one use to catch a canal serpent? She needed an inescapable knot, one that would bind the serpent to her will. She tied an overhand loop, leaving plenty of room. Her hands shook, and her knees were cold from kneeling on the stone.

She pulled the white feather from her pocket and tossed it into the water. It twirled in the air and landed. As it hit the water it vanished, neither sinking nor even getting wet. Margriet drew a silent breath. The pattern of ripples had not changed. Her feather had not startled the water-monster.

The first time Margriet threw the rope, her aim was off. The loop slapped quietly on the surface and vanished. It must have hit the creature's back!

'God's blood.' She pulled the rope back, but the creature had begun thrashing, splashing water in a way that made Margriet suspect it had reared its head. This was a chance. She threw again, and this time the loop at the end of the rope vanished. Margriet gripped the taut, quivering rope that seemed to simply end in thin air. She braced her feet as the invisible thing reared, yanking her toward the water.

'You could pull me in,' she gasped, 'but then you'd have this rope around your neck and no one to take it off! I take it you don't have fingers? I'm a boatman's daughter. That knot won't work itself loose, especially not wet. It will just get tighter and tighter until one day the long end will catch on a nail or an anchor and then—'

'I know what you want,' the creature said in a voice like oil.

She was taken aback. 'What?'

'There are only two things any human has ever wanted of me.'

'Well, I want to know if you've seen my father and my brother.'

'Just like all the others, I see. One of the things humans want is to ask me tedious questions.'

'My father is tall, and my brother has blond curls. They might have taken a boat—'

'I pay no attention to the comings and goings of humans.'

'Then will you take me to—'

'And there it is. The second thing humans always want. No. I will not let you ride on my back.'

Shouting came from the streets behind her, a great inhuman roar. Margriet twisted around, half expecting to confront a dragon. Instead, she saw orange flames staining the sky. The city was on fire. Where would Mother and Katharina go? Where were Father and Nicholas?

'You must pay attention!' she cried, tears thickening her voice. 'The city is burning!'

The serpent's laugh was a wet sound, like the coughing fits that had taken Grandmother before she died.

'I can wait while your city burns. It has burned before and I survived, cosy in my cold home. Those ugly new walls will crumble to the ground, and I will remain. Long ago I lost interest in carrying humans from place to place, or in listening to their boring questions.'

Margriet heard the false note, recognized it from hearing her own voice, her own protestations when the children would not play with her or share their jokes as they walked upon the crane.

'I bet I could ask you a question that would not bore you.'

'Ha! Not likely.'

'If I do, you must take me wherever I want to go.'

There was a pause. Then: 'If you could ask me a single interesting question, I would gladly carry you one time, even if you do smell of sheep's wool.'

In the distance, the cacophony grew. Mother would be beside herself!

'I need you to carry two others as well.'

'Oh ho ho. No question is worth that.'

'I bet I could ask you three questions, each more interesting than the last.'

'That is unlikely indeed. If you could do such a thing, I would carry you and two others.'

'But I might need more than one trip. What if I could ask you seven?'

'If you could ask me seven interesting questions, girl, I would carry you and two others, any time you asked, for the rest of your days.'

'It's a bargain.'

'Ha! We'll see. Remove the rope then and ask.'

'Remove the rope? But how do I know you'll keep your word? I might ask you a question and you could lie and pretend to yawn and say you found it boring.'

'I am a Nix and you are a child, and there are no two creatures anywhere on this Earth who hold a bargain so sacred,' said the serpent.

'A Nix?'

'And I do not yawn, in any case.'

'How do I know? I don't even know what you look like. Do you have to be invisible? It would be easier to get the rope off if I could see you.'

The air above the water shimmered and the Nix showed itself. It was bigger than she'd expected, more like a wingless, limbless dragon than a snake. Its skin was the green and brown of slime and sticks, with a thickly ribbed trunk and a large head. Gleaming golden fangs lined its long flat jaw. The creature swam close. In the night air, its breath, now visible, seeped like smoke out of great nostrils and curled around the shining fangs.

Margriet braced herself against a bollard so that she could stretch her arms out over the water. With both hands she scrabbled at the knot. It had jammed, and she had no knife. She should have tied a bowline! The creature's thick green skin lapped over the rope. She tried not to look at the face, at the great bloodshot eyes. Her fingers were cut and bleeding by the time she pulled the knot loose. Bits of rope fibre floated on the water. A thin red line encircled the creature's neck.

The Nix nodded its great head, enjoying freedom. 'All right,' it said. 'You have injured and insulted me. Ask your question.'

'I am sorry,' Margriet said, and she was. She wished she had considered just talking to the serpent, instead of roping it. It must be lonely in the water, and humans always asking you for things. People were frequently boring, too; the Nix was right about that. Margriet tried to think of interesting things like feathers, bones, and skeins of string. She pictured Mother spinning her distaff and telling stories.

'Why did Reynard the Fox stay away from King Nobel's court?' she said.

The Nix blinked, an oil-paper eyelid sliding over its eye. 'That's your question?'

Margriet shivered from her wet knees to her ratty hair.

'That's the first question,' she said in a small, defiant voice.

'You have before you a creature of long experience and this is what you want to know? Not whether the sun is the centre of the universe, or whether a thing has thingness of itself or only in symbolic reference to a posited ideal, or the number of people who will be saved on the last day, or whether the Holy Ghost proceeds from the Father and the Son or just the Father? I have answers to all of those questions. I don't know the answer to yours.'

'Well, I do,' said Margriet. 'You see, Reynard knew all the other animals would be there, and they all had some reason to complain about him to the king. Chanticleer the Cock came in with the dead body of his daughter on a wagon, claiming that Reynard murdered her. The king sent the bear, Bruyn, to fetch Reynard the Fox. But how did Reynard outwit the bear?'

'I don't know.'

'Well, I do. Reynard knew Bruyn was a glutton. So Reynard said he was unable to come to court because he was too full of honey to move. "That is the food I value above all others," said Bruyn. He promised that if Reynard would show him where he found the honeycombs, he would argue on behalf of Reynard at court. Reynard agreed and led him to a split oak, persuading the bear to thrust his head inside. When the bear was good and stuck, Reynard hid. The villagers came and beat the bear badly. Now if a great bear couldn't bring a little fox to court, what animal would the king send next?'

'I can't say, but I should think a clever one.'

Three questions, Margriet thought. She'd earned a ride

on the beast's back for herself, Father, and Nicholas, too. She might need to get off the Nix to find them, however, and then she would need to get back on again.

'Well, you're right. Next, King Nobel sent the cleverest of his courtiers, Tybeert the Cat. Reynard mentioned that a priest's house nearby was overrun with fat mice that no one could catch. Tybeert thought he was clever enough to catch one, but Reynard scoffed at him. Tybeert marched off to show his skills and walked right into a snare. Now, if a strong bear and a clever cat couldn't do it, who could?'

'Well, this Reynard can talk his way out of anything,' said the Nix. 'What you need is a senseless fool who can't be swayed from his task.'

The din of the waking city grew louder. A baby cried close by. Margriet would not be alone at the water's edge much longer. She needed help this instant, and the creature was just gawking at her, enjoying a good tale. She kept her desperation in her belly, out of her voice.

'You're right! The bravest of all the animals was Grimbeert the Badger. He was Reynard's nephew, which I don't think makes sense, because the nephews of a fox are foxes too. Anyway, Grimbeert appealed to Reynard's honour, telling him that if he kept resisting the king's summons, Reynard's wife and children would be punished. What do you think Reynard did then?'

'I imagine he played some trick, but I can't think what.'

'Well, I know. Reynard said Grimbeert had shown him the error of his ways. He went to court and showed humility before the king. He said he wanted to die right away. He said the people he had wronged should have the honour of building his gallows. So, the king sent Ysingrim the Wolf and Reynard's other enemies to build the gallows. While they were waiting, Reynard told the king he had one more sin to confess. What story do you think he told?'

'How should I know?'

'He said he had listened and done nothing when Bruyn, Ysingrim and Tybeert plotted to kill the king and use their wealth to buy the loyalty of all the noble animals. At the last moment, Reynard said, he got up enough courage to foil their plans by stealing their money and burying it under a tree. In that way he had saved the king's life and got himself some treasure for his old age. Of course, he would never see that old age now, he whined. So, the king pardoned Reynard and set off after the treasure. And where did Reynard go?'

'With the king, I assume.'

'No, he went to the Holy Land. That's seven questions.'

'What?'

'That's seven questions. I've been counting on my fingers. Will you take me?'

'But was the treasure there?'

'Of course not. Now I'm going to get onto your back and you're going to take me to the Belfry.'

The Nix made a strange sucking, clicking sound. It took Margriet a moment to realize this was the sound of a Nix chuckling. 'You have amused me, girl,' it said as it slid along the wall next to her. 'Do you know any other tales?'

'I will come and see you tomorrow and tell you every tale I know,' Margriet said. 'Tonight, I need to find my family.'

Margriet used the bollard for balance and stepped onto the Nix's back as if she were getting into her father's boat. Her foot slid, and she grabbed the bollard with both arms to keep from falling in, scraping her knee.

17

'At some point you're going to get wet,' the Nix said. 'I'm not a barge. Just get on, or we'll be here all night.'

Margriet snorted. She kicked her shoes off and dropped her cloak over the bollard. They might stay dry, if no one stole them. She dropped one leg into the cold water, grabbed the serpent's neck and pushed away from the wall. The Nix swam fast with a sideways wiggle. Margriet held tight. Soon, she was wet through and freezing.

Behind the walls of the beguinage, the home of religious women who did charitable works, the Matins bells were ringing. Did the sisters know what was happening outside their walls? How could they not? A wide, cobbled street opened onto the water's edge. A crowd of people pushed and shouted. They screamed 'Scilt ende vrient!' in tones either mocking and belligerent, or pleading and halting, depending on the accent.

Margriet held tight to the Nix and ducked her head. Her braids were heavy with water. 'Can they see me?' she whispered.

'Of course not. Do you think I would be so foolish? They can't see you, but they can hear you.'

'Nobody will hear my voice in all that tumult,' Margriet said.

It seemed everyone in Bruges had some reason to scream; even the dogs were barking. As the two travelled deeper into the city, the prim bells of the beguinage got fainter, replaced by an irregular, angry clanging. It was coming from the Belfry, the great bell tower that rose from the market square. Someone was up there, pulling with more fury than skill.

To the left, the dark walls of Saint John's hospital grew straight up out of the canal, throwing moonshadow on the other side. There, boats were tied up against a little mooring place.

First Margriet spotted her father's boat among the other small craft, and then she saw her father. He was one man in a crowd, yelling and shoving.

'Stop here, please,' Margriet whispered.

The Nix grew still, snorting like a nervous mule. Despite his protestations, he didn't like all this fire and shouting, either.

Now she had to get Father's attention. What would happen if she ran into the crowd? Would the angry people hurt her or even capture her?

'Do you see your family?' the Nix murmured.

'Yes, Father and my brother Nicholas are there. Father is the one holding the broken oar.'

'Scilt ende vrient!' Father screamed. His face, lit by torchlight, was the face of a stranger.

A small, bald man knelt before him, gasping out French phrases. 'I can't . . . I don't speak . . .'

A knife flashed in Nicholas's hand. The man clutched his belly and screamed in no language at all. Nicholas looked to Father. Father's oar crashed down on the man's head.

'These are your people?' the Nix asked, its voice very quiet.

Margriet wept. She did not know what to do. She ought to bring Father home. She had wanted to protect him, to stop him from getting hurt, to stop him from choosing sides. She did not like the look on Father's face.

'I don't understand. They must have walked here looking for the boat, and when they got here, the other men made them fight.'

'It must be so.'

'Or they're pretending to be with the Claws now because they have to. Like Reynard. The way to outwit your enemies is to make them think you're a friend.'

'Are the Claws your family's enemy, then?'

'No,' said Margriet, confused, watching as Father and Nicholas dragged the man to the edge of the canal.

She remembered the way Father and Nicholas had glanced at each other over the supper table, then looked away. Both of them had avoided Mother's gaze.

Mother must be sick with worry. How could Father and Nicholas have betrayed her so?

'Take me away from here,' she said.

The Nix turned. Margriet clutched his neck, weeping. She should have stayed with Mother and Katharina. Perhaps she could have helped them. Perhaps she still could. She had the Nix, and permission for two more riders. She heard a splash behind them, and cold water lapped over her. She did not want to look back. She buried her face into the Nix's wet skin, letting her fingers trail in the soft water.

In the moonlight, the waves rippling on the water looked like stars streaking across a black sky. She could not see the colour of the water. She fished up a weed. It was red with blood. With a cry she dropped it back in the water. Three bodies floated by. Their bashed faces were turned to the stars. The Nix made a noise and swam around them.

Margriet held on. She must get to Mother. She was almost there, almost back at the Minnewater.

It was not yet dawn but the sky was light in the east, and fires lit the city rooftops like the torches of giants. In the short time since the bells of Matins, when Margriet had left home, the streets had utterly changed. The cobblestones shone with blood or with the orange light of fires. People milled around in panic or leaned from windows shouting to one another.

On the rooftops women knelt, their skirts tucked around their knees. Whooping like boys throwing stones at squirrels, they threw rocks and bricks and roof tiles down onto the fleeing Frenchmen. Half a dozen women and girls knelt on the roof of the Cock tavern. Among them were Mother and Katharina. They had stones in their hands, too. Mother was wielding her distaff just as Father had used his oar.

'Stop here, please,' Margriet said again.

'More of your people?'

'Yes,' Margriet said, keeping herself from crying. 'I don't need you any more.'

The Nix did not move. 'I can swim beyond these city walls, you know. They don't hold me. The canals and rivers go on for days.'

'Swim closer to the wall, please.'

'I can take you with me. Overnight, or until this red, human rage passes. It always passes. I could drop you somewhere else if you like. Some other town.'

Margriet looked up at the faces of her sister and mother. Mother didn't appear angry, like Father. She looked more than ever like the Madonna, triumphant and sad. But up on the roof, she raised her distaff like a weapon. She handed a brick to Katharina and Katharina threw it down. It landed at the heels of a man fleeing a crowd of attackers armed with axes.

'I don't understand,' Margriet whispered.

'There is nothing to understand. It is not worth your while to try.'

'But Mother said . . . No, this isn't what Mother said to do. Nobody tells me anything. I could understand, if they would explain.'

'There is nothing to understand,' the Nix said. 'Humans are a riddle with no answer. Believe me. I've been here since before the first of you came – brutal and boring, then as now.'

'Then why do you stay?' Margriet cried. 'Why don't you just go away forever? Flee to the deepest, farthest water you can find.'

'This is my home,' the Nix growled. 'I was here first.'

Margriet drew a wet sleeve across her runny nose. She wanted to vomit, to let all the anger boil out of her. She wanted to run to Mother and bang on her with small fists like she did when she was little. Mother would hold her close and explain everything. Surely, Mother would be wondering where Margriet went. She had asked God not to let her lose another child. Perhaps that was why she was fighting and not hiding; perhaps it was all Margriet's fault.

No, it was the Lilies' fault. They were the enemy. Father had never looked like that, so angry and frightened, before they came. They had forced him to pick a side, and Mother too. Margriet would never forgive them. She hated the Lilies!

'Bruges is our home!' Margriet shouted.

Mother had been right of course to make the Lilies believe that their family was loyal to them. But that was before. Now the ruse was up. Now was the time to fight. Margriet understood now. Everything was simple, as hard and sharp as rocks.

The Nix was still, floating at the edge of the canal.

Margriet grabbed the stone wall and scrambled off the serpent's back.

'You are visible to them now, don't forget,' the Nix hissed.

She bent and pried a loose cobble out of the street with cold wet fingers. She tried to imagine hurling this stone at someone's head, tried to keep the anger in her belly hot. Her throat hurt from not crying, and from all the unanswered questions.

'Do you think we will win?' she asked, teeth chattering. 'Do you think the Claws will win?'

'What a boring question,' the Nix said.

Margriet trembled, the gritty stone heavy in her hand. She glanced toward the water and the serpent's voice but saw only a distorted reflection of fires and fading stars.

CHAPTER ONE

Excerpt from the Chronicles of Zonnebeke Abbey

In the year of our Lord 1326, a woman drove the beast called Hell up to the surface of the Earth. Its great mouth opened first in the mountains of northern Italy and for several months no one noticed.

One day a wandering French brigand, fleeing revenge, came upon what he thought was a cave. He put his cloak over his mouth and entered, paying no heed to the stalactites that stretched down from the mouth of the cave like fangs, paying no mind to the sulphurous fumes.

Several days later, he emerged bigger than he had been, with his skin bronzed tougher than leather, and with a long metal horn jutting from the middle of his forehead. The woman who drove the Hellbeast emerged behind him.

She was tall and dark and her hair fell in long twists, singed at the ends. She was clad in burnt leather. The woman told Giovanni Saranzo, the Doge of Venice, that she had been so long in the belly of that Beast that she had forgotten her birth name.

'Was it Persephone? Was it Hel? Was it Lilith?' the scholars asked her. She shook her head, and said it might have been, but then again it might not.

'We thought Hell was a place,' they said.

'It is,' she said. 'It is also a beast. A capacious beast; it carries multitudes within it.'

'Are you the Queen of Hell?' they asked her.

She shook her head. 'I have no right to that kingdom as it had no right to me,' she said. 'But I am, for now, its mistress and manager. I hold the keys. You may call me, perhaps, its chatelaine.'

'It is a wonder,' they said, 'that you speak the languages of the Earth so well. Do they speak French in Hell, then?'

And the Italians smirked.

She shook her head, and smiled, showing all her gleaming teeth. She reached up and scratched the horned French brigand behind the ears as if he were a pet. He smiled, too, and said nothing.

The two of them disappeared, then, back into the mouth of Hell, and when messengers from the pope came, they found the Hellmouth gone.

Two years later it emerged again, this time near Paris. It swallowed the village of Minou-sur-Marne and all its sixty inhabitants and all its animals. Out came the Chatelaine and her marshal again.

'Were they all sinners, those of the village of Minou-sur-Marne?' people asked her.

She gave no answer and professed herself confused.

'But then why were they damned? Why did Hell swallow them?'

'They were unlucky,' she said. 'The Beast takes all kinds. It does not require sin.'

Then the emperor warned that one might expect the devil's wife to lie.

But there were some who said the Beast was not truly Hell after all, but only a kind of copy, the way the Earthly Paradise mirrors Heaven. No one had counted all the revenants but there seemed to be too few. If this was Hell, where was Judas? Where was Nero?

One of those who made that argument was the emperor's rival, Philippe of Valois, King of France.

(And indeed some few foolish people whispered that this beast must be Cockaigne itself, for the people who lived within it were never hungry.)

In King Philippe, the Chatelaine found an ally. Here was a man who bore the pale flowers of death embroidered on his clothing. They seemed fated to work together, each to further the other's cause.

King Philippe was in some difficulty at that time in Flanders, where the common people were in revolt against him and against his vassal, their own count. And the Chatelaine had some ambition of her own. Clad now like a noblewoman of France, in ermines and linens, she set about helping the French king by raising an army: an army of the dead or near-dead, and of the altered living. There were many among the weak-minded, the sick and the lame, who were tempted by her gifts.

With this army, and some few mercenaries sent by the king to help, she set about pacifying Flanders.

Whenever anyone asked her about her husband, she refused to answer, and she did not like the question. It was she who held the reins of Hell; that was all anyone could discover about it.

CHAPTER TWO

Bruges, 1328

Margriet de Vos peered at a horizon smudged with the smoke of small fires. Curse her weak eyes. She was too near-sighted to discern a figure against that dirty yellow sky, even had a figure chosen that moment to appear, so she scowled at that blasted, merciless horizon.

It was not that she wanted Willem to return to Bruges, not exactly that. But she had a right to her husband, dead or alive. She had a right to his body, or the little money he earned through the work of that good-for-nothing body. If he was among the dead or captive or changed, she wanted to know. Three weeks now since the battle at Cassel, and so many of the men of Bruges were still among the missing.

Margriet squatted among the dry weeds and thistles, pulled up her skirts. There was no sound but the hiss of her own urine and the hum of insects. It was quiet here, in the no man's land between the city walls and the Chatelaine's besieging forces.

They were out there, somewhere, not far. An army from Hell itself, an army the likes of which could not be found in Christendom or in the imaginations of decent people.

But Margriet de Vos was not afraid. This was her city, and she would not be penned in it. Besides, her milk was failing, her dugs drying up, and she needed her herbs.

She stood and pulled her knife out of the pouch at her waist. Margriet kept her knife sharp. It snicked through the thick thistle stems, through their woolly insides. How strange that God had ordained that the nastiest plants would be the ones to swell a woman's breasts with milk: the furry verbena, the stinging nettles, the sticking thistles. She wrapped her sleeve around her hand and placed the thistles in her apron, tied it deftly, and climbed out of the dry ditch.

The tea from these thistles would keep her milk up for a few more weeks, or so she hoped. And after that, what? Little Jacob Ooste hardly wanted the breast any more, as much as Margriet tried to conceal that fact from his wealthy mother. But soon or late, Margriet would be unwanted.

There would be no work for a wet nurse in a city of widows.

Margriet's legs complained as she began the short walk back to the city gate. She had spent too many of her days and nights sitting. The flesh hung softly on her bones and her back creaked. She stopped, frozen like prey before a predator.

Mary, Mother of God.

A dozen chimeras lounged by the tumbledown stone wall that bordered the cow-path, where it met the main road leading to the city gate. They were facing away from her. She could not see them in detail, but one had a head three sizes too big, clad in an enormous beaked helmet despite the fact he wore no other armour. The others were all the same: each had one straight arm of black metal and one arm, disturbingly, that dangled thin as rope.

Chimeras. The Chatelaine's unholy besieging army. Unnatural, misbegotten bullies, standing in her way.

A little dog circled the chimeras. The first dog she had seen in weeks; they were all dead, within the walls of Bruges. That's right, keep sniffing around there, stupid creature. Keep your nose out of the wind.

A smell of ash and fire. A cloud rose from the little dog's back: curls of dirty smoke or steam. It did not seem bothered. A chimera of some kind; a brazier with paws.

She crouched low, watching them through a screen of meadow foxtail. The chimeras were not facing her, but they might have eyes anywhere, ears of any kind, senses not of God's making. An odd sound seemed to be coming from them: an irregular, echoing knock.

They stood between her and the city walls. Her home and family lay on the other side of the Smedenpoort. She could try one of the city's other gates, but that meant a long, leg-aching walk in either direction while the sun lowered. A dangerous walk, and undoubtedly full of more chimeras, and worse things.

At sunset, the bells of Bruges would ring their tocsin, warning the living to stop their ears and harden their hearts. Then the revenants would come crawling, come calling. Up over the walls, the dead men who had lived in this city a month before would climb, uncaring what the living shot at them or poured down upon their heads. Into the streets they would walk, batting away the few brave souls who fought them hand to hand, and calling the names of the living.

Margriet heard them every night. Every night she wondered whether she would hear Willem's voice, calling her own name. Was he dead? Was he among the revenants?

She would not weaken. She would keep the door shut against him.

Her heart had been shut to him long before.

All the same, the revenants turned her stomach. She did not wish to be out when they were abroad.

This was her path, and Bruges her home, and by God no one would keep her from it.

She hitched up her skirt, the bulge of thistles wagging in her apron, and crawled like a child through the grasses, until she was close enough to hear, and to see a little better. Oh, what she would give for a pair of eyes as sharp as Willem's.

The steaming dog lifted its head and looked in her direction. A man with metal and rope arms followed the dog's gaze, looking out at the horizon just as she had.

'Is Hell ever coming back this way, then?' he grumbled.

'Who knows?' said another. 'The Chatelaine has gone to meet the king at Ypres. Perhaps she will return after the city surrenders.'

The mouth of Hell might open anywhere. Two years now since the Hellbeast had come to the surface of the earth, with the Chatelaine in command.

'This is only a test of the weapons, to frighten the people and see what we can do against the walls,' said a hollow voice: the man in the great helmet. 'Not a full attack.'

A full attack.

Margriet chewed her lip. She had a secret way out of

the city. She could get her daughter and leave – but that would mean leaving her father and sister behind, for there was no way her ailing father could travel, and Katharina would never leave him. Neither would Margriet, if she could help it, but she must keep Beatrix safe.

Until now, the safest course had seemed to stay in Bruges, despite the siege, despite the nightly visits from the revenants. The walls were thick and the moat was deep. Bruges had starved before; its people would survive a long time on whatever tiny fish it could cull from the canals. And there were always rumours: that the survivors of the battle of Cassel were preparing to lift the siege, that the English king had chosen at last to come to save them.

No, it was impossible to leave Bruges. This was their home. How could Margriet and Beatrix live, out in a world infested with monsters? What would become of them as wandering women with little money and no home?

A full attack, said the man with the empty helmet.

It was a familiar voice, underneath the strange echo. How could it be familiar?

Once he had been a man; he had borne a head; he had given it up in the service of the Chatelaine. Had he lost it in battle? Was his head so ugly that he could not bear to live with it?

He lifted his visor. Behind it there was empty space: empty, save for a blue blur. A bird, Margriet realized, squinting. It fluttered and banged into the inside of the helmet every few seconds. The bird seemed unable to find the egress although the visor was up. From its cage, from that void that should have been a head, issued his horribly empty voice.

'But if we blow the doors off, that may be all we need

to do,' he said. 'The city fathers have all been executed. Those who remain are women and children, or old men, and more than half dead of the plague, thanks to the revenants.'

Mary, Mother of God – it was young Julius. It must be. She knew that voice; he had hung about Willem's shop, begging, since his beardless days. Most days he had his earnings stolen from him, poor child, or gave them away to some hard-hearted bully. It did not take much to trick Julius.

And yet here he was, a chimera, commanding other chimeras, by the looks of it. And he did not sound so foolish now.

With his new head, it seemed, came a new intelligence, issuing from what seemed to be empty space.

Margriet did not like to look at that void or the bird within it, so she looked down, to where the gargantuan helmet was welded to a lumpy cicatrice all around his neck.

'Bah,' said one of the men with metal arms. 'The revenants work too slowly. It will be a city of corpses if we leave it to the revenants. Not worth taking.'

'That, my clever friend, is why you are here.'

Julius! What an edge his sweet voice had now.

The gate was so near. She could run to it in a matter of a minute, if it were not for these evil creatures in her way.

In the old days there would have been people, carts, horses, going in and out. She and Willem had gone through this gate so many times, on their way to trade in Poperinge or Roeselare, bickering on their little cart while their pony flicked its ears.

She had eaten the pony last week, she and Father and

Beatrix and Katharina; its lean meat had been as sweet as its disposition, poor thing. And now the gate was shut, although she had no doubt of her ability to get in; she had planned to bang on the postern door, to shout the names of the boys and women who stood guard there with their improvised pikes, even, if need be, to shout the shibboleth the people of Bruges had used in her childhood to separate the city folk from the invading French, who could not pronounce it: *scilt ende vrient*. Shield and friend.

She crawled forward an inch, and waited. The chimeras did not seem to notice the movement. She wished her breath were not so loud, hissing out of her nose like steam from a kettle, and her heart fluttering like that trapped bird.

If only she could go back the way she had come, riding the Nix, secretly by the canal out into the moat. But the stubborn old water-snake would not come to her out here. He obeyed her only within the city gates, in the canals where she had met him all those years ago, when she had tricked him into promising her his service. The slimy serpent was like a wool merchant who picked the last bit of fluff off the scales; he kept his promise to come to her anywhere within the city but offered not one mote more.

How long would the chimeras stand here? They had not been here when she alighted from the Nix's back and made her way with sodden shoes from the moat to the field. Not even an hour before. The barricades were on the roads, a little distance from each city gate.

Margriet crept forward in the weeds, her thighs burning with cramp. She allowed herself a silent grimace. She husbanded her curses.

The men with the metal arms lined up, facing the

Smedenpoort, while the little dog with the steam rising from its back ran back and forth.

'People of Bruges!' shouted the chimera who had been Julius, his echoing voice louder than any human's ought to be. 'You have been warned. The Chatelaine would like to end your suffering. But as you have refused, time and time again, to open the gates to her, we have been sent to take down your walls.'

The silence was filled only by the insects of the afternoon.

The chimera who had been Julius whistled, without lips, and the little steaming dog trotted to one end of the line of chimeras. Each in turn dipped the end of a rope-arm onto its back and rose up with the end glowing red.

'Ready,' said Julius.

He spoke with such authority now.

The chimeras raised their arms and the ropes flailed in the wind, throwing sparks like fireflies, and then came to rest on the metal of their other arms.

A boom and a flash like the day of judgment ripped through the world.

Margriet went flat on the ground, her arms over her head, whispering, 'Mary, save me. Mary, Mother of God.'

Someone was screaming.

She raised her head.

Smoke rose black into the sky.

Two of the chimeras had been blown in half. Another had been blown to bits. His head, with a metal beak like a bird's, rolled straight to her. A man with a new nose and new arms – these men had been lepers, perhaps, before the Chatelaine made her bargain with them.

The smoke filled the air so thick she could not see the

walls. Had the thundering fire breached them? She must get in. She must find her daughter.

Margriet ran through the smoke and the screaming, toward the walls of her city.

CHAPTER THREE

Claude paced the silent nave, alone. He ground his teeth and curled his fingers around the dagger handle. He tensed his right arm and tried, for the eighty-seventh time that day, to raise it with the dagger in its grip.

This time it reached the level of his unbound breasts before he winced and let it drop. It clattered on the stones.

'Blood of Christ,' he muttered.

His right arm, his sword arm, would not obey him.

The wound that encircled his right forearm had healed badly. It left a bracelet of pitted flesh in shining petal-pink, each pock surrounded by square yellow ridges, sore to the touch. The fever had gone, though. There was no reason why the muscles of his hand and arm should be so weak. But he could barely hold a little knife, never mind span a crossbow.

God damn the Chatelaine and all her weapons. The one she cherished most was a mace, attached to one of her arms. A weapon, and more importantly, a key. When she had taken Claude prisoner, he had found a way out. He couldn't steal her own mace, but he did find a way to make a copy. With the mace on his arm, he'd made his way to freedom.

But once he was free, his copied mace had seemed a burden. An obvious sign that he had been in the Chatelaine's keeping. He'd got rid of it. Sold it. And now, his arm wouldn't work properly.

There must have been some enchantment in that mace, taken from those strange forges. It had fitted so perfectly on Claude's hand, like a gauntlet. It had felt like a part of him. Ha. A part of him indeed, more than he knew. Now he missed it dearly. He ached for it. His arm itched and hung useless.

Claude smoothed his hair behind his ear. A swell of panic rose in his chest. He had to get out of this city. Get a weapon in his hand and his own clothes on.

He picked up his dagger with his left hand and paced. One night in Apulia, he and Janos had dined at the home of a merchant who kept a small leopard – a descendant, the merchant claimed, of the great menagerie of Frederick II. It was a rangy beast. Patches of its fur were missing and one eye wept golden tears. Yet it had paced its cage with a warning on its face. Claude felt that warning on his own face now.

A warning for whom? For Willem de Vos, if the man yet lived? Only if he refused to sell Claude back the mace or tell him where he might find it now. No, Willem had nothing to fear from Claude.

Neither did this priest of Bruges, this marked man in a marked city, who had given Claude food and shelter, who had brought him in when he was wounded and close to death. It was more than many men might have done. Claude had, after all, been fighting for the enemy, for the

King of France and for the Chatelaine. The priest had been kinder to him than some others might have been.

But God's nails, the priest had taken Claude's sword. That had been during the fever and he could not remember it. When Claude had woken, he had been wearing a chemise yellowed at the armpits and a rough blue kirtle. Where were the arms and harness he had fought for, wagered for, killed for? Seven years of his life – or was it eight now? – stripped off him.

The priest gave him back his tinderbox and his dagger. Even a woman might carry a knife. He gave him back his own shoes, coated with the dust of many countries, the left one with a small bloody hole through the top. Damn Fleming and his *goedendag*: a long pole with a spike on one end had seemed an impractical weapon to Claude, until he had the spike stuck through his foot.

'Still sore?' he heard, and whirled. The priest was watching him, leaning against a wall with his arms folded. He was a small, pale-skinned man, freckled on his nose and on the bare part of his tonsure where the hair had started to grow in.

'I can manage,' said Claude. He added with a grin, 'Although if you've got any wine about the place, I can't say it would go wrong.'

The priest frowned. No wine, then, or at least not for being merry with. Not that sort of priest.

'What will they do to you, if we give you back to them? If they discover you are a woman, that you have lied all this time?'

What would they do to him? The free company, his brothers in arms? The motley gang of Italians, Bohemians, Spaniards, Saracens and Franks he had slept beside and shat beside and fought beside for all these years? He liked to think they would welcome him back. Claude was pretty sure they had known all along. Or at least, that they would wish to carry on now as if no one had told them. But he'd have to find them first.

Claude, they would say. *Claude, come here and let us get a look at you. Sword arm, eh? Greasy Flemings. We'll soon have you fighting sinister.*

Or perhaps the priest was right, and they would say something quite different.

Could Claude be punished for it, for living in the world as if he hadn't been called 'girl' at birth? He supposed he could. The priest seemed to think so. He had said it was the sin of pride to pretend to be something other than what God had fashioned, that Claude was lucky not to be burned at the stake. His comrades in the Genoa Company didn't care much about sin. Truly, had none of them suspected? None other than his dear Janos, of course, who had reason to know. But Janos was long dead.

'I don't want to see you punished,' the priest said, when Claude did not answer. 'There is no real authority left in Bruges. Most of the burghers who weren't killed in the battle were betrayed soon after, brought out to a parley and killed. I can't turn you over to the French side, and certainly not to the Chatelaine. God knows what she'd make of you.'

He did not know that Claude had escaped the Chatelaine once already and Claude did not care to tell him.

'You are in luck, Father, for I can solve your problem for you,' he said. 'I will be going now. I thank you for your help.'

'Your arm is wounded, a wound the like of which I

41

have never seen, and you have a hole nearly clean through your left foot. And you have had a fever.'

The Fleming had long since wiped Claude's blood off his goedendag. Such an odd weapon. Not long enough to be a proper spear, and the pointed head was all wrong for clubbing. Yet it had done Claude in, or near enough. A knot of Flemings had come upon the cross-bowmen unawares, from behind. He suspected they'd been fleeing the battle and found themselves with a chance to regain some honour or at least some pelf. As he had struggled to drop his crossbow and draw his sword, his god-damned arm throbbing and itching, he had not even seen the goedendag until the pain seared his foot. Claude had fallen under a pavisier, the stalwart Jehan, and was left for dead under his corpse and the heavy pavise.

When the crows and looters had finished, Claude crawled toward Bruges, the only place with food and water he could reach. And he had sensed, for days, that the mace was in Bruges. The strange weapon he had ripped off his arm a few weeks before. The thing that marked him as the Chatelaine's. God's bleeding body, Claude wanted it back.

'I could give you to the beguines,' the priest muttered, looking uncertain about how well Claude would fit into an order of religious women, no matter how charitable. 'But perhaps – perhaps later, once we know a little better what you are.'

What he was. Claude already knew what he was. Claude Jouvenal, a fighter since the day he struck out on his own when he was barely more than a child. But when he had arrived at the gates of Bruges, he was feverish and muttering. That must have been before the chimeras put the city under siege. He did not remember how he came to the priest's empty little church, or when the man had stripped him.

A sound – someone opening the church doors.

Claude held his dagger with his left hand.

A woman walked in. Rich. Surcoat embroidered. Hood trimmed with fur. Her skin was quite dark and a few strands escaped her wimple at the temple.

'Vrouwe Ooste,' said the priest happily. 'You have come.'

The woman smiled slightly. 'I would never ignore a message from you, Father, not even in these terrible days. Is this the stranger who asked after Willem de Vos?'

The priest looked at Claude.

Was this woman a relative of Willem de Vos? A sister, perhaps; half-sister, more likely, given the difference in complexion. If the man were dead, perhaps his property was still here in Bruges. Claude had nothing to buy the mace with and no way to prove he had sold it to Willem in the first place. But he could work.

'God keep you, child,' said the woman. She looked only a little older than he was.

'God has been keeping me here, madame,' he said with a smile. His Flemish was improving. He had picked it up years ago on a campaign near Lille, but it had gone rusty.

Then his smile froze, and he clasped his right arm with his left. The itch was almost unbearable, but his own light touch was so painful he didn't dare scratch.

'You know Willem de Vos?'

Claude answered, 'I cannot say I know him, no. I met him, some months ago. I sold him something, a thing I much regret selling now. I know nothing but his name

43

and that he was a merchant of Bruges. A man of about ordinary height, losing his hair.'

The woman laughed nervously. 'That describes him, yes. Also describes half the city, or it would have, a month ago. Are you a visitor?'

Claude nodded, gritting his teeth against the pain in his arm. A visitor. A burden. A wounded bird.

Claude could overcome being stripped of arms and harness, stripped of coins and horse, alone in the world and wearing women's clothes. He had been that way before. He had gone out into this rotten world as a child with nothing to his name and he had found his own strength within himself. He had breathed that ember into flame.

A man with honour has no need for friends, Janos used to say. Claude had been hurt, the first time Janos said that. Now Claude turned the phrase over on his tongue, in seven languages, before he slept every night.

Given a little time and freedom he could make a life for himself again – but now his strength was not within himself, not entirely. That infernal weapon had stolen his strength, withered his sword arm.

'I don't know what to do with her,' the priest said, gesturing at Claude. 'She was in the Chatelaine's army in some fashion, it seems, but not a grotesque. And not . . . not a camp follower. She was found raving of fever outside the city gates. Dressed as a crossbowman. As a man.'

The woman looked him up and down. Claude felt his skin redden.

'However did you manage that?' said the townswoman.

'Not well enough, it seems.' He smiled as best as he could through the itch of his arm.

'She has been wounded,' said the priest. 'I don't know what to do with her.'

Claude was close to the mace now, so close. If he had the mace and a way out of this city, he could make something new of himself. Find a company of mercenaries. Start again. The first step was getting out of this church and understanding this woman's connection to the mace.

The woman frowned. 'Willem de Vos, I am sorry to say, did not come back from the battle of Cassel. His wife, though, is my children's wet nurse. If you would like to speak with her, come with me. I warn you it is a dour house in these dark times. My wet nurse is a funny old thing and my cook is so frightened she barely does anything but shake.'

The priest nodded his head. 'Vrouwe Ooste, you are a marvel. God will reward you.'

Claude turned to the priest. 'Where shall I find my belongings?'

The priest looked puzzled. Claude listed in French the things he had carried on his body: sword, dagger, crossbow, helmet, cap, camail, mail hauberk and padded aketon to wear beneath it, padded chausses and chausses of mail for the legs, poleyns for the knees, belt, spanning hook, gloves, quiver, quarrels (he claimed twenty, although some had found their marks in his last battle). The priest frowned. Claude went on: shirt and braies for beneath it all. The priest frowned deeper.

'Your man's clothing and armaments have been given out among the guards at the walls. This city is under siege, and neither you nor I would be alive now if the beardless of Bruges were not keeping the chimeras at bay as best they can. Your food, in these desperate times, has cost more than our coffers have seen in a year. We have no help here now from anyone but God. A more than fair arrangement, unless you have some other means of paying for your room and board?'

He swallowed. 'I had a purse, yes.'

The priest shook his head. 'If so, it did not come here with you.'

He might be lying. What did it matter? If the priest had taken it, it would be gone by now, spent on food, most likely.

'Oh, and a phylactery, a little thing on a leather string,' Claude remembered aloud. Given to him by funny old Guillot before he expired of ague in Genoa last summer.

It came to Claude, then, like a blow to the gut, that he had truly lost everything. His tunics and hoods. His game pieces. His good grey courser, with him since Catalonia, his through a very lucky wager, and no doubt stolen or dead now. His friends.

'I am Jacquemine Ooste,' said the woman in French. 'What is your name?'

'Claude,' he said, the name he had chosen at fourteen.

The priest frowned at him. Claude stared back, daring him to question it. He could not remember now, if he had deliberately chosen to call himself Claude because it could belong to a man or a woman. Perhaps he had, perhaps he had been unsure, then, when he had been barely old enough to bleed. He was not unsure now.

'Is that the name you were christened with?'

Claude almost smiled at that. He had not been christened at all. But it hurt to remember the name of his childhood, and anyway that name would not be welcome here. He was pushing his luck enough already, without announcing himself Jewish.

'Claude,' he said. 'Claude is my name.'

CHAPTER FOUR

Margriet ran onto the causeway under the gate, slipping in the dust at the edge of the road, her feet finding purchase in the weeds.

Had the terrible thunder blasted the walls open? As the smoke cleared, she saw it still standing, the wooden door unmarred by the greasy black smoke in the air.

As she approached the gate, she screamed, 'Open, open in the name of Christ! They're behind me!'

Her right leg was still numb from squatting and her breath was in her throat. She fell against the wooden door and banged.

'Open! If you let me die, I swear I shall haunt you. I will come back as a revenant and call your names. By God, I swear it. Let me in, you ninnies!'

She could not hear over the ringing in her ears. Should she leap into the moat? Would the Nix find her there, after all?

Her city. Her city, where she had worked and fought and bled. Its very stones owed her.

The door creaked, and she squeezed through as it

opened. Someone took her roughly by one arm and flung her into the darkness. It was cool and damp, and she leaned against the stone wall to catch her breath.

Young Pieter de Groote, pimpled and scrawny, leaned against the door and barred it, glaring at her.

'What in God's name have you done?' he asked her.

'Me? That was nothing to do with me. That was a passel of chimeras. Blowing themselves back to Hell. They're trying to blow the walls down.'

'And what in Hell were you doing out there?'

'Don't know your job, Pieter,' she said. The words tumbled out of her, a release. She heard how shrill her voice sounded, her throat constricted by fear. 'Letting a woman wait at the mercy of Hell's envoys. You were always a bad one, from the days you ran with a hoop in the street and tortured your little sister with dead rats. Oh, yes, someone was watching. Someone was watching and it was me.' She poked her own chest. 'And now God is watching and sees how you leave a woman out at the mercy of monsters.' She pointed up at Him. Since the arrival of Hell from below, the orientation of Heaven seemed all the more certain.

'Such gratitude,' Pieter grumbled.

Elisabeth Joossens came up to them, holding a broomstick with a dagger blade notched and bound into one end.

'How the devil did you get out there? Lucky I know your voice, Margriet de Vos, or I would have thought you a spy for the Chatelaine. Pieter here wanted to leave you out there.'

'Did he now?'

Elisabeth frowned at her. Would she ask again, how

Margriet came to be outside the city walls during a siege? No, she would not. Margriet recognized that expression. It said: I am not asking. It was an expression they had all learned, all the residents of this cursed city who had been children during the bloody so-called Matins of Bruges in 1302. As Elisabeth and Margriet had both been.

When they were children, Elisabeth used to walk ahead of Margriet on the great treadmill that powered the crane in the market square, that loaded and unloaded the goods on the canal boats. The people of Bruges turned their children into machines and the city prospered.

And then when the French attacked, in 1302, they turned their children into weapons. Up on the rooftops, bricks in hand.

Margriet had sometimes wondered, in the intervening years, whether she would have to pay with one dead child for every Frenchman she had killed in her own childhood. Trouble was, she did not know how many she had killed, how many had died from the rocks and bricks she threw from the rooftop with her family. One had died, at least. She knew about one.

Perhaps, she had thought on more than one silent night, cradling a stillborn baby in her arms, God was taking his due. Perhaps God had not been paying attention the night that Beatrix was born, alive.

Like a market-woman distracted by one thief while the other helps himself to the contents of her cart, God had let her get away with her first child, her only child now.

Margriet must get to her Beatrix, now, to tell her that the chimeras were trying to bring down the walls. They had not succeeded today. Tomorrow, they might.

Elisabeth Joossens, who had also been up on those

rooftops in the siege of 1302, was not going to ask any citizen of Bruges to account for their actions now. This was their code, their silent password.

'Hie to your house, shrew, and be grateful I saved your life,' pimply Pieter hissed, too young to know the code, emboldened by his new position, now that all the men had gone from Bruges. 'Do you not see the sun is nearly down?'

It was. The streets were grey and empty. The revenants would be coming soon and Pieter would be fending them off. Within the city, Jacquemine Ooste would be worried, fretting over little Jacob. But first Margriet must see to Beatrix, tell her to prepare to leave the city. They must go. Tomorrow, they must go. They must take refuge where they could – some religious house, if any were left unburnt.

Damn the chimeras.

Margriet darted up the wooden steps to the top of the city wall, hearing Pieter yelling behind her. She leaned over the wall and shouted at the carnage below.

'Go to the devil, all of you, and save yourselves the shame of leaving with your tails between your legs!'

Margriet stumbled down the stairs again, back to where Elisabeth Joosens was still standing guard inside the gate. She whispered, 'They will take down the walls, Elisabeth. One way or another. It's time to prepare.'

Elisabeth nodded, gripping her broomstick, as if that would help.

Margriet walked into her city crookedly, holding her ribs with her right hand and the bunched-up corner of her apron full of thistles with her left. The city was silent: no horseshoes ringing on the cobbles, for the horses had all been eaten. No carts wheeled over the stones. No children played and the canals were empty save for a few small boats tied up to posts.

Outside the besieged city were the chimeras, but the greater danger to the people of Bruges was within.

With evening coming on, all the houses were shuttered; the only way to tell which walls hid healthy people and which hid those touched by the revenant plague were the marks scratched into the doors: a rectangle, wider than it was tall, with rounded corners. The Hellmouth.

And sometimes, on the richer houses, by the words *Domine Miserere Nobis*. Or the letter H, for Hellpest.

The Hellpest, the revenant plague, meant death. Painful, hideous, but mercifully quick, and mere bodily death was not the worst weapon the revenants carried.

Far, far worse was the Grief, which drove out reason and weakened the will. Every night, revenants flew over the skies of Bruges, and called the names of the living, over and over. Every night, some of the living went mad. They saw strange sights, and tore their hair and flesh, and would not eat or drink.

And, then, one of two things would happen:

The Grief-stricken would go pale and thin until they, too, became revenants, and walked out of their houses to take the hands of their beloveds, and walk away, over the walls, though the living (sometimes) tried to hold them back.

Or the newly Grief-stricken opened their doors and willingly let the revenants in. Once a revenant entered a house, everyone who lived there would be dead of the plague within days.

Buried death or walking death: those were the only outcomes, once the revenants' call opened the heart of a living person.

But Margriet did not fear the dead. Willem might well be a corpse, that she knew. Three weeks since the Battle of Cassel, and no sign of her husband. He might well have been among the prisoners fed to the Hellbeast, in which case he would be a revenant. What of it? If she heard him call, she would be glad, for she would know she was truly a widow. Her husband could call her name all he liked, and she would only smile, knowing he was dead. There was no crack in her heart by which the Grief could enter.

CHAPTER FIVE

The Chatelaine paced the rolling floor of her private chamber, swinging the mace that fitted over her hand like a gauntlet, that bit into her flesh and seemed now to grow out of her arm, at her side.

Her husband's house had many rooms and most of them were red. Great halls that glistened red, deep wormholes that glowed red, wiggling passages that pulsed red. The Chatelaine was fluent in all its hues and meanings.

For more centuries than she could count, she had worn the nine hundred keys of Hell on an iron ring on her belt. They dragged behind her, a long and heavy chain. Her husband had given her the keeping of those keys, given her the weight of them to bear because it made him laugh to see it. That was his first and final error.

The first thing she did, when she finally managed to imprison him in Hell's deepest oubliette, was to change the locks. And she had a new key made, a single key that opened every key in Hell: her beautiful mace.

She would have liked to destroy the keys altogether.

What is an oubliette with a key? Not an oubliette at all. Keys are for remembering.

But her husband had taught her that the beast called Hell could not be destroyed; no part of it could be destroyed. Its keys and its locks were as much a part of its great body as its teeth and its guts.

So she went to the most skilled of her husband's torturers, who used the fires of Hell to mar his victims in the most beautiful ways.

Gobhan Og, a wrinkled turnip of a man who had been a smith once, confirmed that the keys were indestructible, nodding sadly.

'They can change, as all flesh changes. The flesh of Hell may be iron or brimstone or pus or chitin, but no matter what it looks like, it is still flesh, and it may be altered in Hell's furnaces. Altering is not destroying.'

'Then you will alter them, and if you please me, you will be my chief artificer. My weapon-master. I will have no more torturers.'

The Hellbeast required feeding: it must drain the life from revenants, from people held in the moment between death and life for long years. But the Chatelaine would take those people from the wounded who were already dying. She would be a kinder ruler of Hell than her husband had been.

She must keep a key for her husband's oubliette, but she was strong enough to remember. She would remember that she had power over her husband now, that this was a power she had made herself.

'Take all of my keys,' she said to Gobhan Og, throwing one end of the chain of keys onto his great anvil. 'Make them all into a single weapon that I may wear. What sort of a weapon would work like a key?'

Gobhan Og thought. He had been out in the world, getting food for the Beast. He had seen something of the world's weapons.

'A flanged mace, perhaps, if we remade all the locks to fit its flanges.'

'Excellent.'

'In place of your lovely hand, my mistress?' he looked at her eagerly.

She looked at her hand, the dark brown flesh still so young-looking, the nails still so pink.

'I think not,' she said. 'Let me wear it like a gauntlet.'

She had borne the keys already for more than a lifetime. If she must bear them forever, let her wield them as well.

The mace fit over her hand perfectly and worked its edge into the flesh of her forearm. It was heavier than it looked, forged of all the many keys of her husband's many rooms.

She remembered enough about the surface to know that it was safest to arrive with entitlements, with power. Not as some wandering nameless girl, some exile with no land and no memory. No. She would come back to the surface, but with Hell at her back.

She had set the torturers to new work, with an edict that they were to make, not mar. The fires of Hell could fuse anything without killing it, because Hell was a creature in which Life and Death did not rule. Those furnaces could join metal and flesh, and glass and fur, and any other things that the artificers' imagination could compass. She would make an army of chimeras, offering the changes to anyone willing. And there were many willing.

They had started with a French brigand. How miserable he had been when he wandered into what he thought –

he swore he thought – was a mere cave. How he had loathed himself for the sins of his past. He had asked her if he could ever be made pure. And so she led him to the furnace, where her beloved unicorn waited. In they went together, into the fire, unicorn and man. That was her first great sacrifice, her first great gift.

She had not been certain it would work. But it did, and he was beautiful. A body like a man's but larger, bronzed and muscled, and with the great horn in the middle of his forehead.

She asked Chaerephon to name him and he called him Monoceros.

Monoceros taught the Chatelaine his French language. He became her marshal as his reward. The first of her chimeras.

She said the word *chimeras* lovingly, the way one gives a kitten the name of an ogre, to show how fragile it is.

The chimeras chose their own gifts, just as the victims had once chosen their own punishments; will was the bellows that fed the fires of Hell.

But there were risks. Soon after they came to the French court, they met a young noblewoman marred by smallpox, unmarriageable, a reluctant nun. She admired Monoceros and his skin like bronze, asked to be given a skin smooth as Italian glass. The Chatelaine agreed, thinking of the armour she could make.

Gobhan Og vitrified the noblewoman clear through; he let his furnace get too hot.

The Chatelaine demoted him in a fury. No longer head artificer, he would labour with a shovel, cleaning the unmentionable mess made by the forges. The saltpetre from the flying creatures that were Hell's parasites. The brimstone that collected in its cloaca.

In fury, Gobhan Og began to plot against her.

The Chatelaine stopped pacing. She opened her eyes and swung her mace, remembering how pleasantly it had bit into Gobhan Og's skull, how it had spilled his treasonous brain all over the floor of his little chamber, how the Beast had absorbed it into its shining red flesh.

The mantis-man who guarded her door opened it and coughed in the strange way of his kind, and then Monoceros stood there. Her beautiful horned man, the first of her servants. The only one she could trust. The man who was part unicorn, who had shown himself to be as brave and loyal as those creatures were reputed to be.

'What news?' she asked him.

'The hounds think perhaps the mercenary Claude Jouvenal might have gone to Bruges. I gave them the scent off an aketon the mercenary once wore, and they followed a trail to the moat of Bruges. But of course, they could go no further, as the town's walls still stand, for now.'

Her beautiful hounds, made out of a dozen men and women with broken backs or broken necks, whose bodies were frozen and who had been left to rot to death in their bedsores. She put their heads on the hounds and set them off as a pack. The double-headed hounds had the loyalty of dogs, and the anger of nearly-dead humans.

Monoceros stood, waiting.

She paced. Claude Jouvenal was a great danger to her because of the way he'd escaped. Somehow, he had persuaded the smith Gobhan Og to make another mace, an exact copy of the one the Chatelaine wore. He'd used it to unlock the key to his cell, to unlock the mouth of Hell.

She must have the counterfeit mace back – not just a mace but a key, a key to every lock within the Beast and to its very bridle. It meant that the Chatelaine was no longer the only keeper of the key to Hell. Someone else could control it. With the forgery, the mercenary Claude Jouvenal could return, could open any door he liked, could open the doors to Hell's oubliettes, could free any prisoner there.

And the French king was growing impatient. Demanding the surrender of Bruges, but the Chatelaine had lost more than half her forces at Cassel. If she spent any more in attacking a walled city, she would be weakened indeed.

'Let us see if the gonner-chimeras can frighten Bruges into surrender,' she said. 'If all goes well, they will have those gates open by sundown.'

CHAPTER SIX

A woman was picking through a midden between two houses, a rolling pin in one hand. She looked up when Margriet passed. They peered at each other like suspicious crones, although Margriet was still young enough to bear children and this woman looked not much older than she was.

The fingers around the rolling pin were black. She kept clutching and re-clutching it, as if keeping hold of her weapon by sheer force of will. Already taken by the first stages of the plague, but her eyes were sharp. It had not been she who let the revenants into her house.

Soon, her skin would fall away in clumps, leaving bloody welts on her back and chest. The plague killed from the outside in: first the numb, dead skin, then the attacks on heart and lungs and brain. Her breathing was already laboured, although that might be ordinary fear or want.

Neither of them said a word.

Margriet was not afraid of the woman. The disease did not seem to pass from the living to the living. It came only from the revenants who had started to return to

Bruges a few days after the battle of Cassel, men Margriet had known from children. They were dead now: wounded, bleeding, rotting. They swam the moat, uncaring how many hastily made arrows and javelins stuck in their backs. They climbed the city walls after sundown with bare hands and feet. They walked the streets until dawn. They called out names.

Margriet jumped as church bells clanged from all directions, from whatever parts of the city still had a priest or a child to pull a rope.

She turned away from the woman with the rolling pin and the rotting flesh and hurried down an empty street, cleaner than any street of Bruges had ever been in Margriet's life.

She had a little time between the bells and the revenants.

Her daughter would not want to leave Bruges. Beatrix's husband, like Margriet's, had not come back from the Battle of Cassel. Beatrix was living now with Margriet's father and sister, in the house where Margriet grew up.

Nobody lived now in the rooms Willem and Margriet had shared over Willem's shop, where the tables stood empty, waiting for their master's return. Two years ago, after Margriet had lost yet another baby, she had moved in to the Ooste house to nurse little Jacob and help Jacquemine care for her toddler, Agatha. It was a way to make some money. She had not regretted living apart from Willem. She had Beatrix, her first child, the only one of her four children to live past infancy. Beatrix was her blessing and Margriet was finally too tired to ask God for more.

As for Willem, he had been a poor husband and a worse

merchant. Margriet would be able to sell the house, if he was dead.

If she could return to Bruges, that is. If the houses still stood when she did.

She turned the corner into Casteelstrate and nearly barrelled into a man stinking of wine.

'The bells are ringing,' he said, loudly, to be heard over the clanging.

She had not smelled a drunken man for some time. It was hard to find enough wine to get soused in a city that had been besieged for a month. One of the churches must still have had something to be looted.

'I am on my way indoors.' She stepped to one side to get past him.

He let her pass but turned and dogged her steps.

'It's people like you who let the revenants in,' he puffed. 'You think it's hard to block your ears against their calls when you're safely in your chamber? It is impossible when you see them face to face. You must not be in the street.'

Just her luck to run into a man in this city of women. The only men of age left in Bruges now were this sort: stooges or cowards. This bullying fool fancied himself some kind of protector, in the absence of better men. Ha! Margriet had helped protect this city from the French when she was a child, before this lout was even born. She had protected it with the rocks and bricks that came to hand, sitting on the cold rooftops before the dawn.

'Get out of my way.' She pushed him aside.

'Every person in the street when the revenants come will turn traitor. I've seen it happen.'

'Then I suppose you must have been in the street yourself.'

'I go into the streets to protect the weak, you stubborn woman.'

'I don't need the protection of a drunkard. You stink like a friar. Now go, before I make you go.'

'Make me go how, I'd like to know?'

She had nearly reached the doorway of Willem's empty shop. Her father's home was not much farther, but she wanted to be rid of this blackguard.

She stood close to the lock and fumbled for one of the keys she still wore on the chain around her neck, hiding it with her body, as if the key were something secret. She fitted it into the lock.

'This is where you're going? No, too close to the street. Look at these flimsy shutters. You'll stand no chance against them, in here alone.'

He crowded against her. He wanted to come in.

'I have no need of you. Go.'

'I will enter if I wish.'

'This is my husband's house,' she spat, 'and only I and my husband may enter here. Go, before he comes and knocks that dunderpate clean off your shoulders.'

She swung the door open, not caring whether she hit him, and darted through, slamming the door behind her. She threw the bolt across. The bells stopped ringing just as the door closed; it was as if the door stopped the sound, stopped all sounds, separated her from the world outside. In here it was quiet.

On the other side of the door, the drunkard bellowed, 'Troublemaker! Termagant!'

She smiled bitterly and bit back her curses. She would give him a few minutes to move on, then dart out to Beatrix's house.

It was dark inside. She paced. The place was as she left it, if a bit dusty. No squatters or rats to worry about in these times. No oil in the lamp, no tinderbox to light it, but she did not intend to stay.

Yet she did not like to stand in the gloom, with her husband's tables and shelves, empty now of his wares, squatting around her like beasts.

She felt a stare upon her. She turned around and saw, in the doorway, her husband. The shape of him, looming against the dim golden evening.

'Dear God, Willem,' she gasped. 'You gave me a fright.'

'Margriet.'

At the sound of her name she almost was grateful to see him. Old familiarity. Nothing more.

'You're home, then? Might have given me some word, but of course men never think of women, never think how they worry. How did you get into the city, with those chimeras ringed all around the walls?'

She did not approach him. He stood, pale in the dark room; she had to squint to see his face. It was bloodied about the mouth, as if he had walked here straight from the battlefield without pausing to bathe his wounds or rest.

'Margriet, I am come home.'

She stood, unsure what to do with herself, as she had stood on their wedding night. She had last seen him, when? Five, six weeks ago, a little more, as he and the other men went off to wait for battle in their tents, or whatever it was men did. Yet he seemed like a stranger. Perhaps it was a consequence of killing; perhaps it changed a man. Her father on that bloody night of 1302, holding his dagger to a Frenchman's breast, had not been the same man who once plied his boat through the canal, who taught her the boatmen's songs.

And she, as a child, sitting on the roof tiles with a rock in her hand. She had changed that night, too. She had taken up arms, in the fashion of women and children, and had never quite let them drop again.

'Margriet.'

She should be a patient wife to him, and forgiving; but alas, those were not her virtues.

'Have you eaten, Willem? You'll have to bathe, too, before you go to bed. You're covered in muck.'

Blood, she had wanted to say, but changed the word at the last moment.

He shook his head a little too slowly, grinding his head from side to side as if he were trying to rid himself of a crick in the neck.

'Margriet,' he said. 'Margriet, Margriet, Margriet.'

She stared at him and she understood. In the hollow of her stomach. Dead. Her rotten husband, dead. She drummed her fingers against her thigh. Her brain screamed the word she refused to speak.

'You're different,' she whispered. 'You've changed.'

'I have returned.'

'For what?' Her voice was hoarse, as if she had been screaming, or crying. 'What do you want?'

His face was as dull as a doll's. Some of his teeth had been knocked out since she had seen him last.

'I am on the Chatelaine's business.'

She had expected him to say that he wanted her: as his bride, or even as his property. It was a relief that he did not. Even so she felt a lurch in her gut, as if she were all alone in a sinking boat.

She tried not to think of the door, of the plague mark that must soon be set upon it. A revenant. A revenant had entered her house. Was this her house? Not truly, not any more. She just happened to be inside it.

Of course, with Willem dead, it was her house now. Hers and Beatrix's.

'How did you get in here?' she whispered.

'You invited me, Margriet. "My husband may enter here", you said.'

Her stomach turned.

'That's not right,' she said. 'That can't be enough. I didn't want you. You did not even call me. It isn't just.'

Willem stared.

'I am here.'

That goddamned drunkard in the street. May he live to be flayed alive. With a dull knife. And she would use his skin for a book and write all her accounts in it with ink of gall and wormwood. She would gut him, if she ever saw him again.

Willem, or the revenant who had been Willem, walked to a shelf and pulled one of the rough, empty sacks down. He turned to one side and began to pace the floor between the tables, stepping with care, listening to the squeak of each board. She walked closer to him, circling him as though he were a rabid creature. In his back a red hole gaped, a hole as thick as a lance. The hole from which his life had ebbed. She thought she could see clear through it, but it was hard to say, in the gloom.

'What happened, Willem? How did you die?'

He stopped pacing for a moment and looked into the distance, as though remembering. No trace of sadness, or of any feeling at all, crossed his face.

'A poleaxe through the back. But somehow, I did not die, not at first. I lay there as men trampled me. I was so very cold, so very thirsty. I remember that, more than the pain. And I remember looking up into the bluest sky I had ever seen. And then the Crow-women came.'

'Crow-women?'

'Chimeras. They lifted us up into the sky. Margriet, I thought I was being carried to heaven, but it was Hell. The Crow-women dropped us at the mouth of the Hellbeast. Baltazar was there, too. His head was bashed and bloodied and he could barely burble when he saw me. The Hellbeast opened its mouth, and a great tongue reached out and took us, and I knew no more for a time. When I awoke, I no longer felt thirsty or cold, or anything at all. I felt nothing, except that I knew I must come for my life's work, my wealth. It was a great relief, to feel nothing else.'

'Baltazar is dead, then,' she said. Beatrix would be beside herself, poor girl. She would not be safe. 'He is a revenant? Is he here? Willem, is he here?'

He shook his head. 'Not yet. Not tonight.'

She must warn Beatrix, for all the good that warning would do. No, she must keep her safe, take her to Jacquemine Ooste's, where Margriet could be sure to stop her ears. Beatrix had loved her husband. The Grief would find her an easy target.

But Willem – why was he kneeling on the floor? He used his fingernails to pry a board up, fingernails which had grown long, and as he pried, the head of the nail pulled his fingernail off, leaving only a hideous flat of quick, the grey-pink of salmon skin.

He did not seem to notice.

Willem, or the revenant that had been Willem, pulled the floorboard up, then straddled the space and yanked a box up out of the cavity. It was a massive thing, a chest with handles, and with an iron padlock.

'What in God's holy name have you been keeping from me?' Margriet breathed.

'I was a trader,' he said.

'You were the worst trader in Bruges. As wicked as the devil but not half as clever. Always trying to cheat people too smart to be cheated. Always came home with less than you had to start with.'

'I had wealth. I lied to you.'

He said it plainly, baldly. Then he plucked a small iron key from a fold by his waist and opened the chest.

Margriet's breath caught at the gleam of it. Willem had been a trader in cloth, but there was no cloth in this chest. A silver ewer, fine and tall. Daggers. A small sword in a fine scabbard. Bits of plate armour. Piles and piles of coins. She knelt beside her dead husband, leaned forward and ran her hands through the coins: silver and gold in all kinds, groats and pennies and florins.

'Where did you get it, Willem?' She could smell the battlefield on him: clay and decay.

'I kept some of my earnings apart, all the years of my life. I did not trust you with the keeping of it. You would have spent it on women's things.'

'You dishonest, misbegotten knave. I rue the day I married you. What did you do to get all this, then? Was I married to a usurer?'

'Yes,' he said simply. 'Some of this is war-wealth. Some I traded. This,' he said, and picked up a flanged mace, nearly the length of the chest itself, 'I bought this off a young mercenary. The last thing I got before I was killed. He sold it to me for the clothes I stood up in. I hid the goods and came home in my shirt – I told you I had been robbed.'

'I remember.' She snatched the mace from him. It was heavy, but not as heavy as it looked. The handle was strangely hollow.

He took it back from her; he had lost none of his strength.

'This is all the Chatelaine's now,' he said.

He piled it all into the sack, coins and silver, weapons and gold.

'You lying lickspittle, it isn't yours to give her,' she said, hoarsely. She licked her lips. 'Not now. You're dead.' She forced herself to say it out loud, as though the words could break whatever sorcery held his bones upright and bellowed his breath. 'Your daughter is a widow, you tell me, and yet you would take her inheritance?'

He put his head on one side. It flopped just a little too far over.

'Neither of you are widows. Baltazar is the Beast's now. He still walks the earth.'

She shook her head. 'You're dead; you're nothing. Nothing but meat. Food for flies. A bag of bones walking. You're dead. This is mine. Mine and Beatrix's. Flemish law says a widow gets one third, the child the rest.'

He stared at her.

'Everything is the Chatelaine's,' he said. 'She holds the reins of Hell and Hell holds me. I am hers, and all my wealth.'

'No, it isn't. For years, Willem, I have farmed myself out like a cow. Our daughter spins until her hands are raw. My father wears hose that are nought but patches. And all the while you have been sitting on a fortune!'

'You are mine. This is mine.'

He slammed the lid down on the empty chest and stood, holding one end of the sack. It was not quite full but heavy. The sack dragged on the floor as he took one step toward her.

'My husband is dead,' she said again, standing straight up to face him. She had a right to that truth. She was entitled to her widowhood, to the sympathy and respect of her neighbours, to the deference of younger women. To these walls and these tables and to her husband's wealth, no matter how he'd got it.

'I am hers and you are mine. And you are marked by death now, Margriet. The plague will take you. You are not a widow for I am not truly dead. It is right that a wife should die, when her husband has no further need of her.'

'I only married you because I had to!' she screamed. 'Because you had a good business from your father, before you squandered it, and my father was sick from the wars. You selfish bastard.'

He trudged through the open door into the night, dragging the sack behind him like his sins. Willem, stolid, balding Willem, walking out into the road just as he had in life. No one would dare take his wealth from him now.

But it was hers. It belonged to her, and to Beatrix.

She ran out into the empty street and grabbed the sack, but he was too strong; he kept walking and she fell forward. So she grabbed him from behind, her arms wrapped around him almost as though they were lovers. He did not stop. She scraped her nails into his dead flesh, but he kept walking and did not even cry out. She pulled on his thin hair, and it came out in her hands and she fell away from him, tumbled to the ground in horror, looking at Willem's hair falling out of her grasp to the cobbles.

An arm grabbed her from behind and she smelled sweat and wine.

'Got you.' The swaggering drunk, damn him.

Margriet dropped her hips as if she were sitting in her rocking chair, and felt his arms loosen. She stamped her heel on his right toe and then ran after Willem, leaving the drunk cursing behind her.

She ran, calling her husband's name, screaming it, as around her the plaintive calls of the revenants calling the names of their beloved drifted into the sky. Willem had gone. He'd be over the city walls by now, and she couldn't follow, not through the gates anyway.

'You were a great disappointment!' she screamed.

CHAPTER SEVEN

Beatrix let the flax slip through her raw fingertips. It was the hair of a princess. She would coil it and dress it with star-flowers.

'Still spinning?' Grandfather asked with a little smile. She had not heard him come in to their main room.

She dipped her fingers in her dish of water and paused to smile back at him. 'The devil finds work for idle hands.'

'Your mother is late,' said Aunt Katharina.

Aunt Katharina stood behind Grandfather, and everyone's smiles faded. She was holding the bits of wool for stuffing their ears.

'Is it dusk already?' Beatrix whispered.

Grandfather limped over to the doll-sized window he had cut into the shutters and put his eye to it.

'Perhaps Margriet could not get away,' he murmured.

'Mother will come,' Beatrix said. 'No revenant would be a match for Mother, if she met one in the street. Can you imagine? She'd talk it back to Hell.'

'I should hope she'd have the good sense to stay indoors,' said Katharina.

Grandfather closed the little window and sat on his stool by the supper table, shifting the candle so the light fell fully on Beatrix's work.

'I am surprised you still have any flax left to spin,' said Katharina.

'I spin all I have each day, yet every morning I wake to find the kabouters have refilled my baskets,' Beatrix teased. Her grandmother used to tell stories of the little people who would help you or hinder you by playing tricks in the house. 'Actually, this small basket is the last of it. Tomorrow I will have to spin grandfather's belly lint. Get it ready, Grandfather.'

'Really, Beatrix,' Katharina scolded.

Beatrix's stomach rumbled. She wished she could spin them all something to eat. One bony fish between the two of them, tonight. Grandfather looked gaunt. She wished for a chicken. No, a lovely big goose or a swan. They used to land on the fields outside the moat.

'Perhaps I can spin the mist off the canal,' she said. 'Wouldn't that be lovely?'

'You might as well spin air as flax,' said Katharina. 'Who's going to buy it now? The traders are all dead or gone, and the roads shut.'

Grandfather coughed.

'When life gets back to normal, we will be glad of something to sell,' Beatrix said, trying to make her voice soothing, but it came out stinging like a nettle.

Katharina held the bits of wool out to her, two hard white twists. Each plug sighed into shape in Beatrix's ears, suffocating the sounds of the world, as if she were spinning now on the bottom of the sea, fathoms deep.

Grandfather dutifully plugged his own ears. He sat staring at the scratched old table.

A sharp knock at the door. She and Grandfather looked at each other, like conspiring children, as if neither wanted to admit they had heard. If Katharina lost faith in the earplugs, who knew what she would do next to try to keep them safe from the revenants. Lock them in the cellar, probably.

Another knock.

Beatrix let the flax fall from her hand. This could be Baltazar. Any knock, every knock, could be Baltazar, her beloved, her husband, her all, returning to her at last. Hurt in the war, perhaps. Wandering, confused. Or a captive, escaped. She would spin his memories smooth. She would put her fingers to his rough lips, if only he would come back to her.

Grandfather opened the little peephole in the window and put his face right up to it, trying to see around to the door.

'What are you doing?' Katharina hissed.

Without answering, Grandfather unlatched the door.

Katharina stood, a knife in her hand. In the open doorway, Beatrix's mother stood, holding her side as if she had a stitch from running.

'I'm not a revenant yet, Katharina, but I might send a message to Hell and ask to be made into one, if you leave me out in the dark again.'

Beatrix had never seen her mother's eyes shine like that, like a cornered vixen's. She pulled the wool out of her ears and Grandfather did the same.

'There's a bit of bread, Mother,' Beatrix said. She had been saving it to eat before bed, to split with Grandfather.

They did that together every night now, shared a morsel before their prayers. But she wanted now to offer her mother something, to take that hungry look out of her eyes. 'More than half sawdust, but let me see if I can soften it a bit.'

Mother waved her away. 'I'm not hungry. Never mind that now.'

'You're late,' Grandfather said. 'What's wrong?'

'I've been at the walls,' Mother replied. 'I've seen the chimeras, trying to blow them apart with some infernal weapon. They did not succeed, but they will keep trying, I am sure. We must leave Bruges, all of us.'

Katharina's mouth dropped open.

'How?'

'I have a way. It is difficult. Will be very hard for you, Father. But we must try. To stay here means death.'

Grandfather smiled. 'Dear daughter, to go means death for me. I can barely walk from this table to the door without losing my breath. You must go.'

'But we cannot!' Beatrix said. 'Our husbands – how will they find us?'

Mother took a deep breath, closed her eyes. 'I've seen Willem.'

Beatrix knew in a moment what her mother meant. She knew why her mother had not said, 'Willem is back,' or 'Willem is here.' Yet Beatrix could not help herself from drawing it out, from holding hope in her hands for as many breaths as she could.

But Grandfather had never been one to delay the inevitable. He sank down onto the bench, his face slack.

'Yes, he is taken, he is a revenant,' said Mother.

'But you did not invite him in, Margriet,' Katharina

said. It was hardly a question, as if she could not bring herself to make it a question.

'I never wanted that man in my house, even when he was alive.' Mother stared at Beatrix, her eyes now steely. Beatrix squinted but couldn't quite see her mother behind her words. I have no father, Beatrix thought. I have no father now.

Grandfather put his hand to his forehead. 'Willem gone, too,' he said. 'So many.'

'It's done, and past help,' Mother said. 'The main thing is that I caught him carrying off a sack full of clinking money and rich things. We were never poor. The bastard has been hiding a fortune from us. And now it's ours.'

Katharina put a hand to her heart. 'But where? What sort of fortune?'

'He was a usurer, and God knows what else besides. A man may make a fortune during wartime, even a man as gormless as my husband. Now he has taken his fortune off to Hell, but it is ours by right, Beatrix. Widows are entitled to one-third, and children to the rest, by custom.'

'When the siege is over, will you go to the bailiff?' Grandfather asked.

'The bailiff is dead.'

'The count, then,' said Beatrix.

'Bah,' Grandfather said.

'Count Louis is no longer in control of Bruges, not really,' Mother said. 'Besides, he is the King of France's man, and doubtless he would try to apply some barbaric French law.'

'But King Philippe—' Katharina broke in.

'Philippe is no true king,' Grandfather snapped. 'He came by it through trickery.'

'What does it matter?' Beatrix asked. 'There is no one to give us back what Father has taken. We did not even know we had a fortune, and now it has gone. Let us say a prayer for Father's soul and for all the souls not yet at rest.'

'I'll say a prayer for him,' Mother said, 'after he gives me my due. If we leave tonight, we will catch him before long. The revenants walk only at night. I can walk until my feet fall off.'

'And if you catch him and he refuses?' Katharina asked. 'What will you do, then, Margriet? Beat him about the head with your apron?'

It was then, for some mysterious reason, that the grief and worry burst up out of Beatrix's throat and a sound like a sob crossed with a hiccup escaped her throat. She clapped her hand over her mouth.

Mother squatted down to look into her face. Weeds poked out of her apron. Heaven knew where she had been gathering weeds, what garden within Bruges' walls still boasted a few stalks of anything that could be boiled or beaten.

'I must,' she whispered. 'What does Willem need now with silver and gold? It is all going to the Chatelaine and her ally, that pustule. I can't let the Chatelaine and the French king take what is yours by right, Beatrix.'

'It is suicide,' Katharina said. 'How would you even get out of the city walls? What about the chimeras? They will surely kill you if they find you out in the country.'

'Bah. They're only people. You know who's a chimera now? Young Julius, you remember, the boy who was soft in the head. Well he's got a new head now, but he's still Julius. They're only soldiers, and I killed my first French soldier when I was younger than Beatrix is now. A rock to the head is as good as an axe, if you aim it properly. There is no more danger outside the city walls than within, especially now that the chimeras are trying to take those walls down. That's why Beatrix, at least, must come with me, if you and Father will not.'

'Beatrix!' Katharina's eyes went wide.

Her place was here, in Bruges. Once the siege lifted, Baltazar might come home, wounded and hungry, and find her gone.

But perhaps, if she went out there into the world, she would find word of him. Perhaps Father, or whatever was left of Father, would tell her what had befallen her husband. Or she could ask the Chatelaine herself!

'Margriet, you must not drag Beatrix into this foolishness,' Katharina said.

'You go with your mother,' said Grandfather, unexpectedly. They all looked at him. 'It is your wealth, too. The claim is two-thirds yours. You must be there to make it. Perhaps there is enough left of the father in him that the sight of you will soften his heart. There is nothing here for you, nothing to eat and nothing to spin.'

'I cannot leave you here, Grandfather.'

'I cannot come with you, old as I am. I will be fine with Katharina. There will be more food for us with you gone, you little glutton.'

Beatrix laughed. That was true, at least. But to go out there! To go to Hell! She could not imagine it.

St Catherine, she prayed in silence, what shall I do?

Grandfather leaned over the table and whispered. 'A week ago, it was safer inside these walls than outside them,' he said. 'Not so now. We are near starvation,

Beatrix, and I will go more happily to my grave if I know you two have some chance. Your mother is right: I can aim a rock, at least, once they come in. Take care of her. Be her better judgment.'

Mother was stubborn. She would go alone, if Beatrix did not go with her. Beatrix might at least be able to prevent her from getting herself killed. Mother was too sharp, too sure of herself.

'The apples are ripening out there, somewhere,' Beatrix said to her grandfather quietly. 'I will bring you back a bushel.'

'Keep your apples. I want honey. And figs, oh, fine figs like we used to get, do you remember?'

Beatrix insisted on taking her distaff and spindle, although Mother rolled her eyes. She did not want to be without them, and perhaps, she told her mother, they would find something to spin on the journey, and make a little money to buy food. They did not take any food from Grandfather's small store, but they took two leather water flasks, the flasks her parents used to take when they travelled on Father's business, or what everyone thought was Father's business.

They hurried through the dark streets, back to the Ooste house so Mother could take her leave. They filled the flasks at the conduit.

'Do you remember,' Beatrix huffed as they walked, 'what happened when the baker put that mouldy bread in the bottom of the basket, years ago?'

'Hmph,' said Mother.

'You demanded your money back, as was proper. You had every right to that sou. You argued for it until the sun set, and finally you got the sou back.'

'Indeed. That squinting blackguard.'

'And then for five years, we had to walk three streets further to buy our bread. For the sake of a sou.'

'Yes? What is your point, Beatrix?'

'I just wanted to know if you remembered,' she said with a sigh, and hitched up her little bundle of spare linen.

CHAPTER EIGHT

Claude sat at the Ooste table and ate the thin pottage they gave him. Dark, greasy bits of meat – rat, probably – floated in it. No worse fare than he'd had on the Modena campaign, but the company then had made up for it. He and Janos had won six ducats at dice and got drunk on crisp Vernaccia wine. He could still feel the smack of it between his eyebrows.

Claude glanced up at the table. No dice here. Certainly no wine. The dour-faced little girl stuck out her tongue, taking advantage of the fact that her mother was pacing behind her with a mewling baby. The old manservant and the even older cook would not even look at him.

Damn it, all this for a mace, a weapon he barely knew how to wield. But what choice had Claude had? He had not known how it would attach itself to him, how it would worm its way in to his flesh.

What would he take back now, of his choices? Claude had been desperate for a way out of the beast that superstitious people called Hell. But the Chatelaine would not relent. Every day she asked him to submit to the fire, to become one of her grotesques. And Claude might have given in, if the Chatelaine had not been so fascinated by him, had not called him a natural born chimera. Claude did not like to be teased.

When he learned that the Chatelaine's mace worked as a key, that it even opened the mouth of the Hellbeast, he saw his way out. That angry smith was just waiting for a chance for treason.

The smith had not warned Claude. Claude had not known that he would miss the mace after he got rid of it, that devices forged in the Hellbeast always took payment from their users. They were not easily wielded and not easily set aside.

As he ran to rejoin his company, he had considered keeping the thing. It was heavy but he liked the feel of it on his arm.

But it would have made him too easy to find, once the Chatelaine sent someone to look for him, as she would. The Chatelaine did not seem the kind to let a grudge go easily. Besides, Claude was a crossbowman. A mace was good for close combat with armour: a knight's weapon, or at least a squire's. That weapon, if it was to be a weapon and not a mere encumbrance, would reinvent him. He'd need to get a full harness of armour, and a warhorse, and a squire or attendants he could trust to clean out his clothes. And knights and squires would be married off; they had obligations to their lords.

No, he had decided. He would remain a crossbowman. Let him go back to his company without the weapon. The Chatelaine's chimeras would not find him as easily without it on his arm. They would not expect him to get rid of it.

He'd had a devil of a time ripping the thing off his arm.

Every pull in one direction hooked it deeper in the other. Finally, he peeled the edges away from his skin with a dagger and tore it away. He screamed, but the pain would pass, or so he'd thought.

Soon he came upon a Flemish trader. Still wearing the tunic and hose they'd given him in the Hellbeast, Claude wanted new clothes to help him escape the Chatelaine's spies. The trader was not the sort to ask questions.

He walked away in the trader's clothes. The pain in his arm dulled.

But the itch had begun that night and had not subsided, and his arm felt weak without the mace on it. By the time he rejoined his company, by the time the battle of Cassel began, the arm was near useless.

'When that Margriet gets here, she'll get the other end of a tongue lashing for once,' said Jacquemine Ooste, bouncing her baby on her knee and spooning pottage into its mouth. The baby was still fat. A strange sight in a besieged city. Jacquemine's little daughter, Agatha, ate her soup hungrily.

A knock at the door. They all froze.

'That'll be her,' said Jacquemine smoothly. 'Get the door, Hans.'

The old servant looked at her under caterpillar eyebrows.

'The revenants don't knock,' Jacquemine said. 'They call.'

'We don't know that they *can't* knock, though,' said Hans.

They'd be here all night, listening to the knock, at this rate. And if it was the wet nurse, Willem's wife, then Claude was finally getting near the mace. His arm itched as if his very skin knew it, too.

'God's teeth, I'll answer it,' said Claude, with a grin. He rose.

The cook squeezed her face into a sour rictus. There was one who did not approve of swearing. Well, so be it. A woman like her would find some cause to hate a man like Claude eventually. Better to push the righteous away from him quickly, before they could find cause to be disappointed. Much better to force people to choose at once, friend or foe, and then he knew where they stood.

But Jacquemine held her hand out, motioning Claude to stay. She took her knife from the table and held it in her hand, blade out, as she walked. Her baby bounced on her other hip.

Jacquemine Ooste was interesting. Part of it was the way she held herself like a figurehead in rough waters, with her wimple and veil and fine surcoat never out of place. Part of it was that Claude had expected his own golden skin to be the darkest skin in most rooms in Flanders. The woman had spoken to Claude in French at first, but Claude had insisted on Flemish. This was how he had learned seven languages; he might as well improve his eighth. Claude did not like to be at a disadvantage.

Jacquemine went out into the little anteroom and came back with a woman older than herself – that must be the infamous prodigal wet nurse – and a young woman with a distaff as long as a poleaxe in her hand, to which a skinny strand of flax still clung.

'Margriet, you'll feed the baby before you eat,' Jacquemine said sharply. 'Your daughter is welcome to join us now. It's good to see you, Beatrix. I hope your aunt and grandfather are as well as can be hoped. God have mercy on us.'

The girl inclined her head. 'Thank you for your welcome, Vrouwe Ooste.'

The older woman reached forward and plucked the baby from Jacquemine's arms, cooing, 'Oh, come here, little thing. Come here.'

She walked behind the carved screen with the child, and Jacquemine followed her.

Claude stood, at a loss. He needed to speak with Margriet de Vos. How long did it take to nurse a baby? Should he sit and wait?

The girl Beatrix rested her distaff against the wall and sat at the table. The daughter. Willem's daughter? Claude smiled at her and she returned it, looking at him with some confusion. What must he look like, in his kirtle and his loose scraps of hair? Like an unkempt woman, he supposed. Certainly not like a man-at-arms. The wet nurse and her daughter both wore neat linen wimples.

Claude sat next to her.

'You are Willem de Vos's daughter?'

The girl looked up, startled. She nodded. The cook came back from the kitchen with a bowl for Beatrix and she spooned it into her mouth. Ravenous, like everyone else in Bruges.

From the far side of the screen came the voices of Jacquemine and Margriet, arguing.

'The baby's been wanting you.'

'Oh, little thing, heavenly fat dumpling, don't fuss, here you go. Vrouwe Ooste, I was delayed in part by my husband, who has come back to Bruges as a revenant.'

Several spoons clattered onto the table.

Willem de Vos was a revenant. But what of the mace? The manservant, Hans, looked stricken. Beatrix's mouth twisted as if she were about to cry. The little girl's face fell, and her eyes went pink and wet. Claude couldn't have them all weeping. Claude waved his hand dramatically in front of the servant's rheumy eyes, reached over and slid his bowl of pottage to his own place. He slurped it up noisily, looking at the little girl. She sniffed, then giggled a little.

'Margriet, I'm sorry,' Jacquemine said from beyond the screen. 'You don't mean you – you met him out on the street, I hope?'

'I would never invite him in, Vrouwe Ooste. But I must leave Bruges, I am afraid. Tonight.'

'Leave Bruges! I'd like to see you manage it!'

Claude put the spoon down and listened hard.

'I know a way,' the wet nurse was saying. 'A small and secret way, a dangerous way. Vrouwe Ooste, I have been at the walls. I have seen the chimeras. They are going to attack Bruges. Soon. You must think of the children. If you will come with me, tonight, perhaps you can find some shelter in an abbey.'

Nobody spoke or caught each other's eye. The manservant gripped the table. The little girl's lip quivered.

'Let them come,' said Jacquemine Ooste. 'We know how to deal with invaders in Bruges. We will survive, Margriet. You and Beatrix can stay here with us. Surely it is at least as safe here as it is out on the road, or even at some abbey, in these times.'

'I am going to the Chatelaine, to lay a claim on my husband's wealth. It seems I was married to a wealthy man after all. I learned as much from his revenant tonight.'

'Bah. A liar, in death as in life, I have no doubt.'

'I have seen it, Vrouwe Ooste. A great chest with real groats and florins, and a great silver ewer.'

'No golden spurs?'

Margriet chuckled. 'No, but some war pelf, I think. There were weapons. I saw a sword, and some plate, and even a great mace with a hollow handle.'

Claude's heart sped.

'But Willem has taken it all away, away in a sack.'

That trader. The wet nurse's husband. A revenant now, on his way to the Hellbeast, with the mace.

'You would abandon us?' came Jacquemine's voice, quiet as a feather on the air. 'For the sake of some silver?'

'I have a right to it. My daughter does, too.'

'And my baby must starve so you can get your due?'

'The baby is nearly two. He only nurses twice a day now anyway. And I'm losing my milk, Vrouwe Ooste. I doubt I could nurse him much longer in any case.'

'Oh, I see you kept that knowledge to yourself until it suited you. Where will you go, Margriet? Do you even know where to find the Chatelaine?'

'I'll follow my husband. Catch up to him. The revenants only move at night, don't they? We never see them during the day. He must be on his way to Ypres. The Chatelaine has gone there to meet the French King.'

'How do you know that?'

Silence.

'Inheritance falls under canon law,' Jacquemine muttered. 'It isn't the Chatelaine's to award to you.'

'And how do I tell which diocese contains Hell, Vrouwe Ooste? Willem is her servant now, and he has stolen my due. If she is his lord, then let her chastise him. Perhaps she does not know the Flemish customs of inheritance. I will explain them to her.'

'And you will walk? Two women alone?'

'If I may, Vrouwe Ooste, I'll take my pay now. Beatrix and I will not stay here tonight.'

'Mmm?'

'My sou, for the week. Today is Wednesday.'

There was a silence.

'Margriet de Vos, you are a wonder. At a time like this, you are thinking of your sou? I'll have to go to the strongbox. Watch the children.'

Claude waited until Jacquemine Ooste had gone upstairs to the bedchamber. This was his chance. If he could catch up with Willem de Vos before the revenant reached the Chatelaine, he could take it from him. It was his, as much as it was anybody's. He had a right to it. He'd need to avoid the chimeras; they'd take him back to Her.

He rose, kicking his chair back, and darted around the screen.

'Who are you and what do you want?' the wet nurse asked.

'Take me with you,' he said. 'I am a condotierre. I can be your guard.'

The wet nurse opened her eyes wide. 'What sort of jest is this?'

'I am a man-at-arms, I tell you. A crossbowman. I know I don't look like one now, but I am.'

'And I'm the pope.'

'Look,' Claude said, showing her his fingers on his weak right hand. 'The callous from my crossbow string.'

The girl Beatrix joined them, looking from her mother's face to Claude's and back again.

'Hmpf. A callous from the loom or the spindle, more like,' said Margriet, examining his hand and then letting it drop. 'You are some stray whom the good Vrouwe Ooste has taken in. We eat stray cats now in Bruges, do not forget. Why on earth would you want to come with me?'

His arm burned.

'I, too, have business with the Chatelaine,' he said softly. 'You are hunting one of her revenants. You need someone who knows her ways.'

'Indeed? How do I know you won't betray me, call the chimeras on me?'

'You can trust me.'

'But not your arm. What use is a guard with a useless sword arm?'

What good indeed? But even left-handed he could take care of himself. Claude circled around the screen back to the table, took his knife in his left hand, returned to Margriet and threw the knife hard at the wall. He hoped the mere surprise of it, and the sight of the blade quivering in the wall, would be enough to impress, that no one would wonder which part of the wall he had been aiming at.

'I'll take my chances,' Margriet said, after a pause.

Claude burst out laughing despite himself.

'A rotten throw,' he said. 'I'll admit I am not the man I was. But you are going out of the city, where the chimeras roam. I know their ways. I fought alongside them. I will lay down my life for yours if we are attacked, if only you will show me your way out of this city and give me one small thing in payment.'

'Hmph. And what payment would you ask of me, besides the pleasure of my company, which is, of course, a blessing to all?'

He tried to speak as nonchalantly as he could. He did not want to answer questions about the mace, about why he wanted it.

'A share of the pelf if you recover it. I'll take that funny weapon you mentioned, with the hollow handle. It has a heavy ball on one end, with points all around it? A *strijd-knots*, I think you call it? What the French call a *masse*?'

'You can have that. God knows I wouldn't know what to do with the thing and would have to sell it anyway. The sword, too; it's yours. I have no need for arms, God help me. But if we don't recover it for some reason, you get nothing, as I'll have nothing to give. And we can't carry any food. I have no right to anything here, and I can only hope that we receive hospitality at the religious houses on the way. If you can live on very little, and help us find what we can, you can come. If Vrouwe Ooste allows it.'

'Claude is a guest, not a prisoner,' said Jacquemine, standing in the doorway with a little bag in her hand.

'And this person truly was a man-at-arms?'

'Dressed as one, anyway, the priest said.'

They spoke as if Claude were not there, as if his knife were not still quivering in the wall. He strode to it and pulled it out, sheathed it on his belt.

'I am a man-at-arms, I tell you. Believe me or not as you like, but the man part is true. All I need now is the arms.'

'Well,' said Margriet. 'I don't need a guard. But when I meet Willem, or the revenant made from his body, or whatever it is, well, I may need help getting the sack from him.'

'If you are determined to do this foolish thing, Margriet,' said Jacquemine, 'you will take this copper pot and little bag of oats with you, and some waterskins. I would give you more if I had more to give.'

'That is more than I can take, Vrouwe Ooste,' Margriet said. 'I will not take food out of the children's mouths. I will only take what is my due.'

'Then let me give you this in place of that last sou, then, you stubborn thing.'

'A sou won't be much good to you here in Bruges. Oats, though, you can eat.'

'And you think you will find a market outside these walls?' Jacquemine Ooste scoffed. 'You will need something to eat, at least until you find the first religious house, and God only knows how many are yet standing.'

'Mother, take the oats and let's be gone,' said the girl, poking her head around the corner. 'And we thank you very much for your kindness, Vrouwe Ooste.'

CHAPTER NINE

Beatrix was glad of the moon. It was just past full and dappled the streets with puddles of silver. Mother, though, insisted they keep to the shadows.

The bundle tied to her back was light: a few smallclothes, her spindle, and a wooden bowl. Her water flask was slung over one shoulder and banged on her right hip; on the other, her knife weighted her belt. Her fur-lined hood, her wedding gift from Baltazar, opened into a short cape to cover her shoulders.

Beatrix felt like a pilgrim, using her distaff as if it were a walking stick.

Mother carried the small bag of oats and the little copper pot in her bundle.

A revenant came walking toward them and Mother pulled Beatrix into an alley. They stood there, not quite hidden but of no interest to the revenant, who called 'Alberic, Alberic, little Alberic.' He was a young man, about Baltazar's age, and Beatrix could not help but stare at his skin and wonder if it were the moonlight that made it so pallid.

As it passed, Beatrix looked sidelong at the mercenary beside her. Claude was taller than either of them, and he did not seem afraid. He was dressed in woman's clothes, although shabbily, and his hair was plain, undressed and uncovered under the hood. If he was telling the truth about having been a man-at-arms, those slender hands had killed, what, a dozen men, a hundred, a thousand? Had they all been at the end of a crossbow, or had Claude ever fought with his hands, with a knife?

It was the coldest part of night, and the air by the canal was damp. They walked on toward the south end of the city and came at last to the open water called the Minnewater. It flashed like a battlefield in the moonlight. At the far side squatted the beguinage, home to the sisters of charity, silent and dark. Would any revenants dare knock on those doors? Would they have any names to call? Who loved those women, those poor sisters?

Beatrix shivered.

At the edge of the Minnewater, Mother stopped.

'What are we doing here?' Claude whispered.

'Hush. Wait. You'll see, soon enough.'

Mother whistled.

Something happened to the surface of the water. A ripple with intention; a few bubbles; a line of spume and then a collection of dark twigs, slick with green.

A face.

Beatrix stumbled backwards.

Two bulbous eyes blinked open and a mouth widened, from a hole rotted and misshapen like the bole of a tree, into a frog-like grimace. Then it lifted its head out of the water on a neck like a dragon's.

Beside her, the mercenary drew his knife.

'God give you good evening, snake,' Mother said. She inclined her head a little, as she might when she met another merchant's wife in the street.

The creature spat, a long dirty spout that fountained around him. Was it a *him*?

'Margriet,' the serpent spoke, in a low rumble like the sound of the gears that drove the crane-treadmill near the market.

Beatrix decided it was a him. A him who knew Mother. Beatrix looked at her mother as if seeing her for the first time. If Father had kept secrets from them all, then so had she.

'I must go beyond the walls, as far as you will carry me,' Margriet said. 'And these two with me.'

'Hold a moment,' said Claude. '*This* is your way out? Asking passage from a water-monster?'

The serpent moved his mouth around as if he were chewing mutton.

'All three?' the serpent asked.

Mother nodded, as if she were ordering bread.

'The packs, too?'

Mother put her hand on her hip. 'I don't have all night, you mouldy wiggler.'

Beatrix gasped as her rudeness. 'Mother.'

The eyes rolled, the thin inner lids flashed down, and he emitted a grumble like the bubbling of a swamp. To the damp stone wall he swam and drew his long body along it, an expanse of slime and sticks and bits of matted string and floating wood and all the things that lived in a Bruges canal.

'Hop on,' Margriet said, pointing.

Claude took a step backward.

'What is it?' Beatrix asked.

'I've never been very good with boats,' admitted Claude with a quiet chuckle. 'I was very nearly killed in a storm once. I can't – I can't swim.'

'It will bear your weight, don't fret, bag of bones. And don't worry – we won't be seen.'

'And can you promise I won't be eaten?' Claude whispered, with a grin for Beatrix.

'I'll go first, then,' said Margriet. 'Mother of God, what the hell kind of fighter must you have been? No wonder you were found out.'

Mother slung her bag out over the water and let it drop, none too gently, onto the Nix's back. The waterworm shuddered, and a film of darkness slimed up and over to cover it, until Beatrix could hardly see the bag at all.

'Now me,' Mother said.

She stepped on and knelt, steadying herself with her hands. She, too, all but disappeared. There was some sort of enchantment about the watersnake. How long had it lived in these waters, keeping itself unseen? Did it have fellows, or family, in these green depths?

Beatrix put her hand out toward the creature.

'May I?' she asked.

It bowed its head, and she touched its cold skin with her fingertips.

'What is your name?' she asked.

'Oh for heaven's sake, Beatrix,' her mother called. It was strange, hearing Mother's voice but not being able to see her, as though Margriet de Vos had finally been reduced to just her tongue.

'I am a Nix, so you may call me that,' said the Nix.

'And you don't mind bearing me?'

'He is bound to,' said Margriet. 'I beat him in a game, when I was a child. I won the use of him. Hop on, Bea.'

Mother had kept this secret, all these years. To think she could keep silent about anything!

The darkness that came over Beatrix as she crawled onto the creature's back was cool and damp. Not quite wet; more like the million tiny sparks of mist in the air when God couldn't decide whether or not to make it rain.

It smelled, though, much less fresh than rain.

Beatrix knelt on the Nix's back and held her distaff straight in the air at her side like a lance.

Claude stepped awkwardly onto the far side of the creature's body, as if he thought the Nix were a boat that might tip, and his foot slid off and he nearly went into the water. Beatrix grabbed his right arm to help him steady himself, and Claude cried out in pain.

'I'm sorry,' Beatrix said, snatching her hand back.

'No, I thank you,' Claude said, with a weary smile.

'Hush, both of you,' said Mother.

Mother had bested the Nix in a game? Mother never did play games of any kind, not that Beatrix could remember. Beatrix tried to imagine her mother as a child, lying on the Nix's back, perhaps wrapping her arms around it, dragging her fingers in the water. That was what Beatrix would do, if she were here alone. But Mother sat as tall as a lady on a palfrey, and anyway she couldn't have spread out on the Nix's back with Claude and Beatrix riding pillion.

As they passed silently down the Minnewater, Beatrix looked back at the city of beggars and merchants, the city sleeping behind houses shuttered and houses marked. It would be morning soon. In the old days there would be mongers in the streets by this hour, and people shouting and hens squawking. But the hens had all been eaten and the mongers had nothing to sell, and no reason to risk coming out of doors before the sun chased all the revenants back to wherever they slept during daylight.

They floated under the shadow of the walls, holding their breath for fear of making a sound and alerting the women and children who stood guard there, who might demand to be taken too, or might mistake them for traitors or spies. They floated past the first moats, and out of Bruges into the great country of Flanders. And no one saw them.

'Do you grant wishes, Herr Nix?' Beatrix asked.

'He doesn't,' Margriet said.

'Ha!' the Nix barked. 'How do you know?'

'I asked you years, ago, didn't I? You pompous old liar. Don't pretend to be something you're not just to impress the young people.'

'You put a rope around my neck the day we met. Is it any wonder I didn't grant your wishes, you nasty shrew?'

'Bah. You would have done whatever I asked, and you know it. You are becoming a dotard as well as a liar.'

'Hmph,' said the Nix, and plunged its head into the water. A plume of water went up like a fountain; surely anyone watching would see that, even if they couldn't see the Nix or his passengers.

'It's all right,' said Beatrix. 'There's no need to argue, Mother. It is quite enough to ask Herr Nix to take us out of the city, without demanding that he grant wishes as well. It was rude of me to ask.'

'What sort of wish would you ask for, if I did grant them?' the creature rumbled.

Beatrix wondered. She wanted only one thing, and that was Baltazar. Oh, how she longed for just one glimpse of him. She opened her mouth as if she could call him back to her, to her arms, to her lips, to her thighs. Failing that, to call all the creatures of the night to her now so she could ask them: *Have you seen him? Have you word of my love?* Or at least to be able to know a little of the future, to know whether he would come back to her safe, so she could stop her heart from hoping.

Something splashed beside her.

'My distaff!' Beatrix cried, too loud.

She had let it drop from her hand.

'Hush,' both her mother and Claude said.

The Nix ducked its head into the water and lifted it out again. Held in its bared teeth was the distaff. Beatrix gently pulled it out.

'Thank you,' she whispered.

'There,' the Nix said. 'I do grant some wishes, you see. Because you, unlike some people, are kind.'

'By all the saints,' groaned Margriet. 'I'd almost rather swim.'

'I could grant that wish as well,' the Nix grunted.

But he carried them a little further to where the water went as black as pitch and they were out of sight of the city walls, and then they were out of Bruges, and into the Chatelaine's territory. The land opened darkly before them.

The Chatelaine invited the King of France to a feast in Hell. He brought his own food: boars, swans, even a blackbird pie, which erupted in birds when it was cut. The birds fluttered up and into the high corridors, where they woke the bats to screeching and people looked up.

Black feathers floated down over the feast and a bird fell with a thud.

The Chatelaine, along with her chimeras, ate what they always ate: the blood of the Beast. It rushed from the golden spigots along the walls of the Great Hall and splashed into bowls and cups.

A Mantis-man carried a platter of bloodseeds to her. They were piled high, glittering like red gems in the lamp-light. She gestured to Philippe, and smiled when the king cringed at the offered food.

'It feels something like roe on the mouth,' she said. 'And something like pomegranate. Thicker, though. Rougher. We mix the Beast's blood with the Beast's spittle and cook the drops in the furnaces.'

'Your furnaces are the greatest marvel in the world, madame.'

The Chatelaine grasped the handle of one of the long silver spoons and ladled the bloodseeds into her bowl. The body of the Beast; the food of Hell. She had been eating it so long, she remembered no other.

She took a few with her fingers and ate. It was a sweeter, milder taste than the thick, fresh blood that ran from the spigots, that must run even now into her husband's mouth from whatever scratches and scrapes he had made in the walls of his oubliette.

The greasy meat in front of King Philippe hardly looked like food; it smelled like death, not life. But let him cele-brate in his way and she would celebrate in hers.

This was her victory feast, although it was mostly for show, because Bruges had not yet fallen. She had invited the king to remind him: she had done what he required. He had asked her to defeat the Flemish rebels and she had. Her army of chimeras had won the day at Cassel. She had spent nearly her whole army on it, and many of her precious creations had been killed. She had earned her reward. He must make her Countess of Flanders; perhaps even tonight.

And perhaps Bruges was falling even now, if her gonner-chimeras had done their work.

Chaerephon sat to her left. He never ate now. She could remember him eating, years and years before, when her husband was still master of Hell. Chaerephon had always been thin but now he looked like a skeleton wearing skin. She suspected he was becoming a revenant of a kind, that he and the Beast had come to some kind of arrangement. But she had not asked him; she could not think how to phrase the question.

'How does it go with Bruges?' Philippe asked, low enough that people would not hear above the noise of eating and talking.

He ate only a little of his stinking food, from every dish, as if he owed each one a favour.

'It would go better if I had a few trebuchets and ballistas, and a company of knights.'

'It's a city of women!'

'Women can throw rocks and boiling water.'

'It could be worse. It could be Greek fire.'

'When we bring a ram to the gate, they throw down rocks and burning branches and boiling water and kill the men. I don't have enough archers to take them off the walls. When we put up ladders, the women throw them down.'

'But the revenants get in.'

'Yes. The revenants get in. If we leave it to the revenants, it will be a charnel city by the time we take it.'

'All the better for you, since you find the burghers such an obstacle. If you can't control Bruges, you can't control Flanders,' said Philippe. 'When I was a child, in the days of Count Louis's grandfather, the people of that accursed city killed the flower of French nobility. The people of Bruges ambushed Frenchmen in the streets and stoned them to death – the men, women, children all. If you hope to be countess of these vicious people, you must be able to keep them in check without running to me every year, as Count Louis did. If you can't, I shall return poor Louis to his rightful place.'

The Chatelaine bit her tongue. Louis had men, and machines. All she had were ghosts and chimeras. The ghosts worked slowly and strangely, and the chimeras now were few. She would need proper weapons and knights, and if Philippe would not give her them, she would need to make them herself. But it was not so easily done. The forges of Hell only worked on the willing. It took time to convince people, one by one, to become chimeras. And there were losses; there were mistakes.

At the far end of the hall, Monoceros ambled alongside a young man on crutches. A recruit! Missing one leg, but he seemed sound in body otherwise.

She beckoned to Monoceros, who came and knelt by her side, opposite Philippe.

'Do you come from Bruges?' she whispered to him as they exchanged kisses. 'You ran, I think. You stink to heaven.'

Monoceros had gained the speed of the unicorn who had all but disappeared within his man's body when the two went into the forges together.

'The gonner-chimeras are lost,' he muttered. 'They blew

themselves to bits and did not breach the walls. The powder must have been too strong.'

She froze, still embracing him. Her nails dug into the leathery skin of his bare shoulder.

'But the last time it was too weak,' she whispered.

Monoceros said nothing. She thrust him from her and turned back to her place.

She wanted nothing but to run, far from here, to a quiet corner of the Beast where she could think. They had been working with various recipes for the black powder for months, but none seemed quite right. They refined the saltpetre from the bat droppings in the Beast's nostrils; they took the fuming yellow brimstone from the Beast's innards. But somehow the recipes never came out right; perhaps there was something about the sulphur that was not the same as the stuff on the surface. And each experiment cost them more in charcoal, which they had to buy or steal, and which was not cheap in this country, its little woods so few and far between.

'Is anything amiss?' Philippe asked smoothly.

She smiled at him, shook her head.

She looked over the heads of the chimeras assembled at the tables all around the hall. It had been much emptier in her husband's day; he had left most of his guests in the oubliettes or the torture chamber.

So she had shared many meals with her husband here alone, or nearly alone; often in later centuries Chaerephon was there, and anyway no one was ever alone in Hell. Her husband had bought her a throne in Samarkand: lacquered red, wide enough for her to sit cross-legged on a silk cushion, and with two great dragons leaping out on the armrest. She had that throne cast into the furnaces after she cast her husband down into his private hell. She sat now on what had been his throne: a chair made of the carved and polished bones of some unnamed beast.

The noise in the hall was strange and satisfying, even if it did distract her, when she could not afford to be distracted. King Philippe required unstinting watchfulness.

She needed to show him she could manage Flanders. She needed more chimeras, better chimeras.

The Chatelaine turned back to her dear Monoceros, who crouched as though he were trying to make himself small. Dear thing. Dear loyal thing. The first thing she had made for her very own.

Let Philippe see what soldiers she could make, out of nothing but peasants and fire. Let him see his chance to buy her friendship now, while it was cheap.

'Bring me that man with the missing leg,' she said.

Monoceros went silently. Good Monoceros. The pure expression of her will.

She let the young man go down upon his only knee, let him pull himself back up again, red-faced, before she spoke. The Chatelaine showed mercy in her own way and her own time, and the mercy she would show this young man would be subjection to her.

'You have come here because you wish to be transformed?' she asked.

He nodded. 'I ask you for a leg. I am a farmer, my lady. Since I lost my leg, my family has had to pay for help. I have three children.'

'And in return? I must put something into the fire, you see, along with you. What will you give me for my pains?'

He set his jaw. 'I can work. Set me a task and I will do it.'

'Bah, I have no need of peasant labour. Can you fight?'

He bit his lip and inclined his head.

She glanced at Philippe but could read nothing in his expression. Did he not see? Did he expect her to make an army of men such as this? A farmer who had never wielded anything but his fists?

If only she had the use of those mercenary bands that Philippe used, then she would show him what she could do. But they had gone to England, to fight the Scots for the boy king. They refused to fight alongside the chimeras any longer. It was true that her centaurs had trampled through a line of Genoese crossbowmen, but the crossbowmen had been taking too long.

Her poor centaurs, all dead now.

And here was a young man in want of a gait.

'One can never be sure how the fire will do its work,' she said, smiling at the young man. 'When I put Monoceros in with a unicorn, I thought he would come out with four legs, like a centaur. Instead, he barely seems equine at all, does he? The unicorn in him went . . . elsewise. But horses, now, they are more predictable. Every time I have put a man in with a horse, he's come out with four strong legs to gallop and two strong arms for swords.'

The man's red face drained to white.

'And what else of them is horse-like?' Philippe asked with a straight face. 'Always distracted by curious camp followers, I imagine. Give me a knight any day.'

Yes, you son of a whore, give me a knight, she thought. Give me all the knights who owe their allegiance to the useless Count Louis of Flanders, whose battle I just fought. Give me my due.

But she said, 'Knights cost a fortune to harness, and

they need squires and destriers, and after the battle they go home. My chimeras live within their harness, and they are loyal to me, always.'

The man cleared his throat. 'I do not wish to be a centaur. I am no knight, either. I only want something to help me walk the fields.'

'But I can make you better than you ever were, even with your leg! I can do more than fit a new part on you. I can make you whole!'

He said very quietly, 'I *am* whole.'

She threw up her hands. 'Go, then,' she said. 'The fires only take willing men, and you are unwilling. You have wasted my time. Pray this is the last time you see the inside of Hell.'

She called a Mantis-man to take him away. She did not look at Philippe, at his smug face.

But when his Fool began to perform for her, tumbling and farting and juggling coloured balls, she called Monoceros to her side and beckoned so he bent low, so close she could smell his coppery skin.

'We bring down the walls of Bruges tomorrow,' she whispered. 'I cannot wait longer.'

'We will lose many men,' said Chaerephon, leaning in.

She had forgotten Chaerephon was listening; of course he was listening. He listened to every report from Monoceros. He had even given Monoceros his name.

'Then lose them,' she snapped. 'What good are men to me, if they cannot take a city of women? Use all the remaining black powder and blow the gate to heaven.'

'Suicide for whoever carries the powder,' said Chaerephon. 'We could dig mines, if we can get under the moat.'

'No time,' she snapped.

The king turned toward them.

'Go now,' she whispered, leaning closer in to Monoceros, so that his horn nearly rested on her shoulder. 'Ride back to Bruges, my pet. My remaining chimeras are encamped and waiting to take Bruges; let them wait no longer. Do not fail me.'

'I am yours to command.'

'And when you get inside the city,' she said, 'show them mercy, but show them we are not to be trifled with. If you meet any resistance, slaughter to your heart's content.'

Monoceros smiled. 'What low regard you must have for my heart, my lady.'

CHAPTER TEN

It was pointless to negotiate with the Nix. The creature was as stubborn as an ox, always had been, and if anything, it was getting worse. Still, Margriet spoke in its ear, in as kindly a tone as she could muster, whispering so Claude and Beatrix would not hear.

'Carry us down the stream, as near as you can to the abbey of Saint Agatha. It isn't far.'

'If it isn't far then you can walk,' the Nix rumbled.

'You must do as I ask.' She made a clicking sound as if urging on a horse. One must speak the language of boats with boats, the language of beasts with beasts, and the language of bullies with bullies, her father used to say.

'My demesne ends at the outer moat of Bruges. You know that, girl. You asked me to take you to Ethiopia when you were a child, don't you remember? Has your brain gone soft?'

Margriet snorted. Were Claude and Beatrix listening? Beatrix would be astonished, no doubt. But then her daughter was so easily astonished. So susceptible to dreams and wonders, so ready to clap her hands in delight. She had stood no chance against Baltazar and his burning gaze, when he was alive. She stood no chance now against his revenant. Margriet must keep her eyes open.

Everything seemed so quiet out here beyond the city walls; the Nix swam nearly silently. But at any moment the chimeras might appear – or worse, Baltazar. Margriet could only hope her son-in-law's shade was walking the streets of Bruges now, looking for Beatrix in vain.

'We'll walk, then,' she said at last to the Nix. 'And no thanks to you. If the chimeras catch me I'll tell them to fit me with a dragon's head, and then I'll be back to tell you what I think of you.'

'Believe me,' the Nix muttered, 'I devoutly hope that you find a swift road under your feet.'

As soon as the Nix deposited them on the bank of the second moat, with a small unnecessary splash of a tail, they filled their flasks. Then Margriet hurried the younger two away from the water, into the bushes.

'We walk west,' said Margriet as they trudged. 'Toward Ypres.'

'How do you know?' asked Claude.

Damn it, she might have cause to regret bringing this young mercenary along.

But now there was no need to hide the fact that she'd gone out before, beyond the city walls. Her secret of the Nix was exposed. And yet it still hurt a bit to speak about it, as if she'd locked the secret away so long that the key had gone rusty.

'I heard some chimeras talking,' Margriet said, slowly. 'I had an errand, outside the walls. I heard them. They said the Hellbeast is in Ypres.'

'Mother!'

'What chimeras? What did they look like?' Claude asked.

'One had a helmet for a head, and nothing within it – a great void. That was one I knew as a boy. He used to hang about my husband's shop. And the others had metal arms that shot fire.'

'Gonners,' said Claude. 'She's been working on them for a long time. Yet the walls still stand, are still guarded.'

'The fire engulfed them. Is it possible, then? That the Chatelaine of Hell could make arrows of fire shoot out of a man's arm?'

The mercenary shrugged. 'Anything is possible, or almost anything, in her forges. I have seen centaurs and lion-men and a trebuchet with arms. I have seen her forge a visor of glass and steel onto a man's head to give him the keen sight of an eagle. And I have seen the many, many mistakes she cast aside. The human slag that oozes out of her furnace and then goes somewhere to die.'

'A man with the sight of an eagle!'

'He had been blind, before.'

'A miracle, then.'

Margriet looked at the mercenary's face, which was only a few paces from her and yet not quite clear. Nothing had been quite clear to her eyes, since Margriet was a girl. How wonderful, to be given the sight of an eagle!

'I don't think so,' said Claude. 'And you wouldn't think them miracles, either, if you had dealings with them. We must remember that while we are hunting Willem, they are hunting us.'

'Why?' Margriet asked. 'They have no cause. How should they even know we exist?'

'The chimeras hunt everything,' the mercenary said,

after a pause that made Margriet frown. 'Some of them are hounds. Hunting is what they do. Once we left the city walls, we became their prey.'

Beatrix looked back. Margriet rolled her eyes so her daughter could see she was not frightened by this mercenary and his talk. He said he was a man-at-arms, despite appearances, and Margriet had decided to take him at his word. Appearances could be deceiving. But she was not going to be led by him.

'Anyway, I am no authority on miracles,' Claude continued more brightly. 'You can ask the nuns what they think, when we reach Saint Agatha's. That is on the way to Ypres, isn't it? We might try to find out from them if there is a band of chimeras near, find out which roads to avoid. Nuns always know a good deal about the comings and goings of armies, in my experience.'

Margriet frowned at Claude. Soldier or not, that was no excuse for his manner. He was no older than Beatrix.

'Will we catch up with Father tonight?' Beatrix whispered.

'I don't think so,' Claude broke in. Know-it-all. 'He's been walking longer than we have, and is no doubt long past Saint Agatha's abbey by now. But we can walk during the day, and he can't. It will be a long day, tomorrow, but then tomorrow night we should find him if our course is the same.'

The brook ran due south from Bruges, so they walked perpendicular to it, due west or as near as Margriet could reckon, though Claude kept arguing with her, pointing at stars Margriet could not see, and babbling. Margriet had covered this patch of the world several times in the course of her life and needed no stars to guide her. But they were off the road, and she was loth to admit that in the moon-light, every blurry patch of forest on the horizon looked the same.

Then a road cut across their path at an angle.

'The road to Torhout,' Margriet said with some relief. 'If we follow it, we'll be on the right path, and should make the abbey by noon. They'll give us shelter and food.'

'But we must take care when we get there,' Claude said. 'I don't think there are likely to be chimeras at such a small abbey, but if there are any signs of them, we must not go in.'

'Why are you so eager to avoid the chimeras?' Margriet asked. 'We are walking to Hell after all. We'll see them sooner or later.'

'Your faith in my skills as a bodyguard is flattering,' Claude said. 'But upon the road, the chimeras will do to two women travelling what all soldiers do when they come upon women travelling, and I do not wish to test my skills alone against a band of them, if I can help it.'

Margriet only looked at him for a moment. If there was any doubt left in her mind that he was a man, he'd dispelled it. Only a man would spout such nonsense. 'If we were going to stay inside any time we might meet a band of soldiers eager to celebrate a victory upon our bodies, or take their vengeance thereupon, we women would never leave the house.'

Claude shrugged. 'As you like. To the abbey we go, but I say we stay a bit off the road and keep our eyes and wits sharp, that's all.'

'Obviously,' Margriet snapped.

After a few hours, as the sky grew silver-pink to the

east, she noticed that the mercenary had a slight limp, although he walked in front. Stubborn thing.

'You need to rest?' Margriet called.

He turned. 'No. But if you need to—'

'We'll stop to rest in that clump of oaks, there,' Margriet said.

'That's beech,' Claude said. 'But it's a good place to stop.'

'All the better,' Beatrix said brightly. 'Nuts.'

They sat down in the copse together, huddled under their cloaks. Margriet wished the Nix's darkness could cover them still.

Her nose was running, and she was feeling, now, the lack of sleep. There was a time when she could stay up late, with a baby, and not feel it in her bones and her brain. That time had long passed. She felt drunk, ill in the head and the gut. The grey morning light made her sick.

'We can only rest a little,' Margriet said. 'Until we get our bearings.'

'That way's east,' said Claude, pointing at the dawn with a grin.

'I see I've brought a wiseacre along. Lovely.'

Beatrix, thinking of her stomach as usual, gathered a pile of beechnuts, then put her head down on the ground and went to sleep, her arm around her distaff.

Claude looked as fresh as a flower, idly testing his knife on the pad of his finger and staring out into the grey morning.

What unthinking insults these young people were to Margriet, both of them: one who could fall sweetly asleep on the cold damp ground and one who did not even care to. They did not even know to be grateful for their youth, and would not know until it had gone.

Claude turned to her and grimaced. 'Why are you looking at me as if I were a chimera?'

Margriet hadn't realized she had been. She was in the habit of frowning, largely because she was in the habit of squinting.

'I'm wondering why the hell I chose a child for my bodyguard,' she answered.

'I'm well past twenty.' He paused, and then continued with a little bark of a laugh: 'At least, I think I must be.'

'I've lived two of your lives.'

'I've known children who've lived several lives, and old men who've yet to live a single life that counted.'

'Years are all that matter,' Margriet sighed. 'Years are a standard measure. They weigh the same in France as they do in Abyssinia.'

'I don't know about that.'

The face was a child's face, young and fresh, but Claude had a scar over one eye and there was something tough in him. There would have to be. What on God's earth could have sent him off to that life, the life of a man-at-arms?

'If you're not going to sleep, you can build a fire. You have a tinderbox, I hope? If not, you can use mine.'

'You want to risk a fire?' Claude asked. 'There could be chimeras about.'

'You and the chimeras. I almost hope they catch us. It would be a relief. If you can build one without smoke, we should be fine. We need to eat. It's another long march to the abbey.'

Margriet gave up on sleep, and found a large flat rock and a small one while Claude built the fire. Margriet peeled and ground the beechnuts, set the meal to soak for a little while, then mixed it in with a little of Vrouwe Ooste's oats. She spread the dough on the flat rock and set it near the fire.

She stretched out on the grass next to her daughter. Already the September sun was baking some of the dampness out of the ground. Beatrix was snoring gently, her distaff by her side, her bundle under her wimpled head.

Margriet wanted nothing more than to close her eyes, if only for a few minutes. She did not like the thought of sleeping with the mercenary watching over her. He had taken money to fight for the Chatelaine, which meant he had shot crossbow quarrels into many good citizens of Bruges. He had probably killed many of Margriet's neighbours, men she had known her whole life. He might have killed Jacquemine Ooste's husband. Or Beatrix's. It might even have been Claude who killed Willem, come to that, although that hole in Willem's back looked as though it had been made by something bigger than a crossbow quarrel.

But she had made the decision to take this stray in Bruges, and there was no going back on it now, here, out in the open.

'Keep watch on that bread or whatever we can call it,' she muttered to Claude, 'and wake me when it's done, if I fall asleep.'

She rubbed her fingertips together, to make sure they could still feel, that there was no numbness coming upon her. *You are marked by death*, Willem had said, but Margriet could not quite believe it. No, she did not have the plague. Surely not. It had been a trick, and she felt nothing.

'Do you always imitate a cricket before you sleep?' Claude asked with a quick grin.

'Bah,' Margriet said. 'Keep your eyes open and your mouth shut. And don't let me sleep too long. We must catch Willem.'

CHAPTER ELEVEN

Before dawn, the Chatelaine performed her ablutions. What glory to have her own room, with these oils and perfumes given to her by all the kings of Europe and Asia, these caskets of sandalwood and cloves, the bottles of rose water and jasmine water and orange water, the ointments of bay and hyssop and cowslip and myrtle and rue, these powders of brimstone and oils of lavender. The ambergris given to her by the Doge of Venice, the musk from the King of Cyprus.

And best of all gifts, the gift she gave herself: the knowledge that this day would be a day without her husband in it, that tonight would be a night in which her husband would not come to her bed. She stroked her mace-arm. In the early days she had taken it off at night while leaving it beside her in the bed; now she slept with it on, and found that more comfortable.

At dawn she was at the open Hellmouth, waiting.

The revenants came home in the morning. They sought the shelter of the Hellbeast, those who were close enough. The others, the ones scattered out across Flanders searching for their loved ones, would be hiding in caves or other dark places by dawn, whimpering.

The Chatelaine liked to watch them walk in, on mornings like this when she had woken early and been unable to go back to sleep. Around the mouth of Hell bats were swooping, impatient to be home, disturbed by the stretch-armed chimera who stood on a ladder and scraped the guano out. Below him one chimera held the ladder, and another caught the scrapings in a basket, to be soaked and made into saltpetre for the Chatelaine's black powder.

The Hellbeast, annoyed too, but eager for its food, opened its red jaws to receive the revenants from the blue twilight. In they walked, her bleak hundreds. In the depth of the great Beast a rumble of hunger, or of hunger satisfied.

There was a room, deep inside the Beast, where great spurs of bone jutted out of the red walls like broken teeth on bloody gums. Each of those spurs carried venom. That was where the Beast's own victims went: not to the forges that had been her husband's torture chamber, which was always and still for the living. Once the Beast claimed someone for its own, that someone was as good as dead. The venom took a person to the very point of death, to that one liminal moment, after the last breath, when the eyes dimmed and the mouth went slack.

In that moment, the mind of the dying one reached out with one last human desire. A powerful wish. Usually, it was the desire for someone they loved.

In that moment, the Beast gloried, for long years.

The revenants did not last forever – she had seen some

of them crumble into nothing – but they lasted a very long time, becoming ever more skeletal as the Beast consumed them. A long, slow descent into death.

The Beast always needed more.

Chaerephon, now, Chaerephon was a puzzle. Not quite a revenant; he had never had the venom. But he had started to act like one. He was skin and bone. She wondered about that; yes, she wondered. She was not easy in her mind about it. He had been in Hell so long.

The Chatelaine stood to greet each of her returning revenants by name, for that knowledge came with the keys to Hell. 'Jehan,' she said. 'Your labours are over. Fatima, good hunting? Baltazar! You look disappointed, pet. Do not fear, Baltazar. You will find her soon. You will all find them soon, and bring them here with you.'

Beatrix's legs ached wonderfully. What a gift to walk in the open country on a bright morning, after being cooped up in the city for weeks.

The last time Bruges was this hungry, she'd been, what, ten years old? A damp spring came and all the food prices went up. It was so wet that year that when the old King of France, Louis the Quarrelsome, had tried to invade Flanders, his army got bogged down in the mud. The people cheered but they were still hungry. Beatrix had lost most of her playmates, one by one. She asked her mother why none of the other children had taken her with them to heaven.

'Because I told God I would not give you up,' said Mother. 'And he agreed, because He owed me. He has your little sisters and brother already. He won't take you, too.'

The de Vos family went down to one meal a day, at noon, and Beatrix left the table hungry every time.

At her wedding feast eight years later, she stuffed herself, and she swore to Baltazar that they would never go hungry, never let their children go hungry. By then the famine was over but Baltazar remembered it, too.

'I hope not,' he said, with his eyes bright.

She shook her head to show how serious she was. 'I swear it, Baltazar, by my love for you.'

'Do you have the keys to the land of Cockaigne? Will there be roast pigs wandering around our house with forks sticking out of their backs?'

She slapped him playfully. 'I can spin faster and better than anyone. People will always need clothing. We may never be wealthy, but I will always be able to spin enough to keep food on our table. That I promise.'

He kissed her, and said that was supposed to be his promise, not hers.

And now here she was, walking the earth with her belly groaning, and Baltazar was probably dead.

No, this blue sky was too beautiful for that to be true. This world beyond the walls of Bruges, which she had nearly but not quite despaired of seeing again. The smell of decaying leaves and woodfires under a lapis lazuli sky. It made her want to spring up again and walk, no, run. Run to Baltazar on sore legs, in whatever realm of earth or heaven he might be.

If they found her father, or whatever her father was now, Beatrix would ask him about Baltazar. She would know, then, whether she was wife or widow.

If God restored her husband to her, she would go on a pilgrimage of thanksgiving.

Yes, and if Baltazar were dead, she would go on a pilgrimage to free his soul from purgatory, to absolve him of whatever sins he might have committed in war, a war he fought to keep her safe and fed, to keep the people of Bruges from the poverty the French king would impose. She would do whatever she could to help Baltazar into Paradise, where he would wait for her at a table laden with delights.

The sun was a pale groat, up past noon in the sky, when they saw the squat outline of the Abbey of Saint Agatha on the horizon. It would be a relief to feel the beaten earth under her soles. This rolling field had been burnt; scorched stubble pricked right through the leather of her shoes. The whole world smelled of fire.

Mother squinted. 'It doesn't look right. Bits are missing, aren't they? The shape is wrong.'

Claude was a few steps in front and his eyes must have been sharper than Mother's. 'It's been burned. Someone made the chimeras angry. You should stay here. Let me go and see what I can find out.'

'Ha,' Mother said. 'My road goes through that abbey, unless I go around, which I have no intention of doing. My thighs are killing me.'

They trudged toward it. A thin skein of smoke rose still from one of the outbuildings. The guest house, where once Beatrix had stayed with her parents as they travelled this country, Willem trying to sell off-quality wool in one of the hard years. One of the nuns had admired Beatrix's spinning.

'If there's a joint of meat left in this place, I'll be amazed,' said Claude. 'Or anyone left alive.'

Most of the stone walls were still intact but the roofs

had collapsed, and some of the smaller wooden buildings were gone altogether. There was a gaping black wound where the west range had been, a series of rooms reduced to ruins. They walked through the gap and into the cloister.

Inside the muddy garth, dotted on the dark earth, bodies of nuns lay with their faces up to heaven.

Beatrix went to each one and arranged their clothing, covering their legs where they were bare. She spoke a small prayer over each. Why would the chimeras do such a thing? They had nothing to gain from burning this place.

'I'm off to the sacristy,' Claude said at last, when Beatrix had done, and they had each had their moment of silent prayer. 'Coming?'

'And what will you do if you find it full of treasure?' Mother asked.

Claude turned and strode away to the burned walls.

Away beyond the last nun's corpse, something glittered. Bits of coloured glass. Beatrix knelt and picked it up. Mother came and stood over her.

'It doesn't seem right to leave it in the mud,' Beatrix said.

She had never seen coloured glass close up before; it had always been high above in a church window. There was an irregular square in blue and a teardrop in yellow, and a few small shards of red. Mother stretched out her hand for them and held them up to the light.

'No good to us,' she said, handing it back to Beatrix.

Claude came back with a dead chicken in his left hand.

'Found it wandering,' he said. 'Stupid creatures always want company.'

'It isn't ours,' Mother said.

'It isn't anyone's now, except perhaps the Chatelaine's,

and she owes me more than the cost of one chicken. The sacristy is bare. Is there a well?' Claude asked.

'A stream,' Mother said. 'A millrace. Toward the south.'

They filled their flasks at the stream, then they made another fire and sharpened a stick. They took turns plucking and cleaning the chicken.

When the meat was done, Mother pulled it off the stick and broke up the pieces in her hands.

Claude took his piece and then let it drop.

'God's bleeding body, it's hot!' he swore. He always managed to make the nastiest oaths sound almost charming; perhaps it was his funny accent, not quite French, not quite Italian. 'Your fingers must be made of steel, Margriet de Vos.'

Mother looked down at her hands. They shook a little, but they were the same mother's hands Beatrix had known her whole life: a little knobby around the knuckles, shiny and pink in places, the nails pared to the quick.

'Years of hard work,' Mother grumbled.

But Claude was looking off toward the smoke that still rose into the blue.

'The chimeras can't be far,' said Claude. 'There is probably a camp nearby. We should be careful. This fire should be our last.'

'If we don't find Willem tonight,' Mother said slowly, 'they may have word of him in the camp.'

'No,' Claude said with his mouth full of chicken. 'It's too dangerous.'

'Bah. It's dangerous to be alive. And it's dangerous to wander Flanders day and night looking for a revenant who is leading us ever closer to Hell. The faster we find him, the safer we'll be. If you want your reward, we need to be shrewd and quick about it.'

Claude frowned. 'You're right, by God's teeth. But if anyone goes to the chimera camp, it'll be me. Me alone. I know their ways. I can pass among them.'

'Have you forgotten that you're wearing a kirtle now?'

Claude put his hands on his hips. 'I have not. But perhaps you have never been to a soldiers' camp. There are plenty of kirtles there.'

Mother raised her eyebrows. Beatrix stretched and yawned, enjoying for a moment the feeling of being not quite full, but fed.

'We can rest for an hour, then we should get on,' Claude said. 'Willem had at least three hours' head start. We have walked for that long today, while he could not, but I don't doubt he walks quickly when he walks. The revenants are quick, when they're speeding their way back to the Beast.'

To think of Father being a creature of the night, a ghost-man; it was ridiculous and strange. And yet she would like to see him, to say goodbye, as any daughter should, to tell him – what? To tell him that she liked the toys he gave her every year on her name day. To ask him if he had any news of Baltazar.

'Where is Father right now, do you think?' Beatrix asked. 'Where do . . . they go during the day?'

She lay down on the cold ground, wrapped her cloak around her.

'Caves, and dark places,' said Claude. 'They are always, always yearning to be inside the Hellbeast, you see. If they're out of the Beast at all, it's because some other yearning has pulled them. Love, for most of them.'

'Willem walked all the way back to Bruges not for me, not for us, but for a sack full of coin and plate,' said Mother with a twisted smile. 'Even in death, he's a blackguard.'

Beatrix shut her eyes and said a little prayer for her father's soul, for all the souls taking the long road to Heaven.

CHAPTER TWELVE

Monoceros knelt by the side of the lazy Bruges canal and dipped his bloodied horn into the water. When he raised it again there were little clouds of dark blood in the clear green water, just for a moment, and then the water was clear again. Clear save the debris: the cracked planks and tiles floating on the surface, and here and there a body.

The assault had cost them dearly. This city had better be worth its price.

Poor Adolfo. He had been such a bully in his human life, a hard-headed weak-hearted thug. He had asked for the head of a ram and the Chatelaine's artificers had given him one: two great horns, almost as beautiful as Monoceros's own, whorled and graven, curling down past his thick neck, and joined to a plate of bone on his forehead. It had been such a lovely surprise that he lost his thuggishness when he gained his horns, and became melancholy, listless, brooding like a poet though he could give no cause for it.

He was all too happy to carry the canister of black powder to the gate and light the match, shielding it with his massive nude back from the arrows and boiling water from above. Like Monoceros's own, Adolfo's skin was thick, like golden leather. He might have made it back alive, although maimed, if he had not chosen to shield the canister until its final moment, to keep the match alight.

For some people courage came like wrinkles; for some courage came like scars, all of a sudden.

They lost a dozen more chimeras at the gate in the thunderous fire, and many more as the women of Bruges threw rocks and knives and whatever they could from the walls and rooftops. A nasty brood, but they were over-powered now.

And nowhere, nowhere had he seen any sign of the mercenary, Claude Jouvenal. He had checked every human of even roughly the right size and shape for marks on the right forearm, and found nothing.

Monoceros was tired. He had the speed and strength of the unicorn within him; he could run from near-Ypres to Bruges within a night and command a bloody assault in the morning. He had done that, because he always did as he was asked. Yet he was tired.

He lifted his head, canal water dripping from his horn, and there were two Mantis-men there, waiting for him with their long arms folded up before them, their bug eyes bent down toward him. Their patience galled him.

'Well?' he asked.

'We have secured the old castle and the cloth hall. We had to set a fire in the base of the belfry in the market square, but some women who were in the top leapt out, and we believe it's clear now.'

He nodded. 'No more resistance, then?'

They shook their wedge-like heads. They were staring at him with a question in their eyes: *And what have you been up to, Monoceros, while we have been securing the city?*

He had been searching, searching every house for the mercenary. But of course, no one must know the reason for Claude's importance to the Chatelaine. The existence of the second mace, a key to Hell, was a dangerous secret. He was pleased not to give the Mantis-men the satisfaction of an answer to the question they would not ask him.

He stood and leaned his head to one side then the other, hearing the crack in his neck muscles.

'Then this city is now the Chatelaine's, and anyone in it is under her protection. Those without homes can stay in the castle or the cloth hall for now. The beguinage, too, I suppose, if we can spare enough chimeras to guard them. I don't want any crowds gathering where there are no guards.'

The second mantis-man made some sort of chitinous gesture, its upper body clicking and shuffling in place.

'The main thing is the lack of food.'

Monoceros nodded, always a satisfyingly deliberate motion now that the horn weighted his head.

'Tell the people we'll send word north to the coast that Bruges is open to trade again. Tell them there will be food soon.'

He was grateful when the mantis-men strode off on their human legs. He had his own work to do.

Bruges had been the one place in Flanders where he had not yet searched for Claude, the mercenary cross-bowman who somehow worked out what the Chatelaine's mace was for, who had forged a copy of the mace and used it to escape the Hellbeast.

They had had a few beginnings of conversations, Monoceros and Claude, when the mercenary had been a guest of Hell. Though they were prisoner and guard, the conversations were one soldier to another: requests for news from the wars, brief comments about worse places they'd found themselves. Claude had seemed patient, observant, in a way that Monoceros found interesting. When he learned that the mercenary had somehow done the impossible, and escaped the Hellbeast, Monoceros had not felt surprised. He knew well from his years as a thief that very little is impossible to someone with the willingness to plan for the opportune moment and the wit to recognize it when it comes. The only thing Monoceros had ever found impossible was forgiving himself, after a plan gone wrong. The Hellbeast had been his escape, and a chance for a new life through the purity of obedience. It was his task to track the mercenary, now, for the sake of his mistress, but he bore Claude no ill will.

Monoceros walked through the street, weaving around the bodies and the wreckage, until he came to a small stone church tucked between two smashed wooden houses. He tried to remember when he had last been to Mass. Before the battle the month before, in the church in Cassel, with the Chatelaine, and not since.

There would be no Mass in Bruges today. But the chimeras were not as prone to looting as other fighters; so far, few of them had chosen to make their homes outside of Hell, and within Hell they had little use for gold monstrances or silver chalices. So the church might be as intact inside as it was outside.

He pushed the wooden door open.

People everywhere: women, children, more men than

he had expected. They looked up at him with narrow, tired eyes. They filled the nave, sitting or lying in clumps.

A small, pale man in a brown cloak came shuffling toward him. The priest, by his tonsure.

The priest held his hands wide. 'No one here has any weapons,' he said. 'They gave them all in at the castle, as they were told. Not so much as a knife to cut meat, if we had any.'

'I have come to see if the people here may be made more comfortable,' Monoceros said.

The priest made a face. 'They would be more comfortable if they were not starving.'

'That will have to wait a day or two, but hunger is what a city ought to expect when it closes its gates to the world, don't you think?'

Monoceros walked, picking a pathway through the clumps of people. The priest trotted along behind him. They paused at a boy with a stump of an arm, wrapped in bloody cloth.

'Any wounded may ask the Chatelaine for new arms, new legs, whatever they desire,' Monoceros said. 'If they are willing to pledge their loyalty to her, a new life awaits them.'

The boy and his mother stared at him, said nothing.

He kept walking, his gaze hunting for the mercenary. Up and down the nave, and no sign of him.

'Tell me,' he muttered, grabbing the priest by his cloak to draw him in close, 'Have you seen anyone with a weapon on one arm, like a chimera, or perhaps a strange scar on one arm?'

The priest looked like a rabbit. 'Only a woman, who was dressed as a man. As a crossbowman, believe it or not. She is not here any more.'

At last.

These were the moments when Monoceros was most grateful for the horn. It concentrated his thoughts in a knot of mild pain between his brows. It helped him think. It helped him see this priest for what he was: a small man, a frightened man.

'Tell me.'

The priest shook his head. 'I took her to the Ooste house, but she left with some other women, yesterday.'

'Left? While the city was besieged? How?'

The priest shrugged. 'Margriet de Vos and her daughter found some way out. Would you like to speak with Jacquemine Ooste? She saw them last.'

Monoceros nodded, and followed the priest to a dark-skinned woman crouching with two children in a shadowy corner.

Yesterday, the priest said. They could not have got far. If Monoceros could take his swiftest chimeras, and call the hounds, they would capture Claude. The Chatelaine would be so pleased. So long as that thief was free, so long as the counterfeit mace that opened all the doors in Hell was out in the world, the Chatelaine would never be easy in her mind.

'Vrouwe Ooste, you said Claude Jouvenal left Bruges before the assault?'

The woman stared at the priest, and then at Monoceros.

'You are looking for him?' she asked, her voice rough.

'It's that girl,' the priest said, but they both ignored him.

'I wish him no harm,' Monoceros said. 'But yes, I am looking for him. I understand that he left with Margriet de Vos and her daughter.'

'Oh, I believe that you wish him no harm, the same

sort of no-harm you have done to our city, to all its people. My house, burned to the ground, and you mean me no harm. Yes, I believe that.'

Monoceros knelt beside her. The little boy, barely more than an infant, squalled. He put out his finger and the boy grabbed it, and quieted.

'I can offer you safe passage as far as Ypres,' he said. 'I have other business, or I would take you myself. But I have a broad-backed friend who can carry you.'

'Why should I trust you?'

'You are free to stay here with your children and wait for food to come to the city, if you prefer. Wait for your turn, when it comes.'

'And all I must do is tell you what I know about the mercenary with the scar on his arm? What is he to you?'

'A comrade,' said Monoceros. It did not have the feel of a lie. Not entirely a lie.

Jacquemine Ooste sniffed.

'Show me your friend and his broad back and I shall tell you what little I know about Claude Jouvenal.'

Beatrix dreamed of strange hounds with two heads: each had one dog head and one human.

The hounds were nearly home, nearly home to Hell, when one of them stopped, the muscles in its thick chest quivering. It raised one of its heads – its dog head, jowled and brindled – and sniffed the air.

Its other head, with its pallid human face, shushed the other hounds, as if they needed shushing. The faces sometimes acted out of human instinct, still.

'This is not our quarry,' said the one with the brindled muzzle on one head and the jowls on the other. Beatrix felt herself speaking out of that mouth, felt the doggish weight of that heavy body, those strong legs.

'All quarry is ours,' said the one with the black around its nose and the scar on its forehead, and then Beatrix was in that dog, full of rage and gall.

'We are hunting the thief,' growled the brindled one.

'I smell charcoal,' said another, and Beatrix felt it, a loyal dog, a dog who only wanted to be happy. 'If we find charcoal, we will please the mistress. She needs it for her gonners. She will scratch our ears and give us the best meat from her table and call us her good soldiers.'

'It's coming from this way,' said another hound's human face, and they all went racing over wooded hills toward a little millrace that ran ashy and sluggish.

They snuffled along its edge until it veered to the south. They whined with pleasure. They smelled charcoal, yes, but also chickens. Beatrix smelled the chicken meat out of many noses, and in some part of her sleeping mind she thought: this is the chicken on the spit, this is what I ate, giving me strange dreams. Stolen meat, accursed.

The pack of dogs with Beatrix's mind in them came to a road, and along the side of it, the urine of six different humans. A pile of fresh horse droppings, all grass and flies, in the middle of the road.

The pack yipped.

They ran along the road swift and nearly silent, until they came to a place where the scent of horse and human shifted into a nearby field. They found the chickens, and fought and killed a mangy grey dog, revelling in the death. But Brindled would not let them eat before they found the humans, in case they had an archer among them.

Beatrix, inside the mind of the brindled dog, felt the rightness of the argument, sharp as a bone.

They caught the humans in their house, a great square thing with a water wheel. A family of humans, a man and several children, all quivering.

'Where is your charcoal?' asked Brindled out of his human mouth, a mouth Beatrix felt working, the tongue thick and wet.

'In the bloomeries, where we smelt the iron,' said the man. 'Outside. And in the pit beside them. You may take all you find.'

'And where are your weapons?'

'This is a forge-mill,' said the man. 'We have no weapons.'

'This is a place of metal. I smell it everywhere. I smell things that may be made into weapons. You lie.'

'Anything may be made into a weapon,' said the man.

They ripped out the humans' throats and dragged their bodies into the stable and left them, because the chickens made better eating. Beatrix revelled in the killings and felt herself, her human self, writhing and weeping. The small grey nag they left alive, staring balefully at the bodies of its humans. Then they knocked a candle into the stable and watched until they were sure it had caught fire.

After that, the pack was thirsty, so they drank out of the troughs by the stable, slaking both kinds of mouth, before they ran on again toward the setting sun, back to Hell.

Margriet took a sip of her water and collected a stray drop from her chin. She could see the drop on her fingertip but couldn't feel it: not cold, not wet, not anything.

So it was beginning. The plague. How long did she have? Days, yes. Weeks, perhaps, if she were lucky. Long enough to get her due from that greedy bastard and see Beatrix off safe somewhere with money in her purse and food in her belly. On a ship to England, where the new young king had reason to be kind to Flemings.

She glanced at Beatrix, sleeping on the cold ground, clutching her distaff. Poor child. But she was safer here, with Margriet, than in Bruges where any day now the revenant that had been Baltazar would surely have found her.

Perhaps she ought to speak to her more gently about her father, offer to say a prayer for the lying knave. But how to begin?

Claude was sitting on the ground, playing with his knife.

Margriet walked a little way into some trees and stripped off her kirtle. The late September sunlight, however bright, was not enough to warm her, but she must take care of her bindings before they walked any farther. Her chemise was dotted with two spots of milk; she smelled sour. And her breasts were heavy and sore. Who would have thought it, that these old dugs would miss little Jacob Ooste tugging at them, after all this time? She sighed and pulled off her chemise. She started to re-wind the binding tighter to keep them more comfortable and stop the milk.

Another day or two and the milk would be gone, her breasts dry, and her body useless. What did it matter, now that she was nearly a corpse?

She dressed and walked back toward the other two. Beatrix was still sleeping. Claude, cross-legged on the ground, was whittling something.

As Margriet approached, he held up two little bits of wood.

'One thing you learn in the free companies is how to make dice out of just about anything.'

Beatrix shouted, 'No! Stop!'

Her face was contorted. A bad dream.

Margriet knelt beside her daughter. She shook Beatrix awake, shook the strange expressions of horror and cruelty off her beautiful face. Beatrix's wimple fell away and Margriet brushed the golden hair, matted with sweat, off her daughter's brow. Her daughter, her beautiful child, the one thing left to her.

'What is it? What's wrong?' she asked as Beatrix panted and clutched at her.

Beatrix shook her head. Tears streaked her face.

'I had the most horrible dream, of hounds with two heads, one a dog and one human, and they came to a mill and they killed the people there. Children.'

'I have seen such hounds,' said Claude, standing behind them. 'The Chatelaine has hounds like that.'

'Hush,' said Margriet, and gathered Beatrix to her. Someone must have told Beatrix about the Chatelaine's hounds, some fool with nothing better to do than prattle about the works of the devil. And with little food in her belly, little sleep the night before, and her father dead and come back as a haunt, was there any wonder if Beatrix had nightmares? 'Soon, soon, everything will be better.'

CHAPTER THIRTEEN

They walked through a sunset of gold and – what was that colour, staining the clouds? Beatrix ought to give it the name of a flower but instead it reminded her of nothing so much as fish blood, watery red. It used to pool between the cobbles of the streets nearest the canal.

It was over in a moment anyway, the red going out of the clouds and the night reaching around them with cold fingers. Beatrix was not happy to be walking, not any more. Her feet ached and every movement of her legs was an effort. How much worse it must be for Mother, and for the mercenary with his hurt foot. His limp was getting worse as they walked on.

Finally, they stopped and stooped with their hands on their knees, all three of them. It was fully dark now.

'We must be near Willem now,' said Mother. 'And he'll be out, walking. He can't be far ahead of us. But where is he?'

They were near a little wood, walking along the edge of it. In the moonlight they could see the road, a dark ribbon of beaten earth far to their right.

Claude shook his head. 'In this darkness, he could be anywhere. We'll have to get ahead of him, I think, and then try to put ourselves into his path. A bridge, or a city . . . but would he go through a city? I need to think.'

'Well,' said Mother, 'I'll ease my bones for an hour, then, while we think.'

Beatrix laid her distaff on the ground beside her and pulled her cloak against the evening air. The damp from the night before still clung to it.

Something rustled in the copse beside them. Beatrix sat straight up and Mother took a step toward the sound.

'Willem?' she called.

Nothing.

Claude drew his knife and stared. He took a few steps into the woods.

'Nothing here,' he called out after a moment. 'A rabbit or something.'

'Cuwaert,' said Beatrix.

'Huh?'

Claude was sitting back down, with his knife drawn.

'Cuwaert the rabbit,' Beatrix explained. She tried to think of the French words for rabbits and hares. 'You know. *Conyn? Lapriel?* From the stories of Reynard and Ysengrim. Don't you know those stories?'

'Ah,' said Claude. 'Yes, I know them. I doubt I know the same version as you, though. Do you think the travelling condotierres in Spain and Italy tell the same animal tales as merchants in Flanders? Perhaps they do. I suppose we'll have to compare them some time, and find out.'

Beatrix sighed. She and Baltazar had talked, half-joked really, about going to Spain one day. About walking the Camino to Compostela, step by step together in strange lands. What was her place in the world now, a world without Baltazar in it? All her dreams had been with him, or of him.

A sound broke through the night: laughter, and a crash, a little distant. A snatch of many voices, singing.

'A camp?' whispered Mother.

'Perhaps there are some soldiers, some of ours,' Beatrix let herself hope out loud.

Mother shook her head. 'No Flemings would be singing. You have heard the accounts of the Battle of Cassel as well as I have, Beatrix. Chimeras.'

They were silent for a moment.

'That's our pinch point,' Claude said at last. 'A revenant would pass through the camp, if the camp were near his path. He's a creature of the Hellbeast, as are they. He would be drawn to them if he was alone in the wilderness. I've seen them come home sometimes, together, the revenants following on the heels of chimeras.'

What could this young man have been doing in Hell? It was the wrong time to ask, but there was never a right time.

Mother grunted. 'So we go to the camp, I suppose.'

'No,' Claude continued, his fingers kneading his wounded arm. 'We discussed this. I know their ways. One of us will attract less attention than three. You stay here. Keep your knives close to hand. There may be wolves, and other things.'

Mother shook her head. 'We should stay together.'

Claude was right, but Mother would be stubborn until someone gave her an excuse to stop. Grandfather had said, *be her better judgment*.

Beatrix said, 'I think Claude should go to the camp. We

have a friend here who knows the ways of soldiers and even of chimeras. God has brought us together for a reason.'

Her mother twisted her mouth.

The sky was dark purple. Near them, but in the opposite direction from the chimera camp, there was a little ridge with a copse upon it; the shadow of that ridge stretched and covered them. At the edge of that shadow something like a spark appeared, disappeared, reappeared at a little distance.

'Look,' Beatrix whispered, and pointed. 'Fireflies.'

Soon there were dozens of them, lighting up the damp clearing. They sat quietly and watched, pointing every so often to show each other where the fireflies were, their sweaty skin shivering as the air chilled.

Beatrix toyed with her distaff, twirling it so that the patch of moonlight shifted on its wooden shaft. She pointed it at the next firefly when it appeared. And then the next, as if she were scratching a tiny line of light onto the darkness of the world.

'You're quick,' said Claude. His voice sounded loud in the night. For long moments they had been sitting without speaking, listening to the rustle of the leaves in the cool evening wind.

'She always did have keen eyes,' said Mother.

'There's another,' said Beatrix, and pointed. It was a gamble; she began to move the distaff before the firefly appeared, but she knew roughly where it must be, and if she was behind, it would be a matter of a moment.

She was not behind. The firefly appeared where she wanted it to be.

Beatrix stood and whirled and pointed behind, into the depths of the shadows. A firefly appeared.

'Ha,' Claude said.

'We will let God decide our quarrel,' said Beatrix. 'If I can point to the next three fireflies, Claude goes to the chimera camp. If I cannot, he stays here.'

'I like that wager,' Claude said. 'I trust your eyes.'

'God does not care where you point your distaff and neither do I,' said Mother. 'You're silly children playing games at spitting distance from a camp full of monsters who'll run you through if they find you.'

Beatrix let her distaff fall and shivered in the cold night.

'I once pulled an arrow the length of your leg out of my gut,' said Claude tightly, 'and stuck it into the neck of a knight under his camail and held it there while he slashed at me with his sword until he choked on his own frothing blood. Call me a silly child again and see how I like it.'

'Do what you like,' snapped Mother. 'But if you tempt God, you'll get what's coming to you.'

It was not such a thrill, this time, when Beatrix pointed her distaff and the firefly appeared. Still, when Claude clapped, Beatrix sniffed in a new lungful of fresh cold air and tried again. She did not even wait or wonder; she knew she could call the firefly where she liked.

For the third and final firefly, she pointed her distaff far above, and there it appeared.

'Incredible,' said Claude.

'It is, really,' said Beatrix grinning and sitting down on the damp ground. 'I almost think I can call them. I didn't mean to cheat.'

Mother cocked her head. She probably couldn't see the fireflies at all.

'They are only flies, my dear,' Mother said, with an effort at gentleness. Treating her like a child again, always.

'You will see,' Beatrix said. 'Claude, stand, and go where the fireflies lead you.'

Claude harrumphed, and rolled his eyes, but he stood up.

Beatrix pointed, and pointed again. Claude walked farther from them, toward the chimeras' camp. Beatrix nearly choked on fear and excitement as one after another lit up, marking the path.

Claude walked a little slower now, backward, frowning.

'Go on,' Beatrix said, in a loud whisper. She set her distaff down. 'Don't you see God approves?'

'How do you know they're on God's side?' Mother grumbled. 'Might just as well be the other fellow. Might just as well be the other fellow's wife, come to that. Perhaps these flies are her minions. Why should Claude follow them?'

Claude's face looked pained.

'It is my task,' he said. 'I said I would protect you, and help you find what you seek. If I don't return by daylight, don't come looking for me. Keep on your path or find another.'

'Claude—'

'I had a friend,' Claude interrupted, 'who taught me that the best way to help your comrade in battle is to give him no reason to worry about you. Don't give me a reason to worry about you. If I'm delayed, steer well clear of the chimeras.'

He checked that his knife was secure in its sheath and strode into the darkness that lay between them and the halo of lights and laughter on the top of the hill.

'Don't do anything foolish,' Margriet called in a hoarse whisper. 'Keep to yourself. Keep out of danger. Don't eat or drink and for God's sake come back quickly.'

* * *

141

Claude skulked around the tents where once he would have diced, have drunk, have slept with a good sword next to him. Here where he belonged.

And yet he should not have come. Not weak, not wearing these clothes. Still, what choice did he have? He needed the mace, so they needed information. And if he hadn't come, the devil only knew what Margriet would have done. He had promised to protect the women and so he would.

He crouched behind the first tent of the encampment, feeling exposed in the light of the full moon, exposed in his woman's clothing. It was worse, wearing it here. A kirtle was not so different from a surcoat, in a town. But here in a camp, among aketons and armour, he was a fish gasping for water.

He would have liked to steal some proper soldier's clothing first. He was no thief. In wartime, you raided what you could, and this was wartime if ever any time was. He did not know who to be, dressed like a woman; he did not know what to say. The sooner he got back into harness, the better.

It was unlikely he'd find decent clothes just lying around. He might find a chemise, a hood, drying near a fire, or thrown over a tent line. But he needed more than underthings.

By a fire sat three chimeras. One was holding a squirrel on a spit made of his own arm, which was a pike. The chimeras ate the strange food of the Hellbeast when they were within the Beast, but most of them preferred to eat the food of men when they were out on campaign.

Some Christians said the revenants were partly of Hell and partly of Earth. And partly of Heaven? Some said the chimeras lost their souls, when they went through the fire.

Claude did not believe in Hell. He'd once heard someone call the Beast Gehenna, the place of punishment, but he didn't believe it was that either. It was a Beast, and all beasts have to eat. The fact that it came from under the Earth, that it fed on the long-dying, did not make it anything but that.

And the fire? He had not been through the fire himself, but his mace had. The mace that was now a part of him, a missing part of him.

The chimera nearest was squat, with legs twice the length of its body folded up beside it, mantis-like. It turned to Claude; its face was a human face. Some of the chimeras went through the hell-fires with bits of metal and came out armoured. Some went through with animals and came out part animal themselves.

If he found himself again in the Chatelaine's workshop, what would Claude ask her for? Other than his mace back. He wouldn't mind a practical improvement. Give him armour to wear as his own skin, in God's name give him a body that would serve him, and no more bonds and stuffings.

But for now, he was here in the guise of a woman, and he needed information to take back to Margriet, as if that would stop her tongue. If he would have to play a woman, a woman he would play. A woman who belonged in the camp, whose presence would not be questioned.

He stepped out into the firelight.

The chimera holding the spit stood and pointed it at Claude, squirrel and all.

'Good evening,' Claude said, forcing his voice to be loud and blithe, fearing it was tinny; forcing himself to hold his hands out, to show the terrible truth that he bore no weapons. Well, except for the blade tucked into his belt, but that was nothing but an ordinary dagger of the kind every woman – and certainly a whore – might bear.

'I'm supposed to find Robert of Artois,' Claude said, 'but I do not know if he is still here.'

The third chimera, a man nude above the waist with the head of a raptor and great feathered wings where his arms should be, stood and cawed at him. Its companions laughed. Claude laughed, too, hoping it was the right sort of laugh.

'You boys would be delightful company, I am sure,' he said. 'But I am bound for this Robert. I am a gift. He will be angry if he hears that his gift was spoiled or delayed. Tell me where I might find him, and I will come back tomorrow night and give you all a treat for half my normal price.'

Pike-arm sat down again on his stool and put the squirrel-spit back over the fire. The red light leapt and licked the shadows and a fountain of sparks shot up, like Beatrix's flies.

'There's hardly anyone left in this camp,' he said. 'Just us wounded, and those too sick with the runs or worse things. Most are with the vanguard. The others have gone back to Bruges this morning for an assault.'

An assault on Bruges. Margriet de Vos and her daughter had left just in time.

'Ah.' Play it slowly, calmly. Don't rush. 'And where might I find the vanguard? What the devil is a vanguard, anyway?'

'It means her Mercurial Majesty and the Beast,' said the Mantis-man.

'New to this life, are you, pet?' the soldier asked softly.

Claude laughed again. It rang false. He was no good at this, at playing for time and information. That had never been his job.

'Not new to this life but to this circumstance, you might say. I know a lot about men but very little about travelling with an army. I came here from Ghent, hoping for good business, hoping that victorious soldiers might want to celebrate. I made a good impression on a knight and he sent me to this Robert. But now I can't find him, and I'm afraid I'll lose my business and my luck.'

'Hmph,' said the soldier. 'You must be good at the work because God knows you aren't much to look at.'

He'd been too confident. He had thought his body would be disguise enough.

'If you'd tell me where they went....'

'West,' said the squat mantis-man. 'West and south. To Ypres.'

'Ah.' Claude tried to appear disappointed. 'A long walk. And I hear there are revenants abroad.'

'Can't hurt you if they don't know you,' said the Mantis-man.

Claude shook his head. 'Oh, I don't think I'll be going after all. I'll stay here, where it's safe. It is safe, isn't it? Do revenants ever come through the camp?'

'Most nights,' said the mantis-man. 'They crawl into the wagons like vermin during the daytime, give you a nasty shock if you aren't careful. Two came in last night and just left here, at sundown.'

'Two! How strange to think of revenants travelling across country, just like anyone else might. But without any baggage, of course. No need for sumpter horses.' He giggled in a way he hoped suggested nervousness.

'Oh, you'd be surprised,' said Pike-arm. 'One of the two who came through today had a big sack. Heaven knows what he kept in it. But don't worry. They moved on, at sundown. They won't be back tonight. The one with the sack wanted to get it to the Hellbeast right quick.'

'They all want to get to the Hellbeast right quick,' said the mantis-man.

Pike-arm shook his head. 'Not if they're on the hunt for someone. The young one, he went in the other direction. Back to Bruges. Hunting his bride. He went about moaning 'Beatrix, Beatrix.' He won't be back to the Hellbeast until he finds her.'

There were many young women named Beatrix in this land, Claude told himself, trying not to let the gooseflesh rise on his arm. Anyway, if the revenant was headed for Bruges, he would not find Beatrix there.

'Tell you what, my girl,' said Pike-arm, sticking the butt of the spit into the ground. 'Stay with me tonight, I'll keep you safe from the ghosties.'

He gave Claude a hideous grin.

Claude forced himself to smile. 'And who will keep me safe from you?'

He turned and walked away as quickly as he could without running. He was not afraid of this nobody. But he had work to do.

CHAPTER FOURTEEN

The fat moon lay in its bed of silver clouds, holding its belly and groaning in pleasure at all the stars it had eaten. The beech trees were the columns of fairy cathedrals, but the shadows were many and dark among them. What would move there, what would approach, if Beatrix dared close her eyes?

'Will you tell me a story?' she asked.

Mother grunted.

'A fox story,' Beatrix said. 'Reynard and Ysengrim.'

'Tell it to yourself. You know it by heart.'

Beatrix lay on her back and stared up at the moon and the stars, spinning her distaff over and over in her hands. A lovely view but it was a shame one had to be cold and damp and hungry to sleep under it. Perhaps heaven was a sky of stars with a warm, soft bed underneath it, and loaves fresh out of the oven and greasy bacon and as many figs and raisins as you could eat. She licked her lips.

Baltazar was always teasing her about her always

growling stomach, telling her she would be happiest in the mythical land of Cockaigne where food was so plentiful the pigs ran around already roasted,.

If he were here, with her now, what would she say to him? Probably nothing at all, nothing but kisses. And his warm body curled around her, his hand over her own; those knobby knuckles.

She closed her eyes and let herself pretend, for just one moment, that he was with her. In the darkness she slid her left hand through the sides of her kirtle and let her fingers rest between her legs, let them rest there, pushing slightly, a weight, a locus of longing. With her right she held her distaff tight.

Mother's voice shook Beatrix out of a doze a little while later, with a vague tight headache and a sour taste on her tongue.

'Who's there?'

Mother was sitting up, holding her knife out. Beatrix propped herself up on an elbow and pointed her distaff as if it were a spear.

'I don't hear anything, Mother,' she said.

After a while she lay back down, but gently, noiselessly. Her mother stayed sitting up.

'That fool Claude. What can be keeping him?'

Out of the blackest shadows under the trees, a man stepped.

Beatrix recognized him as a revenant first, and as Baltazar second.

It was something about his eyes. Something about the way he looked at her, as if she were nothing.

'Beatrix,' he said. 'Beatrix.'

Margriet sprang to her feet. She brandished her knife.

'Get out of here. You have no business here.'

'So you are dead,' Beatrix said.

Baltazar kept walking forward.

'I'll use this knife,' Mother shrieked. 'Get one step closer to my daughter and I'll cut your balls off. You might not die of the bleeding but it will give me satisfaction.'

Mother had always liked Baltazar. Everyone had liked Baltazar. Because he had a laugh or smile or kiss for everyone. And now that beautiful mouth was slack.

And now Mother was terrified of him.

'My love, where have you been?' Beatrix whimpered.

Baltazar stopped walking and held out his hands to both of them. 'Beatrix, I was a long time dying, before the Chatelaine found me, and saved me.'

Saved him?

'Stay back,' hissed Mother. 'How did you find us here? Do we draw our revenants with us when we leave our homes behind?'

He shook his head. 'We go to the places we lived, we look for our loved ones there. I never would have found you had Beatrix not called me here.'

'What?' Mother snapped.

Beatrix shook her head.

'I did not call him, Mother.'

Did she? Could she have called him to her just by thinking of him? If you speak of the devil, Grandfather used to say, the devil will appear. She thought of the fireflies. And then she shook her head again. She had thought of Baltazar countless times in the last month. She had spent whole hours thinking only of him, under the covers. Why should she be able to call him tonight, of all nights?

She remembered the fireflies.

'Mother, how could I, we have been together the whole time,' Beatrix muttered, talking to Mother but looking now at Baltazar as if she could ask him a question without a word. 'Mother, I have not left your side. How could I have called him here? What am I, a sorceress that I can call the dead?'

Mother frowned. 'Why do you say she called you, then? Are you lying? Are you lying to me?'

He turned his head, oddly, and looked at Mother.

'All I know is I felt myself drawn here. More powerfully even than I was drawn to our home in Bruges.'

'Well, then,' Mother huffed. 'Don't slander my daughter if you know nothing about it.'

'I have no reason to lie,' he said. 'I have left all that behind. I am saved.'

Saved. His face hurt her gaze, his face so much the same, and so changed. She focused on his hand, his left hand, resting at his side as if he were a living man. How strange that the dead should act like the living, should move their hands like any living man. Yet there was something about him, about the way he looked at her. As if his desires were not his own, but only moved through him like water through a wheel.

'Won't you stay with me, Baltazar?' she whispered to him, dropping the distaff and holding out her hands for him to take.

'Beatrix!' Mother hissed.

Her husband looked down at her hands, as if they were an animal that had come begging, an animal with sores and fleas.

Beatrix snatched her hands back. Her throat closed up.

This, this thing that had been done to her husband, was worse than death.

She swallowed. 'What are you? What are the revenants?'

He stared just over her shoulder.

'Some people call us wanderers; have you heard that? Strange, because in fact we cannot wander. We always have a destination. We go either to our homes, to call the people who loved us in life, or we go like moths to Hell. I have come for you, Beatrix. And together we will go. Your father is but a little way ahead of us. We can join him.'

He stood tall as a birch tree but he leaned a little, as if the wind swayed him.

'Father!'

'Where is Willem?' Mother asked, still brandishing the knife.

He stared. No smile crossed his lips and there was nothing in those brown eyes, nothing but the memory of desire, something so sundered now from his thoughts and his soul that it was wordless instinct, like the trotting of a dog after its master.

She had called him, or so he said. If she could call him, she could draw him.

'Lead us toward him, Baltazar,' she said.

He stared. He made no move.

What, then? She had thought – she had been sure that the fireflies went where she pointed the distaff. And she had been holding the distaff when she thought of her husband, wished him near.

Beatrix did not think. If she thought about it, it wouldn't work. She grabbed the distaff off the ground, pointed it at her dead husband and said, 'Walk. Walk toward the revenant that was my father.'

He walked.

There are always ways into a tent. Claude sneaked along the back of a row of tents behind the carts and jumbles. He loosened a peg and wriggled in between the tent wall and the ground, into the darkness. The ground was damp; the kirtle would be filthy. Oh well.

Firelight filtered through the tent walls, weak and red. He stayed down on the ground until his breath eased.

Then he went up on his knees and tried to get his bearings in the dark.

There was one person sleeping on a pallet. A chimera, although of what shape and kind Claude could not tell. Someone important, to have his own tent. At the door, silhouetted by firelight, a guard stood, shuffling. Someone very important, then, or someone guarding something very important. It was hard to tell what sort of chimera it was, from a shape under a blanket. He breathed so softly Claude could not hear him, but the blanket rose and fell.

Claude's hand went to his knife. He had no reason to think the chimera was pretending to be asleep, but if someone wriggled into Claude's tent late at night, that's what he would have done, biding time until the moment of attack.

With the sleeping chimera in the edges of his vision, he stepped to the side, to a small table. Under the table lay a long chest, locked, with half a loaf of bread upon it.

Claude's father had been an arkwright and made all sorts of chests and boxes. As a child, Claude had loved nothing more than to lift the lids, to see what was inside.

Usually it was nothing; the box itself was the object of value, and destined for an owner who had commissioned it. But sometimes his father would leave little surprises in the boxes in his workshop and let Claude find them. Stones, or homemade dolls, or sweets.

He knelt beside the chest, as though he was praying, and held the padlock, letting it rest on the palm of his weakened right hand while he fiddled with it with the fingers of his left. The night was chilly and the metal felt damp against his skin.

Claude thrust the point of his knife between the iron hasp and the wood of the lid. He prised it with all his force until the dagger snapped and the padlock banged against the chest. God's teeth.

The chimera stirred and Claude turned his face back to him, trying to breathe in silence. There was a rustle at the tent flap and Claude shrank back into the shadow. For a few breaths he waited but the guard did not come in and the chimera did not stir under the blanket.

Was the hasp loose enough now that Claude could pull it? He rested the padlock in his withered right hand gently, so it would not bang, and with his left he tried to find purchase under the lid.

In his right hand, the black iron padlock stirred, as if it were alive.

Claude dropped it again, startled, and again it banged. His heart thumped against his ribs but not only now because of the guard outside, the sleeping chimera. Iron that lived? Was this some new sorcery from Hell? What would it do, bite his hand off?

He picked the padlock up again, this time in his stronger left hand, and waited. Nothing.

He put it into his right and there it was, the sensation of stirring, as if the iron were sleeping.

The sorcery was in him. In the hand that had borne the mace. And why not? The mace was after all a key – *the* key. Had it left behind not only this itching wound, this terrible yearning, but something of its power?

Gritting his teeth with the effort, he tightened his grasp and moved his fingertips along the cold, gritty iron. Reluctantly, slowly, something inside it shifted. The shackle popped out.

Claude squatted a moment more, just staring. Then he gently pulled the padlock out and rested it on the trampled ground.

He lifted the lid and saw in the darkness the beautiful gleam of steel.

A sword! And a good one, too, by the rich scabbard. He'd have that. He gently eased the sword out of its scabbard and balanced it in his right hand. A good blade, clean and true, although with an ordinary single-handed hilt, so he'd have trouble putting much weight into it with his weakened right arm. Well. Soon he might be a left-handed swordsman, one way or the other, if he got the mace back for his right. Time to learn.

What else? A pair of gauntlets, heavy and ornamented, and greaves and boots. All too big for Claude but he'd take them anyway and sell them on if he couldn't adjust them. A skullcap and a gleaming bascinet helmet with a visor. Too big but with a bit of padding . . . Chausses! Good God above, wool chausses and a quilted aketon so he could finally dress in man's clothes again. And a mail hauberk which would fall to Claude's knees, but still, useful. No dagger; the chimera probably slept with it.

All of this was the Chatelaine's, ultimately, and poor payment for Claude's weakened draw arm, but it was a start.

Very slowly, he took one item at a time and pushed each through the bottom of the tent to the outside, as far as possible from where the guard was posted. He kept his face turned toward the sleeping chimera.

He grabbed the heel of bread off the ground and squeezed out of the tent.

The easiest way to transport the loot was to wear it. He drew the loathly kirtle over his head, wincing as he pulled his injured arm out. His breath came faster as he tugged on the clothing. It was too big, all of it. Whoever the chimera was, he had a chest like an ox. Claude tied up the chausses and hoped they would not drop around his ankles.

He tried the gauntlets but they scraped over his sore right hand and pained him. For selling, then. He wrapped them up with the bread in the kirtle.

He could not wear the helmet without drawing attention to himself, could he? No one walks through camp armed cap-a-pie. Well, perhaps he could. Here he might be taken for one of the chimeras who had built-in armour. Better that than being taken for a woman.

CHAPTER FIFTEEN

It was foolhardy to follow Baltazar anywhere – the whelp barely knew where he was going himself, half the time, and yet here they were following him into the shadowy woods. Not only following Baltazar, no, worse – following the corpse that used to be Baltazar. With each step in her son-in-law's footprints, with every heart-rent question she asked him, Margriet's daughter walked closer to the cliff-edge that was the Grief.

And yet, what other path would lead them to Willem and his sack, here in the dark, burnt, silent expanse of conquered Flanders? She had imagined, she supposed, that they would find him on the road, the road that she and her good-for-nothing husband had travelled so many times in their donkey cart, looking for someone to buy his good-for-nothing wares. She had been so angry, last night. She had put little thought into the matter of finding Willem, not until they were out into the dim starlit world outside the city, and saw that the road was a hazard, not a comfort.

She had put even less thought into how she would take

the fortune from him. Corpse he may have been, but he seemed at least as strong as he had been in life, and less inclined to recoil or avoid pain. And what wife would contemplate indignity to her husband's body, even a good-for-nothing dead husband's? And yet he was stealing away her right and her daughter's right, and for that she would gladly undertake some small sins, yes, even now when her remaining days might be few.

She would wrest it from him, if she could.

In her pack, Margriet had some rope. She had not taken it thinking of using it to bind Willem – or perhaps she had, if she was willing to admit it. He would not expect her to have followed him, and would certainly not expect her to walk up to him and throw a noose around his arms.

Margriet tied the overhand loop in the rope-end, the same knot she had used to snare the Nix, as a child, all those years ago. She tied as they walked, ignoring Beatrix's inquiring frowns. Margriet needed no light to see her work although she would have liked to feel the rough fibres against her fingertips. No matter. This was a knot she knew like the bonds of love. She was the daughter of a boatman of Bruges. Her knot would not fail.

They followed the flitting corpse that had been Margriet's son-in-law. He was easy to see, even in this murk: his hair was still as blond as flax, though it was matted with blood behind one ear.

He said he had been called. He said he could not lie. Yet what was he if not a deceit, a counterfeit? She could not trust him, and yet he said he had been called. And he seemed to obey Beatrix, when she pointed her distaff and said, *walk*.

As soon as they had the sack, they would make for

Ypres and hire a pair of palfreys, and like pilgrims make their way to Dunkirk or Calais. Margriet would see her daughter on a boat before she died, see her well across the ocean from Baltazar's corpse.

Willem was not blond. They were nearly upon him before they saw him. He turned his head and looked behind them, at his wife and daughter, and then carried on walking.

'Father!'

He ignored them.

'Baltazar, why doesn't he stop? Why won't he speak to me?'

'He is driven by his last desire, my love. It seems it has nothing to do with you, or with your mother.'

Nothing for it now but to act, and quickly. Willem might not care what Margriet did, but he would damn sure care when she took the sack from him.

'Be ready to run,' she hissed to Beatrix.

It was a fine rope, a sound knot, and would have been a good throw if Margriet's fingers had let the rope fly free. Instead, they cramped – the night air, perhaps – no, the plague, the damn plague! The noose dropped sadly to the ground, and she bent to pick it up.

Now she had Willem's attention. He turned and took a step toward her. Her heart sped.

One more throw.

This time she managed to fling the noose, but Willem had enough warning to catch it. He dropped the sack and pulled her toward him, hand over hand on the rope, as if they were children playing tug-of-war. There was no way she would get the rope around him now. Curse her blasted fingers! She should have asked Beatrix to throw it, but she could not have asked such a thing of her, and her daughter would have hesitated anyway. She loved her father; God only knew why.

Willem made no sign that he even recognized his daughter, his face doughy and blank. That face, that irritating face. The face that had watched her lift up dead baby after dead baby for his blessing, and never once given her any comfort.

'You unnatural creature,' she spat at him, pulling the rope. 'Leaving me all those years to patch the patches while you were hoarding like a miser. The shame you brought upon us! When I would go to the cloth hall or the market and all the other wives would look at my poor clothing with pity. And at home, what did I have except the constant, rotting stench of your filthy feet, and a woman can't wear that, or the foulness of your farts, and a woman can't eat that.'

Willem's face did not change.

'My one comfort was that you were so often on the roads. You must have wondered on those journeys whether your wife kept the commandments. Or did the thought never enter into your doddering pate? Do you know how many men asked for my favours, before and after our marriage? But I will tell you now, although you never asked, that never a moment's indulgence did I give any of them, all the while you were doubtless inflicting your belches and groping upon whatever poor maidens you encountered on your sinful business. And leaving me at home to milk money out of my breasts. But do you know how relieved I was to have my milk become our livelihood? Because then I had a reason not to lie with you, not ever again, for fear of souring the milk.'

'Mother, stop!' screamed Beatrix, coming up beside her. 'Father, leave us, for she won't stop until you do.'

'We stay where we wish,' said Baltazar.

'Where she sends you, you mean,' Beatrix snapped. 'You have no wills of your own. If you did—'

Her voice broke. It must be a horrible thing, Margriet realized, to be in love with a man. It always ended badly in stories. If she had known Beatrix loved Baltazar, she would never have let her marry him. Poor child.

Beatrix set her mouth, her jaw clamped. It was an expression Margriet knew well: first from the bad times in Beatrix's childhood, when she had gone days with nothing but sawdusty bread or skinny canal fish in her stomach, and then again from the past month in Bruges, during the siege. She had often wondered what was in her daughter's mind when she wore that expression: prayers for relief or prayers for fortitude?

She let the rope go slack a bit, let the remaining rope run through her hands, let him think he was winning the tug-of-war, and then she gripped so tightly her fingernails bit into her flesh, so she could be sure of her grasp, and she yanked as hard as she could. Willem was not a big man, but he was big enough that her yank made little difference. Still, he stumbled forward just a little. And the sack was on the ground beside him.

She darted forward and took the sack-end in both hands. It was heavy and he was on her before she could drag it a foot.

'Beatrix!' she shouted, and turned and scraped her nails across Willem's face.

He did not cry out, but he did pause, long enough for

Margriet to bend her knees and kick him hard in the gut, so that he stumbled back and fell on his arse.

'Beatrix, take it!' she shouted. 'It is your right. This is not your father. It is a corpse, under sorcery. Your father may not have been much, but would he steal your inheritance, if he were truly your father? Would even Willem de Vos leave his daughter a widow with nothing?'

Beatrix, good girl, was already dragging the sack away in one hand, her distaff in the other. She was younger, stronger; she was nearly running with it. She would make it. Baltazar made no move but only watched her.

'I told you yesterday, Margriet,' Willem said, getting to his feet, 'that neither of you are widows. You will accept this.'

Willem strode toward Beatrix. Margriet ran toward him and grabbed him around the knees. He fell flat on his chest.

'Run!' she screamed.

But Beatrix had stopped, foolish girl, and was staring at her.

'He told you yesterday . . . about Baltazar? And you did not tell me?'

'Run, foolish girl! I kept you safe. Why do you think I took you out of Bruges? I am giving you your chance! Run!'

But now Baltazar was walking toward Beatrix, holding out his hands.

'Wife,' he said. 'I came back for you. You are not a widow. You are my wife. Your place is by my side.'

Beatrix stared at him. What had gone wrong with the girl? Margriet screamed her daughter's name with every ounce of her breath, screamed so loud it rang in her own ears.

Willem had caught up with Beatrix now, and bent to take the sack. It was over. They could not manage this, two women against two revenants. If God had given her a little more time to plan—

Someone came crashing through the trees, a man in mail and helmet, swinging a sword. The sword flashed high in the moonlight and the man yelled and the sword thwacked Willem on the shoulder.

The corpse that had been her husband stumbled back, with a great gash nearly clean through his upper arm. There was nothing on his face, no expression. The wound did not bleed. Whoever this man was, he must want the sack. Margriet had only the space of a moment while her husband reeled back and the man-at-arms lunged after him.

The sack was no lighter the second time, and her fingers slipped on the rough cloth. But this time, Beatrix was at her side, and grasped a handful of cloth on one side and they ran with the sack between them.

'Don't look back,' she panted.

'Do not speak to me, Mother,' Beatrix said. 'Not one word.'

The night breathed cold against Margriet's hot cheek. What cause had Beatrix to be angry? What right? How dared she?

Margriet glanced behind – if the revenants were not dogging their steps, the man-at-arms must be. But no – he somehow had Baltazar pinned to the ground under his knee and was slashing again at Willem's arm.

She cringed; it was hard to remember, when she saw the hand fall away from the arm, that this was not her husband. But it was in any case her husband's body.

'Don't look back, Beatrix,' she muttered again, and tugged the sack, walking forward. Whoever the armed man was, he had business with Willem or Baltazar, it seemed. Her husband had made an enemy. The man who had killed him? People said a dead man would bleed, in the presence of his murderer, yet Willem did not bleed, not even when his flesh was hacked off.

They were nearly out of the copse and into the open field. As the trees thinned, she could see that the eastern horizon was pink. Morning. Two nights and one day now, with only a few hours of sleep snatched here and there. By God, she was too old for this. She might vomit, the moment she got a moment to think.

Over her shoulder, someone crashed through the bushes, coming closer. She whirled; it was the man in mail and helmet.

Margriet put her free hand to her waist to pull her knife and with the other, thrust her end of the sack toward her daughter.

'Run, now!' she yelled. 'I don't care if you say no masses in my name, I don't care if you curse it. I'm a dead woman now and don't you dare stop running.'

But the man in the helmet reached out his empty hands, palms toward them. Then, panting and putting one hand to his side, he lifted his visor.

'It's me, you dolts,' said Claude.

'By all the saints,' Margriet breathed. 'Where did you—?'

'No time,' Claude panted. 'I've bound your husbands, but that bit of rope won't hold them long.'

Margriet peered over Claude's shoulder but could see nothing but dull shapes in the gloom beyond.

'My arm's killing me,' Claude said. 'I could barely make

163

a dent with this sword. But it did what it had to do. If you two can manage that sack a little farther, we need to find somewhere to hide. We passed a ramshackle old sty a while back, at that burned cottage, you recall? We can rest there.'

They stumbled forward. In the sickly daylight Margriet could see now that her daughter's cheeks were stained with tears. She had not cried in front of Baltazar and Willem; she must have been crying as they were running. Poor girl. Let her have her anger. Margriet had never known her to be truly angry, not once in all her years. Come to think of it, if she had not pushed the child from her own womb, she might have wondered whether Beatrix was her daughter; she had so little of Margriet in her.

Claude put his arm across Margriet's path to stop her.

'Wait,' the young man hissed. 'Something's not—'

At the edge of the trees, where the field began, the grasses were tall, and thick, all in among shrubs and saplings. From that grass rose a dozen monsters. She knew them for chimeras by how they moved before she got close enough to see their abominations. Those three sprang from the grass with the smooth-jointed speed of insects; that other one came scampering out of the bush like a frightened partridge.

And, then, out of the darkness of the woods, a line of hounds came running at them. Two-headed hounds, running in a circle around them, their human mouths laughing and their dog mouths snarling.

'There is nowhere to run, Claude Jouvenal,' said the biggest of the chimeras, a brute with a horn jutting from his forehead like a unicorn. The horned man smiled at

Claude as if he was greeting an old friend, but his right hand at his sword belt called him a liar.

If the chimeras wanted them dead, surely they would be killing them by now.

As they drew closer, she could see better that the horned chimera stood a foot taller than any man Margriet had ever seen. Like a vine, the copper-coloured horn grew whorled and mottled with green, so thick at the base that it stretched from his brows to the beginning of his yellow hair. His skin was like leather, plated here and there with grafted armour, and he wore no tunic, only chausses and a belt.

And then he spoke, startling her.

'You took it off?' shouted the horned man, in French. 'You did not like the look of it?'

Margriet had always spoken very good French. Her father had drilled it into her. One day you might find that someone wanted you to say *scilt ende vrient*, he had said. She, being a know-it-all, had informed him that it would be the other way around if the French were trying to test a Fleming, that it would be *écu et ami*, except that *écu et ami* wasn't hard to say, so they would probably pick something with an *r* in it.

In any case, she had not thought that when the moment came the problem would be not that she didn't understand the French, but that she just didn't understand.

She stared at the horned man and opened her mouth as if some words might come out, some words that would work.

'I got rid of it,' Claude said behind her, his French much smoother than his Flemish, perfect *langue d'oc*. 'I sold it.'

The creature's smile grew broader. 'The Chatelaine would have words with you.'

'Take me if you like. But let these women go free. They are not mixed up in this business.'

The horned man's smile faded.

'The whole world is mixed up in this business.'

There was no daylight in Hell. It was difficult for newcomers to tell day from night, there, but after a few years its denizens became attuned to the groans and rumbles of the Beast's digestive system, the telltale borborygmi of its waking moments.

In the evenings it sighed and shuddered before it slept, and that, too, the Chatelaine could feel in her bones.

In the stretches between, people relied mainly on the great clock that stood in the Hall, plunder from one of the Chatelaine's husband's trips to the surface a few hundred years before. Its system of tanks and tubes filled a bowl with oil every hour, when a float triggered a metal serpent to stick out its tongue and ring a small chime. The trouble was that the hours were all the same length; this had been no problem at all underground, but now that they were living on the surface the Chatelaine had a revenant reset the thing at Prime if they were within the sound of bells, and just after sunset if they were not. By the end of each day, to a degree depending on the season, the time in Hell was askew from the time outside.

The Chatelaine was awake on this morning long before the Beast. She lay staring at the red ceiling; there may have been no daylight in Hell but it was never deeply dark, either, for the faint glow of the Beast's blood lit every room.

The messenger had said that Bruges had fallen. And that Monoceros, with a band of his best and a passel of hounds, was looking for Claude Jouvenal. Today, perhaps, the Chatelaine would have him in chains, and the false mace, too, and all would be well. Bruges had fallen – at great cost, yes, but now Philippe could not deny her Flanders. She had conquered it. She would rule it, and she could build up her army again, chimera by chimera.

There was a tap at the door. She rose and put her ermine over her shoulders as Chaerephon opened it and looked in. He looked relieved to see her awake.

'Philippe is here,' he said. 'He brought you a gift, he says.'

'A gift?'

Chaerephon shrugged, all the bones of his shoulders and neck moving under clothing like the levers in her husband's clock. He wore very little now, only a tunic and breeches and, always, a long brown cloak. 'Not a large wooden horse. A bird.'

CHAPTER SIXTEEN

Claude rode behind the horned man, his hands tied around the chimera's thick waist. Monoceros's steel armour was grafted into his skin so that its edges formed welds or cicatrices. Claude felt a childish urge to run his fingers along their lumpy, shiny surfaces, an urge like running a tongue over a sore in the mouth, or picking a scab.

The horned man's skin, where it was exposed, was ruddy, but it was hard to say what colour it had been before the Chatelaine got to him. Her furnace had strange effects sometimes. It was, despite the lumpy joins, a much more attractive result than most. And Monoceros seemed happy enough to serve the Chatelaine.

Monoceros yanked the rein to turn the horse onto the road. His armour shifted strangely over his muscles, pulling the skin taut against his spine. Claude wondered if it had hurt. Had the unicorn been wearing plate when it went into the fire with Monoceros? Or did the Chatelaine throw a bit of plate into the mix, like a cook making pottage?

At the thought, his stomach growled.

Monoceros laughed. 'Been a long time since your last meal, Claude Jouvenal?'

The bite of bread in the camp. He'd meant to give the rest to Margriet and Beatrix. It was in his bundle now with his old clothes and the ill-fitting gauntlets and boots. The women must be hungry.

He looked to his right, where Margriet was riding behind a bird-man. She looked even more foul-tempered than usual.

'Not as long for me as for my companions,' he said. 'You only want me. Let them go.'

Monoceros was quiet for a moment. 'We found the mace in Willem de Vos's sack. Those women were trying to get it. The Chatelaine will want to speak with them.'

'Bah, they don't know anything about it. That one is just a stubborn widow who wants every last sou she has coming to her. And the daughter is a simple creature. They are hungry and footsore and recently bereaved. Have pity, Monoceros.'

'We'll stop soon enough to eat,' Monoceros said.

Claude was a mercenary; he could work for anyone if the pay was right. But the Chatelaine did not hire mercenaries. She made herself servants. Claude was his own master. This was his body, in service of his own mind alone, and when he got the mace back that would be his, too. His muscles and bones were the only truth he could trust. The thought of being bound in service, as Monoceros was, made him shudder.

And now Claude was going back there, to the red place. In bonds. Once the Chatelaine had tortured him into scraps, she would kill him. She would never willingly let him take the mace-key back. He would have to steal it somehow, and his chances of doing that from within Hell's oubliettes for a second time didn't strike him as high.

He had seen Monoceros there, the first time. Usually in the company of many others, and sometimes through the door of the cell, and once alone, in the cell. The Chatelaine had sent him to try to persuade Claude to go into the fire. Monoceros had told Claude then a little of his own origin, but only a little. Only what the world already knew: that Monoceros had been the first of the Chatelaine's chimeras, that a brigand and a unicorn had gone into the furnace and this great-shouldered, hulking, horned man had come out.

People said that Monoceros could run, on his own two feet, faster than any horse. But whether that was true or not, today he rode.

'You never told me your name,' Claude said to the horned man. He spoke more softly now, softly enough that none of the other chimeras riding could hear.

'Monoceros. Have you forgotten?'

'No,' he said. 'Your real name.'

'You first.'

'My real name is Claude.'

'My real name is Monoceros.'

Claude smiled, knowing Monoceros was smiling, too, although neither of them could see the other's face. They rode for a few moments in silence, Claude's sword banging against both their thighs, Claude's helmet and other things nearly spilling out of the saddlebag.

'That's my harness you're wearing, as I suppose you know,' said the horned man.

He hadn't known.

'This mail, and aketon, and helmet, and all? All yours? Well. You shouldn't have left it lying around.'

Monoceros raised an eyebrow; the horn moved. 'I didn't. How did you pick the lock?'

Claude ignored the question. 'Then that was you in the camp? Sleeping in the tent while I . . . while I was there?'

He shook his head; Claude watched the horn coming into view, once twice. 'Ha! I was in Bruges. If I had been there, things would have gone differently for you. I have been campaigning hither and yon and what I did not want to carry I left in my tent, guarded. I had hard words for the guards.'

'It wouldn't fit you any more anyway. What were you going to do, have a hole cut in the helmet?' He imagined the mail straining to fit over Monoceros's armoured chest. He must have been much smaller before he went through the Hellfire.

'I planned to give it to a page, when I got around to getting one. Anyway, it doesn't fit you either.' He paused a moment. 'I remember you, and not just from Hell. From before we captured you. When we fought on the same side at Poperinge. The Genoa Company fought well.'

'I don't suppose you could tell me where they are now.'

'Why?'

'I fought with them for many years. They are my brothers.'

Monoceros paused for a long while, looking away into the trees. Finally, he said, 'I heard they went to Scotland. The young English king is fighting there, you know.'

'Indeed I do know. The Flemings had hoped he would fight for them instead, turn his attention south rather than north, and take down King Philippe. They complain about it in Bruges all the time.'

'Fat chance of that. This parricide King Edward of

England will be just like his father. Not dependable. It wouldn't have mattered anyway, of course.'

'No,' Claude said, but it might have. The chimeras were terrifying but few, and the French forces were divided, uncertain, and unwilling to fight with the chimeras. King Philippe had left the fight against the Flemings to the Chatelaine and to mercenaries like him. Poperinge had gone well for the Chatelaine, but Cassel had been hard fought, as Claude knew too well.

'Your company could have stayed on here to clean up,' Monoceros said. 'They said they would fight for the French king no more because the pay was so bad.'

'You sound as if you don't believe that.'

'I don't. I think they don't want to fight alongside chimeras any more. Alongside people like us.'

Claude heard that the 'us' included him, and he shivered.

'I can tell you, the pay is indeed bad,' he said, but his voice was not as strong as he would like. 'I argued against coming north to fight in this war.'

'Did you now? Well, I suppose your word wasn't worth much, if they thought you were a woman.'

'They didn't think I was a woman.'

'Ah, yes. Tell me, how did you manage that?'

How do you piss, how do you fuck? Not how did you manage to sink seven crossbow bolts into the centre of a target in Toulouse, or how did you manage to fight off three brigands in Florence, half-drunk. No: how did you manage the stuffing and the pissing, Claude? Everyone wanted to peel Claude like a shrimp and see what was underneath.

'I killed everyone who asked me how I managed it.'

Monoceros chuckled. The armour moved on the shoulders again.

'What drove you to that life, anyway? The life of a mercenary?'

Claude opened his mouth to say something clever. Instead he found he was too tired. Too heartsore. 'I wanted to be a man-at-arms,' he said simply.

Monoceros reached up and scratched his ear, brushed one of his bright curls behind it.

'Fair enough,' he said.

They let Beatrix keep the distaff. Probably because it was an awkward thing to pack, and the only sumpter horse was already loaded down with Father's sack. The thing they had come for, to stop the Chatelaine getting it, and now the Chatelaine was getting it anyway, and them, too. Mother never would learn to accept the will of God.

Beatrix was pleased, for no good reason, that the distaff was strapped to her back, the bottom resting against the horse's flank and the top over her shoulder. Probably the chimeras didn't know it was a weapon, and certainly never expected someone who looked like Beatrix to wield one.

That it *was* a weapon, she was sure, although not of the sort anyone might think. It had called the fireflies. It had called Baltazar. It had let her control him.

She was a knight, a captured knight, riding off to negotiations with her weapon still strapped to her back. But bah, the dream popped like a bubble. What negotiations? What could the Chatelaine possibly want with Beatrix and Margriet, other than to feed them to the Beast and turn them into revenants, too?

If she were truly in possession of a weapon, now would be the time to use it.

Beatrix's hands were tied around the waist of the chimera in front of her, a big woman with both arms made all of shining steel, not armour but the very shape of flesh.

Did she need to hold the distaff? Or was it enough to simply have it on her person? She closed her eyes and felt the weight of the distaff between her shoulder blades. She could call – who? How far were they from Ypres? Would anyone get here in time? Perhaps there were people closer who would come, but would they be strong enough and in enough numbers?

Birds. She would try birds. Something dangerous, and she would hope that she could control them when they arrived, as she had controlled Baltazar.

She would call them as she had called the fireflies. For an hour, longer, she stared into the pale sky and called all the hawks, all the vultures, all the eagles.

The sky was empty.

In the cold light of morning, it was silly, of course it was silly. The fireflies had gone where they wanted and she had played a child's game, thinking she could predict their appearance. And then Baltazar . . . well, all revenants were drawn to the people they loved, weren't they? He had said he was called but perhaps he was confused, perhaps the dead lied. He was not Baltazar, could not be her Baltazar. But perhaps he was a shadow, a memory, and she could live as his wife even if he were no longer quite her husband. In the daytime she would grieve him and at night he would come to her, and stand in the doorway, and she would look upon his blood-stained face and love him.

Could such a life be? If only she knew the future, she could begin to grieve the past.

Something on the horizon was moving. Seven black shapes against the sky like insects against a church window.

Her birds – could it be her birds? Had she called them?

The wind rose like the sound of a million insects, then it roared like a whirlwind, and something enormous and dire rose up over the northwest horizon.

A creature of the sky, a dragon with a blunt face like a mole and grey skin gleaming like steel. It filled heaven, and beneath it the people on the horizon were small. It soared without moving its vast wings. The roar grew louder as the dragon approached. There was a flash of fire from the ground to the south, and there were people running, running from the low shapes of buildings that had not been there a moment before.

A city, a city of metal and glass.

The people were dressed strangely and running along roads like ribbons of stone.

Everything was screaming; the world was screaming.

Beatrix screamed, too, and as she screamed she fell, until she was floating in the air and all the ages of the world were rushing past her.

CHAPTER SEVENTEEN

Margriet had been shouting her daughter's name long enough for her throat to get raw. She had started shouting the moment she saw Beatrix slipping in the saddle and kept shouting while the chimera in front of Beatrix stopped her horse and tried to raise the girl, and kept shouting while the whole party stopped, and they unbound Beatrix's hands and lowered her to the ground.

Claude and Margriet were unbound now, but there was no point in trying to run, and anyway Margriet would not have left Beatrix there, staring, unaware, barely breathing.

Another shout and a shake, a splash of water in the face, and at last, at last, Beatrix blinked and rolled over and vomited on the ground.

Margriet knelt behind her and held her, wiped her chin with a linen clout from her pack.

'I saw . . .' Beatrix whispered.

'What?' Claude asked sharply.

'A new city,' Beatrix said. 'And a dragon, or some enormous beast.'

'Some device of the Chatelaine's,' said Margriet.

'It was not here,' Beatrix said. 'The world was changed. The people. There was fire.'

'You chose a poor time to have a vision,' Claude grumbled.

'She doesn't have visions,' Margriet said.

She heard the quaver in her own voice. Damn that Baltazar and his brown eyes! Damn him! This madness was the first sign of the Grief, surely. So many in Bruges had run into the streets, claiming to see things that no one else could. Within days, they wanted nothing more to do with the living world. Their revenants took them away, willing captives.

It would not happen to Beatrix.

'She has not slept or eaten properly,' Margriet said, more firmly. 'It was a dream. Nothing to fuss about. What more do you expect, not even letting us stop to drink and eat and pass water?' She raised her voice at the end and looked at the horned man, who seemed to be the leader of this gang.

'We've stopped now,' he said, looking down at her with a smirk. 'Over there. Hildegard will take you.'

Hildegard was the big chimera with the steel arms. She stood and watched while the three of them relieved themselves in the long grass. Beatrix wobbled a little on her feet but she insisted she could walk on her own; she also insisted on taking her distaff with her. She had always been prey to notions; this was not the first time Margriet had wished she had been able to set her daughter right, set her working smoothly again, the way the men of Bruges used to repair the workings of the great treadmill in the marketplace, where Margriet had once walked with all the other burghers' children.

Margriet's breasts hung heavy and sore now. Two days, only. Two days since she had nursed little Jacob for the last time, nursed any baby for the last time.

And so what? Would she miss it? It was a relief to have her body to herself, to not have to be tied to the household. But yes, she would miss it, would miss the little insistent tug of life, the quiet, the blue eyes staring up at her, content. She would miss it, in the time that remained to her.

Two days since her loutish husband had given her a death sentence.

As they walked back to the fire, with Hildegard's knife at their back, Monoceros gestured for the three of them to sit with their backs to a fallen log. A bird-man tied their legs together, with Margriet in the middle, one ankle bound to Claude, one to Beatrix. Then Monoceros gave them each a bit of dark bread and sausage and a flask of weak ale.

Margriet glanced around. Hildegard was standing, probably within earshot, but not if they spoke quietly.

'Say nothing more about visions, Beatrix,' she said. 'Lest people call you a witch.'

'If the Chatelaine has not been taken for a witch yet,' Claude said, 'I think you're safe.'

'Only because that upstart king of France protects her,' said Margriet.

Claude snorted. 'There is still a pope in Avignon, and although he tuts, you will notice he put an interdict on Flanders, not on the Chatelaine.'

'Hmph,' said Margriet. 'A pope who is as close to the French king as my left breast to my right.'

'People say the devil took her to be his bride,' Beatrix said. 'People say that's who she is.'

'And so where is he, then?' Margriet jumped in. 'Where is the devil in all this? Why does she command the army? Why does she cavort with King Philippe, and not her husband? I think he's dead.'

'But surely the devil can't die,' Beatrix said.

'Why not?' Margriet asked. 'If God can die, why not him, too?'

Beatrix's eyes went wide at her mother's words.

Claude laughed. 'A blasphemer! I never would have thought it.'

'It isn't blasphemy,' Margriet snapped. 'God died and rose again. How is that blasphemy? Tell me? Are you a scholar?'

'I am no scholar,' Claude admitted, 'but I know a little more of the Chatelaine than you do. She is wily. She is secrets upon secrets upon secrets.'

'I may not know much of the Chatelaine, but I am a wife as she is, and I think she is a widow like me, too. Maybe she killed him herself; I can't say I didn't dream of it a few times with old Willem. So if she is a widow, who better to understand a widow's rights?'

Claude's eyes went wide.

'You mean to ask her for your husband's goods?' he whispered, with a glance at Hildegard. The chimera kept her back to them.

Yes, she did mean to ask. Let the woman show whether she meant to be a true countess.

'Mother, no,' Beatrix said.

'Do you remember,' Mother said, keeping her voice low and light, 'how the stories of Reynard the Fox began? How they all began?'

Beatrix nodded. As a child she had asked for those

stories every night, the ones about Reynard, the rogue, and how he bested all the other animals.

'King Nobel had a court at Whitsuntide . . .' Beatrix whispered.

'And Ysengrim the Wolf made a complaint against Reynard, saying he had his way with Ysengrim's wife and pissed on his cubs. And all the other animals laid their complaints, and Cuwaert the hare brought the corpse of his dead daughter on a bier, to show what Reynard had done. And so the king summoned Reynard to court.'

'A fairy-story,' said Claude.

'If the Chatelaine wants to act like the Queen of Flanders, let her show it,' Margriet said. 'We will put our case before her and let her show how she intends to rule, with justice or without. After all she is a woman and a wife. She has an interest in the rights of wives.'

The horned man walked over to them and nodded to Hildegard, who loosened their bonds, at knifepoint, and they were each put back onto a horse with their wrists tied around a chimera again. Beatrix still looked pale, but at least now she had some food in her, some ale.

After they had been travelling on the road a little way, Margriet thought she heard something, footsteps out of rhythm with the horses, behind them. She glanced behind, thinking she'd see the two dead husbands walking behind, staring.

But it was only the hounds, gambolling. Of course; it was daylight, and the revenants would be hiding somewhere, for now.

Philippe looked well-rested, as he always did. His dark curls sat glossy on his velvet shoulders. Philippe of Valois, the thirty-five year old green shoot on the moribund stump of the Capetian dynasty. Philippe the fortunate, who had made himself king, and knew it. It made him gloat.

Beside him, a varlet held a pole with a hooded bird upon it. It was white as ermine, with a scatter of black spots all down its back and wings. The Chatelaine's breath caught with delight, and she very nearly clapped her hands like a girl.

Instead, she knelt, squatting low, her knee not quite touching the muddy ground outside the Hellmouth. She stood again quickly.

'I have brought you a present,' said the king, 'in gratitude for your service. And we shall have a mass of thanksgiving for the fall of Bruges. When you come to one of my estates, we will take her hunting. The hunting here is poor.'

The Chatelaine inclined her head. Was this display of favour from Philippe a sign of more to come? Or a clue that he was preparing her for disappointment? He had said: give me Bruges and you will be Countess of Flanders.

'It is a gift fit for a queen,' she said. 'Or perhaps, at least, a countess.'

Beside her Chaerephon coughed, reminding her to be politic, to be patient. Philippe frowned. She had spoken wrongly, again. She had been so long under the Earth, so long among the people of Hell, who had nothing to hide.

'Fit, I hope, for your famous menagerie,' said the king. 'I should like to see it. I have heard—'

'What?'

'Rumours,' he said, spreading his arms wide.

The Chatelaine did not want him to visit her menagerie.

She wanted him to go away so that she could get acquainted with the marvellous bird. Poor creature.

'You are kind, my king. My menagerie is much depleted of late.'

This was the truth. One of the unicorns had gone into making Monoceros, and that was the beginning, the first of her animals to be sacrificed. She had whole rooms full of insects and others, high-ceilinged, full of birds; the mantis-men and moth-men and bird-men had come from those. When an animal and a human went through the fires of Hell together they emerged bonded, mixed, in an alchemy not even Chaerephon could explain.

Philippe smiled. 'I know you have sacrificed, and that this is only one gyrfalcon. But she is a very pretty gyrfalcon, and she is a killer.'

The bird was very pretty indeed, and when a powerful man asked himself inside your home it was not a request. That much she did not need to learn; that much she remembered.

The unicorn had been a gift. Hundreds of years ago, when she still had the strength to fight her husband in the night, when she still remembered her birth name and the life from which she'd been ripped. It was too late by then for the unicorn her husband gave her to be any kind of test. It was a gift, freely given, but not freely taken, for the new, young Chatelaine of Hell had not been free.

She had loved the unicorn, though, and her husband was pleased.

She loved Monoceros, now, partly on the animal's behalf, and partly because she had made him; he was her own.

'What's this?' the king asked as they entered the first red room, deep inside Hell.

They were four; she told the king he could bring only one of his men because the animals were skittish and the quarters cramped, but she took Chaerephon, too. She wanted him by her, listening and watching the king. This was the room for large birds, the new home for the gyrfalcon.

'I have never seen such a thing,' the king said, laughing.

Philippe held his finger out but pulled it back when the dodo snapped its sharp beak and lifted its wings, angry. The Chatelaine shushed it. In the corner, the old lovebirds twittered. There were so many empty poles in this room. There had been another dodo, this one's mate, but the damn things had never bred. The Chatelaine was a good breeder, of everything from snakes to bears. She made an effort with everything, if she could get a pair. Everything except the blemmyes, the headless people with faces on their chests, and the wodewoses, the hairy men of the forests; it had seemed wrong to breed them and she had secretly been pleased when they died, after the long, unhappy life given to them by the food of Hell. Although her husband had mocked her for it, she had not liked the idea of breeding people.

Now she had cause to regret her squeamishness – the army she might have by now! – but she had been so much younger, then, and had not yet understood that people turn each other into weapons.

'I am pleased with the reports from Bruges,' Philippe said, walking the room and peering at the birds. 'For a moment there I feared the siege would be long and uncertain. They are stiff-necked, these Flemings. Are you sure you wish to rule them?'

He had a way of pulling the conversation out from under her. She would have to watch that.

'I have no doubt of my ability to manage them.'

'That would certainly put you one up on Count Louis. I would be more than happy to find some replacement for him, some man I could trust to quiet Flanders down and let me get on with the English.'

She stopped and looked at Chaerephon, who gave her a little rueful smirk, as if to say, *we knew this would happen*.

'Some man?' she said, speaking lowly, carefully. 'We agreed, my king, that if I could put down the rebellion, Flanders would be mine.'

'And yours it will be. I am a man of my word. We need to find some way to do it properly, though. We'll have to find you a new husband. I imagine it won't be difficult to get an annulment for your . . .'

He'd overstepped, and knew it, looking at her face. She kept her features perfectly still for a moment and let him flounder.

'You are suggesting I find some scion of the ruling house, some cousin of Louis, perhaps, and marry him. Some weak-willed man I can control.'

'I have no doubt you could control any man, no matter how strong his will.'

His black eyes flashed. Sometimes he looked womanish himself, with his soft curls brushing his narrow chin.

She tried to stop her heart from beating. She wanted nothing more to do with marriage. She wanted her demesne to be hers by right, a right no one could challenge. She spoke slowly, looking just past Philippe to where Chaerephon stood.

'I lost my memory of my parentage, as you know. But

I feel sure that your clerks are clever enough to discover who I truly am, to discover that I am in fact the next heir to the county of Flanders, once Louis is . . . dealt with.'

'Wouldn't matter,' said the king, and turned to look at the rest of the room. 'Can we move on?'

She inclined her head and led him to the next room, the wet room.

Water spilled over the top of a large wooden tank, into a second smaller tank, and then again into a third, like three ponds connected by small waterfalls. It was a clever design of her own, run by tubes and floats much like the great clock. It kept the water fairly fresh. Even so it did not smell fresh in here; it smelled like wet fur and mould.

'God save me, is that a beaver?' the king said, putting his hands on his knees and bending forward to get a better look. Philippe's varlet was holding a torch; he walked closer. The beaver stared at them balefully, then slid into the water with a light splash.

'Is it true that they bite off their own balls and throw them at attackers to save themselves?' the king turned to ask her, with a wink.

She knew what he was doing; he was unbalancing her by bringing her close. And it was working despite her wariness. She wanted to show him she could be a friend to him, that she could keep up with his mind. She resisted the temptation.

'Why would it not matter if I had the pedigree to entitle me to Flanders?' she asked doggedly.

He straightened, and sighed.

'My very clever clerks cannot find you to be the heir to Flanders, because my very clever clerks have already determined that a woman cannot inherit in any of the

Salic Lands, which includes Flanders. A very important point of law, that. If it were not the case, I would not be king. The she-wolf Isabella would have a better claim than mine, and her patricide son would be king of France as well as of England.'

He was false. He was a traitor. He had never intended to give the Chatelaine her due. She looked at Chaerephon, not a plea but a hard look of command. If Philippe was going to chop law, well, she had just the man for the purpose.

And Chaerephon did speak, but he said, 'Sire, perhaps you could solve a riddle that has long puzzled me. How would you classify a creature with a bill that lays eggs? Would you call it a bird?'

'Indeed,' said the king.

'What about a creature with fur that feeds its young on milk from its body. A beast, yes? Like a bull or a dog?'

'Of course.'

'And if you will indulge me, what about an animal that poisons its enemies with venom?'

'A snake.'

'Would you like to see the strangest animal in the world?'

Philippe laughed. 'Do you have anything here stranger than man?'

Chaerephon smiled thinly. 'Perhaps not. The strangest animal in our collection, then.'

He pulled the goad off the wall and fished around in the lowest tank until the creature scrambled out unhappily. She was old and her beady fishwife eyes were rheumy. But the king barked with laughter at the sight of the black duckbill, the glistening fur. He circled around it as Chaerephon kept it in place with the goad.

'One of your chimeras?' he asked the Chatelaine.

'No,' she said softly. 'They are born this way. We got a pair of them off a trader in China. He had them in a cage. They cost us a fortune. I bred them and she laid two eggs. One was this creature, which has never lived anywhere but Hell. The other never hatched. I have it in my rooms, still uncracked.'

'Astounding. And what is it called?'

The Chatelaine was silent, not looking at Chaerephon. She had given it a name in the language of Hell, her husband's language, but that tongue was forbidden now, by the Chatelaine's own command. Everyone in Hell was told to speak French.

'It has no name, so far as I know,' she said. 'Perhaps you would like to name it?'

'Me?'

She nodded. 'Who better than a king, to give the animals their names?'

He barked a short laugh. 'I can't think of anything except that the poor thing looks as if God had a few odds and ends left over and couldn't think of a use for them. So I'll call it Hochepot.'

Chaerephon coughed.

'Sire, had you ever heard of a creature of fur that lays eggs, before this?'

The king shook his head. 'Indeed I had not.'

'So when we say, a woman cannot inherit, we are speaking in generalities, just as when we say that birds lay eggs. But in certain circumstances, just as God sees fit to fit a bill and webbed feet on a furred creature, a woman can take on some of the characteristics of a man to suit the needs of the people. Your cousin Joan is Queen of Navarre in her own right.'

187

'And yet she was barred from the throne of France. Different lands, different laws,' he said, as if he were speaking of some far-off and mythical kingdom where monopods and griffins roamed. 'I had no claim on that throne anyway.'

Tread carefully, Chaerephon, the Chatelaine thought. This was not going to work.

'Yes,' Chaerephon continued smoothly, 'but here in Flanders, a hundred years ago, Joan of Constantinople became Countess of Flanders after the death of her father in the Holy Land. Is that not so?'

'Indeed. And there is a man named Pietro Rainalducci in Italy who calls himself pope, and any knave or emperor who does not like my pope in Avignon calls this man Pietro pope, too. But they are not right. The law is the law.'

'You are right, of course,' she said, impatient now with Chaerephon's attempt at sophistry. 'The path of inheritance is closed to me. But the path of simple force of arms is not. This land is mine because I have taken it. If Isabella could take England, if the Empress Matilda could do so before her—'

'It is not right that a woman should rule,' he said angrily, the mask slipping at last. 'It is not God's will. You can command an army, certainly. You cannot be the father of your people. You cannot dispense the law.'

She could command her army indeed; she could command it to fight for the throne of France, and then let Philippe of Valois, Philippe the fortunate, tell her what God intended. But not yet, not yet. It was too risky still. Without knights to command, she needed better weapons, bigger weapons. She needed a fortress on the surface that she could hold, and from there she could grow.

A roach-man scuffled to her side.

'Monoceros is here,' he hissed. 'He has returned.'

He looked nervous, and for a moment the Chatelaine thought something had befallen her army. They had found a way to break them, to destroy them all. She would be left without friends. She would be cast into Hell's depths, in place of her husband. Or worse: with her husband.

But it was merely the way of the roach-man to look nervous. It was his gift, the gift of anxiety. All her insects had it. They made good messengers but horrible spies.

'Monoceros is here?'

'At the mouth. He has brought prisoners.'

She looked back at Philippe, who was watching her, not even pretending not to be listening. Prisoners. Monoceros had found Claude Jouvenal, the man with Hell's spare key. At last.

'Monoceros said,' said the roach-man, with something like an insect smile, or perhaps an insect grimace, 'you would want to see them outside, that he did not wish to bring the thief inside. Shall I tell him he was wrong?'

It looked as if the prospect gave the roach-man some satisfaction. There was something mutinous in him. She would have to watch this one. She would have to watch them all. She had been a fool not to see it in Gobhan Og, but any one of them might harbour a secret ambition, a hatred, a desire. Oh for a Hell peopled only with shades, without desires of their own. But the revenants were weapons, and imprecise ones; they were not soldiers.

'Monoceros speaks with my voice. I will deal with the thief, but briefly, after my audience with the king.'

'Do not delay on my account,' the king said. 'Your men are no doubt tired. I shall come with you. To see how a woman dispenses justice to prisoners.'

The Chatelaine could think of no way to refuse. She walked behind him, Philippe leading the way as if Hell were his.

Even when Hell was at the surface, it kept most of its great body under the earth. When she rode it, the Chatelaine stood in its mouth, holding her mace-key in the mechanism of the scold's bridle that kept its mouth open, that forced it up to the surface.

So the mouth of Hell when it opened looked like a great cave opening out of the earth, like a hill broken open to reveal a sanguine gullet. The great teeth like rocks were wrapped in the bridle of iron, and two great iron chains like columns stretched from top to bottom on either side. She knew how it must look to the king and his men, how it frightened them, no matter which way they approached those rows of teeth.

Let them be frightened.

To that great door the Chatelaine walked, robed in ermine, with her black hair coiled and netted in gold in two points at the sides of her head, very like horns.

CHAPTER EIGHTEEN

A dark hill – that's all it was, from a distance, to Margriet's eyes. But this was flat country and Hell was a big beast. As they approached in the grey morning light, she saw two great circles gleaming like white eggs or blisters on the top of its head. Eyes, she realized with a shock. Unblinking eyes that stared not at the chimeras and their captives approaching on the ground but off into the distance, into the sky.

She was so tired that her head felt like a rotten turnip, and her ears felt as if they were filled with water whenever she moved her head.

The chimeras stopped and unbound the captives and let them slide off the saddles. Margriet's arse was numb, and so were her fingers, for different reasons. When her feet touched the ground they felt odd, too. The plague was progressing.

She stood with Beatrix to her left and Claude on her right. Claude was breathing hard. Beatrix was muttering: prayers, probably.

The great mouth yawned open and Margriet gasped. A row of long ivory teeth gleamed, each one of them pointed like an incisor. One side of the nose was pierced by a copper ring that could have bounded both Margriet and Beatrix with room to spare.

A lick of the lips with a great red tongue, and then the mouth closed.

The horned man walked to the Beast and said something softly, so softly that Margriet could not hear.

Was there a password? The equivalent of *scilt ende vrient* in whatever language this beast spoke?

The Hellbeast opened its mouth slowly, as though someone were cranking a portcullis, and out came a mantis-man. He dropped to one knee.

'Here comes King Philippe,' breathed Beatrix.

'Can you see him so sharply from here?'

'I wouldn't know his face. But look how the man goes on his knee. And look how the king stands. It's him, I know it's him.'

'False-dealing, arrogant, unnatural knave,' said Margriet.

'What shall we do?'

'What can we do?'

The answer rang like a horn in her mind: They could change tack, appeal to the king's mercy as well as the Chatelaine's – or at least his curiosity. His sense of justice? That was a laugh. The man had no right to be king, and no right to impose the rule of a rotten count over the will of the people of Flanders. And yet he had done so, and made a deal with Hell to do it. Could she truly appeal to such a king?

Beatrix grabbed her arm. 'Look.'

Two figures had come to the door of Hell. One was tall

and thin, a man, she thought. The other, by the shape of the white gown and the headdress, was a woman.

'Is it her?' Margriet asked. 'What does she look like? Her skin is dark, that much I can see.'

'Darker than Jacquemine Ooste's. And her hair is black and fuzzy, and coiled up on two sides of her head in horns, and all wrapped in gold threads with gold cloth over it. She is not wearing a wimple. She is very beautiful of face.'

'It's her, then. This is our chance.'

Claude snorted.

It seemed incredible that a human could walk inside and come out again unchanged, but if Jonah could go into the whale, the king of France could visit Hell.

If she were honest, and Margriet could not help but be honest, there was one small part of her mind that held back out of fear, not out of fear of the king's knights or even of the Chatelaine's chimeras but of what she, Margriet, would say. She had practised her speech as they rode, but it was hiding from her mind now.

In all her years, she had never had to speak to anyone higher than a city alderman, and that had usually not gone well. She did not have the gift of smiling speech; that had always been Willem's job, though he did it poorly.

Willem, though, was dead. And Margriet would be dead of the plague soon, and Beatrix would be left with nothing.

The Chatelaine walked out onto a great red tongue that lolled out over the iron-clad teeth and dropped slavering onto the mud. A neat trick. Margriet was close enough to see her better now. She was dressed in white velvet, hair scraped up at the temples, skin flushed and shining on the cheeks. It must be hot in Hell under that fur cloak.

And what was that? A bronze-coloured mace swung

from the end of one arm, as though it were part of her body. So the queen of Hell was a chimera herself, or something like one.

The chimeras knelt. Margriet, remembering that she was a petitioner, knelt too, going down awkwardly on one knee. The ground was cold and damp.

The Chatelaine took the horned man by his giant hand, pulled him up to standing and kissed him once on each cheek. He had to stoop for her to do it, squatting a little so as to keep his back straight and the horn out of the way. Somehow, he made that look elegant. Then the Chatelaine's gaze swept over Claude and Margriet and Beatrix.

King Philippe raised his hand, and everyone stood. The Chatelaine looked irritated, turning to him and turning back again to the assembled monsters and prisoners.

'Where is it?' she snapped, looking at Claude.

Claude sighed heavily. 'My lady, if you think I have a mace secreted on my person, I shall have to disappoint you.'

A mace? The weapon on the Chatelaine's arm looked very like the one Margriet had seen in Willem's strongbox. There was a riddle in all this, and by heaven Margriet would have the answer out of Claude if ever she got the chance, which seemed unlikely now.

'This insolent man is known to me already,' said the Chatelaine, looking at Claude. 'But I do not believe I have seen these women before.'

'We are Margriet de Vos and Beatrix Claes, from Bruges, my lady,' Margriet said, looking her in the eye.

'You'll speak when asked,' growled the horned man.

The Chatelaine raised a hand to him, and smiled at Margriet.

'You were travelling with Claude Jouvenal?'

Margriet nodded. 'He is my guard,' she said. There were titters. 'I bring a petition.'

'A petition! Ah, you pray mercy for your town.'

'No, my lady. That is, of course, yes, I would like you to stop the siege of Bruges. But my petition concerns another matter. I thought to bring it to Count Louis, but I heard people say that you were now lord in Flanders, and in any case I thought that you, as a woman, might understand my cause all the better.'

'You interest me greatly.'

Margriet took that as encouragement to speak.

'My husband amassed great wealth when he was alive, and by Flemish law that wealth must now come to me and to my daughter. One third to me, and the rest to her.'

The Chatelaine glanced back at King Philippe. Next to him stood an ordinary-looking varlet and a tall, thin man in a grey-brown cloak.

'Is that so?' the Chatelaine responded, turning back. 'I am afraid my knowledge of the intricacies of Flemish law is not what it ought to be. And who is keeping you from your inheritance?'

'He is,' Beatrix said. 'Father is.'

'My husband,' Margriet added.

'Ah,' said the Chatelaine, pursing her lips. 'A revenant?'

'Yes.'

'Your husband's name?' The Chatelaine focused on Margriet like a cat on its prey.

'Willem de Vos.'

'Ah,' said the Chatelaine, looking unhappy. 'I thought it was so.'

'You know him, then, my lady.'

'I know the names and hearts of every one of the Beast's denizens. But you are mistaken when you call yourself a widow, Vrouwe de Vos. The dead are dead. The priests tell me they lie in the earth until the Last Judgment. They do not walk. Your husband is a revenant; he walks upon the earth, he speaks.'

Margriet swallowed.

'He has a great hole in his body. A man cannot bear such a wound and live.'

'There are many miracles upon this Earth.'

'He is a denizen of Hell. You said so yourself. Only the dead live in Hell.'

The Chatelaine stepped backward, waving her hand at the great red tongue and the darkness beyond. 'Have you been inside?'

Margriet shook her head. 'But I have met my husband since he took that wound, since he was made a revenant. And I can tell you without fear of lying that he is not the same man. That creature may use his body but my husband, Willem de Vos, is dead. I am his widow. I have my rights.'

'And what form does your husband's wealth take?' said the king, stepping forward. 'Land? Gold? English wool? Or that homely cloth you people weave?'

Margriet pointed at the sumpter horse. 'That bag. We had just taken it back from the revenant when your servants attacked us.'

'Attacked!' the Chatelaine said. 'Really. I don't like the sound of that, at all. Did you attack these women, Monoceros?'

'I invited them to come and meet you, my lady.'

'Indeed. Well, and what's in the bag?'

'All sorts of things: silver cups and lots of clinking money. A sword, and a mace very like the one you wear, my lady. I would have thought there could not be two maces like it in the world.'

The Chatelaine's head snapped around to look at Claude.

'Oh but there are,' said Claude, his voice strangled by laughter or something else. 'Yes, there it is. That mace that once belonged to me. Shall I tell everyone how I came by it and what it did?'

'You stole it,' said the Chatelaine icily. 'You, Claude Jouvenal, are a treacherous liar, a mercenary with no loyalty and no one will believe a word you say.'

'Stole it!' said the king. 'From you? This mercenary stole a weapon from Hell?'

The Chatelaine closed her eyes for a moment, just a moment. When she opened them again she was smiling. 'Not a true weapon of Hell. A poor copy, made to look like one of my weapons. Still, it is the principle.'

'A copy?' the king asked.

'A copy I had made,' said Claude. 'And not a poor copy at all. Shall I tell how I bought it?'

'It seems to me that ought to wait for the trial,' said the king.

'The trial!' the Chatelaine said.

'It is an interesting case,' said the king. 'A case for lawyers, I should say.'

The Chatelaine whirled to face him. 'Sire, it seems simple enough to me.'

'Does it?' asked the king. 'Well then perhaps you should argue it. It seems the inheritance is the central issue, and while Flemish custom is all well and good, inheritance is canon law, so we must have a bishop to decide who owns the goods in this sack, and what parts they receive.'

'Surely, my king, the princes of the church have other matters to occupy them.'

'I am most interested in this case. As you say, madame, it is the principle. The Bishop of Tournai is coming to Zonnebeke for Michaelmas. My lawyers will assist him. Both sides may have their pick of one of my lawyers to help them argue.'

Michaelmas – less than a week's time. Margriet would still be alive, in a week's time, if the plague progressed in her as it had in others. But what wreck of a thing would she be?

Well, if it came to it, she would tell Beatrix what to say.

The Chatelaine inclined her head. 'That will not be necessary. Chaerephon will argue for me.'

'And you, Madame de Vos? You and your companions may stay at Ypres, where I am a guest in the castle. You need fear no harm. And I shall provide a lawyer.'

Margriet did not like the look of him. She had imagined every king must look like a lion, so wise, so fond, that he was nearly foolish; but Philippe looked nothing like she had ever imagined King Nobel to look. He looked like the wolf Ysengrim, conspiring at death, gleeful. She wanted to get away to think.

'My king,' she said, bending a knee again. 'I am most grateful. But I have a daughter, as you see, and we will happily lodge at the abbey in quiet reflection until the appointed day. I have no need of learned men and fine words. God will make the truth of my cause evident, I am sure. No one could dispute it.'

'What of the thief, Claude Jouvenal?' the Chatelaine asked tightly. 'Is his fate to be decided by the Bishop of Tournai as well?'

'At the very least he is a witness,' said the king. 'And he may have a claim. I commend him to your custody, but I expect to see him hale at the Michaelmas feast.'

Claude, still standing in mail and aketon, crossed his arms. 'What cause is there for imprisoning me?'

'The charge of theft,' said the Chatelaine.

She walked over to Claude, grabbed his right hand, and pushed up the sleeve of the aketon.

'Scarred, I see,' she said, so softly that while Margriet could hear, probably few others could. 'You miss it, don't you?'

Claude pulled his hand out of the Chatelaine's grasp.

'Michaelmas is in six days' time,' said the king slowly and looking directly at Margriet, as if he thought the concept of six days to be beyond the calculating of a trader's wife from Bruges, a woman who had kept track of payments owing in sous and groats and shillings and florins, a woman who had kept count of the feedings of two babies at once, who had counted the hours of long nights of grief over the children who had never sought her breast. 'You will present yourself to Zonnebeke Abbey on Michaelmas morning. Good timing, I think. We shall entreat the intercession of Saint Michael the judge, who cast down the devil.'

CHAPTER NINETEEN

It was a leaden morning with a weak sun, and nothing to eat but the last crumbs of the oat bread. But even Hell needed water like any other animal, it seemed. Margriet and Beatrix found a stream not far away and splashed their faces and drank. Beatrix seemed leaden, too. Margriet had never seen her daughter's face so weighed down, so pallid. Every freckle stood out like a star in the sky.

It could be the Grief.

But then they had not slept, had not eaten. She had taken the death of her husband hard. As well she might; she was young, and believed she loved Baltazar. No one could mourn properly, now that the dead were not gone entirely.

'Will you manage a little longer?' Margriet asked, in her softest voice.

Perhaps she should have agreed to the escort the king offered, but it had felt like another captivity. It was daylight, and the abbey was not far.

Beatrix nodded. 'On top of everything, it's my time of the month.'

'Have you got enough clouts? I brought a few.'

'I'll be all right for now.'

When all this was over, Margriet would buy her daughter a leg of roast pork and white bread, and a soft bed to sleep in. Six days, and then they would have enough for Beatrix to start a new life somewhere safe.

'Well,' Margriet said, shouldering her bundle, 'the road is just down that slope, and we follow it east for a few hours till we hit Zonnebeke Abbey. A fine abbey with a good reputation, or it was.'

Some of the richer bishops fought alongside Philippe in his dirty wars; allies of Philippe might not be allies of the Chatelaine, but would they protect the people in their guesthouse if the chimeras came sniffing around? If there were revenants at the gate?

Beatrix took her arm. 'Wait.'

'What?'

'Something moving on the road. Isn't there? Can you see it?'

Margriet squinted. 'I think so. The road will take them quite close to us, where it bends. Let's bide here a moment. Do they look like people?'

'People, or chimeras. I can't tell at this distance. And they are leading a small horse.'

They made their way to a rock and crouched behind it.

'A strange time to be travelling,' Beatrix whispered, watching the figures approaching. 'Not chimeras. Can you see, Mother? A man with a slight limp, and a woman, and a child of about ten. Two young women. An old man and an old woman. And a pack nag laden with a few pots and blankets.'

'I suspect they're making their way to safety,' Mother

said. 'Heading north, to the sea. To Dunkirk, probably, and a ship.'

Where she and Beatrix would go in a week's time, if all went well.

'Surely they are fleeing the Chatelaine, and not in league with her. Should I wave? They have kind faces. Perhaps they have food to share.'

Margriet put her hand on her daughter's arm. 'They have their business and we have ours.'

By the time the travellers were out of sight, Margriet's knees were sore and prickled from the stubbly ground and she was sick of the scent and sight of sun-cooked rock in her face.

Beatrix was lying down in the grass, curled around her distaff, her eyes closed.

'Let's rest for a bit,' Margriet said.

'I can get up,' Beatrix said, opening an eye. 'I don't mind.'

'You sleep, and I'll keep watch. I'll wake you at noon.'

Beatrix closed her eyes and wondered what the travellers would encounter on the road, whether they would make it safely to Dunkirk. Would this land always be burnt and bloody? Would there ever be peace in Flanders?

Her drifting thoughts showed her two enormous eyes, perfectly round, flat circles of glass bounded by rings of metal.

She knew they were eyes because they were in a face, a hideous face of rumpled brown cloth, with no real nose or mouth. Instead, there was a bit more brownish metal at the chin and from there, a long pale snake drooped down to the person's chest – for yes, this was a person, she saw now, wearing a war helmet like that of a man-at-arms.

A chimera, then?

Those eyes. Those glass eyes packed with reflections of Beatrix. Those eyes so round, so lidless, and so huge they hardly left any room for the rest of the face.

Was this the weapon she ought to use against her husband? A chimera of her own?

'God,' she whispered, 'I see the pictures, but I do not understand.'

Hands on her shoulders. She opened her eyes but saw nothing but darkness, and in the darkness the gleam of two round, flat glass eyes.

'Let go,' Mother said. And then she was pulling the distaff, wrenching it out of her hands.

'No!' Beatrix shouted and yanked the distaff back. She could still see nothing but the face, the glass eyes. She heard her mother fall backwards.

Beatrix dropped the distaff.

The vision faded. It was night, but she could see now the true world, lit by moonlight.

'Is it late?' she whispered.

'I fell asleep,' Mother grumbled, raising herself up onto hands and knees, awkwardly, then standing. 'I only woke now because you were having a nightmare. I thought you were going to stab your eye with that thing, the way you were waving it around.'

Beatrix looked down at the distaff.

'I know you think I have the Grief,' she said carefully, leaving no spaces between her words for Mother to jump in. 'But I think it's the distaff. I think it shows me things. And helps me call things.'

Margriet picked it up, peered at it in the moonlight, as if she could see some sign of evil upon it. 'Has it always?'

Beatrix shook her head. 'Just since we left Bruges.'

Mother turned it over and over. 'The Nix fished it out of the water. Wasn't he babbling about wishes? What did you tell him?'

Beatrix shook her head. 'Nothing. But I was thinking—'

'What?'

She hoped Mother could not see her blush. 'I was thinking that I wanted to see Baltazar again, that I wished I could call him to me, or get some word of him that night, and that I could know what would happen to us.'

Margriet shrugged. 'So the old sea-snake did have the power after all, but of course he botched it. I'll throttle him! So you – wait. You did call Baltazar, then.'

'She did.'

Baltazar's voice.

He stood, a little distance away, the blood still caked on one side of his head like a shadow, like a trick of the moonlight.

Mother held the distaff out as if it were a pike. 'Come no further. I'll put a hole in you.'

Margriet turned to Beatrix, shut her eyes tight and thrust the distaff out, pointing it with so much force that her hands shook and it slipped out of her grasp for a moment before she recovered it. It was almost funny to see her trying so desperately to use the distaff to control Baltazar.

But Baltazar only stared at Beatrix and made no movement.

'I suffer,' he whispered. 'It is a terrible suffering, Beatrix, to be without you at the end.'

'The end of what?' she asked, and the air was cold on her skin.

'The end of everything that does not matter.'

He reached out his hand. It was, though, still her husband's hand. The fingers she had watched, in secret, as he set Father's scales or counted out tally sticks. Baltazar had always had a nimble brain and nimble fingers.

She touched those fingers now. Though they were cold, they were still quick; he grasped her hand and took a step toward her.

She could see another kind of vision now. It was very different from the distaff magic, and more real, more warm and true. Like a memory of a thing that had already happened, not a strange sight seen through a glass darkly. This vision was of Beatrix and Baltazar, walking together into warm red halls, hand in hand, with silent joy too powerful to be contained in the laughter rising in their breasts.

This was what would be, what must be. She would never be cold again, or hungry, or afraid. How could she have been so foolish?

She stepped forward and her husband stepped forward, too.

The sharp end of the distaff poked her ribs.

'Get away from him!' Mother yelled. 'Baltazar, you cannot have her. Get away!'

Beatrix was not a girl now, to be told to keep her hands off her husband.

She turned to tell Mother so, and saw the terror in Mother's face.

Margriet let the distaff drop.

'What will you come back for, Beatrix?' she sobbed. 'If

you go with him, if you feed yourself to the Beast. What desire will haunt you? Will you be satisfied with him? Will you both be satisfied in Hell? Or is it the nature of a revenant to come back? Are you certain that you have no other desire than your husband on this earth, that nothing else will pull you out here into the world at night to walk and moan?'

Beatrix's stomach lurched and she dropped Baltazar's hand.

Margriet thrust the distaff at her.

'Do what you must,' she said.

Beatrix grasped the distaff and pointed it at Baltazar. It shook even worse in her own hands than it had in Margriet's.

Baltazar took a step back, stumbled, but did not walk away. She was glad of it, glad that at least she could still look on his beautiful face – no! She must send him away, for now at least, so she could think. She needed to think.

She closed her eyes but she could not will it. She could not stand to watch her dead husband watch her, not for a moment more, and yet she could not send him away.

But she could call . . . what? Fireflies, and what else? What had she asked the Nix for? What could save her from this?

She moved her right hand along to grip the distaff at the middle and pressed the heel of her left hand to her temple, trying to concentrate. Before her eyes she saw again the vision of the horrible face of cloth and glass and metal. She heard a sound like breathing, maybe her own.

The golden metal around the unseeing glass eyes now widened and brightened until she was looking at two round yellow irises, with a great frowning silver brow pressing down between them, and these eyes were seeing eyes but they were not caring eyes. They were as impassive as judgment, as alert as the sun, completely round and open, with black pupils within them.

The eyes of an owl.

It arrived in utter silence so that the first sound Beatrix heard was that of a talon scraping through flesh. She opened her eyes and saw her husband with a dark gash in his head. But the gash did not bleed, and Baltazar did not cry out, because a corpse felt no pain, but he looked to the sky, and crouched and held his arms over his head.

She could not send away her husband, not tonight, but she could harry him. A fine wife she made.

'Now,' Margriet said, and she pulled Beatrix away.

They stumbled and ran, and it was not until Beatrix had stifled several sobs that she realized they were running in the wrong direction.

'The abbey' she panted.

Mother shook her head, and slowed to a walk, her hand at her side. She turned, still walking, and peered behind them.

'Do you see him?' she hissed.

Beatrix turned, too, almost daring to hope, but he was not there.

'I won't take you somewhere he can find you. Come on. Ypres can't be too far north of here, if my reckoning is good.'

CHAPTER TWENTY

Claude slept, despite his rage and terror. The dungeons were quiet, warm and dark, lit only by the glow of the Hellbeast's own flesh. His cloak kept the floor's slight dampness out. Yet he woke with a sharp headache, a dry mouth and the feeling that someone was watching him.

It took him a moment to see Monoceros in the shadows. He stood tall, but his horn did not scrape the ceiling. The room was small but the gently curved ceiling was high.

'Is it time for my torture?'

'My lady does not torture. She creates. And if you think she'd use you now as the material for a chimera, you are a fool. You may be food for the Beast before the year is out, but not just now.'

'A revenant?' Claude shuddered. What would he remember of himself, in such a state? What control would he have over his own actions? He would kill himself first. They had not left him a dagger. He would find a way. Or force them to kill him.

'You don't wish to be a revenant?' Monoceros said.

He took a step closer. In one great hand he held a

wooden bowl. Food. Claude's stomach nearly rebelled at the thought. *Do not show it, do not show how hungry you are.*

'Does anyone want that?'

'To cheat death? Yes. Many do.'

'Do you? Can there be chimera revenants?'

Monoceros stepped forward. He was, as always, naked to the waist like a labourer or a centaur, but his skin was so armoured he did not seem naked. Claude wondered how much of Monoceros was beast now, whether his mind and soul were still human. If the dead truly rose on the last day, as some said they would, would the chimeras rise with all their scales and horns, or would they rise human as they had once been?

Would Claude's arm still itch? Forever? He smiled.

'You smile at me,' said Monoceros. 'You pity me, perhaps.'

'No. Pity you? The Chatelaine's marshal? No, I smile at my own strange fancies.'

'You have fancies stranger than me? Stranger than this?' Monoceros spread his arms wide.

Claude shook his head. 'Tell me what you came here for, Monoceros, and leave me to them.'

'The Chatelaine wishes you to declare yourself.'

'Declare myself what?'

'Friend or foe.'

What had Claude thought he was in for, when the Genoa Company had agreed to take King Philippe's money and ride north to fight alongside the Chatelaine? He had been curious, of course, as they were all curious. They wanted to see the chimeras, and it seemed wiser to see them as allies than not. If only they had not taken the commission. If only Claude had been ill, unable to ride.

He would still have his crossbow and his horse, his money, his good name. He would still have the strength of his right arm. And he would not have this yearning for a weapon he had never even learned how to wield.

'I thought she was my foe, whether or not I am hers.'

'Answer the question.'

'I am a mercenary. I am no one's friend and no one's foe.'

'Do you support the claim of the women you travelled with?'

Claude frowned. 'You mean the claim on the sack full of goods?'

Monoceros nodded gravely, slightly, as if he were in the habit of being careful with the movements of his head.

Claude shrugged. 'I'm no lawyer. I just want the mace I commissioned, and then I shall go very far from here.'

He'd be able to fight properly again, able to present himself to any free company between Gibraltar and Guangzhou, with the mace on his arm. No longer a cross-bowman, but something new. Someone strong.

'My lady cannot agree to that. But she will give you your life, Claude Jouvenal. And all you need to do is speak when you are asked to speak. You will tell the Chatelaine everything about how you turned Gobhan Og into a traitor, how you escaped. You will tell no one else, ever, so long as you live. And then, when the trial comes, you will tell the bishop that you took the mace from here and sold it to Willem de Vos.'

'You wish me to tell the truth at the trial?'

'The truth, but only part of the truth. The Chatelaine does not wish anyone to know that the mace is anything more than a mace. You must not say how it was made or why. Say – say only that you stole it. Say you wanted it for a weapon. Say it was pretty. Say anything but do not tell the secret of how the mace opens the gate to Hell.'

'Not such a secret, if you know it.'

'The Chatelaine trusts me in all matters.'

Claude wondered. She did not seem a trusting woman. But she had made Monoceros, and he was the first of her servants. Loyal to her through and through. It was the unicorn in him, Claude supposed; they were fabled to be noble creatures. How much the Chatelaine must love Monoceros, to have given up such a priceless creature in the making of him.

'I thought the argument was about whether Willem de Vos is living or dead.'

'I am no lawyer either. That is a question for wiser heads than yours or mine. Whether he had any right to every item in that chest in the first place, whether he had a claim on the mace that opens Hell, that is something perhaps that simpler people such as you and I can answer and be rewarded for.'

'Rewarded?'

'You will live.'

'And what would happen to the mace then?'

'It stays with its rightful owner.'

Claude shook his head.

'I don't want the keys to Hell. God knows. But I can't stand the lack of the mace at my side. I feel it there, always, like a ghost.'

Monoceros looked into his face for a long moment and nodded. 'I would feel the same, if I lost my horn. But if you take the Chatelaine's side, you will have a chance to ask her for a new arm.'

'A new arm?'

'Yes. Something to take the longing away. I cannot promise you will get it, but if you say what I tell you to say, you will live long enough to plead your case.'

Claude had done what he promised; he'd kept Margriet and Beatrix safe on the road, delivered them to Hell. After that, what did it matter to him if Margriet and Beatrix got their little coins and plates and cups? They were women in wartime; they would take what was coming to them, and if all that was coming to them was nothing, they should count themselves lucky.

But to say he had stolen the mace was dangerous, too. He might well be let go from Hell only to be hanged for a thief. He could not trust the word of Hell's mistress.

'You wish me to lie to the King of France,' he said, looking into Monoceros's golden eyes. 'And then, you say, I shall walk free from this place, having declared myself a thief?'

'I give you my word.'

Claude laughed. 'God's teeth, your word. Let us put your word and mine on the scales and see which is worth more than a sparrow fart.'

Monoceros looked, if not insulted, then not exactly amused, but pleased and sorrowful all at the same time, like an executioner trying to pretend to a hatred of bloodshed. 'Is that the answer you wish me to give?'

'You may tell your mistress that I am considering her offer.'

Monoceros inclined his head again, this time much less carefully, so that Claude had to shrink back to avoid the dip of the great horn.

'Well, neither fish nor fowl, here is your fish,' Monoceros

said, and put the bowl down on the warm red floor. 'It is Friday, after all. Even in Hell we mark the calendar now. We are respectable.'

Claude had lost count of the days.

After Monoceros had left, after Claude had licked the bowl clean, he lay on the dim dark floor and put his hands over his closed eyes for the length of a wordless prayer. A very old habit of which he had thought himself long cured.

He used to do it in his tent, on Friday nights when he was missing home, in total silence as he slept next to his new comrades, to remind himself of the days when he had helped his mother light the Shabbat candles.

Beatrix was almost grateful for the cramps in her gut, for the pain that she could locate, that she could blame for the way her stomach lurched with every step. She used her distaff like a walking stick, digging it into the muddy ground with violence, using each wound in the earth to pull herself forward.

Baltazar's wounds.

She had called the owl. She had torn apart that beloved body, that face that she had kissed so many times. Claws tearing through the soft skin of the temple, where kisses were light and dry. Claws tearing at the ears she had sucked. Claws tearing at—

'In Ypres,' said Mother, 'we'll get you something to eat. My purse is still tied around my waist, thank God.'

God only knew where Margriet was getting the energy to walk, although it was exacting its cost: Mother was grey-faced and short of breath. Beatrix's thighs were as uncertain as aspic. She'd be happy of a meal at least. Perhaps that would settle her stomach.

'Beatrix, you know that is not your husband. And that is not your father.'

It came out of nowhere, as so many of her mother's pronouncements did. When she was a child, Beatrix had thought her mother must hear her thoughts, for so often she spoke as if in answer to them. Then she had grown up, and learned that her mother did not know her thoughts at all, and she had never quite forgiven her for it.

Beatrix swallowed back tears. She agreed that this Baltazar was not her Baltazar, of course she agreed, but she wanted to make her mother argue. It would be something to distract her, like the pain in her gut.

'They are very good copies, then. Don't you care about Father? Doesn't it hurt to see him?'

'Dear child, desire dies like everything else. In a year, what you felt for Baltazar will be a memory.'

When Beatrix was a child, they had slept all three of them to a bed, and Mother had kept Beatrix between herself and Father. Somehow, they had got babies, the three babies who died. But when she was old enough to have woken in the night, old enough to remember, she had never once heard her parents together, not even talking. How horrible it must be to hate one's husband.

'I don't want to forget him,' said Beatrix softly. 'I pray for him every night, for his soul, although I do not know whether it is still in his body.'

'Of course it isn't. It has gone to where souls go, and on the last day, it will return to take up residence in his bones. Your father's, too. They may find those bodies terribly used by then.'

Beatrix winced. The claws, the silent wings, the flesh opening without blood, without screams.

'It is your inheritance after all,' said Mother. 'If you think I am doing wrong, say so.'

'I am not a monk or a lawyer,' Beatrix said. 'I don't know anything about God's laws except that I try to keep them, in my way. But how do we keep them now? When we do not even know if our husbands are dead or alive?'

'They are dead,' said Mother firmly.

She did not sound as though she grieved.

Together. A living woman and a revenant. His skin cold like leather. And yet his mouth, the twist of his mouth, was as it had always been. Pale, as though in sickness. And perhaps it was only a kind of sickness that had befallen him, the deepest kind of Grief. What sort of wife was she, to abandon her husband in such straits? What sort of lover was she, to let love decay?

If Heloise could love her Abelard after they'd castrated him and he'd shut her up in a convent, having no use for her body any more, could not Beatrix love her husband no matter his condition? If Orfeo could go after his wife all the way to the fairy king's underworld and bring her home again, could not Beatrix bring her husband back from Hell?

They reached Ypres when the sun was high, although it was only a pale white presence between the cold grey sky, like a daytime moon. Beatrix had never been to any other city than Bruges. She looked at each street as if it were a miracle, so familiar to the people who walked them, their heads down as they went about their business.

They had drunk the last of their water flasks hours before, so they bought a drink of beer from a cart, from a tired woman in a floppy hat like a pilgrim's. She had a long steel fork strapped to her right arm with metal bands.

'That's three times what I would have paid a year ago,' Mother grumbled as she handed over the coins.

'A year ago, there was food and drink aplenty in Flanders,' said the woman, almost cheerfully. 'War is a terrible thing.'

They walked through the market lane until they found a ragman, a tall, grey-bearded man with a lean face who had sewn onto the back of his brown cloak two wings as dirty and mottled as a pigeon's, stuffed and quilted but still drooping to the earth. They bought a bundle of mostly clean rags from him; Margriet gave him a denier and he handed back a few bits of thin clipped coins.

It was, it seemed, the fashion in Ypres. Woman peered out of shop windows with brass fixtures around their necks, decorated with wheels and gears. A peddler bent under the weight of a lion's head resting on his own, its ratty and flea-ridden skin falling down his crooked back.

'Does that fool truly believe he looks anything like a chimera?' Margriet muttered as they walked. 'And that woman with the fork on her arm, how ridiculous.'

'Perhaps they don't want to be taken for chimeras, but for people who like chimeras,' said Beatrix. 'They want to be seen to be copying them. Perhaps it's a kind of protection.'

She imagined the ragman turning his face to heaven, the quilted wings lifting and beating until his thin body rose into the sky.

'I don't think a couple of bedraggled wings or a meat-fork would be much protection against the bitch of Hell and her hounds,' said Mother.

They came to a stone inn with a sign of a deer swinging mournfully over the archway and walked through into the courtyard of hard mud, where the horse shit was dry and scattered, days old or even weeks. But a faint smell of food came from the hall door.

Inside, the room was dark but there was a trestle table with several people sitting at it, and they looked up only briefly at their arrival.

A woman came toward them. She wore a brass trumpet at one ear, its stem curving around to fit. The smiths and wrights of Ypres must have been doing a brisk business, these last weeks.

'We have one room only,' she said. 'And one bed.'

'That will do us,' said Margriet. 'What price?'

'No horses?'

Hard-headed woman. The food smell was driving Margriet mad; it must be driving Beatrix madder. The girl thought with nothing but her stomach. And this woman was hell bent on haggling as if the times were ordinary.

'If we had horses,' said Margriet, 'we would have brought them in with us, as heaven knows no groom came to us in the courtyard to take them.'

There were a few titters. The woman narrowed her eyes.

'Two deniers for the bed, and six deniers for three meals with wine and meat. Eight deniers together.'

'Half that, I think,' Margriet said.

'Mother,' Beatrix whispered.

'God save you, but you're a bold one,' said the innkeeper. 'Half that, eh? Not in these times. There is a shortage of roofs left standing in Flanders, if you hadn't noticed, and if you can turn your nose up at good beef pottage, I will be very surprised indeed.'

Margriet held out one Flemish groat, worth about six deniers. The woman looked at it, sighed, and pocketed it.

'Do you know of a good messenger?' Margriet asked. 'I need to send word to Zonnebeke Abbey. We were expected there but changed course.'

The innkeeper frowned. 'I have a reliable boy with a donkey, but that will cost you, too.'

'Of course.'

'You can wash yourselves over there, and by the time you're back I'll have your pottage set. Come to me when you've finished, and I'll give you your candle.'

They washed in a little alcove, where a cistern held water that looked as though it had seen too many travellers.

The pottage was surprisingly good, or perhaps it was their hunger.

As they were eating, a woman came in with a baby on one hip and a child by the hand. Margriet squinted to be sure it was who she thought it was.

Jacquemine Ooste.

She walked toward her and to her surprise, Vrouwe Ooste embraced her, baby Jacob between them.

'Margriet, oh, I am happy to find you alive, at least,' she whispered.

'At least?' Margriet pulled back to look at her face, to read what she could in it.

'The chimeras broke down the gate and took the city. Many people died.'

'My father. My sister.'

Beatrix was behind her shoulder now, listening.

Jacquemine nodded. 'I am sorry to bring you such news. Yes, they are among the dead, and their house burned. A fire started at one end of Casteelstrate and ripped down the whole street.' Beatrix made a little choking sob. Margriet took her hand.

Father's house gone. Willem's house gone. Father, dead. Her sister, dead. And Margriet herself, dying. Beatrix would be alone in the world by Christmas, haunted and alone.

CHAPTER TWENTY-ONE

Beatrix curled up on a blanket on the floor. One bed, the innkeeper had said, and it was barely that, but Jacquemine and the children must have it.

Poor little Jacob was squalling, as Mother walked him up and down, bouncing and cooing.

'If he wants your milk, aren't you just tormenting him by holding him?' Jacquemine asked at last, where she sat on the bed, rubbing her temples.

'I haven't got any milk left, Vrouwe Ooste,' said Margriet quietly.

'Of course. It's not your fault. The poor child hasn't slept,' said Jacquemine. 'I do not blame him. The creature who bore us from Bruges had the most horrible spines all up and down its back, and it rolled like a ship in a storm with every step. But it was that or walk, with the baby and Agatha.'

'And how is little Agatha's fever now?'

Jacquemine put her hand to the girl's forehead. 'Still hot as Hell. Poor lamb.'

'There, there,' cooed Margriet, as baby Jacob choked

and sputtered into red-faced silence, and gave a little exhausted gasp, and closed his eyes. 'Off to sleep, little one.'

'Is Bruges overrun with chimeras, then?' Beatrix asked.

Her throat was hoarse with unshed tears. She wanted to weep for Grandfather, but Mother said perhaps it was God's mercy, that it was a quick death by fire or a long one by starvation.

Jacquemine nodded wearily. 'They blew open the gate, the Smedenpoort, with some sort of spell of the Chatelaine's. People said they heard a sound like thunder and there was fire everywhere. It must have been a fire straight from Hell, to blow the gate open.'

'Was it chimeras with metal arms that did it?' Margriet asked.

'Hmm?' Jacquemine asked. 'No, I don't think so. Some sort of battering ram, or so they thought at the gate. But the ram was just a pretext, I think, for getting some hidden thunder-fire into place. Some of the chimeras were blown to bits, people said. They must have known they would die – do you think they knew?'

'When men go to war, they always know that some of them are going to die,' said Mother.

'Yes, but to be certain that it is going to be you – it must be horrible.'

'It would help to be certain that the weapon would work,' said Mother. 'I suppose if one knew that the gates would fall, that might be reason enough for the sacrifice. Think of how many die long, slow deaths being pecked by crows on the field. Better to die all at once in a blaze and take one's enemy down, too.'

'They very nearly didn't take us down, for all that,' said

Jacquemine, her voice hard. 'Getting into the city doesn't mean taking the city. You remember, Margriet, the Matins of Bruges, when we were children.'

Her voice dropped when she said it, as if it were a secret, what had happened.

'Yes, I remember.'

'We fought back this time, too, as best we could,' said Jacquemine, softly, not waking the baby. 'Even old Hans ran a few of them through with a sharpened stick before they killed him. And my cook Clara, they killed her, too. Our house, like your father's, is burned to the ground.'

Little Agatha played on with her bits of pot, ignoring the women.

'I could not stay there, with no home, little money, no future for my children,' said Jacquemine. 'My husband was one of the aldermen of Bruges. When the horned man offered me passage to Ypres, I had to take it. I hoped they would not find you, Margriet. I lied, and I lied well. I told him you three had gone in the direction of Ghent. I would not have told him that much, but the priest had spilled already that you were together.'

'They have hounds,' Mother said. 'They were looking for Claude. Claude was after something Willem had in his sack – a weapon. They took him. They're holding him in the Hellbeast.'

'No! I had thought he must have left you at the first chance, after you got away from Bruges. Poor stray! The priest put him in my care, and now he is in Hell.'

'The Chatelaine has him,' Mother said. 'But she cannot harm him, for he is to bear witness at the trial.'

'Trial!' said Jacquemine. 'Do you mean over your husband's chest?'

Margriet nodded. 'The Bishop of Tournai is to decide it.'

Jacquemine whistled lowly. 'It must be of some importance to the king, then. What is Willem's argument?'

'Not Willem's but his mistress's. The Chatelaine says he is not truly dead, that the revenants are not truly dead. So, I am no widow, she says.'

'Interesting.'

'Interesting?' Beatrix asked. 'Why so, Vrouwe Ooste?'

Jacquemine Ooste, the alderman's wife, had a mind for politics.

'If the revenants are not dead, and they cannot die, their property would stay with them forever, and their children never inherit. And the Chatelaine controls the revenants, so she controls their property. So all she would need to do, to gain herself a . . . well, a chest of gold or a fine destrier or a palace or a demesne, would be to change its owner into a revenant. Much better than killing them because if she killed them, someone would be around to inherit. Yes, I see why the king wants this case decided in the open, by a bishop. A bishop of his own choosing, I don't doubt. But did he suggest which side he supports?'

There was a sound outside the door.

Someone wailed, 'Alienor! Alienor!'

Mother drew her knife.

'It's a revenant,' Margriet hissed.

Jacquemine was down on the floor, gathering Agatha to her. She pulled her up into the bed and tucked her under the thin blanket, behind Beatrix.

'Who is Alienor?' Jacquemine asked.

'It thinks this was its home,' said Beatrix. 'It came here, looking for Alienor.'

The thing was still calling, plaintive. Beatrix could almost imagine that the memory of Alienor was here with them, that that memory was the true ghost, haunting the poor corpse outside the door.

Jacquemine put her hands over her face and shook with a silent sob.

'It's all right,' Beatrix said. She put her hand on Jacquemine's shoulder. 'We're safe.'

'For today. But what kind of life will we have? What kind of life can I make for my children, now?' Jacquemine whispered.

'You must take them to England,' Mother said, settling herself on the one spare inch of the bed yet unoccupied with a long sigh, and resting the baby on her lap. 'Poor little chicks.'

'I will take them, just as soon as Agatha is well enough for the voyage. And you, Margriet?' Jacquemine asked, shuddering herself calm just as the baby had done.

'Once we regain the money my husband owes us.'

'I envy you your purpose, at least.'

'It's my right. I can't simply pretend it isn't.'

'How did your husband come by this money?'

Mother shrugged. 'A question to which I wish I knew the answer. I can guess, a little.'

'It matters,' said Jacquemine. 'If he came by it dishonestly, and given what we know of Willem, that seems likely, then someone else may have a claim to it.'

'The thing about clinking money is, that no one knows whose groats and florins were whose, once they change hands a few times,' said Beatrix. 'Who is to say who has a claim to any part of it?'

'It may not be possible to trace the coins themselves,'

Jacquemine said, 'but there might be someone who is owed a certain amount, or someone who, like Claude, has a claim on some item, and will not forget it.'

'Then let them make their claim,' said Mother. 'I do not ask more than justice, and I am happy to be just in my turn.'

Outside, the revenant screamed. Baby Jacob screwed his face into a red ball, and then he screamed, too.

Jacquemine buried her face in her hands, then lifted it.

'We can't stay here,' she hissed. 'We need time for my girl to get well, but we can't stay here. I know a family, not far from Ypres. Good people. Only a half-day's walk. I would have gone there but I did not want to show up at their door on the back of a chimera.'

'Will you go there tomorrow?'

'Come with me,' Jacquemine said. 'You can help me with the children, Margriet, and you need somewhere to stay before the trial. Five days? Ypres will bleed you dry in five days, if it doesn't drive you mad first.'

They attended mass at one of the smaller churches in Ypres, for the Sabbath day, and left the city.

Margriet glowered at the low grey sky in the morning. Her nose was running from the chill and the heavy ground sucked at her feet. Let it rain and have done; but the sky held its grudges.

It was slow going, with the children. The three women took turns carrying Jacob on their hips while little Agatha trudged obediently. A good girl, even when she was ill. She nattered to Beatrix and they made up stories about the squirrels and birds in the branches that overhung the road.

'They are making their winter preparations,' said Beatrix. 'They are putting aside food.'

'Because there will be a siege?' Agatha asked with big hungry eyes.

They came to a field burned down to stubble, the wet ground an ashy mess that held their footprints as if in evidence. The whole world smelled now of doused fire; the whole world smelled of Hell.

At the far side of the valley, a mill stood by a creek, and beyond it a dammed millpond. The mill itself still stood, blackened, but charred and tumbled walls around it said there had been a family there.

Jacquemine stood, one child on her hip and Agatha shivering, holding her hand, and stared. 'This is the place,' she whispered. 'This is where the Vermeulen family lived. My friends.'

Perhaps they would find another chicken wandering. Perhaps there were fish in that millpond.

'Perhaps they survived,' Margriet said. 'Come on. Let us see if we can offer some help, at least.'

They walked forward, but Beatrix stood still as a donkey and stared.

'It is the place from my dream,' she whispered. 'The one with the hounds.'

'Nonsense,' Margriet said, taking her arm. 'You have not been here before. Come on, child.'

No dogs walked the yard, no friendly chickens came wandering.

As they approached the mill, something flew over their heads and crashed next to Beatrix. A clay cooking pot, thrown from the window on the second floor. Margriet drew her dagger with her right hand, and then dropped it.

Damn her fingers.

'John, ready the Greek fire!' came a woman's voice from within, screeching in *langue d'oil* French. 'And tell the lads to take up their swords!'

Jacquemine burst out laughing, a laughter just this side of tears.

'Gertrude!' she called. 'Gertrude, is it you? Gertrude, it is Jacquemine Ooste!'

Silence.

'Let's go in,' Margriet said loudly, not even bothering to whisper. Better that the woman hear all their plans, see all their movements. Alone or not, wounded or not, she was afraid.

Any woman in such circumstances would be armed in her fashion.

Margriet shrugged and pushed on the door, which fell off its hinges. But as she was still standing on the threshold, something – an iron pan – hit her hand with such force from above that her arm fell to her side and she screamed, and in the middle of her scream she realized that she felt no pain in her hand itself from the blow, nothing at all, just a dull ringing up into her shoulder.

She screamed louder. 'Curse you! Can't you see we're just women?'

There was no sight of anyone in a window above, but the shutter was open.

'God's bleeding body, of all the millwives in France we had to find a murderess,' Margriet grumbled.

'She's no murderess,' said Jacquemine. 'Gertrude! It is Jacquemine, truly!'

Something crashed onto the ground beside them: another clay pot.

This would go on all day.

'I'm going in,' said Margriet, loudly.

Beatrix, though, walked through the charred door, holding her distaff before her like a priest in procession. God only knew what she thought she would do with it. Bless the place or discharge its ghosts; not likely. If there were ghosts here—

They had not thought to check the door for a mark.

Margriet lifted the ragged, burned wood from the floor with her foot and turned it over. No mark. No plague here, except what Margriet had brought with her. No Grief, either? Could that be the explanation for the woman's behaviour?

They walked in, behind Beatrix. Inside it was dim, and the waterwheel and its workings crouched silently, disconnected from the millstream that burbled below. They walked as loudly as they could up a rickety staircase to the top floor.

The woman crouched in a corner, holding an iron frying pan.

She let it drop to her side.

'Jacquemine, is it truly you?'

Jacquemine handed Jacob to Margriet and walked out to the woman, embraced her. 'Gertrude, where is everyone? Where is Pierre, and the children?'

'Gone,' she said. 'All gone.'

Jacquemine hugged the woman tight. 'We had thought to come stay with you for a short time,' she said. 'My little Agatha has a fever.'

Gertrude nodded. 'There is food. Yes. And water. And beer.'

What kind of army burned a place and left the beer untouched?

'We can pay for what we take,' Margriet said.

'The hounds,' said the woman, and stopped, staring dead ahead. She had a pleasant, freckled face, somehow made even more pleasant by the shimmer of ginger whiskers on her upper lip and chin.

'You see!' Beatrix said. 'I told you. I saw a vision. A true vision. The distaff—'

'Find that beer, Beatrix, and be quick about it.'

Margriet sat beside the woman. They drank beer out of a blackjack that had doubtless belonged to the man of the place. It was good beer and sat kindly on the tongue.

A cup or two soothed the woman into a dull-eyed melancholy in which she was able to speak. Gertrude had been in the privy, which was a little distance from the mill and stable, and she had seen the two-headed hounds coming and hid inside the hole, holding on to the edge with her fingers, wet and shivering, listening to the sounds of the dogs yelping and the cries of her own children, willing herself not to simply let go and fall down into the stinking muck.

'They are all dead,' she said, in a hollow voice. 'All but me.'

'It is risky,' Chaerephon said, 'to have the thief admit to stealing the mace. Even if he does not reveal that he stole the very keys to Hell, the fact that he stole anything at all is a fact we should keep hidden. Do we want the world to know that your artificers can be bribed, or seduced, or suborned? That for a price, anyone could avail themselves of the fires of Hell, for their own purposes? You killed one smith who betrayed you, but where one goes, others might follow.'

'Do you think I don't know this?' snapped the Chatelaine. 'Of course I know this.'

They paced in the menagerie, where no one was allowed except on the Chatelaine's orders, where that had been true even when her husband was at liberty. It was the place she felt most confident of being able to speak freely without being spied upon, although she was surrounded by the ears of all her creatures, and by the Hellbeast, of course.

'Then we must convince the bishop that the revenants are not dead,' mused Chaerephon.

The Chatelaine nodded. If Willem was not dead, none of his property would pass to his widow, including the mace.

'I do not know this bishop of Tournai,' she muttered. 'I do not know his price.'

'We may not need a price,' said Chaerephon. 'The churchmen have held three synods already on whether the Hellbeast is one of death's many kingdoms, and they cannot make up their minds. They want someone to give them the answer. So we will give them the answer they will like best: no, it is not. The Hellbeast feeds on the revenants. They are not dead.'

'Of course they are not. We understand this, we who live in the Beast. But can you prove it?'

'Well, to start with, what is death? My friend Socrates mused upon this very question on his own deathbed. He asked, was it true that death must be the departure of the soul from the body?'

He had the little grin that meant he was enjoying a puzzle, like a rat on a bone.

'How does this help us?' asked the Chatelaine, resignedly.

'If death is defined as the separation of the soul and body, then the revenants must have their souls still within them, somewhere. And what is the soul?'

'Perhaps you should tell me.'

'If we say the soul is eternal, would it change or not change?'

'I'm too damned tired for sophistry, Chaerephon.'

'If we say it does not change, then surely someone who truly knew a man would recognize it in him, even if his face looked different, even if he was wounded or ill.'

'Go on.' The Chatelaine was doubtful that anyone knew anyone's soul, but she knew Chaerephon well enough to let him worry his bone until he got it into a useful shape.

'Plato used to say that there were three parts to the soul. The reasoning part we could try to prove, but with what sort of test? After all, crows and horses can reason to an extent, but do they have a soul? Not according to the Christians. The spirited part, too, but again, a beast can be driven into a temper. But the appetites – well, if we know a man's appetites, and his soul is unchanging, then his appetites could be recognized.'

'The revenants have no appetites,' said the Chatelaine coldly. 'They do as I tell them, and they feed the Beast. They do not care about anything.'

'Then perhaps their appetite is to serve,' Chaerephon mused. 'Perhaps their appetite is to nourish. But that won't do. Somewhere in them there must be the memory of the people they were, and if someone who knew them well could recognize it in them – the wives.'

'What wives?'

'The one from Bruges, who claims to be a widow, and

her daughter. If we can make them admit that they recognize their husbands' appetites within them—'

'But what sort of appetites? Shall we force them to eat their favourite foods?'

'No, no. I mean that if they seem to still be the men who loved them, then some part of them must be the same men. Bodies lust but souls love.'

The Chatelaine considered this. 'I do not think Margriet de Vos can be seduced out of her inheritance,' she said. 'She had a shrewish look.'

'But her daughter,' Chaerephon said. 'Her daughter was quiet. Shall we call the revenant Baltazar Claes to us? Let us see if he remembers how to love his wife. Or at least,' he said with a dry laugh, 'how to seem to love her. We cannot stimulate the impulse but perhaps we can simulate the action. And between the impulse and the action, which is the more real? When a woman wants to know whether her husband loves her, the only way she can know is through his actions, through his words which are a kind of action. She cannot see into his heart.'

'Only if she cuts it open,' said the Chatelaine cheerfully, tossing a bit of Hellflesh, red and dripping, to the wolf cub who paced his iron cage. 'Yes, let us knead the heart of the daughter. And the mother has a price, Chaerephon. We just need to find it.'

CHAPTER TWENTY-TWO

The room was growing dark as the afternoon waned. Soon it would be time to light the cheap tallow candle. Gertrude was downstairs using the pot (she refused to use the privy) and Beatrix was propped with her back to the wall at the other end of the room, a child in each arm, telling stories. Little Agatha was looking better today, thank God. Jacquemine would soon be gone, up to Dunkirk, and safety. Three more days until Michaelmas.

'Vrouwe Ooste,' Margriet said quietly, 'you know how lords and ladies talk, how they think. I wonder, would you come to the trial, and help me prepare? I will need to make an argument, but my tongue always gets me into trouble. If you could speak for me as well, that would be a great help.'

'Ha. I have listened to my husband argue with Count Louis about taxes,' said Jacquemine. 'That does not make me fit to argue with lawyers, and on a matter of canon law!'

'But you are a widow, as I am. A widow whose husband is in the ground where he ought to be, God rest his soul.

Who will stand for the rights of widows if not the widows themselves?'

'Can my children eat rights? Does justice make a dowry? My house is burned to the ground. My children are ruined.'

Jacquemine's mouth hitched up in a strange half-smile, half-grimace, as if she were trying to use the habit of smiling to keep her face from falling into sobs.

Was Beatrix sleeping? Her voice had fallen to silence.

Margriet stood and took a few steps on the creaky floor to where Beatrix and the children lay, all three of them sleeping. She put her hand to little Agatha's forehead, before remembering that her hands were no longer reliable guides to temperature. She snatched her fingers away, even though the plague did not spread from the living to the living.

'Beatrix,' she whispered, testing that her daughter was asleep. There was no answer.

Even so, Margriet spoke quietly. She approached Jacquemine, who sat on the edge of the bench at Gertrude's family table, sewing a small stocking by the waning light, bodkin flashing.

'Agatha?' Jacquemine asked.

'Sleeping peacefully. Vrouwe Ooste, you want a future for your children, and so do I. It would be my honour and my duty to compensate you, if you will help me at my trial.'

'Compensate me?' Jacquemine snorted. 'With what?'

'With my share of the inheritance. Beatrix takes two-thirds. If Claude gets his freedom back, he gets two weapons as his reward for helping me: a strange mace like one the Chatelaine wears, and a sword. The rest is mine. If you help me, it is yours. Not a great deal of money, but enough, perhaps, to make a new start.'

'Why on earth?'

Margriet resisted the urge to rub her numb fingers. Soon everyone would see that she was dying of the Hellpest. But she hoped that would not happen until after Michaelmas, when she could be sure of her daughter's future, when she could crawl off somewhere to die in peace.

'Because I nursed your children as my own, and I do not wish to see them starve.'

'And for them you would give up all your own inheritance? You said the chest was filled with groats and florins and fine things. Even one-third of that would be a great gift.'

'Not a gift. Payment. For all your kindness to me, and for this last one.'

'And how will you live, thereafter? Will you live with your daughter?'

'Perhaps I shall go into orders,' said Margriet.

Jacquemine put her hand to her mouth to stifle a laugh.

'Come, can you not imagine me as an anchorite? Silent for years on end?'

'I can imagine you shouting at the walls.'

'So long as they do not shout back. Have we an understanding, Vrouwe Ooste?'

Jacquemine looked over to her sleeping children. 'I can do only what any merchant's wife could do. But I will do my best.'

'Thank you,' said Margriet, and to her great surprise and shame, tears spilled out of her eyes.

Claude woke to darkness.

God's nails, he would go mad in this place.

The last time the Chatelaine had held Claude, she had let him have more food and drink, more human company. In those days Claude was a mere project, a recruit, a chimera in the making. This time, though, there was nothing. And in that nothingness, nightmares.

His panicked throat pushed involuntary sounds into the silence: a cough, a yelp, a choking gasp. He knew one thing about dungeons: there were always spies and traitors listening within them, even when they held only one prisoner. He wanted to talk, to hear the sound of a voice in the darkness, but he could not trust himself to tell only lies. He was a rotten liar.

The great round door opened and red light flooded his vision.

The Chatelaine stood, not dressed in ermine now but in a simple blue kirtle. At least Claude was still in his chausses and aketon, though they had taken his knife and armour.

She held a torch at her left side and her hair hung down her back in one long dark twist, netted in gold.

From her right hand hung the mace. So very like his own. The key to Hell, but more than that, the key to ending this everlasting pain in his arm, the key to strength of body and clarity of mind.

Claude tried to imagine putting his hands around the woman's throat, pushing her down, aside, out of the way so Claude could go out into the sunlight. A glint caught the mace that swung gently at the end of the Chatelaine's right hand.

'Good evening,' said Claude, in the language of Hell.

The Chatelaine hissed and the door closed behind her. They were alone in the oubliette, made smaller by the light of the Chatelaine's torch.

'Where did you learn that?' She spoke French.

'I picked it up the last time I was here,' Claude said, still speaking in the tongue of Hell. This was true. He had picked it up quickly enough, because it had elements of so many other languages in it. The difficulty was in remembering which words were borrowed from where, and which had shifted meaning. And the grammar was a bit strange.

'Impossible. No one here speaks that tongue now. It is forbidden.'

Claude grinned. 'Then I must be a magician.' He said this in French, because he did not know the word for magician in the language of Hell.

The Chatelaine sighed. She swung the mace on her arm back and forth slightly, like a pendulum, so that torchlight ran like golden water up and down its length.

'Monoceros tells me you are playing for time,' she said. 'I don't have time.'

'Can you blame me? You wish me to damn myself willingly,' Claude said.

The Chatelaine spread her left hand wide. 'You're in the right place for it.'

'I'll swing from a gallows if I admit to theft.'

'Perhaps not. I will argue for your life.'

'And what assurance can I have that you are telling the truth?'

'None.'

Claude wanted to ask for water.

Instead, he said through cracked lips, 'You don't want the mace that opens the doors of Hell to be out there in the world, out of your control. I understand that. Concede it to Margriet and it will come to me; that is the arrangement we made, Margriet and I. You'll know where it is.'

'Ah, yes, Margriet. You know, she was supposed to go to Zonnebeke Abbey. But do you want to know a strange thing? I sent my Chaerephon there, with the revenant Baltazar, and they returned saying that the de Vos women were not at the Abbey at all. Do you think they have chosen to give up their claim?'

Claude shook his head. 'Margriet de Vos would not give up a crumb to a mouse.'

'And you believe she'll win the mace, and give it to you? You are soft in the head.'

'Let me wear it, my lady, and hire me to fight for you. That is what you wanted all along.'

'What I wanted all along? Tell me, did I want you to trick my smith? To forge my keys? To steal from me?'

'You wanted me to become a chimera.'

And so I have, Claude thought, saying it in his own mind for the first time. He had not gone through the Hellfire but the weapon had, and it had altered him. He was altered.

'You are a fool if you think I will let you hold the key to Hell.'

'Can we not alter the mace in some way? Let me wear it, but have one of the smiths change the flanges so they will no longer fit the locks?' He winced as he said it. He wanted it the way it was.

'Whether the mace worked or not, I cannot have you walking around Hell as if you owned it. You will not wear that mace. Give up that foolish hope and think of the matter before you, which is life or death.'

'If you kill me, before the trial, what would the king say?'

'People die all the time. It is unfortunate but I cannot

be held responsible for a prisoner who dies of dysentery. Very common among soldiers.'

They stared at each other for a moment longer, and then the Chatelaine came and squatted next to him. The torch was hot.

'I am giving you a chance at life. Agree to this now and you will stay here as my guest until the trial is over, at which time I will have Monoceros accompany you to a place of your choosing, within seven days' ride in any direction.'

'Where he will gore me to death.'

The Chatelaine smiled indulgently. 'How would it be, then, if you knew you could fight even Monoceros, and win? Tell the story at the trial exactly as we have given it you, and I will take you to the smithy. I will give you a new weapon for that arm. I will make you into a god. What sort of armour would you like? What sort of body? Would you like it so you never had to bind those breasts again? Would you like me to turn you into a real soldier?'

Claude blinked from the torchlight on his eyes, from the glimmering, shadowy image on his mind's eye of himself as he ought to be.

She whispered sweetly as she spoke. Yes, Claude could have put his hands around her throat. And what then? What would the Beast do, if its mistress were attacked? What of the chimeras? He was not afraid of them but he was afraid, afraid of himself. Afraid that what he wanted was within his grasp, and that if he lost it, he would live with the loss the rest of his life, like a missing limb, like his arm that itched.

'I will consider your offer,' he croaked.

The Chatelaine stood. 'Truly?'

Claude nodded. 'I am not a good liar. If I were lying, you would probably know it.'

The Chatelaine laughed. 'It is lucky for us both, then, that I do not require you to lie. Only to tell one part of the truth. In the meantime, I shall send food and water, and you may move to a room with a little more light.'

Claude inclined his head in thanks, so that she could not see his face.

Gertrude eased herself down onto the floor beside Beatrix. She looked at the distaff, leaning against the wall.

'Did you bring your spindle as well?' she asked.

Beatrix nodded. It was in her now much-jumbled, much-stained bundle.

'Ah, that's lucky, then. I have some wool that needs spinning, and I have never been very quick with my spindle, myself. I would be most grateful to have it spun. Later. If you feel you can.'

Beatrix smiled a little. 'I would be so happy to spin again. Thank you. Would you bring it now? I need some occupation.'

Beatrix tried to envy Gertrude, but she could not. To know one's husband was dead, to be free and able to claim the rights of a widow, such as they were, was evidently better than being a widow in reality but not in name. She ought to envy Gertrude. And yet she did not.

She was glad, yes, glad, that Baltazar still walked the world. She did not have to tax her mind to preserve the shape of him, she was not guardian of that memory. So she could give over all her thoughts to preserve the sound of his laugh the night they were married, or the feel of his dry lips the night before that.

He had not visited her at Ypres or at the mill, and she had not called him. But last night she had desperately wanted to.

'Today is Monday,' said Margriet. 'Michaelmas is Thursday. While you're spinning, take some thought for our enterprise, Beatrix. We'll need to spin some fine words for the bishop, too.'

Gertrude shook her head, walking back toward them with the basket of wool. 'I don't understand this matter at all. It seems to me you've lost your husbands, one way or the other, whether their bodies roam at night or not. A widow is a woman bereft of her husband, and so you're widows.'

'Obviously,' said Mother, sharply. 'But they want a trial. They won't be satisfied with a truth that can be said quickly. These are not millers' matters – no, not burghers' matters either.'

Gertrude rose, her lips tight, hands on her hips.

'There is one thing you could do to help us,' Mother said, more softly. 'Vrouwe Ooste is to come with us, to argue for us. She can't be troubled with the care of the children. We'll leave them here with you.'

Gertrude went pale as a revenant. 'They cannot. You must not.'

'I thought you hated to be here alone, anyway?'

'But it would be even worse with children here. Oh no. No.'

Mother sighed. 'Then you'll have to come with us, and mind the children at the abbey.'

Gertrude swallowed. 'If I leave . . . I cannot leave. I cannot.'

'And why not?'

Gertrude paused, wrung her hands. No, Beatrix could not quite envy this woman. Her face was not meant to be so sad; it was a merry face, freckled and broad, pulled now in all the wrong directions.

'The abbot. He owns this mill, and all the land around here. I do not wish to remind him that my husband is dead and the mill is idle. Not yet.'

'Oh, come now.'

Gertrude whispered, 'I am so afraid, Margriet.'

'You have two days to find your courage.'

Beatrix spun. She propped the distaff awkwardly beside her, for fear that if she was holding it, her heart might wish for something, or wish to know something.

'We are out of bread, and flour,' Gertrude said.

'Just our luck,' Mother muttered. 'We come to a mill, and it is a forge-mill. We can't eat iron.'

'There are fish in the millpond,' Jacquemine said, and they all looked at the children, playing with the wooden dice that Claude had made and handed to Beatrix when Mother wasn't looking. A bit of weak ale and fish pottage was barely enough to keep body and soul together, and the children were listless, dark-eyed, sniping at each other as they played. Agatha was doing much better, but she needed proper food, poor thing.

'There is a field to the south, about half a morning's walk, with a large oak in the middle of it. That field often gets mushrooms. Nice big ceps sometimes,' Gertrude said. 'And there is a hedge of blackberries.'

Gertrude looked wistful. She never wanted to leave the mill. Beatrix could almost taste the blackberries, with fresh cream.

'Vrouwe Ooste, will you go with me?' Mother asked.

'I don't suppose you would bestir yourself to show us, Gertrude.'

'It's not hard to find,' Gertrude pleaded. 'The children might have a game of it.'

But Jacob and Agatha were in evil temper. Little Jacob, still chubby, was soon red eyed and gulping with tears, and Agatha burst into angry tears herself when her mother told her to put her shoes on as they were going to hunt for mushrooms.

'Come on, sweetheart,' said Mother, in the soft tones she could muster only for children.

'Mind Margriet,' said Jacquemine, exasperated. 'Mind her, Agatha, or the switch for you.'

Agatha did not stint; Beatrix suspected the switch was not often in use at the Ooste house, as it had not been in hers.

'Why don't they stay here, with Gertrude and me?' Beatrix said.

'Yes, let them stay,' said Gertrude, her voice booming. 'You'll be faster without them. Would you like to see the giant's hammer, Agatha? Would you like to see it pound?'

Mother frowned. 'Don't let them near that thing. Have you got anything to put the berries and mushrooms in, should we find any?'

Gertrude tumbled chunks of iron ore out of two big baskets that stood near the wall in the ground floor of the mill.

'We'll have to rinse these baskets,' Mother grumbled.

'It is fortunate that the millstream is just outside the door!' Gertrude grinned. Beatrix could not quite tell whether Gertrude's fierce good humour was put on, but it seemed as good a defence as any against Mother's frowns.

She also wondered whether Gertrude's loudness came as a consequence of living in the mill. The roar of the water was constant.

When Gertrude connected the cam and let the hammer rise and fall, the clanging made Beatrix and Agatha clap their hands over their ears. Beatrix worried about the baby, but he merely clapped his hands together in delight.

The inner wheel moved faster than Beatrix had expected. Every time the hammer's back end dropped, one of the wheel's teeth lifted it, and the hammerhead hit the anvil with a ringing note. The hammer shaft was a huge piece of oak, about the size of a man or bigger, all wrapped in leather strapping. Its great steel head was relentless.

'We mainly use this on heated bloom,' Gertrude shouted to Agatha. 'That's the raw iron. We bang it and bang it over and over, to make it stronger.'

'How does it get stronger by being beaten?' Beatrix asked.

'What?' Gertrude turned to her.

'Why does beating it make it stronger?' Beatrix asked, louder. Her throat felt weak, constricted from grief.

'I suppose the iron knits together. To protect itself from the blows.' Gertrude turned again to Agatha. 'We use another wheel, downstairs, to run the shaft of the bellows. That shaft, you've seen it? It runs right out to the wall to the bellows outside and the bloomery, where we cook the iron. Would you like to eat iron for supper?'

Agatha giggled and shook her head. She said something too soft for Beatrix to hear over the ringing of the hammer. Gertrude bent in and asked her to say it in her ear. Then Gertrude straightened up.

'Yes, we can put something on it, little chicken. If you like. Let's see. Would you like me to make you a sword?'

Agatha nodded, her eyes still red but clearing.

Gertrude rummaged in a basket and came up with a misshapen bar of black iron with a hole in one end.

'One of our fishing weights from the millpond,' she said. 'We don't have – they took all our charcoal. So I can't light the forge. But it's already been banged around a bit, you see, so now we should be able to give it some shape, even cold.'

She took Agatha's little hand and led the girl to the anvil. Together, they inserted the bar under the hammer. The bar now had a great dent.

Blow after blow and the bar got flatter. Gertrude pulled it out, and looked at it.

'Come over and try, Beatrix.'

Beatrix did want to feel what it was like to hold the bar under that force, and although she was nervous she tried not to show it. They had all thought Gertrude a ninny but here she was wielding a hammer the size of a man.

Gertrude took Beatrix's hand and wrapped it under her own on the bar. They held it under the blows. It wasn't as difficult as Beatrix had thought. It was only the movement in between that made her nervous, when Gertrude shifted the bar's position between blows. After a while Gertrude removed her hand and let Beatrix work alone.

'There,' Gertrude said, pulling it out.

'Well, it's not very even. Spinning is my gift.'

'Can you not spin iron?' Gertrude grinned.

Beatrix shook her head. 'Only gold!' she shouted back with a grin of her own.

245

She did envy Gertrude after all – not her grief, which must be greater than Beatrix could even imagine, but her boisterous presence in the world. Gertrude took up space; Beatrix was always watching from the corners.

Gertrude ran her hands along the rough edge of the flattened bar.

'You have to imagine the point and the handle, but here is your sword, Sir Agatha.'

The girl took it with a grin.

'Well, look at that, my sweet!' Jacquemine stood in the door.

Gertrude unhitched the wheel and the banging, mercifully, stopped.

Mother looked at Gertrude and the anvil. 'A wonder,' she said. 'You can beat swords into ploughshares. Or the other way around.'

'I wish you could have seen my husband at his work. That was a wonder. A shame. A real shame. I shall be sad to leave this place, when the abbey sends a new man to work the hammer.'

CHAPTER TWENTY-THREE

Excerpt from the Chronicles of Zonnebeke Abbey

In those days there was some disagreement about when a soul knows the perfect happiness of knowing God, as it is written in Corinthians: *Videmus nunc per speculum in ænigmate: tunc autem facie ad faciem.*

The true pope in Avignon, who took the name John XXII, expressed the private opinion that a soul cannot know this beatific vision until the Judgment Day, when Christ comes in His Glory and the world will be made new. The Holy Father later came to see that this was an error. But in those days, there were many men of the church who whispered against John and some were secretly saddened that the Imperial Antipope in Rome failed in his attempt to take the papacy.

It was in that same year, the year of the Antipope Nicholas, that King Philippe and the Chatelaine put down the Flemish insurrection.

And, as is the way of things, the words of the wise

came to the ears of the common people like whispers in a cathedral, and the unwise worried that Pope John was uncertain about the life that follows death. What did truly happen to those who died in faith? What would they see in Heaven?

And on Judgment Day, when all souls and bodies were reunited, what would happen to the chimeras?

These were the questions that occupied the pope in those days, as he and his counsellors sought to understand the nature of the Hellbeast, which seemed to be neither the Gehenna of punishment nor any Purgatory of infants or holy fathers. Was this then Sheol, home of the shades, and did Samuel wait in such a place before he was summoned by the Witch of Endor? Was this the infernus where Christ descended after his Crucifixion, for the Harrowing of Hell and the release of just captives? Some hoped that were true, for it might mean that those whom they had loved, who had been swallowed by the Beast, would one day be freed, even before the Last Judgment.

It was clear that many, many of the dead were not in the Beast. There was some other Hell somewhere. For where was Judas?

It was a time of great confusion, and the pope was beset on all sides. For while he had the support of King Philippe, the Emperor Louis was lying in wait for a chance to supplant the pope with a new usurper, someone who would support the Franciscans' contention that Christ and the Apostles had no possessions, someone who would not assert papal authority over the Empire. The pope and all the bishops loyal to him, therefore, were very grateful for the support of King Philippe in those warlike times.

CHAPTER TWENTY-FOUR

Michaelmas day dawned cold.

'You must not leave me,' Gertrude said, grabbing Margriet's sleeve. 'Please.'

'First you throw a pot at us,' said Margriet. 'And now you want us to stay. Well, we can't stay. But before I go, I'll pay for the food Beatrix and I ate, and for the beer.'

'What good is clinking money to me here?' Gertrude asked. 'Where shall I spend it?'

Margriet shrugged. 'I will not steal from you, so I must pay you.'

'You can pay me by staying with me. I – I can't stand it here alone. The water – sometimes I think I hear voices on it.'

'If you truly wish to come with us,' Margriet said slowly. 'That is your choice. But do you have the courage?'

Gertrude was shaking her head. 'I cannot. I cannot go out there. I cannot.'

This quivering widow – this would be Beatrix, if she were left alone in the world. A young woman, afraid of the world outside and the world within, and with good reason. Margriet had coddled her, perhaps. She had let her marry for love. She had made mistakes. But she had thought, somehow, she would be there to watch out for Beatrix, always.

By Christmas, if not before, Margriet would be dead, and Beatrix would be alone.

If she had her inheritance, she would be able to buy herself a husband or, better still, a place at a proper nunnery, high-walled and remote. Protection from the world and from her dead husband.

Without her inheritance, she would have little choice but to cast her lot in with the beguines in some city, working her fingers to the bone and vulnerable not only to Baltazar's revenant but to her own reckless imagination. Why, it was not so long ago that they burned a beguine at the stake in Paris for writing a bad book. The last thing Beatrix needed in her life was mystical women, hard work, and hunger.

And here Gertrude cowered before her, asking for what none of them could have, without money. Asking for a safe place in the world.

Margriet would win this trial, no matter what she had to do or say.

'You are a most exasperating woman,' she spat at Gertrude. 'Stay, then, and mind the children, and listen to the ghosts in the water.'

Michaelmas morning, Claude rode on the plodding palfrey they gave him, the reins held by a mantis-man. And he thought. He always thought best when he was riding.

Three months after he had joined the Genoa Company, or maybe four, a few of the men had cajoled him into going with a small band in the night to recover some dice winnings for Janos. Claude was perhaps seventeen or eighteen years old by then. He had been on his own, or with various bands of ne'er-do-wells, for three years before he joined the Company. Claude had not yet spoken much with Janos, though he had watched him joke with the others, watched him win every contest with his crossbow. Janos was a few years older than Claude; his beard did not look as though it had been glued on.

'What is the plan?' asked Abdul gruffly as they stumbled down the cobbled streets of Barcelona.

'How should I know?' said Janos with a grin. 'The plan is God's.'

'But we must—' Claude had said, his voice as deep as he could muster.

'If I have no plan, then nothing can go wrong,' said Janos. 'I will not waste any time rewriting my plans as I go. I do not want any planners and falterers, Claude, mark me, now, for you are young and desperate, and I want you to stay that way. I want only desperate men beside me!'

But when they reached the alley before the house of Don Carlos, Janos had let the three others go on ahead, and he had pulled Claude to him and spoken to him there in the shadows, leaning one hand on the grimy wall.

'I ask only two things of you, Claude. First, always, you must look after yourself. Will you do that? Don't ever trust anyone to do that for you. Not even me.'

Claude had nodded. He was close enough to feel the warmth off Janos's shoulder, feel his breath when he spoke. 'I may be small, but I can fight,' he'd said.

'I know you can, or I would not have let you come,'

Janos said with a smile. 'There is another reason I will not plan. Planners become schemers, and schemers cannot be trusted. I don't want you to make your decisions here—' and Janos put the heel of his hand to Claude's forehead '—but here.' And he put his hand firmly on his lower belly, so that Claude drew in his breath but did not pull away.

'If you have no plan, you will think with your fists, and the only decision you'll make is whether the face before you is a face you know or not. The face you do not know, you punch. The face you know, you do not punch. That is true loyalty. They say we men of the free companies have no honour, because we fight for whoever pays us. But Claude, my little Claude, our honour is not in whom we serve but in whom we protect. That is the second thing I ask of you: look after those whose faces you know.'

Claude had grinned, for he had never heard Janos be so serious. 'God's nails, have you been drinking?'

'Always,' said Janos, and kissed him, hard, not a kiss of peace but a kiss of war, and they joined the others. They got Janos his money back.

Later they had slower kisses: kisses of joy, and of pain, and of wonder, and many kisses of lust. They learned each other's secrets and the others more or less let them be. For two years they were happy, until the day Janos was felled by an arrow through the eye, his quiver empty of quarrels and eighteen dead men to his count.

A cold day, but not cold enough to harden the mud that clung to their shoes. Margriet was almost glad of the chill air and the sucking mud. It dampened their spirits and stilled their tongues so she could think.

They walked in a line, Margriet in front, Beatrix in the middle, and Jacquemine behind. They walked through empty, burned fields, past charred and desolate farms, keeping a line of low trees on the horizon.

Jacquemine's mouth was a straight line. But they had been right to leave the children with Gertrude. Jacob and Agatha adored her. She let them put things under the big hammer: bent nails and twisted buckles that became, with a little romance and sun-glint, swords and lances and bucklers.

Gertrude had run after the women as they left and watched them go, the children clinging to her.

Zonnebeke Abbey was not far, but by the time they reached it, their hose were spattered and their shoes were caked. Margriet's nose was running. They would not cut fine figures, but they were not there to catch husbands. They were three bedraggled widows with no way to travel but shanks' mare; let them look the part.

The bells were ringing for Terce. A thin, tall porter let them in and escorted them, standing a little to one side as if some of the mud on their clothing might fall on him. A large, rich abbey, this. There were grotesques on the church walls, some of whom looked eerily like the Chatelaine's chimeras. But they were bound not for the church but for the chapter house, a great round thing buttressed and peaked.

It was round on the inside, too, and sunlight striped the floor of green-and-yellow tiles.

Men were arrayed on the benches all in a circle. The chapter house was so large that most of the men were far enough distant for their faces to be blurred. Margriet knew them by the shapes of their clothing. There was the bishop in his golden cope and pale mitre, with dark-robed men, priests or monks. There was the king in his rich cloak and several men beside him, tonsured or not she could not say. One cleric sat at a little table with ink and parchment.

The porter showed them to a cold bench.

The Chatelaine was nowhere to be seen, but as the bells rang again the door to the antechamber opened and she came through it, with the abbot. Behind them came the tall thin man who had stood at Hell's door, who caught Margriet's eye.

'I feel like one of the animals, come to King Nobel's court,' whispered Beatrix.

'I feel like a beggar waiting for scraps,' Jacquemine sighed.

At least they all three had clean and neat wimples and veils, thanks to Gertrude's scrubbing. Beatrix had not been in the habit of always wearing a wimple or gorget, except on days she was out in the streets on some business. She favoured a simple hood or cap at home, and a net or a fillet and veil over her beautiful golden braids on feast days. But she was a widow now, and anyway they had brought nothing else to wear.

'We are no beggars,' said Margriet, not bothering to whisper. 'We are here for what is right. Let us hope this king is wiser than King Nobel.'

The sound carried farther than she'd thought it would and several of the men looked at her.

'Or perhaps if he is not,' whispered Beatrix, leaning close to Margriet, 'let us hope that we are Reynard and not Ysengrim.'

Margriet did not even smile, for she was looking at Claude. She had barely noticed him come in behind the

Chatelaine and her servants. But there he was, dressed in plain clothing, with no arms or armour, looking about as comfortable as a cat in water. Claude sat a little distance from them on the empty bench near the Chatelaine's thin servant. He would not look at them. Had the Chatelaine broken him? What had the hellkite promised him?

The bishop stood and the chapter house hushed.

'We have chosen to hear the petition of this woman of Bruges, one Margriet de Vos, who says she is entitled to this chest that belonged to her husband. We shall ask questions of anyone who we deem to have some knowledge of this matter, but to begin with, let the woman speak. Come forward.'

Margriet stood. 'I am grateful for the chance to speak on my behalf. I know—'

'Come to the middle, so we can all hear you,' the bishop said.

Margriet swallowed and strode forward on uncertain legs. Her feet were tingling, numb, as they had been for days now. She felt as if she might trip on the cracks between the beautiful tiles. The warm patch of parti-coloured sunlight falling from the window made her squint. She bent on one knee, so grateful to have made it without stumbling that she went down like a sack of beans.

'I know my cause is just,' she said breathlessly, 'and I hope for God's mercy.'

'Make your case, then.'

She stood again, creakily. Damn this plague, working its way through her skin and bone! Perhaps she ought to be grateful to seem decrepit, but she was not. She wanted only what was hers, by right, and not through pity or any trickery.

'It is the custom in Flanders,' she said, 'that a widow is entitled to one-third of the wealth of her husband, and any child, male or female, to the remaining two-thirds. In support of this, I ask Your Excellency to consider the case of Anna van Aert, wife of the merchant Victor van Aert, who two years ago was given all her husband's furniture and his home in that town, while their daughter, Mayken, was given all his clinking money.'

There was a pause and a shuffling of cloth shoes on tile. The cleric at the little table wrote furiously.

The bishop said, 'The most gracious king has provided us with an authority on Flemish custom, one Jan Vroom. Do you confirm this custom, Master Vroom?'

One of the dark-robed men, with a bulging red chaperon on his head, stood.

'I do.'

'And do any of the king's lawyers wish to dispute or question on this point?'

'We are not speaking of demesnes,' said Vroom, 'nor even of houses in this case, so the Salic law of inheritance, which has been the subject of so much scholarship of late, does not apply. We have no dispute with the Flemish custom, insofar as it is in accordance with canon law and the restrictions on inheritance that come with remarriage, per exemplum.'

The words rushed past Margriet like murky water. She could barely hear. Her breath was coming short, and her legs were weak. Damn the walk from Gertrude's house. It had been more than her plague-ridden body could bear.

'Vrouwe de Vos?'

Margriet blinked. 'I'm sorry?'

The bishop coughed. 'We are not speaking of houses, as I understand it, but of a chest full of coins and goods. Is that so, Vrouwe de Vos?'

Margriet nodded. 'The house in Bruges was mine, but it burned, as did my father's house, in the attack. If there is some compensation due me for that, it is only the same as what is due all the other people of Bruges whose houses were destroyed. This chest, this wealth, I never laid claim to, because I only learned about it after my husband's death.'

A quaver went through her at the thought that if they asked her outright about where such and such happened, and how – or God forbid if they asked about Willem – then everyone would know she had the plague, and no one would need to listen to her or provide her due, for they would know that she was walking into her grave. Stumbling, more like.

'You did not know your husband had collected such wealth?'

She shook her head and tried to speak but coughed instead.

'Someone bring this woman water,' someone said.

Margriet waved it off and recovered her voice.

'When we were married, the priest asked if he would share his body and his belongings – and his belongings, mark – and treat me in all ways as a husband should treat his wife. He said yes. And instead, he hid his goods from me, kept them from me, so that I had to go out as a wet nurse, and our daughter, Beatrix, there, had to spin her poor fingers red and raw.'

Vroom stood. Margriet squinted to see if she could

recognize his face. She had known a few Vrooms but could not place this one. He spoke French with a Paris accent.

'You speak of wedding vows, but what of your vow to treat him as a woman ought to treat her husband?'

Margriet blinked. 'I do not understand.'

A few of the men chuckled unpleasantly.

'We have made inquiries,' said Vroom, 'among the people of Bruges. We have heard that this woman is a notorious shrew, eager to revenge any slight, even perhaps an invented one. We have heard that she mistreated her husband, giving him both sides of her tongue even in the public market.'

'If I argued when he gave me cause to argue, then I was no different to any other wife saddled with an oaf for a husband.'

A few more titters among the king's men.

'And did you share your belongings with him? When you were paid for nursing? Did you share every sou?'

Margriet shook her head. 'That was to keep my body and soul together and my daughter's, too. It was all I had. He gave me nothing. He said he had nothing to give. He lied.'

'Then we have established that you were not treating him as a wife should, if you were a scold to him and withheld your belongings.'

Margriet's mouth was sour. She should have eaten more on the road, but she was in the habit now of saving food, and anyway what good was food to a dying body, beyond what it needed to keep stumbling from today into tomorrow?

She did not know how to answer them, when they

asked if she had been a good wife. She had been the only wife she knew how to be. In the early days, she had tried to dull her tongue and wait upon Willem. But then Beatrix had arrived, and then it was a never-ending cycle of pregnancies and confinements, and she did her duty by him in bed, and she gave birth to his stillborn babies, and she lost the will or the strength to be anything but a mother to Beatrix.

'You may say it is a woman's duty to be kind to her husband, but what is the duty of a mother? When I was a child, I trod the treadmill with the other children to work the crane that lifted the barrels for the boatmen. When my Beatrix was a girl, she broke her ankle walking that treadmill and I paid for the bonesetter out of my savings. And when she could not walk it any longer because it made her ankle ache, I went out to wet nurse, for my husband told me we were destitute. When Beatrix was married, she had for her dowry a silver ewer that I bought for her with the money I had set aside from double-watering our wine and eating the day-old crusts from the worst baker in Bruges. When the Devil puts up walls, men smash them, and if they cannot smash them, they despair, or they walk away. But women must trickle through the cracks, they find a way through because they have no choice, because they have nowhere to go, and nothing to smash with. No one would feed my daughter but me, and so I fed her, with whatever sous I could earn as an honest woman. I have been a faithful wife to Willem de Vos and served him in the truest way I know: I have borne his children, all four of them, though three are in limbo now, where I pray for their souls every day.'

She would have said more but she ran out of breath and drowned from the lack of it. Her eyes went dark and she only dimly felt herself hitting the tile floor.

CHAPTER TWENTY-FIVE

Margriet woke in a small, dim chamber. She was lying on a bed and a monk was tutting over her with a sharp-smelling cloth in his hand.

'Brother Infirmerer, she has come around,' murmured a voice.

She turned her head. There was the bishop. Close up, she could see his face at last. An ordinary face, within all that finery. Not a kind face, but not a cruel one either. The face of an alderman or a lawyer. Solid and weary, pale and fleshy about the neck.

'I am better,' she said, propping herself on an elbow. The world lurched.

'It is taxing, for a woman to occupy herself with the arguments of churchmen and lawyers,' said the bishop. 'We understand. Take some rest, here.'

'I can continue now.'

The bishop shook his head. 'We have an office to keep, in any case. We will continue in an hour's time, if you are well enough.'

The bishop and the monk slipped out through the plain

wooden door. Where was Beatrix? She would be beside herself with worry.

Margriet sat up, to see whether she could. Her head was light, but she thought she could manage to stand again.

The door opened and a man came in. The tall, thin servant who always stood near the Chatelaine. He had an ancient face.

'You have nothing to fear,' he said, holding up one bony hand. 'My name is Chaerephon. I am in the Chatelaine's service. I have come to see whether you wish to put a stop to this madness.'

She swallowed. Had the monks let him in? Kept her daughter from her, and let this ghoul in to harry her?

She shook her head. 'Please leave me be. We will argue before the bishop, when it is time.'

'But you are unwell.' He stepped closer to her, cocked his head.

'It has been a difficult time, as I am sure you appreciate, sir.'

'Difficult, indeed, for one who has the plague. Oh, there is no point in hiding it from me. I have lived in Hell so long I know death's marks when I see them. When you collapsed, and I rushed to your aid with so many others, I took a moment to look at your hands.'

She looked at them: her fingers blotched with black, and shaking.

'I have only a very little time,' she whispered. 'I wish to have my right, before I meet God. I wish to see my daughter safe and provided for.'

He nodded. 'Of course. We would be happy to provide for her, if you were to withdraw your claim. We would compensate you, with twice the worth of your husband's goods.'

She frowned. 'Why, in heaven's name?'

He turned from her. 'If you win, that creates some . . . difficulties for us. If you lose, that creates difficulties of its own. We would much rather leave the status of the goods owned by revenants as a . . . political question, not a legal one.'

'You speak to me as if I have a brain, sir,' she muttered. 'Not like the bishop.'

'Because you do have a brain, Margriet de Vos. That much is evident. But not for much longer. It will be as useless as a bowl of tripe before All Souls' Day. And if you lose this trial, as well you might, your daughter will be alone, and penniless. One hates to think what will come of a girl, alone and penniless, in time of war.'

Margriet drew a long, ugly breath.

'If I take your offer, will you declare her right to it?'

'To the payment? No, I am afraid it must be done in secret, or it would be taken as evidence that we believe it to be her due.'

Margriet shook her head. 'Then I must refuse. How do I know you won't take it away from her, after I am dead? How do I know you will not pursue her with your hounds, as you pursued Claude? No, I want the world to know it is her right. I want my due, sir, and nothing else.'

He threw up his hands, turned away from her, and paced a bit.

Then he turned his face back to her. Such an old face, and yet there were hardly any wrinkles in it. Smooth as a skull.

'There can be no way to know she is safe, Margriet de

Vos, whether you wrench some declaration from us or not. After you are dead, anything could befall her. Ruffians could steal it all from her. As for that, if you mistrust us so, what prevents our hounds from pursuing her even if you win the trial? Of course they would never be directed to do so, of course not, but mistakes do happen. The only way for you to watch over her, would be for you to live, and to be stronger.'

She snorted. 'But no one lives, once they have contracted the plague.'

He had no eyebrows, but if he had, they would have risen.

'Not someone who has gone through the fires of Hell, and been bonded with something that cannot be killed by the plague.'

She gasped, and then coughed at the intake of breath in her ragged throat. 'You are asking me to become a chimera?'

He spread his arms wide in their mouse-coloured cloak. 'I say it is an offer we are willing to make. You are intelligent, and you fight. These are the qualities the Chatelaine seeks in her chimeras. Your disease is as nothing to us. We will give you new fingers – claws, perhaps. And new eyes – yes, I have seen you squinting – something far-seeing. Would you like to be an eagle, Margriet de Vos? Armoured with steel, so that nothing could harm you? You could watch over Beatrix every night, and keep her safe not only from ruffians and hounds, but also from . . . well, I believe her husband is a revenant, is he not?'

Blood beat in her ears. If only she could think properly! She wanted to vomit at the thought of being mixed with something inhuman, of claws and feathers and armour in her skin. She had a right to her own body, riddled with plague as it might be, at the end. She had a right to go into the ground sole, and whole.

But to see clearly, to be strong again. To live. To live.

To live as someone else's beast – who could say what will would enter her mind, once she went through those fires? Would she be the Chatelaine's creature, then, like the horned man, like this bag o' bones in front of her?

To live . . .

Margriet shook her head until the world rang.

'I want none of it, none at all. I will not hear any more of it. Get out of my way, if you don't mind. I do not wish to be late when the bishop reconvenes.'

The bishop asked if Margriet had anyone to testify to her marriage, to whether she had indeed been the wife of this Willem.

Jacquemine stood by Margriet's side.

'And you are? A Moor, by your skin.'

'Jacquemine Ooste. My father was indeed a Moor. I am a Christian woman, wife to the late Jan Ooste, alderman of Bruges.'

More rustling, as the men wondered if he were one of the aldermen of Bruges murdered by the king's henchmen. Jan had been an alderman, yes, but he had died at the Battle of Cassel, mercifully. Died and been buried in the ground, not fed half-dead to the Hellbeast and turned into a revenant like some women's husbands.

A good man, Jan Ooste had been, always kind to Margriet.

'Say your piece, then, for pity's sake,' huffed the bishop,

'and let this de Vos woman's tongue rest in its sheath a while.'

More chuckles. Margriet felt herself swaying. She stared at Jacquemine to keep herself anchored. Jacquemine stood tall, her wimple neat and a lovely white veil falling over her shoulders. She looked none the worse for the walk from the mill, at least if one did not look at her shoes.

It was not in Margriet's nature to ask a favour from her employer. But Willem's sack would ensure a full belly and a safe roof for not only Beatrix but for little Jacob and Agatha too, for all the children who had drunk the milk out of Margriet's body.

'Margriet de Vos is a virtuous and respected woman of Bruges. She has been in my employ as a wet nurse for several years. Yes, she is known in the cloth hall and throughout the city for her honest and forthright ways, but she is no scold. I know her to have been married to Willem de Vos since the twenty-third year of Philippe le Bel's reign. It would have been twenty years for them soon.'

'We shall consider these matters,' said the bishop. 'If a wife is not a good wife, that seems to me it does not dissolve the marriage, nor her husband's obligation to her. Does the Chatelaine wish to speak about these questions of marriage, or about the Flemish customs of widowhood?'

Margriet felt a dull pressure against her left hand, a pressure with purpose, with insistence. She glanced down and saw that Jacquemine was taking her hand in her own, to offer comfort. Margriet did not trust her fingers to grasp so she smiled a little and hoped that was enough. She needed nothing from Jacquemine, who had already given her more than she needed. Indeed, Margriet was already in debt to her. She would never have asked this of her employer had it not been for Beatrix, had it not been for the war and hunger in this world she was leaving her daughter in alone.

The Chatelaine stood and all the men turned to her. She was a marvel to behold, so beautiful, with the elaborate gold netting in her hair.

'We find it a very simple argument,' said Chaerephon, standing just out of the sunlight. 'It is untrue that this woman Margriet de Vos is a widow. Her husband is not dead.'

CHAPTER TWENTY-SIX

Beatrix watched Mother and Jacquemine and clasped her hands tightly together. What was it about Jacquemine Ooste that she always looked like one of the fine ladies of Bruges, even when there was no more time or space for finery? She wore no brocade or silk today, only her deep blue velvet surcoat and a red linen kirtle, and she looked like a woman out of a church window as she stood in the slanting sunlight.

'What evidence do you have of your husband's death?' asked the bishop.

'I have seen him, your excellency,' said Mother. 'With a great gaping hole through his chest. No man can have that much air whistle through him and live, excepting our Saviour, of course.'

Beatrix winced. The pain that must have caused Father, before he died. He had never been good with pain; he used to have Beatrix pull his splinters out.

'May I speak, your excellency?' asked the thin man who stood near the Chatelaine.

'Chaerephon, your response would be most welcome.'

'I have seen Willem de Vos walking the earth,' said Chaerephon, walking to the centre of the chapter house. 'Dead men do not walk.'

'He has no breath in his body,' said Mother.

'Yet he speaks,' said Chaerephon.

Jacquemine put her hand out to stop Mother from answering. 'I have heard that a murdered man will speak the name of his killer, if the killer approaches. Yet the murdered man is no less dead for this miracle.'

'The revenants are not dead,' said Chaerephon. 'The bodies of the dead rot in the ground.'

'Until they are resurrected at the last,' said the bishop.

'Indeed,' answered Chaerephon. 'Yes. But you have seen that this Willem is not rotting in the ground, although the Last Judgment is not yet upon us.'

'Some have seen the bodies of saints, preserved whole,' said Jacquemine.

'Surely this woman does not mean to imply that this Willem de Vos was a saint.'

Laughter circled the walls like a drunken swallow and rose up into the rafters and drifted out the windows to where the gargoyles watched the world.

'Father bishop,' Mother said, in her chastened voice, which was never a good sign, 'my husband is no saint, certainly, and I am no scholar of religion. But help me to understand. If my husband is not dead, why can he only walk at night, with bats and other evil creatures? I do not claim to understand these revenants, or anything about the state of their souls, but I do know that the man I knew all my life as Willem de Vos no longer inhabits that body.'

'A man may be greatly changed,' said the Chatelaine,

standing, 'and in that way his family may consider him as one dead. But that does not mean the law regards his wife as a widow.'

The bishop considered. 'Is there anyone else here who has had dealings with this Willem de Vos, in the days since he went to Hell?'

Mother turned to her with an apology in her face. Beatrix wished she could crawl into the earth and lie there until the nightmare was ended. It was warm in the hall. Her damp shoes were warm now, warm and still wet, and she could smell the tang of wet leather and wet wool.

She stood.

'I have seen my father.'

'And was he alive or dead?'

Beatrix looked at her mother. She spoke slowly. 'I do not understand how he could be alive.'

The bishop leaned back.

'No,' he said. 'Indeed, it would be a wonder. Then again, it is a wonder if the dead walk the earth. It is a difficult question for one humble man to answer, but the king has tasked me with deciding this case.'

The Chatelaine pulled Chaerephon aside and conferred with him. Then she addressed the bishop.

'Your Excellency, I fear we tax your time and delay the Michaelmas feast already, but there is another matter to decide. Not all of the wealth she claims was lawfully her husband's. What a man does not own he cannot bequeath. Part of it was stolen from me. Indeed I would not be surprised to learn that much of it was stolen.'

She smiled, but the bishop did not. The room was silent, the word 'stolen' echoing.

'Indeed? Which part do you claim?'

The Chatelaine gestured to Claude. 'This man stole a weapon from me, and later sold it to Willem de Vos.'

'Stand, then, and give your name and your account.'

Claude stood.

'I am Claude Jouvenal, formerly of the Genoa Company, and I have never stolen anything,' said Claude in his deepest voice. 'I have raided, I have taken my due after battle, I have bought and I have bartered. I am not a thief.'

The Chatelaine gave him a look like a basilisk.

If the Chatelaine wanted to hunt him, let her call her dogs. Claude would look after himself. He would not step into a trap.

'He is lying,' said the Chatelaine. 'He admitted his guilt to me, and now he denies it.'

Claude smiled indulgently.

Chaerephon coughed and stood. He was cloaked, even in the warm hall, as though the heat of the sun could not touch his skinny body. He said nothing, but a shiver ran through Claude. He remembered the priest in Bruges, saying Claude had been lucky not to have been burned at the stake. If Chaerephon thought it would help their cause, would he advise his mistress to tell the court that Claude was not a man? It was not something the Chatelaine had ever doubted, before, but it was a weapon she held against him.

The Church could charge him with heresy.

There was a long moment, a moment with all sorts of possibilities in it, none of them very good.

'Are there any witnesses who can speak to the manner of this crime, then?' the bishop asked.

Claude blinked. Crime? The bishop meant the mace.

'I shall,' said the Chatelaine. 'He was a guest in Hell, and many saw how he greatly admired my arsenal, in particular this mace I wear myself. Then one day he was gone, and with him he took a mace, forged by one of my smiths, in copy of mine. He sold the mace to Willem de Vos, the husband of this woman Margriet. That is how the mace came to be among this wealth that she claims, but the mace is mine by right. It was forged by my smith in my fire. It is mine.'

The bishop sighed. 'We shall have to see it.'

The Chatelaine inclined her head and lifted her hand.

The mantis-man brought her a long casket of fresh wood and opened it, holding it out to her. The Chatelaine reached in with her left hand and pulled it out with a triumphant snarl, so that she held one mace in her left hand that was an exact copy of the one she wore on her right.

An intake of breath echoed round the chapter house. Claude's arm jumped and quivered. It called out to him. It was his.

'Your Excellency, if I may?' the king asked.

The bishop nodded.

'Come here,' said King Philippe to Claude, 'so I may question you.'

Claude knelt to one knee, then stood and walked toward him.

'Closer.'

He did not like the king's smell, perfumed and oily. Claude had known men like him before. Vainglorious. There was a kind of violence that went with such vanity, an unwillingness to let anything else in the world be beautiful. The king grabbed his arm and felt it up and down. He took his chin in his hands and looked into his eyes.

'You are a twisted thing,' he said. 'Unnatural. What did you want with the Chatelaine's weapon?'

'I wanted to use it to escape,' Claude said, the full truth rolling from his mouth like a ball of fire. 'I knew that the mace could open the mouth of Hell.'

This time it was not a mere intake of breath but a gasp.

The Chatelaine blanched. A servant brought the copied mace to the king. He turned it over in his hands, and peered into the hollow end that had fit over Claude's arm. It was all Claude could do to stop from grabbing it from him.

'God be praised, this is a marvel in truth,' said the king. 'Not quite as beautiful as the one my lady the Chatelaine wears, of course, but a marvel. And who was the one who made this weapon for you?'

The Chatelaine whirled to Chaerephon, who stood beside her. He stood, putting out a hand toward her, as if in reassurance.

'His name was Gobhan Og,' Claude said. 'An angry man with a long, forked beard. He made it for me as a gift, in the hours he was given to rest. He was in the habit of making small secret items, as a sort of practice, I imagine. As you have said, my lord, my mace is not nearly as beautiful as the Chatelaine's. It is rougher at the ends and has no adornment. If he gave away some of his practice-work that would make him no different to any smith I have known, and it does not make me a thief. You cannot ask him, because now he is dead. Perhaps the Chatelaine would like to explain how he came to be that way.'

Claude almost laughed as the truth, like a cat o' nine tails, whipped where it was least expected. It had been a gift, of a sort, although given in exchange for the gift of

Claude's silence about the little arsenal Gobhan Og had been making for himself. Claude had not yet decided whether to tell that part of the truth, or to hold it back, and had not yet decided which would be the mercy to the Chatelaine.

'Ah,' said the king. 'Now I begin to see. The question, it seems, is whether this armourer was free to make and give the piece, what his terms were as he saw them. What a pity he is dead and cannot speak about it.'

'The mace itself is a small matter,' said the Chatelaine, her voice sharp, 'I use it only to make the point that this Willem de Vos was like a magpie, picking up things of unknown provenance. All of it could have been stolen.'

'But who can ever say, with coins and cups and even weapons?' said the king. 'It was all in his possession, and it seems the task before me is to decide who should leave here with it. That is the reason I called for this trial. After that, if anyone wishes to make a claim on a particular piece, let them bring it to whatever local bailiff or petty lord they wish.'

The Chatelaine inclined her head. Claude could see her breast rise and fall a few times, and her right hand clenched. Then she raised her head and smiled.

'As you say, of course. We have made our argument.'

'Good bishop, do you have enough evidence to make your decision?' said the king.

Claude watched the bishop's face. He looked strangely nervous and would not meet the king's eye. Ah, then the king had ordered an outcome – which? – and the bishop was not easy about delivering it.

'I believe we need to devise some sort of test,' said the bishop. 'Some way for all to witness the truth, rather than the opinion of one man, no matter how humble and prayerful.'

Chaerephon coughed. 'As it happens, we have already devised just such a test,' he said.

The bishop smiled at him. An arrangement, or a happy accident for this bishop? And what sort of test?

Chaerephon stood. 'It remains to be proven that these women are truly widows, and that their husbands are truly dead. So we must see a revenant, and then all can judge.'

A murmur spread around the chapter house.

The bishop raised his monumental eyebrows. 'Then let us pause for the noon meal and take some time for prayer, for I suspect this procedure will have to go on past Vigils, if we are to question revenants.'

Claude looked for the first time to Margriet and Beatrix, to the faces that he knew. And he almost smiled because the weight was off him, because he had not given in to the Chatelaine's offer. But his smile died when he saw the pallor on Beatrix's face.

Mother insisted they avoid the refectory and eat their own food, outside, away from prying ears. Jacquemine and Mother muttered together while Beatrix nibbled an apple.

Soon she would be asked to deny her father. And then that would be it, over, the last time she would see him. And Baltazar? Would he come to her again, after all this was done? Would he know that she still loved him, would always love him, even after death?

The sun was nearly setting when they gathered outside the chapter house, where they could see a revenant without bringing the plague upon anyone.

Monks brought torches and they stood in a circle: the king, the Chatelaine, Chaerephon, Margriet, Jacquemine, and Beatrix. And Claude. The knights and squires, dressed in velvet, stood near the king, looking all around as if they hoped to see a wonder. Did they not know to be frightened? Had they not seen what the Grief would do?

Beatrix was grateful she had left her distaff at the mill-house. No one could blame her now for what came in the night, be it fireflies or apparitions.

Someone took Beatrix's hand, with cold fingers.

She turned to see the face of her husband and screamed.

He looked even more battered now. Some of that was her doing: long scratches down his head and face.

'Oh, my love,' she whispered.

Everyone had moved away from them.

Mother took her shoulders, pulled her away and said, 'That's the wrong one. That's Baltazar.'

Beatrix let her mother move her into the crowd of people, leaving Baltazar standing alone.

'You call him by name,' said the Chatelaine.

'This is the wrong one,' said Margriet.

The bishop strode forward and looked at Baltazar in the torchlight. He stood impassive, staring at Beatrix. He only wanted her. He wanted her, and nothing else, just as he always had. And yet she had spurned him, had called an owl upon him.

She thought she could see, around him like a golden miasma, all his love for her.

'This is your husband, I believe?'

Beatrix nodded.

'Beatrix!' Mother hissed.

'It was,' she managed.

'Speak, then,' said the bishop. 'Are you alive?'

Baltazar looked at the Chatelaine and back to the bishop. 'I am.'

'This is not the man in question,' said Jacquemine.

'One is as good as another,' said the Chatelaine.

'If one revenant is not dead, none of them are,' said Chaerephon.

'Is he your husband?' the king asked Beatrix. 'What do you say? Look at him and tell us the truth.'

Beatrix turned to see him. The wounds on his face and head were as fresh as the day she gave them to him. His gaze was on her.

'Come closer,' Baltazar said.

Mother's grip was strong, but Beatrix pulled her arm away and stepped to him.

'Are you the man I married?' she whispered, so quietly she could barely hear the words herself.

He put his hands on her shoulders and pulled her to him. When he whispered in her ear there was no breath, no warmth in it.

He whispered, 'I remember all of it. Every word we spoke outside the church door. Every bite of pigeon pie, including the one that fell on your kirtle, and the way you blushed. Every touch of my fingers that night, and how all we did was use our hands on each other, and kiss, that night. I remember all of it. I am very much changed and for that I am sorry but if you deny me you deny those memories.'

She pulled away and looked at him. His eyes were so dull, his face like stone. He might have been reciting the month's cloth sales. He knew, he knew it all. But did he still care? And did that matter? She had sworn a vow to him before God.

'Deny me and I will pester you no more,' he whispered, and his lips quivered as if he were trying to remember how to smile.

Of course, he cared. It was his only care now. Everything else had been stripped away.

'Do you deny him?' asked the Chatelaine. 'Do you deny that this is your husband?'

If she said yes, she might never see him again. Mother would take her over the sea, where, people thought, the revenants would not walk. Mother wanted to give her a chest full of gold and a new husband. Beatrix did not want a new husband. She would rather live a pauper, shut away in some hut, like Heloise, clutching to her heart the precious scraps of the love-promises her husband had made. The ghost of Baltazar was worth ten living men.

'Do you deny him?'

'I don't know,' said Beatrix desperately. 'I don't know.'

'Then you are no widow,' said the Chatelaine gleefully.

CHAPTER TWENTY-SEVEN

The bishop said he would pray on the problem and render his decision in the morning, after Lauds.

The three women slept in the little guesthouse outside the gate. They were invited to the Michaelmas feast, but they chose not to go. Claude, accused of theft, was not invited to the feast, which was just as well. He stayed under guard with the Chatelaine's lesser servants in the dormitory, but all night long he could hear Baltazar calling Beatrix's name.

Was Beatrix covering her ears, or would she have let him in if Margriet and Jacquemine had not been there to stop her?

Claude wondered what he would do if he heard Janos's voice on the wind, now, after all these years. It was an idle thought to torture himself with, for Janos had died before the Hellbeast broke the surface of the earth, before revenants became an ordinary sight.

Claude slept in shallow fits until Monoceros came to collect him at dawn. He found he was relieved to see the horned man. Was it merely that prisoners become fond of the wardens, after a time? Or that Claude recognized in the brigand-turned-marshal a man of the same sort of solitary honour as himself? Or was it only, if Claude were to admit it, that Monoceros's kind eyes and strong shoulders were fair to look upon?

He smiled, despite himself, as they walked to the chapter house.

'You are confident, Claude Jouvenal,' murmured Monoceros.

'Not in the least,' Claude said. 'I expect I'll be dead or wish I were, by morning.'

'You had a chance to earn the Chatelaine's mercy,' said Monoceros evenly. 'You didn't take it.'

'I never did expect mercy from anyone,' Claude said. He felt as if he were leaving his body behind already, as though he might as well be a revenant.

'Well,' said Monoceros, and stopped walking. He glanced around, as if to see whether anyone was in earshot, but the little clumps of people scurrying back to the trial were not close enough to hear. 'It is not mercy, and not pity, but if you do find yourself free today, you will find something buried at the crossroads just south of here on the road to Lille.'

'Something?' he breathed, looking up into Monoceros's face. It was a well-lined face, the grooves determined, engraved.

'My old hauberk, gauntlets and helmet,' said the horned man. 'They don't fit me any more anyway.'

Claude had to take two breaths before he understood.

'You're giving them to me?'

'Don't tell anyone. A man has to have proper harness. You can't very well rejoin your company with nothing.'

Claude swallowed his only response, which threatened to be tears. He wasn't sure he could rejoin his company anyway, not with his arm as it was.

At last he recovered his voice, and nodded. 'Will you do me another kindness, Monoceros? If it goes the other way. Will you try to make sure that my death is a clean one? Clean and quick?'

Monoceros did not smile. He closed his eyes for a moment, and gave a very small nod of his head, just enough to dip the horn a little.

Claude nodded, too, the movement of his head an anchor, keeping him from weeping, from pleading.

'My mistress is not cruel,' Monoceros said. 'She is only . . . well, all great lords and princes do as they must. She will want to be rid of you, but I do not think she will want to see you suffer.'

But she might want to feed me to the Beast, Claude thought, and see me spat out as a revenant. She might relish that indeed, being able to order me hither and thither as if I were one of her dogs. There is no honour in that life, a life without will. If it comes to that, I could wrestle a knife off a guard and cut my throat.

In the chapter house, Margriet sat on the edge of the stone bench, her hands in her lap. Her face was grey. Her right leg trembled; impatience, Claude reasoned.

The bishop rose and said, 'On the question of whether these so-called revenants can be said to be truly dead, on the question of the state of their souls, I am disinclined to rule.'

Disinclined to rule? Was that it, then?

Claude looked at Margriet. Her face was like stone. He

looked to the king: he looked angry. Indeed, he had wanted a particular outcome, then, and this was not it.

'I shall send a delegation to Avignon,' said the bishop, 'to convey our evidence on this question to our Holy Father the pope. As for the question before me, though, that is a narrower one. I do not need to rule on whether a revenant is truly dead, but whether his wife is a widow.'

Blood of Christ, this bishop could out-argue Chaerephon. Men who lived in their own heads were bloody dangerous.

'As to that,' the bishop continued, 'it seems clear to me that the husband, whether he is dead or alive, is still able to work and provide for his family, and I see no obligation for the husband to hand over all his goods to his wife, no matter how vigorously she scolds him. However, I caution that this means Willem de Vos still has the care of his wife, and that God's law requires him to keep her as a man would any wife, in the way he sees fit.'

Margriet's face was a mask of anger. He pitied her. She had very little to hold onto, this woman, and yet she held on with a warrior's strength.

Still it was over, and there was nothing Margriet could do about it now. And Claude did not have the mace, or his freedom, or soon, very likely, his life.

'Do you understand this judgment?' asked the bishop of Margriet.

Margriet stood. 'I understand it. I will go now a widow, although this court does not recognize me for what I am. But I wish to take my companion with me.'

She looked at Claude.

Claude looked back, frowning a question at her, until he remembered that she could probably not see his expression with her dim eyes, from that distance. Convenient for her. What was she thinking?

'Who, the mercenary?' the king asked, after a silence.

'He is my prisoner,' snapped the Chatelaine.

'I thought he was your guest,' the king replied smoothly. 'I am not satisfied he has stolen from you. He is no one's man, as I understand it. So Claude Jouvenal is free to go as well.'

All eyes looked to Claude, and he was not sure, for a moment, what to do. Was this meant to be mercy? Was it a gift or his due?

'Come here,' the king said to Claude, and Claude stood up and walked to the king, without looking at his face.

The king grabbed Claude by the shoulders and whispered in his ear, 'Go with care.'

Claude stumbled away, and did not remember to kneel again as he took his leave. He walked past Margriet and out of the door.

Margriet caught up to him, dragging Beatrix with her. Jacquemine stood on the other side of Claude, saying nothing.

When they had put a little distance between them and the abbey, Claude said, 'I owe you my life.'

'You owe me nothing,' Margriet snapped. They all stopped walking. 'I have repaid you for the bravery you showed in fighting my husband's corpse, a week ago, when you might have left us to our fate. As for the mace and sword I promised, that is forfeit, your words in the trial notwithstanding. It is your fault that we failed. You brought the Chatelaine's attention to us too soon. You hid from us the fact that you had stolen the mace in the first place.'

Claude felt as if he had been slapped.

Beatrix put her hand on his arm. 'Don't listen to her—'

'Oh, the traitorous daughter speaks!' Margriet yelled.

Jacquemine said, 'Margriet—'

'I never agreed to deny my husband,' said Beatrix, her voice low and shaking. 'You demand that those who love you must harbour your grudges. You ask too much.'

'Is loyalty too much to ask of a daughter? None of this was for me in the first place! This is how you repay my love?'

'It is an impoverished, twisted love,' Beatrix retorted.

'You have impoverished yourself, you foolish girl. You will starve, if you do not contract the Grief first. How long will it be before you let him in to whatever hovel you inhabit? A day, a month, a year? You can no more close a door to him than you could close your legs. And now you have nothing, and you will die a pauper.'

'I am happy to have nothing,' Beatrix said in a small voice. 'Anyway, I can spin.'

'Ha!' Margriet said. 'And what will you spin? Cobwebs? And where will you spin it, where you can be safe from him? He will get you, Beatrix. He may already have started to get you.'

'She can come with us, Margriet,' whispered Jacquemine. 'If we can get the money.'

Margriet shook her head. 'We have no money for passage. And no time. We will go to Ypres, quickly, today, before sundown. And there we will take you to the beguinage because we cannot afford to buy you a place at a rich abbey. You will join the poor sisters, and work for your keep. You will need strong walls and strong women between you and your dead husband.'

She turned and walked away from them, down the

narrow muddy road to Ypres. There was smoke coming from the chimney of a farm cottage away to the right, and a nuthatch calling from the bushes. And the small, stout figure of Margriet de Vos, trudging through whatever future remained to her. Claude watched her, numbly.

Beside him, Jacquemine embraced Beatrix. 'It will be all right.'

'And you?' Jacquemine turned to Claude.

'I'm going south,' Claude said without thinking about it, because it was what he had done every time he had been broken down into nothing, every time he had found himself alone and penniless. South where one did not need to worry about keeping warm, at least. 'Italy, most likely.'

'So you'll be a man-at-arms again,' Jacquemine said.

'We'll see,' he said, putting on a smile. 'And perhaps in time I can train my left arm to draw a crossbow.'

Jacquemine embraced Claude. She smelled of lavender; Claude smelled of sweat.

As Jacquemine walked after Margriet on the road north to Ypres, Claude stared after them, idly scratching his right arm.

At the king's invitation, the Chatelaine and her retinue stayed the night at the chateau in Ypres. She could hear her hounds circling under the window, whining, and she was ready to be gone with them. She turned Chaerephon away and paced the room.

This was the sort of place she would have, if she were Countess of Flanders. A big cold stone place, with tapestries and fireplaces. But it would not be for her, not most of the time. She would make Monoceros marshal, and let him stay in the stone chateau, and she would stay in Hell where she could check on her husband.

He kept her there, even now, although he was the prisoner. She would never be rid of him, never be free. That was why the Beast was Hell – not because it shat brimstone or belched poison, not because of the revenants, not because it burrowed under the earth. The Beast was Hell because it was home to her husband.

She paced to clear her thoughts of him.

They had given her this room with a great stone fireplace, and a fire within it. Fireplaces were new to her. When she remembered her life before her husband, she remembered a warm country, where fires were outside.

The Chatelaine opened the chest and lifted out the mace. It gleamed in the firelight. Each of the irregular points on the flange caught the orange light like a jewel. Gobhan had wrought it well. This would, she had no doubt, open Hell and all its rooms, even the deepest. That traitor, Gobhan. To think a twisted smith like that could leave her so vulnerable. If he had chosen to open her husband's dungeon – she shook her head. The smith was dead now, and no more worry for her.

She could trust no one. Certainly not the half-wild Chaerephon, who was lying wrapped in his cloak in some dark hallway like a dog or a servant, waiting and watching, although he had been offered a good bed. She had never asked why Chaerephon had betrayed her husband. She had assumed – too much. She was learning, too slowly.

She was tempted to try the other mace on her left arm, but she needed her hand, and Hell could only have one key.

There came a knock at the door.

She put the false mace under a pillow. Then she opened the door.

King Philippe stood there, smiling. She hesitated. He was fully dressed still, his blue cotehardie to his knee embroidered with gold lilies. His face was stern.

'I have no designs on your person,' he said, as if in answer to her expression. 'May I enter?'

She stood back and swept her left arm wide to let him in.

'Are you pleased with the judgment today?'

'Of course, I am pleased that the thief was not rewarded, although he got away with his life,' said the Chatelaine, inclining her head.

'And to the larger question? Do you believe that those women were widows?'

She laughed. 'Do you take me for a scholar, my lord?'

'I know you are no fool. I know you understand that what we have done here today will create fear, and not only among my enemies but also my friends. We have had a bishop declare that the revenants may keep their property, that their family may not inherit, for however long a revenant lasts.'

'A very long time,' said the Chatelaine softly.

'Indeed. And the revenants serve you, because they are creatures of Hell, and you are the mistress of Hell. If you may obtain a knight's property simply by making him a revenant, all of France could be under your control without so much as a battle.'

He looked pleased. Had he designed this outcome?

'That is not my design,' she said. 'I do not wish to control the land of others. I wish to have a demesne of my own, in my own right.'

'Yes, well, about that. I cannot be seen now to be giving you even more power. I have decided to let Count Louis keep Flanders. It would send the wrong message if I used my strength to uproot him rather than support him. And now he is afraid, he will be a more useful idiot.'

She gaped. She had seen the blow coming, but it still hurt when it fell. Nothing for her, then, after all this. 'And what of my reward? What land shall be mine, then, if not Flanders?'

'I have one more task for you, and then if I am pleased, we shall find another count for you to marry. I am pleased with this bishop of Tournai. He did as I asked him today, although his conscience was against it. I like a man who can fight his conscience. I shall ask for his help in declaring your husband dead, and you a widow.'

She bit her lip against the answer she wanted to return. They called him Fortunate but there was no chance behind his success. He took what he wanted, and kept what he wanted. Well, she could do the same.

'And what is this task?'

'You must feed a man to the Beast, and make him a revenant.'

'Which man?'

'Edward, the young king of England.'

'Ha!' she laughed and put her hand over her mouth. 'And shall we make war on him, then?'

'No, of course not. He is a boy of fifteen. Surely you can find a way to manage it. A revenant king would be unlikely to press his claim to the throne of France, don't you think?'

The Chatelaine swallowed. This king would never give her what she wanted.

She must leave him, and find a new place. This time she would not seek an ally. This time she would take what she wanted. She had a few dozen grotesques now, not enough to fight, but she would make more. And she would make more gonners, who could use the black powder to frighten anyone into giving her a little land, a little place to begin anew.

'Tell me,' the king said, walking toward the fire, 'how do you manage it? How did you wrest control of Hell?'

She stared into his back. 'I have always been the Chatelaine of Hell, since my marriage. The keys of Hell are mine by right.'

Tomorrow. Tomorrow she would go to Hell, and close the mouth, and send the Beast deep under the earth. They would go east, a very long way, and they would come up again, somewhere quiet, and begin to rebuild her army.

'And what does your husband say?'

'My husband is no longer able to speak to anyone.'

'He is old, then.'

'Yes,' she said through tight lips. 'He is very old indeed.'

CHAPTER TWENTY-EIGHT

They spoke little and walked fast. Beatrix was sullen. Margriet had nothing to say to anyone and besides, her bowels were clenching and griping. She had to stop three times on the way to relieve them and was glad she'd had nothing but water for hours.

She blamed the abbey food but it was the plague, she knew. She had seen it before: the bowels went, and the skin, and then the brains.

Jacquemine was eager to get her children at Gertrude's mill, but she agreed to walk to Ypres with them first. She had a few things she wanted to barter for, without the children clinging to her skirt, she said. A rich woman, unused to having no servants, unused to having children at her ankles all the time.

Probably she also wanted to be there with Margriet when Margriet delivered her daughter to the nuns. Jacquemine Ooste was kind in a way that drew no attention to itself, and Margriet was grateful, although she did not know how to say so. After Ypres, Margriet would walk with Jacquemine to Gertrude's, for two were better than one on the road. And then – then she would find some solitude, like a dog finding a quiet corner of the yard, in which to die.

'Margriet,' said Jacquemine, as if reading her thoughts, 'will you come with us? To Dunkirk and England?'

'You have no need of a wet nurse now,' said Margriet dully. She had a dry headache now to go with the wrench in her guts.

'We cannot pay a servant, until we find some work, or some man to marry me.'

'I am surprised you do not return to Bruges, where people know you, and some would help you.'

'Yes, but in Bruges I will fear the count's retribution for my husband's actions,' said Jacquemine with a sigh. 'And now I have made an enemy of the Chatelaine, too. I will never feel safe, not until I put the Channel between my children and Flanders.'

At that, Beatrix walked faster, putting more strides between them as if she did not want to listen.

The streets of Ypres were strongly shadowed. A dog barked and Margriet started. She was still unused to the sound of dogs; in Bruges they had all been dead for weeks, along with everything else on four legs.

Two chimeras approached, of the kind called men-of-arms, with bits of armour breaking through their skin – but no, as they passed, Margriet could see they were men of about their own age, with pieces of metal sewn into their leather aketons and caps. To hell with her dim eyesight.

'They would have fooled the Chatelaine herself,' said Jacquemine.

Margriet was startled. It had not been her eyesight alone

that had created the illusion. Would the Chatelaine have been fooled? Could she be?

She stopped walking.

'What is it?' Jacquemine asked.

'I need one more favour, Vrouwe Ooste,' Margriet said. 'Before we part ways.'

'If it is within my power, name it.'

Margriet thought as quickly as she could through her raging headache. If men could be made to look like the Chatelaine's chimeras, could not a group of women? The helmets would disguise them perfectly. They could be in and out of the Hellbeast without anyone knowing. They could recover what had been stolen from them.

Was it madness? Was her brain plague-addled already?

They would need someone with an ability to get past locked doors, and to fight their way past guards. Claude.

'Margriet, what is it?'

Beatrix turned at last, and frowned at her.

'I need – I need to get a message to Claude.'

Jacquemine's eyebrows raised. 'Claude! Is this to salve your conscience?'

Margriet nodded. 'After a fashion.'

'Mother—'

Margriet took three long steps toward her, the world reeling as she did so. She grabbed on to her daughter's shoulders, in part to keep herself upright.

'Beatrix, what if I did not have to lock you away after all. What if there were another way to get your inheritance?'

Beatrix's brown eyes were brim-full of sadness, and yet there was a gleam in them, too. A glimmer of a future without a husband, if the girl would but let herself see it.

'Mother, you're mad.'

'Yes, but listen,' said Margriet absently. She scratched her neck under her wimple.

A long piece of grey skin came off in her hands.

Beatrix stared and Margriet saw the understanding in her daughter's face. A worse sentence than death itself, to see her daughter grieve again.

Jacquemine grasped the edge of Margriet's wimple and pulled it away, yanked it off her body.

'Dear God,' she said. 'Dear God in heaven, Margriet. The skin – your neck—'

Margriet swallowed. 'Is it bad?'

'It is the plague!' Jacquemine hissed.

Beatrix took Margriet's hands and looked in her eyes. It had been a long time since Margriet had looked in her daughter's eyes for more than a moment, years perhaps. This, more than anything, made Margriet want to weep.

'It's true,' she said. 'I have the plague. I am in no pain. Well, not much pain. But I need your help. God has given me an idea. We are going to recover your inheritance, Beatrix. I will see you safe and provided for, before I go. I will have my rights before I go. God has shown me how to do it.'

A hundred different expressions crossed Beatrix's face, and all of them were some form of pain.

Jacquemine put her hands on her hips. 'But when – Margriet de Vos, where did you see your husband in Bruges? Where was it?'

There was to be no more denying it, then. She was a dying woman now. Margriet took a long, painful breath.

'He tricked me. He entered the house, taking my words as permission although I did not mean them that way. A villain, even in death.'

'Before you came to me? Before you nursed my child?'

Margriet frowned. 'It does not pass to the child.'

'How could you know? How many wet nurses have you known who contracted the plague from a revenant and then watched to see how the curse would manifest in the child in the months, the years afterward?' Jacquemine's voice was shrill; she put her hand to her mouth.

'I did not mean any harm to Jacob. You know I love him as if he were my own.'

'I have seen how you love your own,' Jacquemine said more quietly, her eyes flashing. 'I should have known better than to listen to one word from you. You have always been a stubborn fool and you have brought me great misfortune. When we get to the mill, I will take my children and go, and you will not come near them, lest you – lest you frighten the wits out of them.'

The gorge rose up to Margriet's mouth and she managed nothing better than a nod.

They found a messenger at The Deer. He charged twice what he ought to have, but these were dangerous times.

'Find a young mercenary named Claude Jouvenal, in Lille, and tell him to come to Ypres, to meet me at The Deer tomorrow.'

'No,' said Jacquemine. 'Tell Claude to meet us at the mill. Beatrix will know which one.'

Margriet nodded. 'All right. Yes. At the mill. Bring Claude there and I will pay you the same again.'

'And if this person will not come?' the messenger asked.

'Tell Claude—' Margriet rubbed her tingling hands together. 'Tell Claude I am dying. And I need help, urgently. Tell Claude there is another chance at the reward. Go!'

The messenger rode off, not fast enough for Margriet's wishes.

They decided to stay at the Deer for a night after all, for the sake of Margriet's tired legs, and because Claude would not get the message until that night anyway. Beatrix and Jacquemine asked Margriet for her plan, but she begged them to wait until the morning, said she did not have the strength to talk now, which was for the most part true. She wanted to think, first.

At the Deer, she ate nothing but a bit of bread and water, and slept sitting on the privy, leaning against the wall in the cold. Jacquemine did not want her in the bed with her, and Margriet did not have the strength to go up and down the stairs to the privy with each clench of her guts.

Beatrix thought she heard, from time to time, the roar of a metal dragon, the squelch of mud erupting, the boom of thunder deep in the earth. Her distaff was still at Gertrude's and yet with each step they took toward it, she relived the visions it had shown her.

These visions were true, in some way. They were not true now. But she had asked the Nix to tell her what would come for them, and so the distaff was showing her – some future. Must it come to pass? Surely God had ordained all things – and yet, if that were so, he had also ordained that Beatrix should see these sights, and do what she could to prevent them.

She shook her head. What could she do? She could not even stop her own mother from dying. Mother, whose brain was clearly addled already, who was convinced that she could get the inheritance back. Beatrix could not care less about her father's sack of goods if it were a sack of offal. She hated to think of good people like Gertrude Vermeulin cowering in fear when the metal dragon came. And all this beautiful country, which Beatrix had only just started to see!

She was grateful, yes, in spite of everything, that she had at least this one day to walk this beautiful world, that she was not shut up in the beguinage. She was – dear God, she was happy to be alive.

They bought bread, meat, and apples from the Deer, and bought a new flask to share between them and filled it with ale. Margriet's purse was getting light. But if God smiled upon her enterprise, she would have plenty in a few days' time. Of course, in a few days' time she would also be dead, or close to it.

Her stomach took a bit of bread and small ale without complaining, which she counted as a good omen. Her hands and feet tingled, and she itched everywhere. For now at least, all the patches of dead skin were hidden under her wimple or her kirtle (there was a fresh patch on her ribcage), which was a mercy. Jacquemine and Beatrix knew, though.

Margriet on her weak legs struggled to stay abreast of them. It had rained in the night and the road clung to their shoes.

The millrace gurgled merrily down the slope toward the little dark building where Gertrude and the children waited. It was otherwise quiet as they approached, and Margriet almost expected another pot to fly from the window. The quiet annoyed her, and she called, 'Gertrude! We are here!'

They took a few more steps and the door creaked open. Gertrude put her face to the crack, then opened the door.

'Thank God and all His saints,' she said. 'I was beginning to think you would be gone a week.'

'What's happened?' Jacquemine asked sharply. 'Where are the children?'

'They're fine, fine,' Gertrude said, but tears welled in her eyes and she began to blubber and fell, hanging on the door.

'Saints save us,' Jacquemine muttered, and elbowed her way past Gertrude, into the mill. 'Agatha? Jacob?'

Beatrix gave Gertrude her hand and helped her up.

'Come on,' she said, and pulled her into the mill.

'Where are they?' Jacquemine shrieked.

Gertrude pointed toward the back of the mill.

'In the privy,' she blubbered.

'What, both of them?' Margriet asked. 'Jacob, too?'

Jacquemine darted back out the door.

She returned in a moment with a child under each arm, both of them blubbering like Gertrude. 'She put them both in and barred the door with a rock,' Jacquemine muttered.

'What in the name of Christ were you thinking, foolish woman?' Margriet asked.

Gertrude put her head in her hands. 'I wanted to keep them safe. I kept thinking I heard the hounds coming, and that's where I was, and I was safe. I stayed in with them at first, but then I thought I should stay here to distract the hounds when they came. I was going to run off so they would chase me. And so I just went in every now and again to bring them food and water and cuddle them a little. I was so afraid.'

'God have mercy on you, Gertrude, for I cannot,'

Jacquemine said, but there was nothing more to say, and her voice had gentled now that she had her two children, one on either side, an arm over each.

Beatrix put her arm around Gertrude.

Margriet wanted desperately to kiss each of the children on their foreheads, on this the last day she would ever see them. These children who had nursed from her breasts, these children she knew like her own mind, from their eyelashes to their toenails. Lost to her now, like all else. Would she see them in Paradise? She might not recognize them; they would doubtless be grown, then, perhaps even old.

Margriet told Gertrude about the trial while Jacquemine gave the children apples and rocked them until they both fell asleep. She leaned against the wall of the mill, her face wan.

'We'll wait here until they wake,' she whispered.

'And then you're all going again,' said Gertrude.

Margriet shook her head. 'Vrouwe Ooste is going to Dunkirk, with the children. But Beatrix and I will wait here for Claude for another day or two, if you are willing.'

CHAPTER TWENTY-NINE

The Chatelaine rode home on her pale palfrey, its hair braided with red and yellow ribbons. This horse had been with her in Hell two years now, stabled in one of the narrow chambers with uneven floors that were useless for anything else, and it was starting to show signs of it: it was ever more bony, its eyes wild, its nostrils flared. She had not given it a name, not even in secret, for she knew well enough that this beast might soon be destined for the fires of Hell, to make a chimera.

The mantis-man and roach-man had gone before them. Her hounds ran alongside, yapping with delight in the cool, bright day. Their human faces grimaced at Chaerephon where he sat. He made them nervous, and this pleased him.

'You are out of humour,' he said mildly.

'If you hadn't noticed, we have lost all hope of reward from the king, the ally we have served two years now. We are betrayed.'

'Not so. He asked you to do a task for him. Kings only ask their most trusted favourites to do their dirtiest business. *Ergo*, he is showing you favour.'

'He is showing me who is king,' she retorted.

'Yes. And did you ever challenge that? At the very beginning, when you came out of the earth, you came looking for a man to bestow land upon you, instead of seizing land for your own.'

'Perhaps that was an error. It was your advice, as I recall.'

'And still good advice. What could you have done, with your revenants? Slowly throttle Bruges, the greatest and richest city of Europe, into grey death? Leave it waste? If you want land, good land occupied by living people to farm and mine and trade, you need to earn it, not conquer it.'

'Unless I can make better weapons, and win faster.'

'Yes,' said Chaerephon. 'Or you could do as the king asks, and gain his trust.'

The Chatelaine frowned. She would have thought Chaerephon, of all people, would understand. It was one thing to send her armies to war alongside Philippe as an ally, even as a vassal. It was another to put Hell itself at his command, to make revenants of whomever he wished. Who would truly hold the key, then, even if it remained upon her hand?

They were nearly home now. Hell was before them, its mouth shut tight, its eyes closed nearly completely, with just a slit of red light where the lashless lids met. The Beast seemed to have piled up fresh earth around itself in a kind of burrow.

The Chatelaine dismounted, strode to the mouth and put her mace to the lock at one side of the Beast's bridle. She used her left hand to twist the mace, the end of which rotated until the great bridle creaked open and the sulphurous red mouth yawned before them.

The sooner they were gone from here, the better.

She walked her palfrey into the mouth, the hounds trotting alongside on the thick red tongue as if it were a Roman road.

She twisted the mace again to close the mouth, and then they were enclosed inside the beast. The air here was warm and close; safe.

'Where should we go, Chaerephon?' she asked.

'You are running away, then?'

'I am finding a new place, where I will be the mistress. No more asking for scraps.'

Chaerephon shrugged. 'If you are determined to give up the work of these two years—'

'Not give it up. We have dozens of grotesques now, and more revenants than before. We have learned a great deal about war and we are perfecting the black-powder weapons. We will be stronger the next time.'

Chaerephon sighed. 'Then let us find a place where the people are more civilized, and the weather is warmer.'

The Chatelaine left her mace in the bridle and said to the Beast in the language she had forbidden, 'Go south. South and east, until you come to water.'

The Beast shuddered but did not move.

'Go now,' she said. 'Down into the earth. I hold the keys of Hell. You must obey.'

This time the Beast did not so much as shudder.

'It will not obey,' she whispered, hearing the high note of panic in her own voice. 'Chaerephon, what do I do?'

'Perhaps it is injured,' he said. 'Let us go out again and see what we can see.'

For a moment the Chatelaine wondered whether the Beast would never listen to her again, whether they were trapped in Hell forever. But it opened its mouth obligingly, letting the daylight in.

She sent the dogs scampering and whimpering inside, and she and Chaerephon stepped out into the cold world. Chaerephon nosed his way around the Hellbeast's mouth, to the side of its head, where there was a very narrow space between its body and the wall of its burrow.

'In there?' the Chatelaine asked. 'We'll be buried alive if it so much as sneezes.'

'Wait for me, then,' he said, and was hidden behind the earth.

In a moment he came out again.

'I think you will find this worth seeing with your own eyes,' said Chaerephon.

They squeezed in. The fur of the Beast was as slick as velvet. The Chatelaine ran her hand along it to keep herself upright in the shifting tunnel, until her hand came to a matted protuberance. She looked, and saw the sleek body of a tick, the size of a rat. She winced and kept her hands to herself.

'Here,' said Chaerephon. 'Step very carefully.'

He squeezed over into the body of the beast to make room for her to come beside him. There beside the Beast were three pale eggs as large as boulders, the shells like ivory.

'What are these?' said the Chatelaine. 'Surely not.'

'Your husband,' said Chaerephon carefully, 'was always in the habit of calling the Hellbeast "she". "Hell is a female creature", he used to say.'

'But what – what is in the eggs?'

'I would very much like to see them hatch. Hmm. That is fascinating.'

'Indeed, that is one word for it.'

'Eggs! Who would have thought it, of a furred creature? Just like the – what was the new name the king gave it? The Hochepot, in your menagerie.'

The fool was in love with the sound of his own voice. The Beast had eggs. A nesting creature would not be easy to move. They were stuck here, and meanwhile the King of France would be sending an army against them. Philippe wanted control of the Beast, and if he could not control it through the Chatelaine, he would take it. Soon she would be in a dungeon somewhere, and God knew what would happen if the King of France was foolish enough to find and free her husband.

'The question is,' said Chaerephon, 'if Hell is the mother, then who is the father?'

She did not care to know, or even to wonder.

'Can we smash them with our hands?' she whispered, in French, although she was not entirely confident the Beast had not learned French. It only obeyed the language of Hell, and spoke no word itself. 'Shall I fetch a rock?'

The Beast rumbled and earth fell onto their heads.

Chaerephon put his fingers to his lips. 'I would not harm Hell's young, not for all of Midas's gold.'

'Then what?'

'Eggs hatch. We wait.'

'But for how long?' she asked. 'We don't know how close they are to hatching. Once they hatch, she may not want to move, even then.'

The Chatelaine shut her eyes. How long could she stall with Philippe? She could pretend to be on his side, pretend to be preparing to take the King of England. She could even tell the truth about the Hellbeast and the eggs, although she did not want to give Philippe any information he might try to use to his advantage.

Without saying another word to Chaerephon, she walked toward the burrow's exit and waited for him to follow. She had been so pleased when he took her side. He had even encouraged her to act against her husband; without him, she might have waited longer.

Had he known about the eggs? Was it all a plot against her?

A thought came to her, a beautiful, horrible thought. Whatever hatched from those eggs would be hers, hers to guide and guard from birth. Hellbeasts of her own, whose loyalty was not in doubt. She would not need a key for them. She would make them into a new army, her third army.

The only thing she could trust was strength. She would need more chimeras, too, and more powerful ones. She needed weapons that could level a city. She would put Philippe off as long as she could, but in the meantime she would get stronger.

'While we wait, I want to make more gonners, better ones, and more black powder,' she said to Chaerephon over her shoulder. 'Set the mantis-men to scraping the bat grime off the walls of the great hall. I've never been so happy that the Beast shits brimstone. But we'll need more charcoal. Check on our burners and send riders out farther this time to collect more from the smithies and forges.'

CHAPTER THIRTY

The wait for Claude turned out to be nearly two days. Margriet found herself feeling grateful for the chance to think and to rest, and that gratitude irritated her. She should begrudge the time. Her body betrayed her in some new way with each day that passed, and no amount of rest would stop the plague from taking her. Meanwhile, the Chatelaine might decide to burrow back underground, taking Beatrix's inheritance with her.

Jacquemine waited with them. She and Gertrude took care of the food, and chattered away like the old friends they were. Beatrix spent her time with the children, smiling and playing with them, but her face couldn't hide her grief. Margriet avoided her gaze whenever possible. She needed to think. She had work to do.

None of them asked what her plan was, or what she wanted with Claude, which was just as well. She had the sense that none of them even expected their mercenary to come. They were waiting, but not for that. Waiting for Margriet to die.

But on the afternoon of the second day, someone hallooed outside the door. Gertrude flinched.

'That's Claude's voice,' Margriet said, and pushed herself onto her unsteady feet. She opened the door to Claude and the messenger.

Claude was wearing mail, with a helmet under his arm. He looked at her with wary concern.

'You came,' she said, and tossed the messenger his coin. 'Come in, Claude, and have some food.'

Claude grabbed her arm. 'Margriet. What did you mean by your message?'

Margriet pulled away, walked into the mill where it was dim. The sun was shining today; it made her head hurt.

'I have a task for you,' she said.

'Margriet,' hissed Jacquemine. 'You will tell him. There is no point now in lying.'

Margriet shut her eyes. Jacquemine was right. Claude would see it for himself soon enough. Margriet might start to gibber and screech at imaginings, or fall to the floor and shake. What did it matter if the whole world knew? Beatrix knew, and that was the hardest thing, and it was done.

'You have the plague,' said Claude.

Margriet looked up, caught Claude's eye. It had not been a question.

'Yes,' Margriet whispered. 'Keep your voice low. No need to frighten the children.'

'I should have guessed earlier,' said Claude. 'I saw you touch a hot cake and not notice it. Since Bruges, then?'

Margriet nodded. All was made plain now.

Claude stared in disbelief while Margriet told him why she'd summoned him.

'We will go to Hell, you and I, and get the sack with my husband's wealth in it.'

The plague must have reached Margriet's brain already.

'That is your plan? It's madness. That's why you sent for me? You want me to fight anyone who needs fighting? You forget. My sword arm is wounded.'

'You fought my husband well enough,' Margriet said quietly. 'But anyway, I hope there will be no fighting. I want you because you have been there and know what Hell is like, inside. And I want you to get past any locked doors.'

'I do not have the key, or do you forget?'

'Of course, I don't forget,' Margriet snapped. 'But you managed to steal a suit of armour from what was doubtless a locked chest under guard.'

Yes, he remembered the click of the padlock in his hand, the strange magic of it. Margriet had squirrelled her questions about that away. She probably only thought him a lockpick.

'Somehow,' Margriet said, 'you escaped from Hell before. If anyone can get me into Hell, you can. Don't you want to get the mace?'

'Yes, and I would also like to fetch the golden fleece from Colchis and the waters of youth from Prester John's kingdom and Holy Grail from the castle of the Fisher King. What you ask is not possible. I have been in the Hellbeast. I have been a prisoner there. You will not succeed.'

'But you got out,' said Margriet. Her shrewish eyes were narrowed. Damn her. She thought she knew everything. She knew nothing.

'God's teeth, woman. Yes, I got out. I was invited in, taken with some of the best fighters in my company. I will tell you what I learned while I was there. The Chatelaine said we were guests, at first, and set about trying to convince us that we should become chimeras. One of my comrades was made into something she called a gonner: she gave him a metal arm that shot bolts using an explosion of black powder. It worked like a charm. We all watched him shoot targets in the great belly of the Beast. When he missed, the Beast would rumble, but that was all. It has a hide like iron.'

'I am not suggesting we try to cut its hide.'

'No? And how would you get in and out? Through its mouth? There came a day when I thought that I, too, would let the Chatelaine choose a weapon for me. But that day, my comrade was practising, and the powder exploded too wildly and he was killed. Blown to little bloody bits.'

'Yes,' said Margriet, which was the last thing Claude expected her to say. 'I saw something like that, before the gates of Bruges, the day – the day we left. I saw chimeras with metal arms attack the gate, and blow themselves up in the process. But you found your way out.'

'Only because I convinced a smith to make me the mace, which took him many days. The mouth is shut in an iron contraption like a bridle. The Chatelaine is the only one who can open it.'

'How will you get out?' Gertrude asked.

'By then,' Margriet said, 'we will have the mace, won't we?'

Again they looked at each other, and again were silent.

'Even if I were to get in,' Claude began, and stopped. He did not like this scheming; there were so many cracks in it. Yet could he live the rest of his life like this? Would he have to cut off his right arm to stop this infernal itch? And would that be enough to stop it, this phantom torture that did not need mere flesh to make itself known?

'If we were to get in,' he said, 'we'd need weapons, and there are none to be had anywhere.'

'There, I can help you,' Gertrude said.

'You?' Claude asked.

'Why not? We have a scythe, and we have hooks and hoes and all manner of things that can be beaten into shape. We will beat our ploughshares into swords, or something sharp to poke people with anyway.'

They stared at her.

'Good,' said Margriet roughly. 'You can also help us make ourselves look like chimeras.'

'Not me,' Claude said, shaking his head. 'I don't wish to be anything but myself.'

'You are the best known there of any of us!' snorted Margriet. 'You will be recognized. At least wear a helm or something to cover your face.'

'All right,' Claude said, and nodded. 'So long as I can see well enough to fight, well enough to see which are my enemies and my friends.'

'You're all mad,' said Jacquemine.

Beatrix knew it was mad. Jacquemine was right. It was death, probably. And yet it was better than a life locked away, listening to her husband call her name every night.

'You propose to raid Hell,' said Claude slowly, 'with one spinster, one wounded man-at-arms who can barely hold a knife, and one wet nurse who is half-dead of plague.'

'No,' Mother said. 'The spinster stays here.'

Beatrix looked up. So, Mother didn't want her, after all. She was to be disposed of, again.

'If you wish to kill yourself,' Claude said, in a soft, infuriating voice, 'there are easier ways.'

'Why would I want to kill myself?' Margriet retorted. 'I'll be dead in weeks anyway. But I want to see Beatrix settled before I go.'

'As likely to see her a revenant, if you bring her to the Beast,' said Claude.

'That's why she isn't going near.'

Beatrix frowned. 'What do you mean? It's a mad plan, it's suicide, but I have nothing to live for anyway. If you want me, Mother, I'll do it.'

Mother smiled at her. 'That's my girl. But it is too dangerous for you.'

Beatrix shook her head. They were worried about Baltazar. But she had met Baltazar three times – the night of the fireflies, the night of the owl, and the trial – and three times she had denied him, or nearly had. If Mother was going into Hell, then she would need help.

'I'm not going inside,' she said. 'But I will be near. I will call the revenants out.'

They all looked at the distaff, leaning against the wall.

'All of them?' Gertrude whispered.

Beatrix nodded. 'All of them, all of them who are in the Beast that night anyway. It will create confusion, and the mouth of Hell will open, and you can get in unnoticed. And you will have less to deal with, inside.'

'Draw them out,' Claude said, as pale and as quiet as Beatrix, her face like an ash that might flame up any moment. 'Draw them to where?'

Beatrix swallowed. She would need to call them to

herself. 'They can't hurt me. Only Baltazar can, and I can deal with him. I've done it before.'

'They can send you mad,' Margriet said. 'Or drive you into a river, or off a cliff.'

'This is Flanders,' said Gertrude. 'There are no cliffs.'

'You, too?' Margriet whirled on her.

'If Beatrix wants to do this, I think we should not stand in her way,' Gertrude said, and walked over to sit beside Beatrix and take her hand in her own. 'I know she can fight off a whole army of ghosts.'

'Not Baltazar,' Margriet retorted. 'If she calls them all, Baltazar will be among them.'

'What is one dead husband, Mother?' Beatrix said.

'If he knows where you are, the Chatelaine will soon know it, and send her hounds after you, or something worse.'

'I will do it,' said Beatrix, her jaw set. 'If getting my inheritance is what will bring you peace in your last days with us, Mother, I will help. Father's wealth is for me, you said. It is mine. Therefore it is mine to claim as my right. It is only just.'

Mother stared at her for a long time, and then she laughed.

'My girl,' she said. 'My dazzling girl. Deep waters, but with something like a Nix in them, just waiting to flash up into the air. Yes, it is your right. You shall do it. And Claude and I will go inside.'

'And what about me?' Gertrude asked.

'You!' Mother said. 'Who would go to Hell for a lark? We have business with the Chatelaine.'

'My children's murderer,' said Gertrude, her eyes now fever-bright.

'Will you smack her with a frying pan?' Claude asked, smiling.

'Her frying pan or your sword would be about equal use against that hellkite and her minions,' Mother grumbled. 'Come to think of it, why shouldn't Gertrude settle her debt with the Chatelaine? Is it not customary for a lord to pay restitution for the actions of his troops? And the Chatelaine owes Gertrude a great deal.'

They all stayed quiet for a moment. The air still smelled of burning.

'I have as much cause as you to see the Chatelaine brought low,' Gertrude said. 'I cannot stay here hiding until they come and cart me away. Please.'

'We are in your debt for the food and shelter,' Margriet said slowly. 'And so it seems to me that if you name this as your payment, if you truly want to come with us, that is your choice. But do you have the courage? What if we are set upon on the journey?'

'Frying pan,' Claude mumbled with the cup to his mouth.

The children woke and Gertrude and Jacquemine set about preparing the day's meal, and Beatrix took up the distaff and excused herself.

Outside, the day was cold, with the sun slanting through the trees on the horizon. It was quiet. Here, at last, let this distaff be of some use.

She shut her eyes and held the distaff out in front of her. Will we succeed? Will we get the mace, and the rest of it, and get out alive?

Her vision blurred and she saw a great fire, and Gertrude walking away from it, her face bloody and sooty, but smiling, and in her hand was Willem's sack.

Beatrix took a step toward the vision, but Gertrude vanished.

Then the ground erupted and there was the wail of something horrible coming from above, and the ground boomed again. This was another vision, another possibility?

Another screeching wail and something hit her and she fell to the ground.

Someone was shaking her, calling her name.

She looked up into the faces of Mother and Jacquemine.

'Foolish girl!' Mother said.

Beatrix shook her head. 'I have seen a vision, Mother. I think we shall succeed. But the distaff always wants to show me another vision, every time I think of the future. It is as if that vision is so strong, so stamped on the future memory of this land, that I cannot help but call it to mind. I have seen again this vision of terrible war, of chimeras and thundering fire. Weapons of the Chatelaine's, I think. She will bring war the like of which we have never seen. All of Flanders turned to mud, flattened by this horrible war. Burned to the ground. All of it.'

Margriet frowned. 'Then we must get far away from here, as soon as we have got our due. You must go, Jacquemine Ooste, as quickly as you can.'

But Jacquemine was shaking her head, her face so pale it was nearly grey.

'You have seen what the Chatelaine can do,' she said. 'If you can weaken her, if a band of women can raid Hell and live, then perhaps the people of Ypres and Roeselare and Poperinge will rise up. Do you think so? Do you think they might?'

Mother nodded. 'Yes. We have seen them rise before, haven't we?'

'I cannot bring the children to Hell, and I cannot risk leaving them an orphan, but I will stay and help you until you are ready. I – I am a good hand with a needle!' She laughed. 'Agatha is doing better. We can wait a few more days. I will help make your disguises, and cook your food.'

'But the moment we leave,' Mother said, 'you must take the children and go, quickly. If we fail, the Chatelaine may send her hounds, looking for our friends.'

Jacquemine Ooste nodded, her face set.

'Vrouwe Ooste,' said Beatrix wonderingly.

Jacquemine knelt by her and smiled, taking her hand. 'This is what we have always been taught, Beatrix de Vos. It is in the tradition of Bruges, in the tradition of our fathers, who always found a way to bite the hunter's hand once the trap had sprung. Has your mother never told you the stories of the Matins of Bruges of 1302, when the women of our city fought off the French soldiers with rocks and bricks?'

CHAPTER THIRTY-ONE

Margriet sat and brooded while Gertrude and Beatrix set about making a pottage with some uncertain mushrooms and cress.

She rubbed her chin with the back of her hand. There was a patch of three or four stiff hairs poking through, just long enough to be annoying. Her fingertips could not feel the hairs, only the skin on the back of her hand. That annoyed her, too. She missed her tweezers, sitting in her little chest in the Ooste house. She missed chairs and beds. She missed the bells of Our Lady's church. She missed Bruges, when it came to it: the city where she was born, where she had lived her whole life. The greatest city in Christendom, it had been, until the Chatelaine had decided to strangle it.

'Anyway,' Margriet said, pulling her hands away from her chin with a tiny act of will, as though someone had spoken, 'has anyone got any tweezers?' she asked.

Beatrix laughed. 'Tweezers, Mother? You're worried about your eyebrows at a time like this?'

'Chin hair,' Margriet grumbled. 'It's not about how it looks. It's annoying, that's all.'

'I know exactly what you mean,' said Gertrude, who was between Beatrix's age and Margriet's. 'You are too young to know but one day you'll understand. Margriet, I had some lovely tweezers, but they were in the house. If they are still there, they are somewhere in the ashes.'

'Bah, never mind,' said Margriet.

'I could make you something,' Gertrude said.

Margriet waved her away. 'I can live with a beard if need be.'

Claude was looking at her. His own chin was narrow, little bird bones coming to a sharp point beneath smooth, sun-brown skin.

'What did you do about it?' Margriet wondered aloud. 'Didn't they ever ask why you never shaved?'

Claude raised his eyebrows. 'Everyone always wants to know the most boring things. How I pissed. How I shaved. Nobody wants to know how I shot eleven soldiers with only ten bolts at the battle of Zappolino.'

Impudent fool. As if it were a thing to be proud of, killing people. As if any child couldn't do it, if they were forced. Margriet shrugged. 'I assume you slaughtered people, as mercenaries are paid to do.'

There was a pause.

'Well, I want to know all of it,' Beatrix said. 'The soldier parts and the other things. I guess you could just pretend to shave, couldn't you?'

Claude shook his head. 'I didn't care to. When I was very young, though, I made a false beard. A useful thing, sometimes. Glued on with pitch in spirits.'

'It sounds like a hassle,' Jacquemine said.

'It was a pain in the arse,' Claude answered with a grin. 'Which is why I stopped doing it. But for a while, I got used to it. No more a pain than braiding one's hair or plucking one's eyebrows or whatever it is women do.'

'Yes, but if our hair comes tumbling down out of its braids, we won't be—' said Gertrude loudly. She said everything loudly. She was loud just sitting there. The women looked at each other. 'Anyway,' she continued, red in her round face, 'what I mean is that it would matter so much, that beard. I imagine it must have always been a worry. I admire you. For being able to fight and everything and keep everything else perfect. Keep your breasts and everything hidden and whatnot.'

'Not much to hide,' Claude said with another grin. 'Not like you and Margriet. How do you walk around like that? Isn't it a great weight? Don't they flop around? I don't know how you manage it.'

'We all have our crosses to bear,' Gertrude said seriously, with a heavy sigh, and Beatrix giggled and Claude laughed out loud like a soldier, and even Margriet had to smile.

'Come on, then,' said Margriet, patting her lap. 'Agatha, come over. Who wants to hear a story?'

'Will you tell us about Reynard?' Agatha asked, scrambling over.

Margriet looked up at her daughter. She wanted to show her in her face that she forgave her, that she understood. But she knew how her own face looked. It scowled. It grimaced. It was incapable of anything kinder.

'What would you like to hear, Beatrix?' she asked. 'Reynard, or something else?'

'Reynard, always,' Beatrix said with a little smile.

'Sometimes,' Margriet said, 'you think you know what an animal will be like, because of its kind. So you think all foxes are tricky. Did you know that Frenchmen won't even say the word *goupil*, the word for fox in their language? They think it is unlucky. So they call them *renard* instead. Isn't that silly? I think Reynard laughs.'

'I am not afraid to say it,' said Agatha. '*Goupil*. Is that right?'

'That is right,' said Margriet. 'But my name is Fox, too, isn't it? Margriet de Vos, Margriet the fox. Yet I am not tricky at all.'

'But you have whiskers,' Agatha said with a grin and put her little finger to Margriet's chin.

Claude and Beatrix roared with laughter.

Margriet kissed Agatha's forehead, held her close, for what might be the last time. She nuzzled her with her whiskered chin. A few more days and she would be dead. She would go to her grave with whiskers on her chin. At the Day of Judgment, when her body was raised, would it go to Paradise with whiskers on her chin? Or would all her imperfections be taken away? If God took away Margriet's imperfections, she would look nothing like herself.

The chausses were still too big. As he had walked in the grey, drizzly pre-dawn from Lille, following the surly messenger, the blue wool had gapped and flapped around Claude's thighs. Worse than that, the chausses were much too long. He had to roll the tops, which meant he was walking around with extra itchy, sweaty fabric near his crotch. And the laces at the tops didn't fasten properly, so the whole contraption kept slipping down.

He was hungry. His legs were wet with this clinging cold mist, and his wounded foot ached, and his arm itched. By the time he had arrived at the mill, his initial surprise and delight at Monoceros's gift of the heavy hauberk, gauntlets and helmet had vanished, and he was in a foul temper.

Strange to say, his mood had lifted. Yes, it was suicide, this plan of Margriet's. But it was a plan. There was something familiar about preparing for a raid. He had never quite agreed to Margriet's plan, never quite said yes. He didn't need to. Margriet knew, well enough, that he would not refuse.

Claude borrowed a bone needle from Jacquemine Ooste and sat, stitching the chausses, making them fit.

The first law of going into battle: make sure your underthings don't ride up.

He smiled. Janos would have liked that.

The true first law, of course, was to make sure you weren't bringing your own death with you, because death had a way of spreading to one's comrades.

He stretched out his weak right hand, the hand that shook with the needle in it.

'I can mend them for you,' Beatrix said.

Claude shook his head. 'A man-at-arms knows perfectly well how to handle a needle.'

His foul mood was still there, lurking.

He put the needle in its case, sighed. Then he rummaged through his bundle.

'Listen,' Claude said, and tossed the heavy gauntlets to where Margriet and Beatrix sat, drawing with bits of charcoal on the floor, trying to think of what they could wear to look like chimeras. 'These gauntlets don't fit me at all. You have bigger hands, Margriet. Would you like them? Or you could sell them.'

Margriet ran her knobby fingers over them. They were

steel, with little brass pieces on the knuckles in the shapes of beasts.

'What are these?' Margriet asked, running a fingertip over them.

'They're to protect your hand, mainly. They're called gadlings. Usually they are just little knobs or bits of steel. Sometimes they make them in shapes, animals and whatnot. A bit showy, aren't they?'

'They aren't even real beasts. This one is a leopard or something with wings. This bird – well, I've never seen any bird like this.'

'Are you saying you want me to steal you gauntlets with gadlings that resemble the courtyard chickens of Bruges, or some other animal with which your vast experience has made you familiar?'

That seemed to quiet her, for a moment at least. Margriet put the gauntlets on slowly and stretched out her fingers in them.

'They fit well,' she said. 'They looked far too big but they fit rather well.'

Claude had been sure at first that Margriet's message that she was dying and needed his help was at least part lie, and then on the road he had begun to remember things like the hot cake, and to wonder. Although even if Margriet were dying, he did not know what she wanted him for. But truth be told, he was curious, and Italy would wait.

Of all the things he had thought Margriet might ask of him, he had never considered it might be a plan to raid Hell. And now they were sitting on the floor drawing disguises, like monks drawing monsters in the margins of books.

He looked down at the scratched drawing of a stick figure with a cauldron on its head, and grimaced.

'It'll be a bear to wear, unless we can make it lighter than it looks,' Claude said. 'Talking of beards has given me an idea. Have you seen some of the animal chimeras? If I can get some fur and fix it on my face and hands, and wear my mail and helmet—'

'Not strange enough,' said Margriet.

'I don't know if you have forgotten, but we do not actually have access to the forges of Hell,' Claude snapped.

'We have brains,' Margriet snapped back. 'What could you wear on your head other than a helmet?'

'What about horns?' asked Gertrude. 'There are two drinking horns in the little church across the field. I am sure even now they are in the sacristy.'

'You would steal from a church?' Beatrix asked.

'Not steal. Borrow. I know the priest. Or I did, when we were young.' Gertrude smiled, and Margriet raised her eyebrows. 'They have silver work but only on the edges, and I think it could be hidden.'

'All right,' Claude said. If Gertrude got talking about her romances, they would be here an hour. 'Then where shall I put them? If I can get a leather coif, we could make two holes and poke them through.'

'But how will you affix the fur?' Beatrix asked. 'We don't have pitch-in-spirits.'

'I have some birdlime,' Gertrude said. 'Perhaps—'

Claude shook his head. He had tried birdlime, with his first false beard, at fourteen. It had been a messy business, and the hair had come off when he sweated. 'I should be able to get pitch-in-spirits in Ypres, at the apothecary.'

'In Ypres?' Margriet asked.

Claude nodded. 'I won't be long, and can get anything else we need, while two of you fetch the horns. I'll need money, or something to trade.'

'Have your food first,' said Gertrude.

CHAPTER THIRTY-TWO

The Chatelaine stood and everyone else in Hell's great hall stood as well, if they had legs to stand upon.

'Let us eat and drink, and give thanks for our victories,' she said.

The chimeras cheered, if they had mouths to cheer with. The revenants flitted around the edges of the hall; they required no food, but it was night and they were restless. She had called them home. They all looked at nothing, their faces blank. There were Willem and Baltazar; she would have liked to give them some reward, not because it would mean anything to them, but because it would remind Chaerephon how close they had come to losing, and what they had lost by winning.

A woman, small-bodied, knelt before her. Her torso was a piece of wood, the sides curved voluptuously. Three strings and a bar of wood ran down her middle.

Beside her stood a tall man with a long pipe where his nose ought to be, running down to his waist, and another sticking out his back from between his shoulder blades.

As he breathed, his chest wheezed, his abdomen puffing and collapsing like an enormous bladder.

'Fresh from the smithy, I see,' the Chatelaine said. 'You're the two who wanted to play music.'

The woman nodded. Little mouse. They had both been rotted in the lungs when they came to her, and near death. Small good she would have been in battle anyway. It was an annoyance that the Hell-forges would not work on unwilling subjects, but perhaps there was a wisdom in it.

'Go ahead and play for me, then,' the Chatelaine said, waving her hand. 'Be good for something, before you die.'

A monkey-man ran around the room as they played a quick tune, wheezy and uneven. He was too conscious of himself. He was hoping to be made her fool, but what need had she for another fool? She was surrounded by them, and she was disinclined to laugh.

Monoceros came and knelt at her side.

'I am sorry for being late,' he said. 'I was bringing in the last of the grotesques from Bruges. There may be a few strays about the countryside but the good ones, the sound ones, are all in. We could leave now any time.'

'Oh, could we?' she said sweetly. 'Could we leave? Do you give your consent?'

Monoceros knew better than to say anything. He tried to bow his head, giving only a hint of a movement before he checked himself, and kept his head high so as not to gore her. Even on his knee he was as tall as she was sitting in her great chair made of the carved bones of extinct beasts, the chair that had belonged to her husband.

She pitied Monoceros a little, the first and most loyal of all her creatures.

'I am peevish,' she said. 'Here, sit next to me and I'll tell you the reason.'

Monoceros took his chair, an ordinary wooden chair with its bars and finials and roundels painted blue and red, like you might find in any chateau. He leaned close to her.

'The Beast will not move,' she said softly, holding a goblet in front of her mouth. 'It refuses. It has laid eggs.'

'Eggs?' He raised his eyebrow, making the horn shudder.

'Chaerephon did not want me to smash them, but I am not so sure. I do not trust him, Monoceros. He is not mine, you see.'

'I am,' he said. 'You know that I am.'

'Yes,' she said. 'You are my very first. And best, still.'

She reached her hand out and patted his huge shoulder, his skin like smooth and burnished bronze. She almost expected him to purr like his great cat.

'I need more chimeras and better,' she said. 'Chaerephon is getting me black powder. I need you to find me some people who want to be weapons. Strong young people.'

He nodded.

'And Monoceros—'

'Yes?'

He leaned closer, understanding that this was a secret. She swallowed and spoke as quietly as she could, holding out a small iron key.

'Go into my chamber. I have kept everything that came from Willem de Vos there in a chest. Open it and take the counterfeit mace. Destroy it.'

He nodded.

Claude went in search of what he needed. Margriet had given him some of the contents of her dwindling purse.

He bought a bit of pitch-in-spirits from an apothecary, and three skinny rabbits from a hunter. Fur, and meat. It was not a market day, but the ragman had some bits of leather and wire that might come in handy when making their disguises. He even had the beak of a giant bird, and a long bit of metal that looked like a bone. The people of Ypres were doing a brisk trade in chimera fashion.

It felt good to walk the streets in chausses and aketon with money to spend, to have people call him sir. He strode into a tavern.

The moment his eyes adjusted to the light he saw Monoceros.

The horned man was sitting at a table, talking with three boys. They looked terrified, but were trying not to look terrified. New recruits.

Monoceros looked up, caught Claude's eye, and smiled. He stood. His horn nearly scraped the ceiling.

'The clothes are fitting better,' he said quietly, coming closer.

Claude nodded. He reminded himself that he was free, that the Chatelaine had no hold on him.

'I thank you for the armour,' he said. 'It was a great kindness.'

'I was impressed by your testimony,' Monoceros said. 'You are an honourable man.'

'An honourable man who'd have nothing to his name, otherwise.'

That was a mistake. Monoceros glanced down at his clothing, and his eyes lit on the bundle of leather and cloth scraps and the little bottle in Claude's left hand.

'Then you must let me buy you a drink,' Monoceros said. 'Let us tell our best war stories and see how strong the hearts beat in these whelps before I let them become chimeras.'

'I would rather a sturdy crossbow and passage to new lands, but if a drink is all that is on offer, I will not say no,' Claude said.

Monoceros laughed.

Beatrix and Gertrude walked in silence to the church to fetch the horns. Gertrude seemed to sense that Beatrix needed to be silent, needed to have an argument with her mother in her head, which was the only place it was possible to have an argument with Margriet de Vos.

As they were leaving, Beatrix had tried to be light and joyful with her mother.

'We will have to give your gold to the Church,' said Beatrix to Mother. 'If we even get it.'

'The Church took my brother,' Mother snapped. 'Now the score is even.'

'Do you really think you can settle scores with God?' Beatrix had asked quietly.

'I do not, of course, my daughter,' Margriet said. 'But if I can raid at the gates of Hell, surely I can ask for a small dispensation at the gate of Paradise, where I shall be shortly, so let's finish this business.'

She never thought about Beatrix, never thought to apologize to her, or ask her opinion. Stubborn to the last. And she would be in her grave soon, and there was no point in trying to change her now, but Beatrix wanted to all the same.

The ground was cold but firm and she and Gertrude went quickly.

'I should just keep walking,' Beatrix said out loud, to have it said, out in the cold air.

'You know, I have always been a good walker,' Gertrude said. 'I wanted to go on pilgrimage.'

'So did I!' Beatrix said. 'Well, Baltazar and I spoke about it, often. We were going to go together, one day.'

'And why not go without him?'

'Oh, I don't know,' Beatrix said. 'I never thought of it. Every time I thought of the future, Baltazar was in it.'

'Let's walk there now,' said Gertrude and took her hand. It was warmer than her own, despite the cold air, as if Gertrude were more alive than she was.

They swung their arms like children.

'We'll walk for three days to Paris,' said Gertrude, 'then on to Spain.'

But their feet took them to the little tumbledown church, where Gertrude said a prayer and smashed a window.

CHAPTER THIRTY-THREE

Late into the night, they worked. Gertrude used the forge-hammer to shape metal. Beatrix and Jacquemine sewed and wired.

They armed themselves in the morning.

Claude was cutting rabbit skin. Gertrude had stamped the holes in her copper cauldron with her forge-hammer and a sharp bit of twisted scrap iron. She put it on and looked ridiculous; she had meant it to look like a helm, but it looked like a cauldron with holes in it.

'I am not wearing that,' Margriet said.

'Good,' said Gertrude, taking it off. Her face was even redder than usual. 'I'll wear it. I'll die the same with a cauldron on my head as I would with a great steel helm with an ostrich feather.'

Margriet had picked up a stone at the age of eleven, and clambered up onto the rooftops of burning Bruges, and hurled her stone down at the first lurching, bleeding figure who came into sight. That stone had missed but the next brick hadn't. She had brained him, a killer at eleven, her first blood before her first blood. It did not require a fancy blade or a plumed helmet to be a fighter.

'How would you all like to die, if given the choice?' Margriet asked. She had been thinking about death, when she was alone, in the night, retching her bloody guts up in the privy.

There was a long moment when no one spoke. They were all thinking of her plague, of the fact that she would be dead in a moment. Damn her loose tongue. They were pitying her.

'Is that a threat?' asked Claude at last, a little too lightly.

'I suppose I'd want to go painlessly,' said Gertrude after a moment, with a world of pain in her voice.

'You know,' Margriet said, remembering childbirth, 'I don't want a painless death. I would rather have pain, and no fear.'

'It isn't one or the other,' said Gertrude.

'It is,' Margriet retorted. 'I remember with my third baby, the pain and blood would not stop. I got so cold, and all I could think about was the pain. I did not care whether I lived or died; my sister was there to watch over Beatrix. And a few days later when I had recovered I took comfort, and in that moment I knew I would not fear death, so long as it came when I was in pain, because then I would welcome it, and so I would not be afraid.'

Beatrix said, 'You need not fear anyway, Gertrude, because you will live again in Paradise.'

'Yes,' said Gertrude with a sigh, 'but I won't be here, will I? And what if there is something I'll miss? What if there are no figs?'

'I think there will be figs,' said Beatrix with a smile, a smile that faded to a look of horror. She was remembering, no doubt, how she had promised to bring figs home for her grandfather. Remembering that her grandfather and her aunt were dead, that she would have been, too, if Margriet had let her stay in Bruges.

Gertrude had made a smaller helmet out of a piece of iron, hammering it over and over again, shaping it into something like a bowl.

'I'll take that,' Margriet said. She put it on her head. 'I don't need much. I have my gauntlets. I'll wear those. And a breastplate, Gertrude, if you can make me one. Punch a couple of holes in that silver plate from the church, for a leather strap.'

'What would you ask for, if you were going to be a chimera?' Claude asked.

Margriet looked sharply at him.

'Why?'

'Well, why not?'

Margriet thought. 'There was an alderman of Bruges, dead now, who had a pair of spectacles. He was insufferable about them. Every time the boys would play outside his house, he would tut and hold his spectacles up high. Folding things, you know, bits of glass set in frames of bone.'

'You want a set of spectacles?' Jacquemine asked.

'I did not know your vision was so poor,' Beatrix said.

'It isn't,' Margriet snapped. 'Not for things that are close up. But sometimes I want to look at things that are far away.'

The Chatelaine looked over the new recruits. Boys. Boys would be willing to do what she asked.

She had so little – not enough armour, not enough swords. She had to make what she had stretch farther. She needed to sow fear; she needed chimeras.

331

But these were the boys left over after wartime. The dregs. Cowards who used violence only in small mean ways, to feed off the women and children left behind. They looked at her resentfully, though she had given them no cause.

'You are my warriors,' she said to them in a loud, clear voice like a horn of war blown across a battlefield. They shuffled their feet.

'You have a choice before you. You can choose any enhancement you like. But because you are strong, I will offer you a choice many never get. Would you like that?'

The biggest one nodded.

'Good. Now have any of you ever heard of the fire powder from the East? No? Let me demonstrate.'

She held out her hand and a match-woman handed her a little sack full of black powder. She was one of a half-dozen match-men and match-women the Chatelaine had made a month before; the only one who had not yet blown herself up. Her left arm twisted and narrowed into a thin rope. She snapped the flinty fingers on her right hand and sparked the end of the rope a few times, until it caught and glowed orange.

'Stand back,' the Chatelaine told the boys.

The match-woman's rope-arm snaked into the air and she brought the glowing end down to the powder. A bang, a puff of dirty smoke. One of the boys yelled, but the Chatelaine thought it had something of a war-whoop in it, under the fear.

'Good,' she said. 'Good. Now imagine what this powder could do, if we put one end at the bottom of a jar, and a crossbow bolt or a quarrel at the top. Imagine if you had such a weapon on your arm all the time, a weapon that could never slip or miss, a weapon that would obey you as easily as your own fingers and feet obey you now. Who would not fear you, from here to Prester John's kingdom? You would be the most feared men in Christendom, maybe even the world. Are you ready for it, boys?'

She looked at their eager faces. Five. She'd lose two in the smithy, most likely, and perhaps another later. But that left two, which was two more than the King of France would have. Ha! Let him come. A few more days and she would be ready for him. She'd scare him away.

They bade farewell to Jacquemine early in the morning, while the children were still sleeping. Claude watched Margriet kiss their foreheads, and wondered. She was such a kind-hearted woman, really. She just husbanded that kindness, as if it would run out.

The walk to Hell was long. They avoided Ypres, turning south when they saw its spires on the horizon. Claude was in front, as he knew he would be, and he walked even faster so as not to think. Margriet was tripping over her feet, of course, and Beatrix walked like a puppy and Gertrude strolled, comfortable in her big body, swinging her ersatz helmet as she walked.

In the thin sunlight, they found a copse where they could watch the road. Gertrude handed out bits of salt fish. Claude was so sick of salt fish and weak ale. It was long past time to get back to the countries of olives and wine.

He pulled something out of his pocket: a bundle of dried figs he had brought in Ypres to surprise them. It had been Margriet's money, but he had saved that money by letting Monoceros buy him a meal and a drink, so it had seemed to even out.

Beatrix squealed. 'Figs!'

'Who's that?' Margriet hissed, as a merchant jingled past them on an ass.

'The Queen of Sheba,' said Claude, and the others tittered.

In the distance, a church rang the bells for Nones. Nobody else came along the road.

As they trudged south, nobody spoke. It felt familiar, four fighters walking to battle. But his companions were not soldiers, only women dressed in fur and strange metal. And they were not going to battle but to a raid.

They stopped after an hour to rest and drink. Margriet struggled to pull her helmet off. Her fingers scrabbled at it uselessly until she finally used the heels of her hands to yank it off. A trickle of blood ran down her temple, which she seemed not to notice.

She looked very grey and very old.

'I want you to pledge something,' Margriet said, to Claude quietly, looking at the ground. 'If I am killed and you recover the sack.'

Claude nodded. 'I will bring it to Beatrix, if I have it, and if I have breath in my body.'

Margriet looked at him balefully. 'I believe you,' she said. 'And I believe that you have a right to that mace. The key of Hell! To think of it. But you made it. You have a right to it. And I will see it on your arm.'

Claude nodded again. He owed Margriet nothing. But she was his friend, in the only way she knew how.

'My father was an arkwright,' Claude said slowly, remembering. 'He made the loveliest little boxes, with gold and silver clasps. I used to love to open them with the little keys he made. I wonder what he would have thought, to learn that his child could open locks, any locks, the locks of Hell itself.'

'Where is your family now?' Gertrude asked, wide-eyed.

'Dead,' Claude said. 'Long dead. Long after I ran away to become a man-at-arms. It was some years afterward that I heard what had happened. You remember, the Shepherds' Crusade came down from the north. They killed the Jews in Cahors and in Toulouse.'

He had not even told Janos all of this, only bits and pieces here and there.

He could not interpret the way they looked at him. Some mixture of revulsion or pity, and something else. Admiration, perhaps? Guilt? Hatred of his Jewishness?

He spat a soggy fig-stem into the earth. There were only a few more hours of daylight left to them, and if they hoped to reach the beast that the superstitious called Hell before the revenants awoke, they would have to be on their way.

'No sense dallying,' said Margriet, and stood up.

He smiled. Margriet always had to be the leader.

CHAPTER THIRTY-FOUR

Beatrix kissed her mother, who smelled the same as she always had: slightly sour, like old milk. Though everyone said the plague couldn't spread from the living to the living, Margriet had been keeping herself at a distance, even so. But Beatrix knew any embrace could be their last. She walked away with the wetness of her mother's kiss on her lips, and forced herself not to look back.

Beatrix trudged with her distaff, away from the road and across an open field.

She needed to get well away from the others, well away from Hell. She could not call the revenants before sundown, so she knew she should be wishing the sun would hurry up and go to bed. But she wished the opposite: just one more breath of daylight, and another, and another, before she had to do it.

The sun was melting into the edge of the world and the shadows were long, but Beatrix still didn't feel she'd gone far enough. She finally stopped and looked back. All she could see was the horizon, without even the line of the road. But in the half-light it was difficult to know how far she had gone.

The field dipped down to a little stream, where willows grew, bending their pale arms in the dim. A good place to get a drink – she had not thought to bring a flask with her – and to keep herself hidden. A strange thought, since she was calling her enemy to her.

Beatrix clambered down and found a little rock, flat enough and dry enough, on the bank of the stream. She held her distaff high although she didn't think it mattered; she had simply had it beside her, in her hand, when she'd called Baltazar. Still, it felt good to wield it, to pretend for a moment she had a weapon.

She shut her eyes and wished. She wished for all the creatures of night to vacate Hell. All the bats and the night moths, all the revenants. No shudder went through her distaff, no lightning crashed. There was nothing to tell her whether it had worked. So she kept wishing, imagining the horde of them. How many were there?

The bats came first, like swallows blackening the woad sky. She held her distaff high, her face wet with tears. Around her, they circled, chittering and swooping, confused as baited cockerels.

She stayed there, kneeling, holding her distaff, as the night grew darker. It would take longer for the revenants to walk here from Hell. She said all of her prayers. She told herself all of the stories of Reynard the Fox. She marked the passage of time with stories, each tale like a line marked on church candles.

The most frightening creature in the stories had always been Ysengrim the Wolf, despite his dull wits – or perhaps, because of them. Because he could be vicious without even knowing himself to be in the wrong. He could have done anything, and thought himself right, while Reynard knew himself to be a villain.

A figure stepped in front of her, and she feared for a moment it was Baltazar, but it was Chaerephon, the advocate. He too was a night thing.

'What have you done?' he asked gruffly, in French.

She opened her mouth to respond and then remembered she did not need to tell him; she owed him nothing.

He reached for her distaff and she pulled it back, away from him.

She stumbled into Baltazar, who did grab the staff.

'Beatrix,' he said. 'My wife.'

And Beatrix opened her mouth and laughed, a horrible laugh, hollow and rotten, spilling out dust and woodlice, decaying before it died.

They were all around her, the silent figures she had summoned. Silent, except for the one who had been her husband.

'What do you want from us?' Baltazar asked.

'Yes, husband. Now it is my desire that matters, not yours. Now I want something. I am very surprised to learn that I want things, for myself, things that have nothing to do with you. I want many things, in fact. Do you know what I want? I want to eat some roast pork, first of all. And then I want to walk the Camino de Santiago on sore feet with a song on my lips. I would like to travel on a ship, also. And I would like to learn how to play dice.'

Father stepped out of the crowd of revenants and came between them, looking angry. She was shaking, but not with fear. With the cold air, with the hum of the distaff in her hand, with so much energy she wanted to run, run as the revenants had run.

'She wants the money. Where is your mother?'

It took all of Beatrix's will not to answer.

Instead, she thought of Ysengrim. She called him.

'The Chatelaine must be warned,' said Chaerephon, and put his hand out. A bat alighted on it, folding its wings, as if waiting for instructions.

'No,' said Beatrix, wresting the distaff away from Baltazar. It came toward her easily out of his grasp, but he pushed, so it knocked her in the face, and she fell. Her cheek stung and she saw nothing but mud and bright blackness.

She could not best him with strength. But the distaff was a weapon in more ways than one.

Let me see, she prayed. Saint Catherine, show me a vision of time to come. Show everyone here the horrible sights that will pass.

For one long moment nothing happened. She felt the revenants pressing all around her. Perhaps it had not been the distaff after all, but the Grief, creeping into her mind with every sight of her husband. Oh God, how she wanted him, even now, to enfold her in his arms and take her away.

The air overhead filled with the screams of metal dragons and the thunder of fire. The earth beside her exploded and all the revenants were scattered. She lay in the mud, holding the distaff over her head, thinking only of the sights she must show.

'I will show you, my husband,' she screamed. 'I will show you such awful sights that you will never wish to be near me again.'

She did not dare to look up, but no one pulled at the distaff or bothered her. They were still near. The sounds of thunder and a rain of fire – what sights were they seeing? Not even Beatrix's horrible visions could break a revenant's heart, she suspected, but it might confuse them, distract them for a while.

Then she heard a sound, a howl on the air, and the vision shattered like glass.

The wolves came.

They ran almost silently and from all directions like shadows and fell snarling upon the revenants.

She looked up, holding the distaff out, and began to stumble through the fray, outside it. But just as she was getting clear of the wolves, a revenant put his hand out and touched her shoulder.

Baltazar, looking at her as if he owned her. She expected him to say something, to protest that he would always want to be near her.

But he said nothing. His face was like stone. There was no need now for him to pretend for his mistress, to trick Beatrix into believing he still had love within him. He was a corpse.

Any moment now, a wolf would set upon them. She could stop that; she could control them. The distaff hummed in her hand.

Then something came flying around her like a grey rag on the wind, and plucked the distaff out of her hand, and took Baltazar up.

Chaerephon. Chaerephon, flying like a bat, his grey cloak fluttering, holding Baltazar by the hand as if he weighed nothing at all.

She jumped to grab for the distaff, to call Baltazar back,

but they were gone. And now she was without her distaff, and could not call anyone, enemy or friend.

She rose to her feet and ran, praying that the wolves and the revenants would keep each other occupied, that neither would follow her.

Hell had its mouth shut tight like a child refusing to eat. Its great pale eyes looked out toward them as they approached. Margriet felt sure that this beast knew them for what they were. It saw through their disguises. But somehow, she could not imagine that a beast who wore a bridle like that would share any secrets with the woman who held the reins. That bridle looked as if it hurt.

'Good morning, beastie,' she whispered, though they were still too far away for it to hear.

'What?' Claude asked.

Claude was wearing fur all over his face and hands, and a leather cap with the two drinking horns coming out of it. In the forge-mill, he had looked ridiculous. In the waning light, he looked like a demon.

'Ready?' Margriet asked.

'I don't like it,' said Gertrude. 'I don't like the look of it, just sitting there, staring. I'm sure it knows we're here.'

With her weak eyes, Margriet could make out very little of the details of the Hellbeast's face, but she could see the great eyes gleaming. Then they closed, and the great head heaved once or twice, as if it would vomit. Was the bridle a lock? Or was it only there to open the mouth when the beast wanted to keep it closed?

She soon had her answer. The beast opened its mouth and vomited blackness. The revenants screamed as they ran past.

To see the revenants running was a strange sight. Oh God, what had Beatrix brought upon herself?

Gertrude slammed her pot-helmet over her head. Margriet checked her own helmet. She wore no disguise on her face but in her chausses and tunic, her helmet and breastplate and gauntlets, she doubted anyone would recognize her.

She tried to catch a glimpse of each revenant, but they were too quick, and she was ducked down under the branches of a willow, so they would not see her.

Claude tugged on her sleeve. This was the moment; if they waited, the mouth would close.

Margriet ran and stumbled right away and landed face first in the black mud. She heard Claude swear, 'God's blood,' and felt Claude's hands under her armpits, lifting her.

She ran on again, trying not to think about it, letting movement alone carry her forward as it had done for something like forty years. She had not run in a long time, not since the day at the gate of Bruges, which seemed an eternity ago now. The day she had contracted Hellpest. The day she had started to die.

Margriet's breastplate banged from side to side as she ran. She wanted to yell, with rage and purpose, but her breath was short. They dodged the revenants. She hoped they would see them only as chimeras coming home, not as raiders. How long would they have, after that? It depended on Beatrix, and on luck, and on God.

The Hellbeast was still vomiting as they neared the great lips, the great teeth reaching down and out. They had to push past the last of the revenants. There were so many. All of them running toward Beatrix. Margriet elbowed past a reeking, headless thing and grabbed on to one of the teeth. It did not look slippery but rather pitted like dull stone. But her fingers scrabbled and shook and could not grasp. She was pushed backward again, roughly, and then someone pressed her back more gently and she moved toward the mouth.

It was damply warm inside, and still packed with fleeing revenants. Margriet could see nothing but flashes of red and here and there her friends, fighting their way through. Claude rushed by her, pulling Gertrude by the hand.

The tongue rolled beneath them and Margriet was down again, down on a surface like damp earth, except that it was warm. She wanted to cry like a child, to pound her fists against the Hellbeast's tongue. But she could not act like anything other than a chimera now, now that the revenants were thinning around them.

A crowd of bats flew past them, and they put up their hands. Behind them the mouth closed and it was dim, and they did not have to fight anyone off. But as they ran down the Beast's throat, Claude pulled them into a branching off to the side, a warm wet room with heaving, sighing walls so close around them that Margriet could not help but lean against them. She was grateful for a chance to catch her breath, although the air was so close here it was like trying to breathe through a wet cloth.

Three chimeras went running past them. They heard one of them shouting in French, wondering why all the revenants were leaving at once.

'There must have been orders,' one of them said.

'There were no orders,' said Monoceros. Margriet saw

him, standing just opposite them. Claude tensed beside her. 'All the orders come through me.'

'Then what? What made them leave?'

'I don't know,' said Monoceros. 'Where's Chaerephon? Still sleeping?'

'He left with them.'

'With the revenants? Where has he taken them? Come on. You stay at the mouth, Oplo and Mantis, and if they come back, one of you come and tell me. I'll be in the Chatelaine's chambers.'

Monoceros and the two with him ran down the throat. Claude pulled Gertrude and Margriet out and whispered, 'Don't sneak. Walk as if you're angry. Walk like they were walking.'

The passages of the Beast opened into a chamber and there were chimeras gathered there, talking among themselves. There were fires bursting up now and then from the floor like guttering candles.

The chimeras looked up when the women came in, but no one seemed to take much notice. The idea that these cobbled together bits of metal and fur could make them pass for ordinary here made Margriet want to laugh; she could not think of the last thing that had made her want to laugh. Perhaps it was the plague, eroding her mind.

'This is the smithy,' Claude whispered.

They strode through to the other side, into another corridor.

They kept walking until Claude told them to stop, hissing that here was the entrance to the Chatelaine's chambers, in time to see Monoceros go in, alone. Where the other two had gone they did not know.

'The Chatelaine will be leaving, no doubt,' Claude said

as they crouched and watched the entrance. 'She'll want to know where they have gone. She'll go after Chaerephon herself, perhaps.'

But as they waited, they heard behind them the mouth of Hell opening again.

'If it's opening without the Chatelaine working the bridle, that must be the revenants returning,' Claude said. 'The beast always takes them back. God's nails. We've lost. They'll tell her.'

Margriet pulled him around and looked into his face.

'I'm trying something. As soon as you see the Chatelaine leave her chambers, as soon as she is well gone, look for a chest with my husband's things in it, and get out of here. And keep Beatrix safe, or I'll haunt you when I'm dead.'

'Don't be a fool,' said Claude.

But Margriet was already creeping away from them. She thought of Beatrix's sweet face, the lovely rosebud mouth that had sucked at her breast, the round blue eyes. She was a good girl and she would get herself a proper husband and a baby. She would be fine.

Margriet walked as quickly as she could back toward the large chamber where the smiths were hammering at their forges. The furnaces blew and she felt for a moment like what she was: a small creature inside the bellows belly of a great beast.

She walked to the middle of the room and pulled off her goggle-helm.

'Call the Chatelaine!' she screamed. 'Call the hellkite! Tell her Margriet de Vos has come to be transformed!'

CHAPTER THIRTY-FIVE

Claude heard Margriet scream. Gertrude darted forward but Claude pushed her back, despite the fact that he wanted to run down the hall himself. But there was no point in trying to save the dying.

'Walk,' he muttered, and he and Gertrude walked deeper into the beast, past the Chatelaine's door. As they walked, he heard the Chatelaine's voice, behind them, giving orders to someone.

'Go to the mouth and see what Chaerephon is about, and bring him back to me. Bring me his head if he answers back anything but "yes, Monoceros".'

Monoceros was there, then, behind them. Claude's face flushed. Would he recognize him from behind? Claude kept walking away. They must look like two chimeras on their way somewhere. They must keep up that pretence.

At last after they had heard nothing for several long moments he stopped, and put his hands out to Gertrude, and looked behind.

Too soon; he had miscalculated. There was the back of the Chatelaine, her dress sweeping behind, and a step or two behind, Monoceros, glancing back over his enormous bare shoulder.

Monoceros looked at Claude and knew him for who he was.

Claude was sure of it. The golden eyes widened and the pupils within narrowed, and Monoceros stood taller for a moment, like a beast ready to spring.

Claude's right arm shuddered with instinct but it was no good to him, so he reached his left over to his dagger.

And then the lids dropped a little over those eyes, and Monoceros's head drooped, and he shook his head a little. His expression reminded Claude of the time a general had told the crossbowmen to hold their fire, and one had not heard, and had shot and alerted the enemy to their position. Monoceros looked as if he were mourning someone yet alive.

Without looking at him again, Monoceros turned and walked away, following the Chatelaine.

It all happened while Gertrude was still turning; she did not see.

'All clear?' Gertrude whispered.

Were they? Would Monoceros betray them? Was he playing some game? For now, Claude could only hope that he would not give them away.

Claude did not answer but crept towards the door of the Chatelaine's chambers. He had been inside them once before. It seemed a lifetime ago; he was different now. Desperate. Let me have desperate men, Janos had said, once. Desperate men can be trusted. He pulled his knife out. The last time he was here, there had been a porter in the antechamber. If the forged mace-key were in those chambers, there would no doubt be a porter there now, perhaps more than one.

But the main thing he was worried about was the lock. He made a fist of his weak right hand and winced in pain.

The interior doors of Hell all opened to one key only, and it was on the Chatelaine's arm. It was certain that she had locked her own chamber, if the treasure were inside. But Claude's right hand had opened a padlock simply by holding it. Whatever magic the mace had left behind, he hoped it would work on the doors of Hell. He also hoped that the locked door would be on the inside of the antechamber, after the guards, where he could pick the lock in peace – having first dispatched the guards.

He was not so lucky.

The outside door had a great lock on it, a shining scar set into the flesh of the beast. It matched the pattern of the flanges, like a cruel reminder of what Claude did not have.

He pulled Gertrude toward him and whispered in her ear.

'I've got to get that door open but I can't make a sound. You stand here and cough or something if someone comes.'

Gertrude nodded like a frightened coney. It was strange to see her quiet, for once.

Claude crept to the door and put his withered right hand out, felt the flesh of the beast meet his own flesh. Between them there should have been a key, and he felt the lack of it, and the beast felt the lack of it, too. A shudder went through the skin of the door.

'Shh,' Claude said softly.

He moved his fingers against the scar, feeling the polished uneven surface against the skin of his fingertips. Pain lanced through each of his fingers. He sheathed his dagger, gritted his teeth and used his left hand to prop up his right arm, under the elbow. He could feel the scar tissue shifting, closing in on itself, the keyholes tightening against his efforts. He gritted his teeth so as not to swear.

It wasn't working. The Beast knew what he was doing, and was working against him. And what would it do if he kept at it? Bellow? Vomit him out? Claude had never been quite sure whose side the Hellbeast was on, and this seemed like the worst possible way to find out.

Gertrude came to his side.

'Not working?' she whispered, not quietly enough.

'You're supposed to be on watch,' he said.

'Can't we cut our way through or something? It's not like wood or stone, is it?'

Bloodthirsty woman.

'Not without letting the guard on the other side know we're here.'

Gertrude looked at him.

'There's a guard on the other side?'

He nodded.

'Then why not let him open the door?'

Claude shook his head. He wanted a quick, silent throat-cutting in the antechamber, not a fight out here in the hall that would call all the chimeras to them.

He concentrated again on the lock, but it was even worse with Gertrude looking over his shoulder. Hadn't he told her to keep watch? He should have come on his own. He should never have made common cause with these women.

Gertrude coughed.

The lock moved and the door started to swing open.

'Speak,' came a voice in French. 'Friend or foe?'

Claude's dagger was already in his left hand, and he

thrust it up into the place where he expected the throat to be, but it was a mantis-man, and the throat was higher than Claude's head. So instead of shutting up the guard, it made a sound like a great chittering insect as black blood bubbled out of the wound.

'God's nails,' Claude muttered, but Gertrude was down on the ground, pulling the legs of the mantis-man. The mantis-man fell backwards, and Claude pounced on its narrow green chest and felt something chitinous snap beneath his weight. A poor choice of guard. The Chatelaine should have left someone like Monoceros behind; but she had probably thought the danger was above, not below. And Margriet now was doubtless caught, and soon they would be bringing her down, deeper, for questioning.

The mantis-man was struggling; its razor pincers snapped. Claude slit the mantis-man's throat and rolled off him, through the door, Gertrude crawling behind him.

Margriet was in shackles by the time the Chatelaine and her horned lackey came through the door of the smithy. Margriet stood tall, her blood pounding, her hands shaking.

She had a terrible idea. It had taken hold of her, been building in her since – when? Since Beatrix's first vision, or since the day Jacquemine told her about the Hellfire that destroyed the Smedenpoort? Or perhaps since the day she saw the gonners blow themselves and their yappy dog to pieces?

The Chatelaine came to her and walked around her sniffing, as if Margriet were some vermin brought in by her hounds.

'Explain, and do it quickly,' she said. 'If I lose patience, you lose your viscera.'

'I am offering you my service,' Margriet said. 'I would like to become a chimera.'

The Chatelaine came closer, spoke more quietly.

'And why would you do that?'

'Because I am destitute, thanks to you,' she answered, hewing as close to the truth as she could, knowing she was a rotten liar. 'Because I do not wish to be a burden on my daughter, and because I would go sour in a convent.'

'You're sour now,' the Chatelaine muttered, walking around her. 'And why this performance? Can you explain, then, why my revenants ran out of here like rats fleeing a ship?'

'I did not know the best way to knock on your front door. I was afraid I would be killed outright by one of your guards. So my dear daughter called the revenants, to give me a chance to get in, and get your attention and make my case.'

'Hmm,' said the Chatelaine again. 'A strange way to earn my trust.'

'I don't want your trust,' Margriet snapped. 'I want you to make me into a weapon.'

'Truly? Well now, and what sort of weapon would you be?'

'Something with power. Something like the thunder weapons I saw at the walls of Bruges.'

Margriet thought of the visions Beatrix had, the wars she had seen that had not yet come to pass. If Margriet could succeed, perhaps those infernal wars never would happen. Perhaps that gift she could give her daughter, a life with no more of those horrible visions in it.

The Chatelaine drew away from her, frowning.

'But more powerful,' said Margriet. 'I don't want to just

351

make a sound like a little fart and throw some smoke. If I'm to be a weapon, make all of me a weapon. Make it count.'

'You've got a mouth on you,' said the Chatelaine with a cruel smile. 'I could make the thunder come out of your mouth. I could make a furnace of your belly. I could make you a Hellbeast on wheels. Would that suit you?'

'It would,' said Margriet, with her stomach lurching and her skin cold.

The second door was locked, too. And this time there would be no one on the other side of it. Or so Claude hoped. He and Gertrude pulled the mantis-man's body into the small antechamber and stood there in the darkness, lit only by the red flesh of the Hellbeast, by the fiery blood that coursed through its body. How old was it? Claude would have liked to speak to it – or to speak to the Chatelaine's husband, who some said was still alive, and kept here in the deepest oubliette. He could free him – that would be a fine revenge.

But that was not why he was here.

He put his sore right hand to the scar again. Again, the keyholes shrank and squirmed.

'God's bodkin,' said Claude, and drew his dagger.

'Good,' said Gertrude. 'Do something, and quick!'

Claude wrapped the fingers of his weak hand around the knife hilt, and held them in his strong hand, and thrust the knife in. A few twists and the beast groaned. Blood poured out from the scar. He had been right to worry that this would have alerted the mantis-man; but now the mantis-man was dead, and they would soon be caught if they stayed much longer.

The door cracked and swung in.

The Chatelaine's private chamber was hung in tapestries that showed strange scenes, with no humans in them. Claude had had a chance to study them before, when the Chatelaine had asked him what he wanted to be.

'I want to be myself,' he had said, over and over, unwilling to be made into one of her lackeys, mistrusting any transformation she could give him.

And in the end he had transformed himself, into something very like her.

They strode in, not speaking, each of them looking in the corners for the chest.

Into the next chamber, where the Chatelaine slept. Here it was more bare: a bed, a table with a book upon it.

There beside the bed was a great chest.

Claude used his knife again and cracked the lock. This one was much easier; it gave way willingly. An ordinary padlock, to hold the wealth a man had tried to keep from his wife and child. An easy thing to break, a pleasure to break.

There was the sack, full of Willem's goods. Still not distributed or melted down. But the mace-key was not inside.

He stood, seething. Where had she hidden it? Was it possible she had destroyed it already?

'We should take this and go,' said Gertrude.

'It isn't all there,' Claude answered.

'They'll find us.'

Claude paced the room. 'What would you do with something you wished did not exist?'

'I'd throw it away.'

'No, you foolish woman, not something you wished you didn't have. Something that should not exist.'

'I'd throw it away, and don't call me foolish. I'd throw it somewhere no one could find it, like the sea. Or into a fire.'

Claude whirled. There was no fireplace in this room, or any other room inside the Hellbeast. It was always warm in here. But then where could they find a fire?

'The forges,' he said, despairing. 'But she'd have to do it quietly, privately. She didn't want anyone to know. Did she do it already?'

'We must go now,' Gertrude urged.

Claude picked up one side of the sack and Gertrude the other, and they pulled it out of the strongbox and walked out, stepping over the Mantis-man's body, not bothering to close the doors. If anyone saw them now in the hall there would be no denying their purpose. No running, either. They would have to fight.

But not without a search of the smithy furnace, if Claude could manage it.

The hall was empty save a cloud of bats and a few scrappy revenants who ignored them.

'They weren't gone long,' Claude said.

'What do you think happened to Beatrix?' Gertrude asked.

Nothing good, Claude thought. Not for them to have come back so quickly. Or perhaps Beatrix had simply lost her nerve and sent them all back. The most likely scenario, really. He said nothing to Gertrude, who seemed so fond of Beatrix. Let her think what she liked. Nothing Claude could say would make it any better or any worse.

They paused as they came near the door of the smithy where there were crowds of people hanging at the edges. But everyone was looking inward, where a fire was raging and some victim was screaming. There were hoots of laughter. Margriet. It must be Margriet.

Claude looked at Gertrude's face and saw she had realized it, too. What could they do? She had asked them to get the chest to Beatrix. Although now Beatrix was very likely dead, and there was nothing in this sack Claude wanted, and Gertrude had wanted only to hurt the Chatelaine and would have a very hard time convincing herself she had.

Claude shut his eyes for a moment to steel himself and saw only red, the glow of fire through flesh, his or Hell's, it did not matter. Then he opened them and walked to one side, yanking Gertrude along.

'Wait here,' he told her. 'And if any chimeras come, scream. And run. Run first then scream while you are running.'

'But—'

He walked away from her, elbowing his way into the crowd of chimeras watching the scene at the smithy. He glanced at each of the fires in turn, at the scraps of bone and charred fur, of horns and blades. He could not see the mace-key. Of course not; if she had brought it here she would have seen it done, in private, not left it lying here. Still, he could not help himself.

He was closer in through the crowd now and could see Margriet lying prone on a great anvil. She was shackled, no, more than shackled – she was ringed with iron all down the length of her body and her mouth was open, open wider than Claude would have thought possible. It was hard to tell from a distance but her face did not look pained at all; she looked ferocious, like a lion receiving its prey.

He looked to one side and there his eyes caught Monoceros's again. The horned man leaned in toward the Chatelaine, who was exulting over Margriet. He said something, and the Chatelaine looked up, toward Claude. Claude turned and walked through the crowd as quickly as he could without causing alarm. As he passed one of the working tables, he saw one of Margriet's gauntlets lying there and he picked it up, like a champion's token, like a trophy, like something to give Beatrix of her dead mother. For there was no doubt Margriet would be as good as dead, soon enough, that she was now a weapon of war.

Claude strode out through the room and into the hallway. He glanced back just once to see that Monoceros was following him, although silently and alone.

When Claude got near the hall, he could hear a hound yelping and someone screaming. Gertrude!

He ran through the corridor, uphill on the damp surface like loamy earth. He put the gauntlet on his weak hand and with a thought, sent the steel gadlings flying off his knuckles like living things out toward the chimeras gathered there.

He had known, somehow, when he gave these gauntlets to Margriet, that they were more than they appeared. Had Monoceros known as well? Had he given Claude the gauntlets to try to trap him, to turn him into a chimera for once and for all?

But the creatures gathered before him, shooing away the flying gadlings, were not chimeras after all but revenants. Gertrude must have angered them somehow, or else the Chatelaine had given them orders.

Gertrude was struggling with one – Baltazar. The revenant whirled as one of the gadlings hit him in the forehead, and Gertrude managed to grab Beatrix's distaff from him. The hound leapt up and took a gadling in its dog mouth but then it wheeled like a mad thing, as if it had swallowed a hornet, until Gertrude thrust the end of the distaff into the hound's chest, hard, and it yelped, and its legs shook.

The face on the back end was a woman's. It grimaced.

The gadlings returned to Claude's hand. The hand, his mace-hand, throbbed from the chafing of the gauntlet upon it. But the itching, the horrible itching, was gone.

Now Gertrude was pulling the distaff out of the dog, and it wouldn't come, and Gertrude was yelling something Claude could not make out. Baltazar seemed at a loss. He stood and watched Gertrude.

'Come on,' Claude said. 'Monoceros is behind me.'

Gertrude pulled once more on the distaff and it came free. She whacked Baltazar across the head with it, and he fell to the ground.

'Ha,' Gertrude said.

Claude swore, grabbed one handle of the sack and ran, dragging it, but the thing was too bulky and it was a relief when Gertrude came up alongside him and took a handle. They were nearly at the mouth when they heard Monoceros behind, calling, 'Claude!'

All was lost.

Claude took the distaff from Gertrude and jabbed it up into the roof of the mouth, but the beast only groaned. Damn thing.

He could open locks if he had a tool. He thrust the distaff into the scar hole and twisted, bending all his thought on it.

Blood poured out of the scar and the Hellbeast gnashed its teeth.

With a groan, the bridle creaked. Just a crack but it was enough. Claude and Gertrude fell to their knees and pushed the sack out. They half-crawled, half-rolled out into the cold night air.

CHAPTER THIRTY-SIX

The Chatelaine did not believe Margriet de Vos, or trust her. A city woman, who smelled of dry fish and babies. A woman who measured her life in coins and cloth, and yet wanted now to be made a weapon. The Chatelaine could not understand it, and the sooner Margriet was put onto the anvil, the sooner it would be clear whether she was lying.

So she had a smith put rings around Margriet. The rings were ready, for she had wanted to try this for some time now. To make a powder weapon more powerful – or at the very least more frightening – than the gonner-chimeras who had blown themselves up at the wall of Bruges. If this worked, she would make more tomorrow. And then Philippe would see what she could do.

Monoceros whispered to her, 'I want to see what Chaerephon is up to.'

She nodded. Good of him to remember. Loyal Monoceros, little better than a beast. She must remember not to have any more philosophers around her.

The smiths put the ringed woman through the fire, face first.

'Wait,' said the Chatelaine. She took her fingernail and found a place where the flesh of the woman showed through the rings. She scratched the words ULTIMA RATIO MULIERUM in the blood; the final argument of women. The skin shuddered and bled but the woman did not cry out, for she had iron in her throat.

Margriet de Vos came out with her arms and legs fused, with her mouth open and her skin bronzed darker than Monoceros's, as if her whole skin were armour. She came out silent. The Chatelaine crouched and looked into Margriet's unblinking eyes, at her mouth, now wide open, but silent.

They put a long tube of iron down Margriet's throat, and she thought nothing could hurt more than that. She would be dead soon and she was glad of it.

And then something did hurt more: the fire was everywhere as her flesh melted into the metal and became metal, as her open mouth became the mouth of a cannon. She felt her eyes sliding backwards, like the eyes of the great sea monster figurehead on the boat that her father had most admired. He had taken her to see it, many times, when she was a child, before the violence of the Matins of Bruges, before he became a smaller man, a reduced man.

When she came out, the pain was a dull throb. She could not hear very well any more, but she could see, and the worst of it was how cold she felt. How cold the hot air of Hell felt against her metal skin.

They set her on a cart that did not fit her. They rolled her, rollicking and bumping, up through the throat of the beast. The Chatelaine opened the lock. No sign of Claude or Gertrude. Margriet hoped they had got themselves well clear.

'No sign of Monoceros?' the Chatelaine asked one of her mantis-men.

They loaded the powder in and set the match. They put a bolt in her mouth, a long bar of wood that had been a spear, she thought. They did not care much about the bolt itself, how true it would fly; they just wanted to test the powder to see if it worked. They loaded the powder. The Chatelaine retreated to a safe distance.

Margriet swallowed it down when the powder ignited. All of her bile, all of her hate. She swallowed dampness out of the air and it worked.

They thought it had failed.

'It's a new mix,' said the chimera loading her, his voice echoing in an empty helmet. 'We were hasty, perhaps. We did not mix it wet and let it dry. No time.'

'Add more, then,' said the Chatelaine.

They added more. Margriet swallowed it down. She let the fire rumble through parts of her they did not know she had. She destroyed it.

The third time, they spilled all they had into her. And the Chatelaine, growing impatient, stood a little closer.

Margriet asked God to bless her enterprise. She honed her thoughts. The only task that remained to her in this life was to explode, the way the gonner-chimeras had, but bigger. More powerfully. Enough so that the Chatelaine herself might be killed, and if not, at least a part of her army would go. Revenge for Margriet's lost life. For her daughter, wherever she might be now. For Bruges itself, her beautiful city, the city of canals where Margriet had learned to love the world.

This time Margriet forced the fire out of herself, out through all the cracks. She knew nothing more.

Beatrix walked through the darkness. She did not even know in which direction to walk. The smell of brimstone was on the air but she could not follow it.

A boom resounded through the air and a great light lit up the horizon. The very clouds became bright wounds in the sky, with clouds of black smoke swirling in front. This must be her vision come to pass.

St Catherine, she prayed. *Where are you? Will you help me?*

She wanted to run as far as she could from the fire, but Mother and Gertrude and Claude might have been there, and they might need her help.

And indeed, as she walked closer to it, shielding her eyes against the light, she saw the head of the great Hellbeast. But it was bloodied and torn, a gash breaking through one of its eyes. There were bodies all around, chimera bodies.

A giant egg rolled in front of her. It was as high as her shoulder and cracked clean across. A very thin hand almost like a human hand, and a long arm, reached out of it.

Then she saw a half-dozen of the eggs lying around, all cracked, with thin arms and legs coming out of them.

The beast itself groaned, and retreated until there was nothing left but the mounded earth where it had been.

'Beatrix!' she heard behind her.

She looked and her eyes had to adjust to the darkness. She saw Gertrude holding her distaff, and she ran to her.

Gertrude handed her the distaff and then kissed her cheek.

'We must leave,' Claude hissed. Some of the fur had

fallen off his face in patches but he looked fearsome all the same.

'Mother,' said Beatrix.

'She's gone,' Claude said. 'Dead. She's the one who did this.'

It was not possible. It was a mistake.

'But how?' Beatrix asked

'No time. It was quick, quicker than the plague would have been. Come on.'

Beatrix picked up her distaff and felt it wet. She sniffed her hand; blood.

'What happened in there?' she asked Gertrude as they ran.

'I speared a hound,' Gertrude yelled, and laughed.

After a few steps they nearly tripped over the sack.

'You got it,' Beatrix breathed.

'Yes, we got your stupid coins. All that for this,' Claude said, heaving it.

They walked a little more and then they heard a voice in the darkness say, 'Claude.'

CHAPTER THIRTY-SEVEN

Claude drew his knife when he saw the horned man approaching. He didn't want to hurt Monoceros, but he wasn't going to let him get in the way.

'Your mistress is dead,' Claude said. 'You have no more business with me.'

'I'm not sure she is,' Monoceros answered. 'But Hell seems to be going beneath the earth without me in it.'

'Then let us pass,' he said gruffly.

'I am not here to stop you. I am here to walk beside you, if you will allow it.'

Claude squinted at him. The earth rumbled and rolled.

'Come over here,' he said, and pulled Monoceros by the hand, away from Gertrude and Beatrix.

They stood close to each other in the cold night, with the bleak little trees still burning on the horizon. He felt as if he could not see Monoceros very well, that he needed to see him in better light, but there was no better light to be had.

'Why?' Claude asked. 'Why did you let me go? You saw me. You knew who I was.'

'I told you before,' Monoceros said slowly. 'I know you are an honourable man.'

Claude stepped back, thinking hard. Monoceros knew the shape of his body. He had looked it over often enough when he was crouched in the Chatelaine's cell.

'Yes,' Claude said simply. 'A man who failed to become a chimera.'

He held up his right hand with Margriet's gauntlet still chafing it.

Monoceros, in answer, put his hand to it, and pressed it down to Claude's side, and in that moment he moved closer to him and kissed him on the mouth. It was a hard kiss, a soldier's kiss. He smelled of brimstone.

'You are trying to trick me,' Claude said after a moment. He let his hands linger on the skin like armour.

'No,' Monoceros said. 'Yes. I am a brigand. I can't be trusted. And I am a unicorn. The noblest of creatures.'

'I don't understand you.'

'Then let me walk beside you for a while, and we'll see if we understand each other then.'

Claude glanced behind his shoulder, at Beatrix and Gertrude.

'I have to see her to the coast, so she can get a ship for England. It's what Margriet wanted.'

'No,' said Beatrix, stepping forward. He had not known she could hear. 'We're going to Spain. As pilgrims. But we'll walk with you as far as Paris, and farther, if you're going south from there.'

The Chatelaine lay dying. She knew she was dying. She knew from the froth of blood in her own mouth, the bubbles of blood pushing at the packed soil in her nostrils. From the sense that she was distant from her own body.

At the edges of her vision, she saw eggs running on spindly legs. The beast's spawn. The reason she was dying. The beast screamed and opened its mouth wider than it ever had before. The egg-creatures scampered inside and down came those jaws, clamped tight. The Hellbeast slid into its burrow, back beneath the Earth.

Carrying her husband in its belly, her husband locked away with a key that only she held. She sobbed and turned her face into the cold mud.

They would find her body, and her mace-key on it.

A tree was afire, a little way into the distance. If she could get to that fire, she could thrust the mace into it, and hope to destroy it. No one should have the key to Hell.

And the other mace? The one she had given Monoceros to destroy? Her loyal Monoceros. He had said he would destroy it, so no doubt he had.

She crawled in her torn kirtle and surcoat through the mud. Every movement was a dagger in her breast. She crawled under the burning tree and when a flaming limb fell, she lifted her arm, the one bearing the mace, and slammed it down into the fire. A small fire, but perhaps it would be enough.

CHAPTER THIRTY-EIGHT

Excerpt from the Chronicles of Zonnebeke Abbey

In the year of our Lord 1328, the beast called Hell was driven under the Earth. No one knew what became of its mistress. Some say she walks the Earth, still, and some claim to have seen the Hellspawn, scrawny creatures hatched from the eggs of the Beast.

Nine years later, the King of England challenged the right of Philippe of Valois to the throne of France, and those two countries began a war that would last a hundred years and more. A new plague came to the world, and at first many feared that it was a return of the Hell-plague, but it was instead something far worse.

There were many stories born during this time, as the people were afraid. People told stories of a band of women, led by a Flemish widow, who donned armour made of pots and pans, and raided Hell itself. People called this woman Dulle Griet in the Flemish tongue, or Margot-la-Folle in French, or Mad Meg in English. The city of Ghent constructed a great bombard and named it Dulle Griet.

From time to time there were stories of revenants left wandering, the remnants of the brief sojourn of Hell on the surface of the earth.

The wise say the creature was not Hell, but only some chthonic creature, whose doings have been so confused in the imagination of ordinary folk that it might as well have been. The wicked say that this beast must have emerged from time to time in the story of the world, and that it might one day rise again to trouble us.

AFTERWORD

I started writing this book in 2014, and its first edition was published as *Armed in Her Fashion* by ChiZine Publications in Canada in 2018. Thank you to my early readers who welcomed this weird book of my heart, and particularly to its first editor, S.M. Beiko.

I'm grateful for this chance to bring it back into the world in a revised edition.

I thank my wise editor Jane Johnson, the wonderful team at HarperVoyager UK including Natasha Bardon, Vicky Leech Mateos and Elizabeth Vaziri, my agent Jennie Goloboy, and my whole family, especially my partner Brent and my son Xavier, to whom this book is dedicated. Thank you to Andrew Davis for the beautiful cover.

The tale of Margriet's childhood included in this edition first appeared as the story 'Lilies and Claws' in *Trouble the Waters: Tales From the Deep Blue*, published in 2022 in the United States by Third Man Books and edited by Sheree Renée Thomas, Pan Morigan and Troy L. Wiggins.

The list of books and articles that informed this book is long. Here are a few I found invaluable: *Bruges, Cradle of*

Capitalism, 1280–1390 by James M. Murray. *Of Reynaert the Fox: Text and Facing Translation of the Middle Dutch Beast Epic*, edited by André Bouwman and Bart Besamusca. *Transgender Warriors* by Leslie Feinberg. *A Plague of Insurrection: Popular Politics and Peasant Revolt in Flanders, 1323–1328* by William H. TeBrake. *Medieval Handgonnes* by Sean McLachlan.

Finally, I acknowledge the visual artists whose work inspired mine: in particular, Pieter Bruegel, whose painting *Dulle Griet* is the foundation for my story.